I was s_____ _____ _____ _____ d, but
I made my_____ _____ _____ ___ __or way. What
was that di____ ___ ___ g ngnt?

I don't know which I noted first; the innocent
sound of the hall door closing, or the quick flaring
burst of light that had been so low and dim.

Like a badly managed marionette, I turned my
head with jerky movements, seeking the source of
that dreadful light. My indrawn breath was like a
dried thistle barb in my throat.

The color of the light was gold and red and quite
beautiful. Even as I stared, it leaped and swelled
and grew, moving up the sides of the windows,
biting into the dry wood of sills and frames. God
help me, the entire side of the room was ablaze!

MANSION
OF
DARK MISTS

EVA ZUMWALT

LEISURE BOOKS   ∞   NEW YORK CITY

To Donna
and her wonderful family,
with love and appreciation.

A LEISURE BOOK

Published by

Dorchester Publishing Co., Inc.
6 East 39th Street
New York, NY 10016

Printed in the United States of America

Prologue

Last night I stood again upon the shores of hell!

With a thousand other souls, I was sucked into its greedy, thundering maelstrom of waters. Faces I knew moved about me; Rebecca, Mrs. Pinkham, Joshua. Joanna was there too, her pale hair floating, her eyes filled with accusation. I tried to reach her outstretched hand. Smoke and water came between us. Frantically I looked for the others, but they had gone. There was no one with me. I was all alone with the roaring, screeching mountain that now loomed over me, and fell, and fell—

I woke screaming, my body drenched with clammy sweat.

Shuddering, I buried my face in my husband's shoulder, grateful for the arms clasped tightly about me, the reassurance of his voice. "Katherine, it was nothing, only a dream."

He was mistaken. It was more, much more than a dream. It was the refleshing of the bones of memories I have striven uselessly to bury.

The nightmares occur with less frequency as the years pass, yet each night I dread to close my eyes lest those phantoms from eight years ago rise to snatch me back to the cataclysmic day when my sane world was swept away in a space of ten minutes.

In the blessed daylight hours I am able to capture the illusion of serenity. I am absorbed in my family, in the prosaic business of my household. With Eileen, who is more a member of the family than a hired girl, and dear, difficult Mrs. Potter who rules the kitchen. I shape my days, finding contentment in the ordinary.

"Eileen," I will remark comfortably, "we must let down the hem of Louisa's dress again. How the child grows!"

"Ah, she'll be lovely and tall like yourself, Katy," Eileen teases, for she knows I have wished myself of lesser height and more fashionably-rounded form.

"Flattery will not make me put off beating the parlor rug another day," I reply.

A mock sigh from Eileen. "No more did I think it would, Katy-ma'am, but 'twas worth a try."

And we smile together, and I am at peace.

Yet even in the smallest events there may be a seed of a reminder. Only yesterday my small son came to me scarlet-faced and in tears, his grubby hand closed about a polliwog that had spilled from the jar he keeps on his night table.

As always, Thad's chubby knees were skinned, and his shirt did not resemble the spotless garment Eileen had wrestled over his squirming, freshly-bathed little body an hour before. Wailing, he held out to me the tiny, dead creature.

"What's the matter with it, mama? Can papa fix it?"

I held my child close and tried to explain about death. Together we took his red sand shovel and buried the polliwog in the rose garden. The ceremony appeared to ease Thad's distress. Today he seems to have forgotten his first experience with mortality.

I wish that I could so easily be made to forget the day that haunts my life. Then there would be no nightmares to invade my sleeping, unguarded mind; to drag me cruelly back across half a decade, to a cold, wet afternoon in May, in the year 1889.

Never again would I hear in memory that unbelievable sound, that hideous, mind-numbing symphony composed of crashing rumbles and jars, or the rending atonal screeches like a viola played by madmen, underlying a tangled theme of human voices raised in terror and agony. Never again would I relive the moments when I watched the black mist and the mountain of water tumble greedily upon its victims, or feel my chest ready to burst in utter fear, or wake to hear my own screams hanging in the night like splintered shards of glass.

In my heart I know there is no miracle of forgetfulness. Half-healed wounds of mind and spirit will inevitably be reopened by dreams, by the hard spattering of rain on the roofs, or perhaps by the sudden, frantic crying of a child.

Then, however much I wish it were not so, I will remember.

Dear God! I will remember.

Chapter One

Until the day I was summoned so unexpectedly into Mrs. Blackwood's office, my life had been very quiet. Orphaned at six, brought up in a modest Pittsburgh house by a spinster aunt who died when I was seventeen, I had found employment at Mrs. Blackwood's Home for Aged Convalescents.

It was not the most cheerful environment. The work was hard and poorly paid, the hours exhausting. There was never time for the reading I loved. Until my aunt's death I had attended public school, with the hope of winning a scholarship that would have allowed me to attend Bryn Mawr. Aunt Betsy was a great believer in the benefits of education, and had encouraged me in my study of French, history, mathematics, English and science. Her swift terminal illness spelled the end of these endeavors, as well as leaving me alone and deeply grieving.

Yet in spite of the unwelcome and sad change in my circumstances, I reminded myself that matters might be worse. I had a roof over my head, employment and enough to eat. I tried also to believe that my work was of some comfort and help to the elderly women in residence at Mrs. Blackwood's establishment.

Some of the patients were completely helpless and unable even to speak, and must be tended like infants. On occasion, changing the linens of some long-bedridden woman, I wondered if she might be more aware of what went on about her than her speechless condition indicated. If so, she surely must be humiliated and cast down by the necessity of being turned and lifted, washed and fed by strangers, helpless to direct her own life to even the smallest degree.

Often I talked to even the most unresponsive patients as if they could understand, as if individuality and human dignity might yet be acknowledged in their poor, almost vegetable bodies. I never knew if my efforts were of any use. Yet, somehow I felt better within myself for having tried.

On the day Mrs. Blackwood sent for me, I was hanging out freshly laundered sheets and towels in the cold March air, hoping that the threatening rain would hold off long enough for the linens to dry. Even in the chill air, it felt good to be out of doors. I sang to myself, and at first I did not hear the impatient call of Edie Jones, one of the cooks.

"Katy Livingston! Katy Livingston! Come in at once. Mrs. Blackwood wants you."

Startled, I left the laundry. Drying my hands on my big apron, I hurried to answer the summons. It was most unusual to be called into the proprietor's presence. Mrs. Sibyl Blackwood had a separate apartment in the east wing, and she was seldom seen in the other parts of her sprawling house. She never attended her charges personally, although she was reputed to have nursing experience, but hired others to do the actual work. She merely interviewed the families of prospective patients, kept the books, and considered the requests of the staff for kitchen or sickroom supplies. On fine afternoons she drove out on Pittsburgh's bustling streets in her carriage.

I had met Mrs. Blackwood only briefly when I applied for my position nearly two years ago. At that time she paid so little attention to me, interested only in my capacity for labor, that I certainly would not have expected her to recall my face or name.

Hastening along the corridor to her office, I tried to pin up straggling hair which had slid out from under my cap as I rubbed laundry against the washboards in the big tubs. I knew that my dark, blue serge skirt was wet, despite my apron, and my white blouse wrinkled and untidy, for it was near noon and I had been working since sunup.

I needn't have been concerned about my appearance. It was not noted by my employer. As I stepped into the office, I saw that she had guests. Upon the horsehair sofa sat a heavyset, floridly complexioned woman laced tightly into her corsets, and still straining the seams of her pink, silk afternoon dress. Beside her sat a tall, thin man with very

9

fair hair and a tiny moustache. His sharply molded face and small, even teeth made me think of a rodent.

Sibyl Blackwood was seated behind her large desk, which was fitted out with a handsome silver inkwell and pen holder. The blotter was strewn with various ledgers and papers.

One might have expected the owner and proprietor of a nursing home to be a plain, buxom woman of middle years. On the contrary, Sibyl Blackwood was not much over thirty, and might have passed for several years younger. Dark-haired, she had smooth, very white skin and was at first glance a beautiful woman. Then one might note the small-ness of her eyes, and the rather thick-lipped mouth that opened to reveal gapped teeth.

Mrs. Blackwood always dressed at the top of fashion. She was a widow, and considered handsome, yet I had never seen her with a gentleman. When she rode out in her carriage, it was always with Miss Spendquill, who was her assistant.

Today Mrs. Blackwood wore garnet velvet, with a high, lace-trimmed collar. Her coarse black hair was dressed high, with many coils, puffs, and ringlets. And she was glaring at me with such unsuppressed fury, that I came to an un-certain and wary stop halfway across the room.

"I sent for you some time ago, Livingston!" she snapped. "What kept you?"

"I came as quickly as I could," I began. Rudely she interrupted.

"Be more prompt in future, or you will regret it! Now, I think you should make the acquaintance of Mr. and Mrs. Horace DeWitt."

I nodded at the man and woman, wondering what their presence had to do with me. Mrs. DeWitt's eyes were fixed on me, her fat face frozen in a look of disgust as if I were something she had discovered crawling across her salad plate. Mr. DeWitt, looking me over with offensive thor-oughness, gave me a quick, very shiny glimpse of his teeth.

"No doubt you find the name familiar," Mrs. Blackwood was saying, with heavy sarcasm, as I turned back to her. "I'm sure you have guessed why Mr. and Mrs. DeWitt are here. What have you to say for yourself, Livingston?"

I drew a nervous breath, trying to think what I might have done to displease these total strangers. The name was vaguely familiar, but with Sibyl Blackwood's accusing eyes on me, I could not for the life of me think where I had heard it.

"Forgive me, I don't quite recall—"

"Don't try your lies with me!" Mrs. Blackwood warned, eyes narrowing. "Do you dare deny that you knew Mrs. Bertha DeWitt? She was a patient in your section!"

And then of course I did remember. Mrs. DeWitt had been brought to the Home after a stroke that had left her almost unable to walk, her speech sadly impaired. She was one of my responsibilities, and from the first I felt a deep compassion for the woman with the thin, beautiful face and sad eyes. At first she was very listless and indifferent. I encouraged her to eat, helped her to bathe and dress and brushed her white hair. As she slowly improved, I urged her to walk a bit. With my support, she first managed to circle her room, and then in a few weeks I took her out into the side garden.

But in this I fell afoul of Miss Spendquill, Mrs. Blackwood's ever-present spy. When she caught me returning Mrs. DeWitt to her room after a brief outing, Spendquill lost no time in warning me that Mrs. Blackwood wouldn't like my efforts.

"Surely you know it's against the rules to take a patient from her room. You take far too much authority on yourself!" she informed me.

Indignantly I protested. "I am certain that activity helps Mrs. DeWitt! She feels happier and eats more after a walk, and she's already much stronger than she was. She even speaks more clearly."

As if afraid of being overheard, Miss Spendquill glanced swiftly over her shoulder. "If you know what's good for you," she hissed, "you'll listen to me. I'm trying to do you a good turn, can't you see? Sibyl don't like her patients to improve too much, for then they want to go home."

"What could be wrong with that?" I asked, honestly puzzled. "Surely it would be a kindness to help these people

11

to be able to return to their families, where they might be more comfortable and content.''

Spendquill's face grew red. She eyed me as if I were being intentionally stupid.

"It takes money to keep this place going, you little fool! Patients all nicely cured and gone home don't line our Sibyl's pockets. Nor do their families want 'em back on their hands, neither. If you want to keep this job, Katherine Livingston, you'll think twice before you step out of your place and meddle in things that don't concern you.''

After my chores were done that night, I tried to think it all out, and I was appalled at the ugliness of my conclusions. It seemed that elderly, unwanted people were being held prisoners by means of their illnesses, and milked of their money. I would never be a party to such a thing!

Nevertheless, I could not afford to resign my job. After my conversation with Spendquill I confined my work with Mrs. DeWitt to her own private room, careful not to be caught helping her exercise.

After a few months, Mrs. DeWitt was able to walk with the aid of a cane that I smuggled in to her, and she had recovered her speech until she had less difficulty. Only certain syllables eluded her. She loved a friendly chat. I spent as much time as I dared with her, letting her reminisce. Her voice slow, and enunciating with care, she talked about her girlhood, and old friends, mostly dead years ago. Patiently I sorted out her halting sentences.

"I want . . . must . . . go home to die,'' she said again and again.

"You're not going to die!'' I protested. "You're ever so much better now.''

She patted my hand. "I'm not . . . young. I . . . feel my time coming. I must go home.''

"Then why don't you? I am sure it could be arranged through members of your family.''

With great effort and mounting agitation she explained that she had written repeatedly to her nephew, Charles Marchand, but received no reply. I knew how difficult it was for her to write, and I was furious with the indifference of a man who would not make the effort to answer a sick

12

woman's letter. She seemed to read my expression, and shook her head.

"No, no. Charles . . . loves me. He . . . he didn't . . . the letters, the . . . "

She was so anxious, her hands fluttering as the words she wanted escaped her, that I tried to help. "Are you trying to say that you think Mr. Marchand has not received your letters?"

She nodded gratefully.

"Why can't you simply tell Mrs. Blackwood that you wish to be taken home?" I asked.

Slowly, stumbling over words, she enlightened me. After her stroke, when she was helpless for a time and could not speak, her affairs were taken over by the son of a distant cousin, the only kin available, as Mr. Marchand was abroad. This much younger cousin thought it best that Mrs. DeWitt remain at the Blackwood Home.

She seemed so unhappy that I made a suggestion. "Give me your nephew's address. I will write to him myself. I will . . . "

I stopped, for a sudden small memory had popped into my mind, of an afternoon when I had surprised Miss Spendquill examining the outgoing mail on the hall table. Startled, she had laughed and in a shrill, nervous voice offered the explanation that she had laid a letter here to be posted, then changed her mind about sending it. I had thought little of it at the time, but now for some reason I remembered her nearsightedly peering at the envelopes.

Thoughtfully I finished my sentence. "I will write your nephew and post the letter myself. It is my turn to do the marketing for the kitchen tomorrow."

Eagerly, with hope flaring in her kind eyes, Mrs. DeWitt gave me two addresses for her nephew, one in Johnstown, Pennsylvania, the other in Kentucky.

The next day I saw to it that the notes were properly mailed to Mr. Marchand. Within a week Mrs. DeWitt had been removed from the Home. Her departure was completely unexpected. I was again marketing when she left, and I felt a pang at missing the opportunity to wish her well and say goodbye.

But after work that night, Eileen O'Donnell, the kitchen maid who often brought Mrs. DeWitt's meals, came to my tiny attic room.

"Katy, I do wish you could have seen the uproar!" she grinned. "Mrs. DeWitt's nephew came striding through the halls, with that witch Mrs. Blackwood trotting at his side, mind you, sweetly arguing with him. 'I assure you, you are making a grave mistake, Mr. Marchand,' she says, 'your aunt is better now, but if you remove her from our tender care, I won't answer for the consequences!'"

Eileen was a clever mimic. She sounded so much like Sibyl that I smiled. She continued breathlessly. "Old Blackwood was *that* furious, I could tell, but she made her voice all oily and persuading, and even put her hand on the gentleman's arm! He brushed it away as if it was a nasty wasp, he did, and asked which was his aunt's room. An' Mrs. Blackwood had to tell him.

"Then he hisself packed his aunt's things, and he carried old Mrs. DeWitt out in his arms, telling me to bring her little trunk. Sure an' I was glad to do it, for you'd ought to have seen the glad look on Mrs. DeWitt's face."

"I'm so glad for her. She wanted to leave here, and who can blame her?"

"She gave me something for you," Eileen said conspiratorially. "She said I was to tell you most particular that she would bless you to her dying day for all you'd done."

"I did nothing."

"Here's what she left for you. And this money, too."

Eileen pressed something into my palm. "Ain't it lovely, though?" she breathed.

It was a ring, a translucent, pale, red stone with shifting irridescent fire in its depths. Seed pearls surrounded it in a heavy gold setting. I slipped it on the third finger of my right hand, where it was only the least bit too large. "Oh, I *shouldn't* take it!" I whispered.

"Don't be a silly goose, Kate! You'd break that old lady's heart if you sent it back. Surely you wouldn't be doing such a cruel thing, for the sake of pride?"

Perhaps she was right. I examined the stone in the lamplight. Mrs. Blackwood had not had gas lighting installed on the top floor of the house.

Eileen touched it with a fingertip. "'Tis a fire opal, Mrs. DeWitt told me, and very, very old. It belonged to her great grandmother, and came from Honduras."

"I shall treasure it always," I sighed with a mixture of delight and guilt at keeping the gift.

"An' the money, too. Don't forget the money. She said it was for a time when you might need it particular bad, that you was to hide it away and keep it for such a time."

"But money! What would Mrs. Blackwood and Miss Spendquill say to my receiving a money gift from a patient," I worried.

"Huh! They'd say it was property of the Home, that's what." Eileen gave me a significant look. "An' that's the last you'd see of it, and Sibyl Blackwood would be sportin' a new dress, like as not. Hide it like Mrs. DeWitt said, an' let that fine old lady be happy in doing someone a kindness."

"Eileen, you're wiser than I, I think."

"O' course!" she agreed, with a giggle.

I made her take half the twenty dollars that Mrs. DeWitt had left. I did as instructed by my elderly friend, pinning the currency within my clothing daily, so that I always knew it was there. It was a comfort to know I had that much security, for it seemed I could not refrain from displeasing Miss Spendquill, and I wondered daily if I would be dismissed.

I wore the lovely old ring upon a faded ribbon tied about my neck, and tucked into my bodice. I sent Mrs. DeWitt a letter in care of her nephew, thanking her for the gifts and wishing her well. But I never received a reply, and after some eight months, I had almost forgotten how much I missed the kindness and gratitude she'd shown me.

Now, called upon the carpet in Mrs. Blackwood's office, hearing Mrs. DeWitt's name again after so long, I could only think that my part in helping her leave the Home had at last been discovered. I stood quietly, waiting for the blow to fall.

"You great dolt," Mrs. Blackwood slapped the palm of her hand on her desk top. "I have asked you a question. What have you to say for yourself? You have disgraced yourself and my establishment, working slyly to influence an old sick woman. You are a conniving, scheming little cat!"

The plump woman seated on Mrs. Blackwood's sofa sprang up hotly. "As I said to Mr. DeWitt, I never heard of anything so outrageous as what you have tried to do," she shouted. Her hat plumes bobbed wildly, she held her gloved hands up like a preacher exhorting his congregation on the certainties of hellfire and brimstone. "The house was to have come to us, I know it was, until you brought your evil, vicious hints to bear on that poor old woman's befuddled mind! I'll have the law on you, see if I don't!"

"I know nothing of any house," I began, but Mrs. Horace DeWitt shouted me down.

"It's stealing, pure and simple, that's what it is, outright thievery—"

"I haven't the faintest idea what you are talking about," I cried, exasperated and bewildered by the attack.

"Read this, and then tell me you don't know what we're talking about!" sneered Sibyl Blackwood, handing me a sheet of paper.

It was a letter, with the sedate, printed letterhead of a Johnstown, Pennsylvania attorney. It was addressed to me. I drew myself up, angrier than I had ever been before in my life.

"This is *my* letter! Your name is nowhere upon it, Mrs. Blackwood. Why have you opened it—read it?" I demanded. "This is completely improper. You had no right—"

"You dare accuse *me*?" shrilled my employer, but her eyes darted sidewise. "You're a fine one to talk about rights and propriety, scheming and conniving to rob a dying woman of her property!"

Startled, I stared at her. "Mrs. Bertha DeWitt is dead?"

"A week ago Tuesday morning," Mr. Horace DeWitt spoke up for the first time. "God rest her soul," he added piously.

I looked from him to Mrs. Blackwood. "And this letter came for me, but was given to you instead. By Miss Spendquill, no doubt." .

"I have a right to know what is going on in this household," Sibyl spluttered.

"You have no right to pry into another's private corre-spondence, about matters that do not concern you. How many other letters have you intercepted?" I asked coldly, struggling to keep my voice from rising. "I am leaving your employ at once. I must ask you for my wages for this week to date."

But she would not give me the two dollars that were owed to me, and at this point I was not surprised. Folding the letter without reading it, I thrust it into my skirt pocket.

"I will bid you good day," I said, and left a roomful of silence behind me.

The silence did not last. As I shut the door I heard Mrs. Horace DeWitt babbling something about the law and a question about Mrs. Blackwood's part in the plot.

Mrs. Blackwood responded with an enraged roar, and the argument waxed hotter as I hurried away. From a distance their voices took on the sound of contentious animals snarling over a bone.

Chapter Two

Midway through my meagre packing I realized that I had rendered myself without employment, and further, that I had no place to go.

Stunned, my anger running out, I sank to my narrow cot, trying to think what I must do. There was a tap on the door. Eileen came in, her round, freckled face rosy with excitement.

"Is it true then? You're really going? Oh, what shall I do without you?"

She squeezed my hand until it hurt. "Well, never you mind, Katy. You're doing the right thing. Mrs. Blackwood had no right to yell at you so. We heard, even in the pantry."

"She opened a letter meant for me," I said dully, still trying to take in the abrupt change in my situation. I felt in my pocket, realizing that I had no idea what the letter contained. Taking it out, I smoothed it with trembling fingers.

It was brief. The sender was a Mr. Joshua C. Galbraith, Attorney-at-Law. He stated that Mrs. Bertha Louise DeWitt, late of Johnstown, had been found dead of an injury suffered during a fall at her home on the twenty-seventh day of February. If I would come to his office at soonest convenience, I would be given news of a beneficial nature.

"What is it, Katy?" Eileen asked anxiously. She had capably taken over my packing, and was now tucking my Thurston's Ivory Pearl tooth powder and a bottle of witch hazel into my old Gladstone bag.

"I—it's probably nothing." I frowned at the letter.

"Where will you be going?" Eileen laid my aunt's Bible into the bag.

I hesitated, but only for a moment. "To Johnstown," I said.

"That's up east. It's in the Connemaugh River Valley, ain't it? I know a lad that works in the Cambria Iron Company mills. Now, promise you'll write to me."

"Of course I will. You've been a good friend. Perhaps," I said recklessly, "perhaps I shall find a good job in Johnstown, and you can come too. We could room together."

The girl stared at me in delight. "Mercy, do you mean it, Katy?"

Feeling a little better at having even the ghost of a plan, and a first step to take, I stood and closed my bag. "I'll write you as soon as I have a place to stay. There are surely jobs in that town for both of us."

It was a two hour trip from Union Station to Johnstown, Pennsylvania. My anxiety kept me from noting much about the scenery as the train climbed into the Alleghenies, following the course of the Connemaugh River.

We rocked along the valley, making stops in the several towns along the way. We left Bolivar and New Florence behind. At Sang Hollow, four miles from Johnstown, a brash young man came aboard and seated himself next to me, despite the fact that I gave him only a very cool nod. Ignoring my lack of encouragement, he demanded to know if this was my first trip to Johnstown, then began to point out landmarks, some of which I confess I found interesting. For instance, we saw the Connemaugh Gap a mile out of Johnstown, which is said to be the deepest river gorge between the Rocky Mountains and the Alleghenies. He showed me the Cambria Iron Mills, where steel rails and plowshares were made; Cambria City where the immigrant millworkers lived; and the new and impressive stone railroad bridge that crossed to the north side of the river just below the point where the Connemaugh was joined by Stony Creek.

I ignored my persistent seatmate as well as possible and turned to the window to see Johnstown.

It was not a very pretty town. To me it seemed quite crowded and busy and raw. Boarding houses of pine lumber stood next the river. There were countless two or three story family homes of frame construction, with tiny front yards.

·However, there were also a few handsome dwellings.

"Them fine houses belong to the Company men," my unwanted companion informed me. "Ain't that brick one a fine sight? They even got indoor bathrooms, some of 'em!"

I felt annoyed at his indelicacy, and did not reply. I noted large office buildings on the main street, some of them as tall as five storeys, and there was a park that in summer would be appealing, with its many elm trees.

To the town's credit, I saw numerous church steeples. The young man breathing over my shoulder informed me of other advantages.

"We got swell band concerts in the park in summer, and there's even a opera house. Course, I haven't been there. How'd you like to go buggy riding with me up to South Fork sometime? I'll take you to see the lake them rich men got up there. They even got sailboats."

Politely I demurred. I was grateful when the train stopped and I could escape his attentions with a murmur about my uncle meeting me. Regretfully he jammed on his wool cap and swaggered off the train ahead of the other passengers in our car.

When I had my bag, I went into the station to make inquiries as to inexpensive rooms, and was directed to a quiet house two streets away. It was owned by a Mrs. Carew, who gave me a plain square room overlooking a muddy backyard. But if this outlook was depressing, I could look up onto the steep slopes that hemmed in the town. There was still snow among the evergreens and other thickly-crowded trees up there.

I took time to wash and change into my best dress, a dark green merino, plainly-fashioned and not of the most recent style. Aunt Betsy had made it for me. Her fingers had lovingly placed each jet button on the tunic top, draped the cloth over the modified bustle and fashioned the large bow that tied upon the left side. I wished that I had had time to borrow an iron and press the creases out of the skirt. I shook it out as best I could, and reflected that at least the cloth was still in excellent condition, and the color reflected itself softly in my gray eyes.

At last, having done all I could for my appearance, I set out to find Mr. Joshua Galbraith's office. Mrs. Carew kindly gave me directions to Alma Hall. I could see the avid curiosity in her eyes, but she refrained from inquiring my business with Mr. Galbraith.

It was precisely four-thirty in the afternoon when I entered the lawyer's outer office on an upper floor of the building. I stated my need to see Mr. Galbraith to the pretty young woman who sat at a reception desk, using a typewriter with self-conscious skill.

"Yes, miss, please be seated, won't you? Mr. Galbraith is with a client at present."

A few minutes after my arrival the door between the two offices, not quite latched, swung open an inch or so as some stray draught of air caught it. I heard a man's voice, low and intense.

"You and I both know it was a clever swindle. Yet you say that nothing can be—?"

The receptionist looked up, startled, and hastened into the attorney's office, with a hasty preliminary tap on the door. She was gone for several moments, and when she returned she shut the door firmly behind her.

She glanced at me with an odd look, almost speculative. "I'm sure it will only be a few more minutes," she said. "I've informed Mr. Galbraith that you are here."

I nodded. I had never been in an attorney's office before. Aunt Betsy's affairs had been handled after her death by a lawyer who was an old friend, and who had kindly come to my aunt's small rented house to tell me compassionately that debts had taken everything Aunt Betsy had been able to save, and that her few pieces of furniture would have to be sold to satisfy creditors.

I felt uneasy and uncomfortable in this place of business, very young and gauche. Perhaps it was foolish, but I was most disquieted by my lack of gloves. My work-reddened hands were an embarrassment. I kept them folded so that the office girl would not notice them.

The inner door opened suddenly and a squarely-built man with sandy moustache and crisp, red hair looked out at me.

"Miss Livingston? Come in, if you please."

I stood, knees trembling, and went past him. Catching my toe in the hem of my skirt, I stumbled awkwardly. My cheeks flamed.

"Please take a seat, Miss Livingston," the attorney said. "May I present Mr. Charles Marchand?"

Only then was I aware that there was another man in the room, a man who came forward and took my nerveless hand with cool courtesy.

Witlessly I acknowledged the introduction, realizing that here was Mrs. Bertha DeWitt's nephew, the man to whom I had written.

Mr. Marchand was an overwhelming person. He was very tall, quite dwarfing Mr. Galbraith. Perhaps thirty years of age, he was strongly built. His hand on mine was firm, the fingers long and much browner than my own. Black hair, thick and with only the slightest tendency to wave, fell forward over his brow, above blue eyes strongly accented by stubby black lashes and eyebrows like the gleaming wings of some mythical, ebony-feathered bird.

In the moment I dared stare at him, I gained the impression of icy reserve. His sternly-carved mouth gave only the barest hint of a smile of greeting. I noticed that his cheekbones were his most distinguishing feature, high and slanted and strongly apparent in his lean face. He was a country man, I thought, noting his weather-darkened skin. By contrast, his gray suit, the gleaming white perfection of his collar, and the dark silk of his cravat might have come from New York's finest men's shops.

"Miss Livingston, I am pleased to make your acquaintance," he said.

"Mr. Marchand heard that you were here, and asked to meet you," the attorney explained, taking a seat behind his very cluttered and high-piled oak desk, as I sank into a straight-backed chair. "It's a fortunate coincidence that you stopped by today. Charles tells me that you were instrumental in alerting him to Mrs. DeWitt's situation at the Blackwood home."

"My letter was merely one of several written to Mr. Marchand," I said. "Mrs. DeWitt wrote more than once, even though it required great effort." I remembered her bewilderment at his failure to reply, and temper began to demolish my diffidence. I gave Mr. Marchand a direct look, and I suppose my eyes accused him, for he blinked and raised his winging eyebrows.

"I am sure you are mistaken about that, Miss Livingston," he said curtly. "I received no such letter from my aunt. Had I done so I should have come to her assistance at once. I was abroad when she became ill, attending a sale of Irish thoroughbreds, after which my presence was required at my farm in Kentucky. However I had returned to Johnstown several weeks before your letter arrived.

"Of course I was told of Aunt Bertha's illness, but I was given to understand that she was not cognizant, nor able to be out of bed. It was my intention to visit her, but I was delayed by . . . personal business. When your letter came to me, and I read of my aunt's incarceration against her will in that damnable place, I lost no time in coming to take her home!"

Was it possible he spoke the truth? "There *were* letters, I am certain of it," I insisted. "I took them from her hand myself and laid them to be mailed upon the table in the anteroom of the Home."

"I fear you labor under a misapprehension. I received not one word from my aunt," he insisted, with a look that seemed to relegate me to the ranks of innumerable souls not worthy of his further consideration.

"Miss Livingston, is it possible that Mrs. Blackwood or some of her people tampered with the mail?" asked the attorney quietly.

"That thought had crossed my mind," I admitted. I pulled from my reticule the letter I had taken from Sibyl Blackwood's hand. "When this came for me from your office, it was given without my knowledge to Mrs. Blackwood, and I only received it after Mr. and Mrs. Horace DeWitt went to her to complain about me."

The men exchanged a startled glance. "The Horace DeWitt's have been to the Blackwood establishment recently?"

I nodded. "This very morning, sir."

"To complain about you, you said."

"Yes, Mr. Galbraith. They came," I said steadily, "to accuse me of using undue influence upon Mrs. DeWitt in a matter pertaining to a house. They did not explain exactly what they believed I had done."

"Allow me to enlighten you." Mr. Galbraith placed the tips of his fingers together and studied me intently. "Mrs. Bertha DeWitt, in a will written shortly after her return to Johnstown, made you one of her heirs. You are now the owner of her residence in this city."

I stared at him, speechless for a moment, then struggled to express my thoughts. "Surely there is some mistake. What you say is simply not possible, Mr. Galbraith. She knew me for only a very brief time, and I am in no way related to her family."

He sent an enigmatic glance towards Charles Marchand, who had moved to a spot behind my chair, where I could not see his face.

"I assure you, Miss Livingston, it is quite true. I can show you the documents, signed in my presence by Bertha DeWitt."

I was utterly dumbfounded by the news. Naturally I had taken Mrs. Horace DeWitt's remarks about a house that should have gone to her, to mean that she suspected me of advising Mrs. DeWitt to leave it to another relative, perhaps the nephew, Mr. Marchand. Now, remembering the fury on the woman's face, and her accusation that I had used an old lady's confusion and gratitude for my own purposes, I felt quite ill. The room blurred and began to spin about me.

"Charles, she's—"

Strong hands caught me, held me upright in my chair until the dizziness went away.

Slowly the mists cleared. I ran a shaking hand over my eyes. The familiar feel of my own work-hardened fingers, rough against my eyelids, helped me to find a sense of reality. I drew a deep breath and straightened my back.

"Please forgive me," I said.

"Are you all right now?" Mr. Marchand asked, stepping away.

"Yes. Thank you." I cleared my throat. "Mr. Galbraith, I cannot of course accept Mrs. DeWitt's legacy. She owed me nothing, and yet, when she was leaving the Home, she gave me twenty dollars and a valuable ring. I now realize, it was very wrong of me to accept these gifts."

I drew the ring out of the collar of my dress, and untied the worn ribbon. I laid the opal ring upon the desk and fumbled in my purse for the ten dollars belonging to Mrs. DeWitt, less my train fare. This I put beside the ring. "I wish to return this. Half of the money I gave to the maid who was kind to Mrs. DeWitt. I will repay that and what I have spent from my earnings when I find another position."

The men stared at me in silence. I felt that Mr. Marchand in particular had found my statement unexpected.

"What's that you say?" Mr. Galbraith asked sharply. "You won't accept the house?"

"That is correct, sir. Please give me a paper to sign to that effect." Already I felt better. I regretted having to give up the lovely opal ring, but I knew it was the honorable thing to do.

"May I ask your reasons?" the attorney inquired almost gently.

I paused, sorting out thoughts and words. "This morning, sir, I was accused of something utterly despicable. I did not fully understand the accusation at the time. Now that you have explained to me the alteration of Mrs. DeWitt's will, I see that quite naturally members of the family must suspect me of having tried to gain materially from my attentions to Mrs. DeWitt, who was ill and helpless. Caring for the lady was my job—nothing more. For that service I was already receiving a stated wage. Not one penny more is owed to me."

I knew that I sounded pompous and silly, and hastened to finish. "It was never my intention to ask more than I had earned, and I do not like the feeling of . . . of . . . "

"Miss Livingston!" Charles Marchand interrupted, his blue eyes focused narrowly upon me. "It is obvious that Bertha DeWitt *did* feel deeply indebted to you. I for one accept your statement that you used no influence on her, and were ignorant of her intentions. I knew my aunt very well. She was strong-willed, and in sound mind right up to the day of her death. Mr. Galbraith would not have taken her will down verbatim and without question had he suspected that she was not clear in her mind.''

The gentleman's voice had the sound of conviction, yet I was not convinced of his sincerity. Of course he had suspected me! Why else had he insisted upon this meeting? I met his look, and lifted my chin proudly.

"Mr. Marchand, I am sure *you* are Mrs. DeWitt's rightful heir, you and perhaps Mr. and Mrs. Horace DeWitt. It would be ludicrous for me to claim any rights in this matter.''

"I see we have here a very stubborn young lady!'' chuckled Mr. Joshua Galbraith. "I do believe this is the first time anyone to whom I attempted to hand over a legacy has refused it. What shall we do about it, Charles? Miss Livingston seems quite sure of her decision.''

Mr. Marchand smiled suddenly, and his cold features lighted with a wicked charm. The change was startling, as if he were suddenly another person altogether. "Why, we shall take the lady to dinner, of course. Miss Livingston will think more clearly when she has eaten. I venture to guess that she has not had a decent meal since early this morning, if then.''

I viewed his astonishing switch of personality with uncertainty and suspicion, but he was more correct than he knew. I had been too agitated to think of food during the trying day.

Mr. Galbraith followed his client's lead without hesitation. "Capital idea, Charles. Come, Miss Livingston.'' The attorney rose and moved rapidly across the room with a sort of bearlike stride, taking his coat and derby from the corner rack. Before I could more than murmur an instinctive protest, we were on our way from the office.

Soon I was being handed into Mr. Marchand's handsome carriage, drawn behind the loveliest horses I had ever seen—matched blacks with elegant high heads and a lively trot.

They took me to the Hulbert House and ordered an enormous meal. I confess that I could not resist the delicious food—I was hungry. For that matter, I have never suffered from an indifferent appetite. After I finished, I felt a trifle ashamed, thinking they had surely never seen a lady so ravenous. Ah, well, it scarcely mattered what these gentlemen thought of a poor working girl.

They had been conversing without apparent attention to me. Mr. Marchand was describing a new tower being built in Paris, France.

"It is almost complete. I saw it when I was abroad again in January. A man named Eiffel has designed and erected it for the World's Fair to begin in May."

"I hear it is very impressive," nodded Galbraith.

"It is said to be nine hundred and eighty-four feet in height, and will cost one million dollars."

Galbraith whistled. "Will you return when the Fair opens?"

"Possibly. I have made no decision as yet."

I laid down my napkin, and both men turned to me with instant, alarming attention. I felt that I should take my leave. Thanking them for the meal, I rose to go. Mr. Marchand tilted his face to one side and looked at me like a terrier eyeing a bright rubber ball just before pouncing.

"Where did you think to go, Miss Livingston?" he asked.

"I have rented a room in Mrs. Carew's rooming house," I said. "I thank you for—"

"And what do you propose to do for a living?" he asked bluntly. "I take it that you have thoroughly burned your bridges at Mrs. Blackwood's Home?"

I flushed. "I am sure I can find employment of some kind. Perhaps I could learn to work a typewriter, like the young lady in Mr. Galbraith's office."

Mr. Marchand shook his head sadly, but something told me he was laughing at me, and I began to be angry. "Then, who is to care for my aunt's beloved old house?" he asked.

"Why," I replied tartly, "I should imagine that you will, sir."

"No, it is impossible. You see, I have the responsibility of my horse farm in Kentucky, and while my partner often takes over when I must spend time elsewhere, I am afraid I cannot take the time to oversee all that needs to be done to the house. Since, after you, I am clearly next in line to inherit, I must follow your example and decline the property.''

''Charles, no!'' spluttered Mr. Galbraith. ''Then it will certainly go to Horace DeWitt and his family, and you know how your aunt felt about them. It would break her heart, were she living, to know Lily DeWitt would handle her possessions with her greedy fat hands!''

Mr. Galbraith's face was so grim that I was sure he, at least, spoke from deepest conviction.

Charles Marchand shrugged big shoulders. ''I can't be blamed. That house has liabilities, as you well know. I don't wish to pay those overdue taxes.''

''Then you would really let it go to Horace DeWitt?''

I remembered those unpleasant people, and how they had kept Mrs. DeWitt in Blackwood's Home against her will, and when it was no longer necessary. Now they were to win what they had sought. I felt deeply disturbed at the thought.

''I won't have it!'' Mr. Galbraith was shaking his head. ''I simply won't turn that house over to those—those boorish social climbers!''

Marchand sighed with finality. ''Then there is only one solution. Miss Livingston must accept it, after all, if only because she owes it to my aunt to do so.''

He turned to me earnestly. ''You wouldn't want to be ungrateful to a fine woman who befriended you, Miss Livingston, surely? Would you flout her dying wishes?''

''But—but I have no right to the house, you cannot deny that!'' I stammered.

''*She* gave you every right.''

I sensed that I was being adroitly maneuvered. I grasped an irrefutable argument. ''It's no use. I could never pay the taxes, either!'' Somehow it had become a contest between my wits and those of this bewildering, domineering gentleman.

''Ah, but you can,'' Mr. Marchand said. ''And you will. I intend to rent the house from you for a year. My wife and family are already living there, and I dislike uprooting them.''

''But–you just said—'' I was thoroughly confused now.

''I said that I could not personally superintend the house and estate, and it is quite so. I am forced to be absent a good deal of the time. Now, the rent will pay for the taxes, renovations, and other expenses. I will expect you to live on the premises and oversee the necessary work. When the place is in good condition, either I shall purchase it from you, or you may sell it to people who will appreciate a spacious family dwelling. It is what my aunt would want. Certainly she would have been appalled to think her old home would fall into the hands of people she despised, who took every advantage of her generosity in the past, and thought of her only as a future source of possessions!''

There was more persuasion that flowed from the man's lips in a passionate stream. My arguments were like straws in a gale, blown away before being clearly seen.

In the end, weakly, I agreed. At which both men offered congratulations and hurried me back to Mr. Galbraith's office to sign necessary documents. Then Mr. Marchand bid me good evening and went rather hastily on his way.

Mr. Galbraith drove me back to my room. He left instructions for me to be ready to travel across town to the DeWitt house next day, and then, he too, was gone.

I went up to my room in a state of bemusement. The events of this day had been not at all what I expected. I found myself the reluctant owner of property, a landlady with tenants—and all because of Charles Marchand's magnetic persuasion.

None of it was what I wanted. I had not forgotten the accusations made by the Horace DeWitts. By accepting the legacy, had I not lent truth to their suspicions?

Unfairly, perhaps, I began to blame Charles Marchand for turning me from what my judgement told me was the best course of action. I puzzled over his determination to persuade me to accept his aunt's house. Why on earth had he done that, when it could have gone to him?

I did not, on reflection, believe that he could not afford the taxes. After all he had himself arranged to pay a very generous rent.

I grew increasingly uneasy over my decision, suddenly convinced that the man who had artfully manipulated my decision today was not the real Charles Marchand at all. He had been putting on an act. But why?

Doubtless I would be meeting Mrs. Marchand tomorrow, and I wondered unhappily how that meeting would go. Mrs. Marchand was bound to resent the fact that a complete stranger, a young woman out of nowhere, had taken over the house where she resided, a house she might fully have expected to own.

Sighing, I took off my hat and unpinned my long, thick hair. Removing the green merino dress, I inspected it carefully for spots or mud upon the hem. I must look my best tomorrow, if only for the tiny added bit of confidence it would afford.

Chapter Three

My first sight of the DeWitt house is engraved deeply in my memory. It stood near the small river called Stony Creek perhaps half a mile from where it joins the Connemaugh. A very large house, set back amid wide lawns, it commanded a view of the bustling town from its small hill. Yet it was very private.

We arrived there in Mr. Galbraith's buggy in the late afternoon. He had been delayed by business until four. Before we turned into the drive he stopped the horse to let me see the place. A tall house of frame construction, of no particular style, it rambled over a large space. There were many chimneys and steeply pitched gables. A wide porch and second floor balcony swept comfortably about two sides. Once this must have been an imposing house, but now the paint was peeling and no longer white. I noticed two broken windows upon the third floor, and wondered that someone had not seen to their replacement. That must be done immediately, for winter was still very much with us, cold, raw, and wet with a stubbornly drizzling rain that had kept up most of the day.

Lawns and gardens ran in all directions about the house and they too were much in need of care. Last summer's growth of grass had apparently been allowed to stand rank and thick, and was now yellow and dead. Leaves from the many lovely old trees—oak and maple and elm—littered the lawns, and dried weeds were rampant in every spot where grass had not crowded them aside.

There was a small barn or stable, and the usual outhouses and sheds. I saw two horses in a small pasture that lay along the river and halfway up the hillside back of the house.

"The place needs someone to take hold of it again," Mr. Galbraith remarked. "It was a fine house once. When Mrs.

31

DeWitt was well, before her fortune was lost by unfortunate purchases of worthless western mining stock, she kept a full-time gardener and a handyman who tended to things. She had gardens and a cow and hens—''

"Oh, I would love to have hens!" I surprised myself by saying.

He smiled at me. "I see you are going to be good for the place. You're not afraid of work, and with the rent Charles is paying, you can do wonders. I want you to feel free to call upon me for any advice."

"We must have a hired man," I decided at once. "Can you find one for me? Someone who will work willingly."

"I know a man who might do. His father was Mrs. DeWitt's employee for years, and he's a first-rate gardener. He loves growing things, and he's handy with tools. I happen to know he's free just now."

"Then we must have him."

"Before you decide to hire Johnny Brock, I feel I must warn you—" he hesitated, as if reluctant to go on.

"Warn me?" I prompted.

"Yes. John Brock has a drinking problem. He lost several jobs because he cannot stay away from the saloons. But I know him well, and basically he's a good man."

"I don't hold with imbibing spirits!" I said, knowing that I probably sounded dreadfully prim.

"Certainly not. I quite understand. If you give Brock a trial, I shall impress upon him that he must not drink during working hours. If he will not agree to that, we'll look elsewhere."

"Under those circumstances, I agree."

The feeling of competence in making decisions that had sprung up in the last few minutes vanished like a child's soap bubble, leaving me uncertain again. "Will you advise me as to proper wages for Mr. Brock? And—I shall need a maid, I suppose. There is a girl at the Blackwood Home I should like to send for."

"Hire at least two girls," Mr. Galbraith said firmly. "You mustn't expect to do the cleaning yourself. Charles tells me they kept on the cook when Bertha DeWitt passed away, though the woman had it in mind to retire on the very generous bequest Mrs. DeWitt left her. Mrs. Potter will continue to be paid by the Marchands, no doubt. I believe Mrs. Marchand also has her own maid.''

"Mr. Galbraith," I blurted suddenly, badly needing re-assurance. "Did I do the wrong thing in accepting the house? I find that I feel very guilty, very—presumptuous.''

He clucked to the horse. "You did exactly the right thing. It is what Mrs. DeWitt wanted. Put any anxiety upon that score right out of your mind.''

"But—" I twisted my hands, and realizing how gauche that appeared, made myself stop. "But won't Mrs. Marchand think—?''

"Don't always ask yourself what others think!" he scolded. "Nine times out of ten you will be in error, and you only rob yourself of confidence you need. You are a young lady of good judgement and upright character. Remember that and ignore the opinions of others.''

He sounded quite cross. I glanced at him sidewise, biting my lip. He grinned suddenly and patted my hand. "Forgive the sermon, my dear, but you will find I am right. Have a little faith in yourself! Will you try to do that?''

Grateful for his kindness, I nodded. "I'm sure your advice is excellent. I shall try my best to follow it.''

"Good." He reined in the horse at the front of the house. Somewhat heartened, I allowed him to help me down.

The front door was opened to our summons by a woman who was still wiping flour from her hands as she let us in. She was a big woman, with graying, ginger hair skewed into a knot on top of her head, and a generally untidy appearance. She looked harrassed and not in the best temper.

"Ah, Mrs. Potter! This is Miss Livingston, the new owner of the house. Miss Livingston, Mrs. Potter is in charge of the kitchen; and from what Charles tells me, is a most excellent cook.''

"Pleased I'm sure." The woman nodded. "I've got a pie in the oven." Without another word, she hurried through a door at the back of the large entry hall, past the stairs.

Startled, I smiled at Mr. Galbraith. "I seem to have made a poor impression on Mrs. Potter.''

"Nonsense. She is just single-minded. Her kitchen is all that occupies her mind."

"I suppose you're right." But uncertainty assailed me again. What was I to do now? I hoped Mr. Galbraith would not desert me until I had made the acquaintance of Mrs. Marchand. "You will stay—stay to dinner, won't you please?" He looked down at me quizzically as if he very easily saw through my sudden attack of hospitality. And then I realized something dismaying. "Oh—perhaps I shouldn't be inviting guests—" and that sounded even worse.

He laughed heartily. "I often stay, and I'm sure no one will be offended by your invitation of a family friend. Now let us see if we can find Mrs. Marchand."

Timidly I walked at his side, feeling like an uninvited tradesperson, soon to be given a sharp reprimand for venturing into the private home of strangers.

We looked into a large, dim parlor full of heavy old furniture. Finding no one there, we glanced into a study situated along a hall that ran the length of the house at right angles to the entrance. We stepped into a drawing room, what might be called a music room, a library, an office or perhaps another study, even a conservatory. We found no one, and had started down the other way, when we heard light rapid footsteps on the stairs, and went into the hall to intercept them.

And so I saw Joanna Marchand for the first time. She came flying down the stairs like a mere girl, her silvery, pale, fine hair floating loose about her small face. At first glance one must think of a fairy-tale princess. She was quite lovely, small and delicate.

She came to a halt, obviously surprised to find us here, and my stomach knotted with frightened anticipation.

"Why, Joshua!" she cried. "Forgive me, I didn't know you had arrived." She came swiftly down the remainder of the stairs, hands outstretched to both of us. "You must be Miss Livingston." She smiled at me. "My husband was here briefly this morning, and he told me to expect you. It is such a pleasure to meet you. I had heard much of you from our Aunt Bertha."

"I am delighted to meet you, Mrs. Marchand," I murmured.

"Not half so happy as I am to meet you," she laughed, charmingly. "I am so glad the estate is settled at last, and that you were kind enough to allow us to stay on here. I so dreaded moving." As she spoke, she gestured theatrically with her beautiful hands. On another woman, it would have seemed affected. "Charles tells me you will be having the place attended to, and believe me, much is needed. It used to be so comfortable when Aunt Bertha was able to manage it."

"Why didn't you have some necessary things done, Joanna? The estate would have borne the coasts."

"Oh," she waved with airy indifference. "I have no head for such things. I notice my own discomfort, but I dislike planning how to remedy things. Now that Miss Livingston is here, perhaps things will get done."

She turned her bright blue eyes on me. They were round, very childlike, yet they seemed to probe beneath my face. The effect was not offensive, but rather flattering, as if she bestowed her deepest interest upon me. Her small, rounded figure seemed almost to vibrate animatedly within her blue faille dress. Next to her vitality, her delicate smallness, I felt too tall, too passive, too—still.

"I am sure you want to see your quarters. Charles said the former housekeeper's apartment would probably be your choice, since it is most private. But I assure you that if there are other rooms that you like better, you must feel free to choose."

"I—wouldn't think of intruding upon the portion of the house you have rented," I said.

She shrugged airily. "It would not disturb us in the least. You must do whatever you wish. Come, I'll show you the housekeeper's apartment. Joshua, you'll be staying for dinner, of course?"

"Thank you," he said with an amused glance at me. "I shall be delighted. I must see to my horse. May I drive my buggy around to the stable?"

"Of course."

"First let me carry Miss Livingston's bag to her rooms,"

he offered.

"Don't be silly. I am sure Miss Livingston can carry one bag." Joanna laughed at him.

Hastily I assured him that it would be no trouble, and picked it up. He bowed us out of sight.

Chattering steadily, Joanna Marchand led me into the corridor Mr. Galbraith and I had been exploring, but in the opposite direction. The second door let us into a suite that surprised me. I had pictured very modest quarters. This was more than comfortable, and in better condition than the rest of the house.

"Aunt Bertha had these rooms redone—at an expense greater than she could truly afford, I might say. The housekeeper Old Mrs. Welcome, had been with her for years. She died about a year before Aunt Bertha, and no one has occupied this apartment since. It's quite nice, don't you think?"

"Indeed yes. There is so much light!"

"The rooms face the south side of the house. Bertha had more windows cut into the walls for Mrs. Welcome because she suffered from cataracts and was slowly losing her vision. The wallpapers were ordered from New York." She gestured as expansively as if she herself had planned every detail. "I only wish the rest of the house were in such good condition!"

We entered a sitting room. The walls were covered in a delicately striped blue-and-white patterned paper, with tiny sprigs of white blossoms sprinkled over it. The drapes at the many windows were a darker blue scrim with embroidered hems. The matching rockers before the small marble hearth were of gleaming cherry wood. They were ladder-backed chairs cushioned with some sturdily woven cloth, a shade that matched the drapes. A Banjo clock stood upon the mantelpiece, together with assorted knickknacks and figurines. On the painted wooden floor lay various rag rugs and a Smyrna rug occupied the center of the floor.

Upon one wall hung a cheerful painting of sailboats on sunlit water. As for the other furniture, there was an old but still beautiful Duncan Phyfe settee with a reeded mahogany frame, various small tables including a lovely little sewing table, and a tall secretary with painted glass doors. But the long room was not overcrowded, an effect I found restful. Everything was very dusty, the windows badly neglected, but these things I could easily remedy. It would be a pleasure to have such duties in a home of my own.

For a moment my mind spun with a combination of realization and disbelief. Was it possible that this place was mine? All of it, even beyond the apartment that would be my refuge?

Mrs. Marchand showed me into a bedroom, fitted out with a grand old four-poster bed in some dark wood, a dresser, bureau and wardrobe. For winter warmth there was a small wood-and-coal heater.

A narrow hall led past the bedroom to a small corner room that had been made into a kitchen. There was a wood range, just the right size, with a cooktop and warming ovens on top. There was an assortment of copper-bottomed pots, dishes and cups and various supplies in glass-fronted cabinets. There was kindling ready—had it lain ready in its basket for more than a year, since the death of the woman who had placed it there? A chipped blue teakettle that had seen much use stood invitingly on the cold stove. There was a zink-lined sink. Beside it upon a counter stood a small pitcher pump.

I exclaimed with pleasure, and Mrs. Marchand smiled widely. "What do you think of it?"

"I adore it! I shall make some tea at once. Would you join me, Mrs. Marchand?" I invited impulsively.

"No, no," her white hands fluttered apologetically. "I must go and see if Mrs. Potter has the dinner well in hand. We have been dining at eight."

I felt sudden anxiety, fearful of misunderstanding her remark. Was she assuming that I would dine with her family? If I guessed wrong, how very embarrassing it would be. She seemed to sense my worry, and nodded her head briskly like some exotic bird with sweeping silver plumage.

"You will have time to rest and dress for dinner. Charles will probably be a little late, as usual. Mr. Galbraith and my son will join us at table also."

She hurried out before I could adequately thank her. What

··a wonderful person she was, so beautiful in her ethereal way. In spite of her obvious wealth and position she seemed not at all condescending. Her warmth and generous welcome under these unusual circumstances brought a sting of relieved tears to my eyes.

I puzzled briefly over her remark that her son would be joining us for dinner. I was aware that the Marchands had two children, for I had asked Mr. Galbraith about the size of the family. Was the second child, a daughter, away perhaps? Or maybe she was too young to dine with the adults.

Catching sight of my comfortable old teakettle again, I shrugged my shoulders, dismissing small mysteries. How foolish I had been, worrying needlessly about my reception here, thinking that I would be regarded as an intruder, when nothing could have been further from the truth.

Kindling a small fire in my very own cooking range, I looked happily around the tiny kitchen. Tomorrow, I promised myself, everything should have a thorough scrubbing. I would soon have my quarters spotless. And I would give Mr. Brock, when he arrived, instructions to scythe down the overgrown lawns at once, and to replace the broken windows upstairs, and to purchase paint for the exterior of the house–

Oh, there was so much to think about! I unpinned my hat and removed it, and somehow it was symbolic of my feeling of homecoming. I knew suddenly that I would thrive upon the task of putting this dear old house to rights. It was a whole new life opening up before me.

"Bless you, Mrs. DeWitt," I whispered.

Even as I said it, the little kitchen was invaded by a draught of cold wind, and misgivings moved over my spirits again.

Aunt Betsy had been fond of saying that one needn't expect in this life to receive something for nothing. There was always a price to pay, and sometimes it was the greater for first being hidden.

The thought disturbed me. I stood very still, my hat held tightly, as if something in me feared to lay it down and thus signify that I was here to stay.

On the surface of the situation, I had received a very valuable and certainly unearned windfall. But there *would* be some cost involved. I knew it with a disquieting certainty. A shiver crept along my spine.

What would be the price that I must pay?

Chapter Four

Predictably, I felt better and had banished silly notions by the time that I had finished my cup of tea. Rinsing my cup, I positively longed to begin scrubbing the little room. But I had little time before dinner. I must bathe and find something to wear.

I rummaged about in the cupboards until I found Mrs. Welcome's irons. I replenished the fire again and set the irons to heat upon the stove-top, along with water for washing. Then I returned to the sitting room where my Gladstone bag had been left.

There was not much to unpack. I had never owned a great many garments, and there had been no new things since my aunt's death. The green wool dress I was wearing was my best, and it was travel-mussed. Yet something acceptable must be found for evening.

For the first time in months I knew the sensation of worrying about proper attire. It was not entirely unpleasant, for it meant that my life had opened out. But I realized that I should have to buy cloth and sew some decent dresses now that I was living in the same house with a family of means.

Lifting out my wrinkled clothing, I thought suddenly of yesterday, of Eileen, packing them for me. I had promised her that if I found a suitable position, I would send for her. And now I could do just that, and offer her a wage myself! It would be good to have a familiar face here, and Eileen was capable and hardworking.

There was little to choose from in my stack of clothing. Sighing, I picked up my best white shirtwaist and the least worn of my skirts, a brown bombazine. With Aunt Betsy's glass cameo, perhaps my dress would be acceptable.

I took the garments into the kitchen, set up an ironing

table, tested the iron, and carefully pressed out the creases. I washed hastily in the china washbowl in my bedroom, slipped into my hose, petticoats, chemise, and my netted, wire bustle. I put on the skirt and blouse and sat down at the dressing table to arrange my hair.

My hair is like my mother's, heavy and straight, too light to be called brown, too dark for blond. It fell to my waist, and to my disappointment had never exhibited the first sign of a curl. At the Home there had never been time to do more than braid and wind it about my head, but tonight I was minded to try something different.

Accordingly I brushed it well and coiled it into a chignon high upon the back of my head, with wings draped smoothly to cover my ears. I pinned it with care. Looking critically at my reflection, I sighed. The effect was still unfashionably simple.

I stood and turned about before the cheval glass in one corner of the room. Not that I expected to discover the duckling turned into a swan. I was too tall and slender for real beauty. My neck was too long, my face a passable oval, but betrayed by a wide mouth, and a nose too short and childlike. And did I really look so starved? My gray eyes overwhelmed my other features. If these were not sufficient defects, I thought my chin too pointed, giving me a stubborn look.

Squaring my shoulders, I turned away. One must accept the face and form the good Lord had provided. At least I was young and strong and had never known a day of sickness except for the usual childhood ailments. I was well fitted for my new life as landlady and housekeeper.

Nervously I left my part of the house, and made my way along the hall, wondering if I could find the dining room.

Hearing voices in the entrance hall, I followed the sound.

Joanna Marchand had just opened the door to new arrivals. Embarrassed to be intruding, I hesitated at the junction of the corridor.

The visitors stepped into the house and stood under the gaslight chandelier. With astonishment I recognized Mr. and Mrs. Horace DeWitt. With them was a young woman.

"Come in Lily, Horace," Joanna greeted them viva-

41

ciously. "Yolande my dear, how are you?"

"Very well, thank you," murmured the girl. She was perhaps seventeen. Black curls tumbled out from under her Neopolitan braid hat. She was wearing a Worth cloak of fine black mastic wool with pearl velvet bands embroidered with rows of jet beads and cabochons. Strings of tiny jet beads looped over her hips. The cloak was very stylish and expensive, but I thought the young woman's pouting babyface with its pink, rounded cheeks looked out of place in the sombre black.

"You are just in time for dinner," Joanna exclaimed. "We didn't expect you, but there will be plenty for all, I am sure."

At that instant Mrs. DeWitt glanced round and saw me in the background. She drew an audible gasp, and her double chins quivered righteously.

"You!" she cried, as if I had been the serpent in Eden's perfection.

I stood wishing myself anywhere else on earth, but I could hardly turn and run, although the impulse was with me for a craven moment.

I drew myself up and came forward with an attempt at undisturbed dignity. "How are you, Mrs. DeWitt?" I inquired.

She made a sound like the gobbling of a turkey as she seemed to test and reject words as not strong enough for the occasion.

"Who is she, Mama?" Yolande languidly inquired, but her black eyes were snapping with curiosity.

"This!" thundered Lily DeWitt, pointing a rigid, white-gloved hand at me, "This is the penniless upstart who has stolen this house from its rightful heirs! To *think* that she has the effrontery to insult decent people with her presence, to actually invade this house!"

I had the impulse to suggest to her that if one steals, traditionally one takes possession of the stolen item.

"Now, now, Lily," Horace DeWitt murmured pacifically, taking his wife's arm. "Let's not create a scene, dear. After all—"

"After all, what, you fool?" his wife interrupted, jerking her elbow away. "Maybe *you* have an idea of giving in to

42

this scheming hussy, but I won't be flimflammed by a pretty young face. You!" Again she pointed at me dramatically, her imposing bosom heaving with emotion, "You will be good enough to leave at once. I do *not* wish to see your smug tabby-cat face again!"

I am not exactly sure how I should have responded to my eviction, but from the dangerous leap of my temper, I fear I might not have spoken with the courtesy and dignity that my Aunt Betsy had been at pains to teach me. I felt my face heating, and I had just opened my mouth when the doorway behind the DeWitt's revealed a tall, broad form. Mr. Charles Marchand stepped in upon the scene. Doubtless he had heard some of the argument. However, he stood silent for a minute, taking it in. He did not interrupt when Mrs. DeWitt began a vituperative spate upon the topic of the underdeveloped state of my immortal soul, my shocking lack of common decency, and my advanced moral condition of basest depravity.

With a freshly drawn breath, she began upon her thoughts about my upbringing and ancestors. My hands clenched into fists and I stepped toward her. I had heard as much as I could tolerate.

But Mr. Marchand stepped forward, rather jostling Mrs. DeWitt aside as he came past. He turned to face the family, and his broad back was between me and my adversaries. My purposeful advance was frustrated. I was ready to do battle, and he was squarely in the way. I was obliged to move to the side even to view my enemies.

"What are you doing here, Horace?" Charles demanded curtly.

"Why, why—" the thin, fair man began nervously. Characteristically, his wife cut in.

"We have every right to be here, Charles, and you won't deny that, I am sure. We have instituted legal proceedings against that—that barefaced thief, Katherine Livingston, and until the case is settled we intend to stay on the premises."

"I am afraid that is impossible," Marchand said. "I have leased the house for the entire summer from Miss Livingston."

Mrs. DeWitt was not at all distracted. "Then you have

43

. . not leased it from the owner," she said.

"You are mistaken, Lily. Joshua Galbraith has assured me of the validity of the will. I am convinced that Miss Livingston is the rightful owner, according to the wishes of my aunt, Bertha DeWitt."

"Joshua Galbraith is a fool. *Our* attorney assures us that he will be able to break the will. We intend to prove that that sly little cat used your dear Aunt Bertha's illness and uncertainty of mind to weasel her way into the poor old lady's good graces."

"How *dare* you accuse me of such a thing?" I cried, maddened, but Charles Marchand's cold blue glance and abruptly lifted hand stopped me.

"Such an accusation may be difficult to prove, Lily, since Miss Livingston had not spent a moment's time with my aunt for eight months prior to her death. All of us here, if you will recall, were constant companions of Aunt Bertha after she left the Home. Even you and your family resided in the house up until the day of my aunt's death. If there was opportunity for influencing the will, it was ours, not Miss Livingston's."

Lily DeWitt made a hissing noise between her teeth. "Why would one of us do that, since Bertha's original will undoubtedly mentioned all of us? Besides, that girl's insidious suggestions had already had time to work, before poor Bertha came home for the last time—"

Here her voice appeared to break, and she dabbed at a tear I did not quite see. "If you cannot see that Bertha was worked on until her poor mind was turned, then you are as gullible as your aunt was!"

"Please!" Joanna came forward anxiously, hands fluttering in a placating gesture. "Must we have such a scene? Truly, I cannot bear it. I feel quite faint, Charles. Make them all stop!"

I felt mortified at my own contribution to this undignified brawl, and I bit my lip, ready to throw up my hands in defeat. I think Mr. Marchand sensed from my uneasy movement that I was about to capitulate, and again his icy glance challenged me. There was not a trace of kindness in the look he gave me. Instead it held a warning as potent as

44

words, and it held me still, although I could not have said why.

"We shall have no more of this wrangling," he decreed. "Lily, if you feel that you must contest Bertha DeWitt's will, do it through your attorney, if you please, and not under this roof. Now, I must ask you to leave."

Surprisingly, Joanna interceded for the DeWitts, gazing up at Mr. Marchand imploringly. "Must they go, Charles? After all, they are family, and we have lots of room. I have already told them they might stay for a time. I am sure if Lily will promise not to bring up the subject of the will, everything will be quite amicable."

He stared down at her frowningly for an instant. To my intense disappointment, he bowed to her request. "As you wish, Joanna." Gently he lifted her hand away and turned toward the stair. As if he had had more than enough of the subject, he strode away into the upper regions of the house without another word to any of us.

Like cats that have fought to a standoff, the rest of us were left to eye one another in impotent hostility and suspicion.

"Will *she* be allowed to remain here?" Lily muttered to Joanna as if hesitant to challenge me again directly. "I feel I cannot bear to draw breath in her company!" The final sentence was almost a wail.

"Why, Miss Livingston is going to act as housekeeper, and supervise the renovation of the house and grounds," Joanna reassured her, with a faint smile in my direction. "You do realize that the place is in very poor condition, and we need someone to make us more comfortable, do we not? I am assured by Charles and Mr. Galbraith that Miss Livingston is most—most capable."

Thus she neatly relegated me, at least in the DeWitt's eyes, to the status of a servant. I disliked the sensation, so quickly had I grown used to my newly elevated position as the owner of property! But I could see that it was the perfect diversion to soothe the DeWitt woman's ruffled feathers. If I stood in a menial position, she could accept me.

In a few more moments, Joanna had encouraged the

DeWitts to go to their rooms to freshen up before dinner. They went with varying looks at me. Mrs. DeWitt, of course, sent a malevolent glance, her heavy face still mottled with temper. The daughter, Yolande, seemed merely interested, and I could not quite read the look given me by her papa, who glanced sideways as he smoothed his skimpy moustache. It was not an inimical look, I felt, yet I could not quite like it, either.

As soon as they were out of sight, Joanna turned to me and, to my astonishment, giggled.

"My! Wasn't that a rare set-to? I have never seen poor Lily so ready to explode."

It did not seem a laughing matter to me. I had been twice accused by Mrs. Horace DeWitt of stealing, or worse. I had been ordered from the premises, and drawn into an embarrassing quarrel with strangers. I felt myself to blame for this—I should have used more restraint.

"Mrs. Marchand, I am sorry for the unpleasantness," I said. "I hope you will realize that the entire situation took me as much by surprise as anyone. Until yesterday, I had no idea of Mrs. DeWitt's generous bequest, and I—"

I had been about to tell her that I had tried to refuse the legacy and been talked out of it, but she waved me to silence.

"Oh, please, Miss Livingston! I am sick to death of the whole dreary business." She sighed. "Well, I fear dinner will be delayed. Come into the parlor and we shall get acquainted while we wait. Ah, here is Joshua. Perhaps he will join us in a glass of sherry before the meal."

The squarely-built attorney was coming down the stairs, lips quirked with amusement.

"What was all the ruckus down here?" he asked, looking my way with a friendly wink. "Did my eyes deceive me, or was that the illustrious Horace DeWitt delegation bustling along the upper hall just now?"

"You are not deceived," Joanna laughed. "Come, I'll tell you all about it."

She took his arm and they led the way into the parlor, where she gracefully served us with tiny crystal wine glasses filled with sherry. This was my first experience with wine.

I hesitated, for Aunt Betsy had drummed into my mind the virtues of total abstinence from spirits of any kind.

I heard Mr. Galbraith chuckle and looked up to find him regarding me amusedly. "Drink it. It's good for you," he advised.

Feeling very naive and foolish, I sipped the stuff, promising myself that I should do no more than that.

Joanna had launched into a humorous account of the scene with the DeWitts. I did not attempt to add to it in any way, allowing her to enlighten the lawyer.

"Mrs. DeWitt has begun a suit against Miss Livingston's claims to the property?" he asked, brows raised. "Well, we shall have to look into that. Don't worry, Miss Livingston, there's little they can do."

I sighed. "I hate the whole thing. It was never my wish—"

With a rather strange look, he quickly overrode what I had been about to say. "Well, what do you think of Johnstown so far, Miss Katherine? We're rough and new, but those of us who have been here since the mills converted to the Bessemer process, and set the area booming, have learned to like it."

"If it weren't for the noise of mill whistles, and the Hungarians!" Joanna put in, with a charming wrinkle of her nose.

Galbraith laughed. "Not only Hungarians, although most folk rather unkindly lump the workers together. There are Italians, Poles, Russians and Swedes."

"Enough, enough!" Joanna protested. "It makes me quite nervous to think of all those—those—"

"Hunkies?" Galbraith suggested with a teasing smile.

"No, indeed," Joanna shook her head. "Of course I should never use such a vulgar term!"

"Whatever you call them, they are the manpower to keep the mills going night and day, turning out the steel rails and plowshares that will expedite the settling of the West."

"Now, Joshua," Joanna smiled indulgently. "We all know you wax poetic over the dream of Western migration. But, if you will forgive me for saying so, I have noticed that *you* have not ventured into those untamed areas as yet."

"Give me time," he grinned. "I have not yet grown dissatisfied with—Johnstown."

Joanna flushed, her perfect skin tinted a charming rose pink. I thought she was about to make a spirited reply. She was interrupted by the opening of the parlor door.

A boy of ten or eleven entered. He was tall and coltishly slender, with fine fair hair that marked him as Joanna's son. The child's face was sensitive, and it seemed to me, too grave for his age. He did not smile as he grasped his mother's outstretched hand. His eyes were on me, as the only stranger in the room, and he studied me with a disturbingly adult intensity.

"Sidney! Come dear, you must meet Miss Livingston, who now owns our house, and will be staying here. Miss Livingston, this is my son, Sidney."

I put out my hand. "Hello, Sidney. I am happy to meet you," I said.

Soberly he shook hands, still looking me over with round blue eyes very like his mother's. He was a very handsome child, indeed.

"How do you do?" he murmured. As if satisfied with his scrutiny of me for the time being, he moved away.

I turned to Joanna. "I understand that you also have a daughter," I remarked. "Is she younger than Sidney?"

Too late I read the frantic warning in Mr. Galbraith's eyes. Puzzled and alarmed, I saw Joanna's lovely, animated face go as rigid as stone, her warmly twinkling eyes ice over. What on earth had I said?

I felt my lips part upon an apology—but since I had no idea what *faux pas* I had committed, I could not think how to make amends.

Joanna turned abruptly to Galbraith, and began to chatter very rapidly, in a high, brittle tone, about the weather—so cold and so unusually wet.

Stiffly I sat, the forgotten and scarcely tasted sherry in my hands, feeling like a child severely and unfairly reprimanded.

There is no adequate way to describe the sense of dismay I felt at having offended Mrs. Marchand. She had been so kindly welcoming to me. I had begun to hope that I had found a new friend. She was everything admirable, to my young eyes. I wanted, already, to learn from her, to copy her polished, vivacious conversation. She was a lady of elegance and taste.

And I had blundered, had said something to distress or anger her.

I sat puzzling over my mistake, trying to swallow the sharp ache of embarrassment in my throat, and blink away the moisture that had risen in my eyes. Was I going to weep like a scolded baby? I, who had endured Miss Spendquill's spying and Mrs. Blackwood's tirades, who had not folded up under Mrs. Lily DeWitt's poisonous insults?

Somehow I got a fingertip grasp upon my pride, yanked it back into place and anchored it well with inner admonitions. By the time Mr. Marchand and the DeWitt's joined us, and we went in to dinner, I had control of my emotions once more.

Considerately, Joshua Galbraith was beside me. Charles Marchand sat at the head of the table, with Joanna to his right. Lily DeWitt sat at the end with Yolande and Horace on either side of Sidney.

Mrs. Potter brought in the soup. I realized that she must have no kitchen help, if she must serve as well as cook. I must remedy that at once. There was so much that needed attention. As I glanced about the long room, I could see evidence of clutter and dust. The tablecloth was clean, or at least washed, but it was stained, and I mentally saw it in a tub of boiling water with chloride of lime, sal soda, or aqua ammonia.

The drapes at the long windows were furry with dust, and the lace panels were definitely dingy.

At least the food was deliciously prepared. Mrs. Potter took away the soup dishes and brought in tender roast lamb, whole small potatoes in some kind of very delicately seasoned sauce, and yeast rolls that were light as a baby's breath. There were other dishes too numerous to list, and it was plain to me that Mrs. Potter was most expert in her own domain.

Still very conscious of my earlier mistake, I was quiet, listening to the conversation around me. Most of the talk was between Charles Marchand and Mr. Galbraith, spiced with Joanna's comments, and now and then jarred by some heavy remark from Mrs. DeWitt. Horace DeWitt said little, seeming more interested in the food than in talk of politics and horses. Charles was describing his latest purchase, a stallion from England which he believed would prove very fast. He had great hopes for the get of this powerful thoroughbred. His somber face lighted with enthusiasm as he spoke of his horses.

In this mood he was a most attractive man, blue eyes warming with interest and humor in that strong, weather-darkened face, his smile boyishly amused as Mr. Galbraith made some jesting comment.

I was fascinated, in spite of myself, for I had never known a gentleman like Mr. Marchand. I cannot say that I liked him, for I was still uncertain and suspicious of his motives in insisting that I accept Bertha DeWitt's legacy. And there was that about him that almost—frightened me, a kind of forceful masculinity that both attracted and repelled.

I watched him as he talked, trying to puzzle out the odd effect he had upon me. Unexpectedly he turned from his animated conversation with Mr. Galbraith, and caught my eyes upon him.

It can have been only the briefest flicker of time during which Charles Marchand's ice-blue eyes held my flustered gaze, yet it seemed minutes—an hour—an eternity of consciousness.

One corner of his expressive lips moved in the barest beginning of a smile, and was released from the spell. I tore my eyes away, shaken as I had never been before.

With trembling fingers I took up my water glass. I had just swallowed a sip and was setting the glass down when there was a thunderous clatter of footsteps outside the dining room. We all looked up, startled, as someone charged into the room.

50

Chapter Five

It was a girl, possibly eleven years of age, very fat and misshapen. The first thing one must notice about her was her head, grotesquely overlarge, with heavy, dirty, fair hair that fell in tangled hanks to her waist. Her face was a flat white pudding set with current eyes, a wide nose, and a mouth that gaped open to show large, uneven teeth.

The poor child's nose had been running, and had not been wiped. She snuffled and snorted, mouth open, with an unpleasant sound.

"Siddy!" she honked, in a low, hoarse voice. "Siddy!"

The boy across from me seemed to stiffen and cringe down over his plate, as if he hoped not to be seen. But the big girl was at his side in an instant, shaking his shoulder urgently. "Siddy, play!" she demanded.

At that moment she caught sight of the food on Yolande's plate, and with a cry of delight, she reached out with both hands, filling them and bringing them dripping to her mouth.

Yolande gave a scream and managed to flee from the table. The other girl did not notice her departure. She was busily eating—cramming meat and vegetables into her mouth, dribbling food down the soiled front of her dress.

I heard Joanna's strangled cry, and turned my mesmerized eyes to see her sink back into her chair. She had apparently stood to go to the girl. Her face was whiter than the linen cloth beneath our plates, her eyes blazing. I saw that Mr. Marchand had a tight grip upon his wife's wrist. Joanna had overturned her water goblet; unconscious that the stem of it was gripped in her right hand, almost like a weapon.

It was then that I understood why my innocent question about a daughter of the family had had such an unfortunate

51

effect. *This* was Joanna's daughter, this pathetic, feeble-minded caricature of humanity.

A woman ran into the room from the kitchen, a maid in a black-and-white uniform and white cap. I guessed that she must be Mrs. Marchand's personal maid. She took the arm of the gobbling girl, tugging forcefully.

"Come, Becky, come with me!" she ordered in a high, frightened voice.

"Where is Mrs. Archer? Why is she not watching over Rebecca?" Charles Marchand's voice was staccato with disapproval.

"She quit today, sir," explained the maid. "I've been trying to see to Miss Becky myself, but—"

"Has Rebecca had no supper?" Marchand coldly inquired, standing and laying aside his napkin.

"Well sir, no, that is, not just yet, sir!" babbled the middle-aged maid, her eyes alarmed as she looked at her employer's husband.

"Why has she not been fed?" Marchand's voice rose by a bare degree.

"There was plenty of time, Charles," Joanna spoke up. "I told Lottie to have her own supper in the kitchen first."

"Lottie, has the girl been fed at all today?" he continued grimly interrogating the maid. "She appears famished!"

"Why, certainly she has, sir!" muttered the servant.

But something in the way her eyes slid sideways made me think she did not speak all the truth. Was it possible that she had forgotten to tend the girl—or dreading it, had simply put it off?

"You will prepare Rebecca's supper at once and bring it up to her room!" Marchand came round the table to the fat girl. "Lottie," he stopped the maid on her way to the kitchen. "Ask Mrs. Potter to come and take Rebecca back upstairs."

Rebecca had slowed down a bit in her eating. She turned, her face smeared almost comically, to look at her father. She watched him warily, like a fearful animal. He took her elbow firmly, and with a quiet command, drew her away and out of the room. I was minded of the way a man might give orders to his dog. I ached with pity for the sad wreck of a child he was leading away.

Since Mrs. Potter was otherwise engaged, I rose and cleared away the mess left by Rebecca. Sidney slipped away out of the room and did not return. I thought the boy looked quite ill.

Yolande, who had burst into nervous tears at having her dinner plate invaded, sat down at another place. I provided a clean place setting from the sideboard, and brought her food from the kitchen. She resumed her meal.

But her mother was not so easily pacified.

"Joanna, I've told you for years that you ought to have that girl locked away, for her own good!" she boomed. "How *can* you inflict that hideous spectacle on all of us?"

Joanna did not respond to Mrs. DeWitt's remarks, but rose and excused herself from the room. All the lovely animation had gone from her face. She looked older, and desperately unhappy.

I waited only a few minutes before I also left the table. I had a longing to go into my own part of the house, away from them, for suddenly they were all strangers. I even felt a foolish longing for my cramped, cold room at the Home, and the familiar faces I had known.

It was blessedly quiet and private in my apartment. Yet even with the relief of being alone, I could not wrest my thoughts from the people into whose lives I had been so suddenly tossed.

How deeply I pitied Joanna and Charles Marchand. What would it be like to have a flawed child like Rebecca? To watch her babyhood fading, watch hopefully for the signs of developing intellect—in vain. And yet the child was more to be pitied. I shuddered to think what such a life would be.

And the parents doubtless found consolation in their son. Sidney did not lack intelligence, that much was obvious.

I shook my head, looking about me for a distraction from my thoughts. Absently I had wandered into my tiny kitchen. As before, I felt the urge to clean the room. Well, why not do it now? The hour was not late. My day had been emotionally tiring, but I was used to hard physical work, and long hours, and I felt restless.

In moments I had found a big apron, built my fire and put on water to heat for scrubbing.

There was a kind of comfort in the odors of yellow soap and ammonia as I emptied the cupboards and began to wash every inch of the shelves—dumping dusty dishes, an earthenware crock and small japanned trays into the dishpan. I heated more water, grateful for the pitcher pump.

From cupboards, I progressed to walls, sweeping down cobwebs and washing the paint with Fuller's Earth. I promised myself to clean and black the stove tomorrow, and I scrubbed the painted wooden floor with a brush.

The gaslights hissed overhead, showing me a kitchen set nicely set to rights. I removed my wet apron and tiredly dried my hands.

When I crept into my bed a half-hour later, I had no trouble sleeping, nor did the scenes of the day disturb my mind. I had literally scrubbed them away.

I woke at first light, a habit built during my years at the Blackwood Home. What a pleasure it was not to be forced to leap from my warm bed, wash with chilled water in an unheated room, and rush down to a meagre and uninspired breakfast. Sighing with realization that my life was changing in almost every way, I lay back, thinking about the day ahead.

There was much to do. That did not worry me. It would have been very much more dismaying had there been no duties. I had never been of an indolent nature. I was happier when busy.

But there was a question about what matters should be placed first. On an impulse, I deserted my bed, built a fire in my sitting-room hearth, and settled at the secretary desk with paper and pencil. I would make a list and try to organize things properly.

It was not difficult to see that I must hire servants immediately. The house had been neglected for so long that there was work for a half-dozen cleaning women.

I wrote down a notation to the effect that I must find and hire maids. Naturally that brought Eileen to mind. I found notepaper and had actually begun a letter, when it occurred to me that I might bring my friend here more quickly. The night before I had noticed that one of the new long-distance telephones was installed in the entrance hall of the house. Mrs. Blackwood's Home also possessed this convenience. In my three years at the Home I had used the telephone only on rare occasions, but I felt that this situation warranted use of the rather frightening instrument.

Accordingly, I went back to my bedroom and dressed quickly in my everyday clothing, a blue, serge skirt and clean, striped blouse.

I took time to build a fire in the range, feeling a surge of pleasure at the cleanliness of the kitchen. I pumped fresh water into the teakettle and put it on to heat. Then, pausing only to brush my loosened hair and tie it back with an old ribbon, I entered the still sleeping house.

Feeling very much above myself, nervously I took down the receiver of the Bell telephone. I signaled the operator, and in an incredibly short time she was ringing the phone at the Blackwood Home.

I knew that Mrs. Blackwood would still be sleeping. It gave me a sinful pleasure to disturb her. She always answered the phone herself, as no one else had sufficient importance. The help were allowed only to ring out to the stores and make necessary orders.

When Sibyl Blackwood's voice came drowsily over the line, I did not give my name, merely asking peremptorily for Miss Eileen O'Donnell.

"Who?" Mrs. Blackwood asked tinnily.

"Eileen O'Donnell, one of your maids," I repeated. "This is an emergency call. Please be so good as to get Miss O'Donnell for me at once."

I had to cover my mouth to stifle a giggle when she actually obeyed my order without question. If she had known who was calling, doubtless she would have hung up at once. And if she had been fully awake, she might have demanded to know my name.

After a short wait, Eileen's voice tremulously reached my ear.

"Hello. Did someone wish to be speaking to me, please?"

"Is this Miss Eileen O'Donnell?" Some imp of mischief made me alter my tones to a businesslike drone.

"Oh, yes sir. I mean, yes ma'am, this is her!" Eileen shouted into the instrument.

I could not help laughing. "Eileen, it's Katherine Livingston. I'm calling you all the way from Johnstown."

"What? Glory be!" She stopped, seemingly speechless with surprise.

"How soon can you pack and come up?" I asked eagerly.

"Come—come to Johnstown?" she gasped.

"Yes! I'm here in Johnstown, and you'll never guess what. I have inherited a house. A whole house, Eileen! And I want to hire you to help me."

It required a few moments to explain the situation to her. Her excitement grew until she was almost babbling.

"Glory be, yes! I'll pack me things and catch the first train, Katy, I will! I'll be there just as fast as I can."

"Do you still have Mrs. DeWitt's money?" I asked.

"Sure, and 'tis safely pinned in me shimmy," she informed me in a loud whisper.

"Well, then, buy your train ticket with some of it, and I'll pay you back with your first week's wages."

Soon it was all arranged, and she had hung up. I went to make my breakfast.

I spent the morning cleaning rhe remainder of my apartment, a cloth tied about my head to keep the dust from my hair. My satisfaction grew with every cobweb swept away, every curtain shaken free of dust. I wished for a day fine enough for the beating of rugs and airing of pillows, but since it was drizzling again out of a gray, unpromising sky, I must resign myself to doing without those details for the moment.

By noon I had finished. I made a simple lunch for myself on my newly-blacked stove, then gathered a bundle of sheets and cleaning rags to be laundered, and started toward the kitchen.

But I was halted in the corridor by Mrs. Marchand's call. I turned inquiringly. She hastened toward me, with Mr. Joshua Galbraith in tow. I was very conscious of the dirty linen in my arms, the dust on my face. Doubtless I looked like a scullery maid in my working clothes. Mr. Galbraith smiled teasingly under his ginger moustache.

"You waste no time in beginning a task, I see!" he said.

"I've—I've been cleaning my apartment. Did you want me for something?"

"I've brought you your hired man," he said. "Oh, and something else."

As Joanna stood by, watching curiously, he dipped a big, freckled hand into his pocket and took my own hand to press something into it. Puzzled, I opened my palm to find the ring Mrs. DeWitt had given me, and the money I had placed on Mr. Galbraith's desk the day before yesterday.

'I forgot to return this to you last night," the attorney explained. "Charles said you are to keep them, and he'll hear no more nonsense on the subject."

"Why—isn't that Aunt Bertha's ring?" Joanna asked.

"Yes. When Mrs. DeWitt left the Blackwood Home, she gave it to Miss Livingston as a gesture of appreciation. This very foolish girl thought it should be returned to the estate," Joshua explained, smiling.

At once Joanna smiled also. "Why certainly if it was given to Miss Livingston, then of course she must keep it."

"I don't know how to thank you—" I began.

"Not me. Thank Charles." Mr. Galbraith shrugged. "Now then. Are you ready to interview Mr. Brock?"

I felt instant consternation. "Oh, I am not dressed properly for seeing anyone—"

Again he interrupted. "Come now, don't be foolish. If you were in fine feathers you would scare poor Johnny away. He's a very plain young man."

I was not convinced, but had little choice since I don't believe in keeping people waiting unnecessarily. I took the laundry into the kitchen. Mrs. Potter looked up from her giant range where pots boiled and burbled, and told me to place the bundle on the back porch.

"Mrs. Smith from down the street does all the wash. She'll send her boy for it this afternoon."

I took off my apron and the cloth I had tied around my hair and added them to the pile before I went back to Mr. Galbraith.

I found him alone in the hall. We went out to find Johnny Brock standing, hands in pockets, by Mr. Galbraith's

·buggy. He was studying the ground, tracing a circle in the mud with the toe of his big brogan, his head bare to the cold wind and rain. He wore no coat, only a wool-flannel shirt and baggy, woolen trousers.

"Johnny," Mr. Galbraith said, "this is Miss Livingston. She owns the house, and will be telling you what needs doing."

The man looked up, but glanced away at once, and I was reminded of a starving mongrel who had been kicked once too often, and could trust no one.

"Mr. Brock, I am happy to meet you," I said. "Do you think you would be willing to help me put this place into good repair?"

He met my eyes again, this time with surprise. "I gotta have a job, ma'am. I reckon I'd take most anything."

How well I understood that attitude. I studied this thin, youngish man, whose coarse dark hair, in need of a barber's skills, blew over his pinched face.

It was not a bad face. There were lines about the eyes as if Johnny Brock had suffered, and he did not smile. It was as if he stubbornly refused to fawn and wag his tail in hopes of a handout. I was uneasily mindful of his weakness for strong liquor, but somehow I felt that there was decency in this man, and that he deserved a chance.

"If you want the job, you may have it. I am not sure what wage would be appropriate, but I am sure Mr. Galbraith can name a figure. When can you begin?"

"Why—right now, ma'am." He shrugged bony shoulders under the galluses that held up the waistband of his trousers. "I got nothing else to do."

"That will be satisfactory. Let me think—" I found myself at a loss to tell him what to do first. Joshua Galbraith helped me out.

"Why don't you look around the grounds and the exterior of the house for awhile, Johnny, and make a list of things that need doing," he suggested. "Then we can decide what materials you will need." He rummaged in his pockets and found a pad and pencil which he handed to Brock.

With a shy nod, Johnny Brock left us, disappearing around the corner of the house.

Chapter Six

"Come, let us go back inside. You're cold," Mr. Galbraith said.

Once indoors, I started toward my own sitting room, but he took my arm and led me in the opposite direction. "Come into the study. There's a fire there, and you might as well get used to being in the Marchand's part of the house. You can't hope to begin renovations if you hide away in your own rooms and are too shy to come out!"

Mr. Galbraith was too astute by far. Sighing, I followed him into the dim and dusty room. He perched on the edge of the heavy old mahogany desk and tilted his head inquiringly.

"What is your opinion of Johnny Brock? Will he do?"

"I trust your judgement," I said. "And—I like him, I think. But I have to confess that I have little experience of hired men."

"Or perhaps—of any men at all?" he asked, with a glint in his eye and a raised eyebrow.

Slightly offended, I straightened my shoulders. "What should I pay Mr. Brock? And for that matter, how do I go about paying? There will be expenses for materials and food for the household—"

"If you want something, you will write a bank draft. I'll show you how, and give you a ledger to keep an itemized list of expenses, so that you can budget properly. Mr. Marchand has already set up an account for your use. As for Brock's wages, he'd be happy with eight dollars a week. He might make more at the mills, but he lost his job there because he was caught drinking."

"How much could he make as a mill worker?" I asked.

"Ten dollars at the most," Galbraith informed me.

"Then I would like to pay him that much."

He studied me almost lazily. "Perhaps you are wise to do so," he said at last. "If you build up a man's morale, and sense of worth to himself, he is more inclined to apply himself to the task at hand. But I do caution you to expect the most from him, and let him know it. If he thinks you are a soft touch, and gullible, he might be inclined to take advantage of your generosity."

"And that would be detrimental to him as well as to me."

"Quite right. You have a good head on your shoulders, Miss Livingston!"

"Thank you. Now, can you tell me where I might find a girl who would be willing to work very hard to get this house in shape? I have sent for a friend of mine to fill one post as maid."

"I have made inquiries, and found two likely girls," he said. "They are sisters, Lena and Marie Watson. I think you have ample work for both, in addition to the girl you have already hired."

"But—I cannot afford so much help, surely."

He stood. "Well, yes you can, as a matter-of-fact. Charles Marchand himself specified that you must have all the help you need, and has agreed to pay whatever expenses are incurred. This is in addition to the flat figure for rental of the house."

I stared at him, dumbfounded. "Mr. Galbraith, I would be taking advantage of the Marchands to accept such an arrangement. I expect to fit the expenses of hired help and materials into the rent figure!"

"Then argue the point with Charles." He shrugged and smiled. "Katherine, take my advice and allow Charles to handle such details as he wishes. Whatever you can accomplish—even in the way of cleaning this place," he drew a finger through the dust on the desk, "will make the Marchands more comfortable. And, I venture to guess, even if you refused the offer, Charles would simply hire maids on his own, since the house definitely needs a great deal of work."

Still I felt uneasy, but was not allowed to express further doubts. Pleading an appointment for which he was already late, Joshua Galbraith took his leave. As I saw him out, Mrs. Potter, looking more forbidding than ever, approached me, saying that there was a man in her kitchen asking to see me. No doubt, Johnny Brock had completed his preliminary survey.

On the way to the kitchen, I stopped the cook with a question. "Are there any old, still usuable men's overcoats stored in the house, Mrs. Potter?"

She turned to me, curiosity in her eyes for the first time. "Yes, miss. There are some old things still in the attic."

"Would you mind looking for a warm coat that would fit Mr. Brock?" I asked.

"Who?" she blinked.

"The man waiting in the kitchen," I explained. "I hired him to do repairs and yardwork, and he has no coat. I cannot allow a man to work in the rain without a coat."

She stared at me without expression for a long moment, and I wondered what she was thinking. Perhaps she considered me a soft-headed fool. Nevertheless, she nodded.

"I'll go fetch one. Best let me give it to the lad, though, or 'twould embarrass him, I've no doubt."

"You're perfectly right." I smiled at her. "Thank you, Mrs. Potter. Is there anything that needs attention in the kitchen while you're getting the coat?"

"Well, I s'pose you might peek at tonight's roast duck," she said grudgingly. "It may need a mite of water—but only a cupful, mind you, and that hot from the kettle, so's not to toughen it!"

Johnny Brock was standing stiffly just inside the enclosed back porch.

"Mr. Brock! Do come in!" I noted with distress that his shirt was wet through. "Come into the kitchen, and I'll see if Mrs. Potter has any coffee left. Sit down at the table while I see to the duck, then you can tell me about how we should go about house repairs."

Silent, frowning as if distrustful of the most ordinary courtesy, he obeyed me. I found a thick, earthenware mug and poured hot black coffee from the pot on the back of the range. Mr. Brock appeared to relish the coffee, at least. He drank it almost too fast for it to have cooled, without waiting until I had brought cream and sugar. As soon as I had tended the deliciously steaming bird in the oven, I brought him more coffee, and poured a cup for myself, hoping Mrs. Potter would not resent my taking liberties with her domain.

I sank into a chair across from the man.

Woodenly, bringing out a paper with a scrawlingly penciled list, he recited what he had concluded after his tour.

"The grass needs cutting, ma'am, and them weeds. The stable needs repair, but maybe it'd be better to wait until the house has been seen to?" I nodded, and invited him to continue.

"I seen there's some broken windows upstairs. I'll need new glass, but I can fix them, right enough. Maybe that needs doin' first?"

"I thought the same thing myself."

He seemed to relax the tiniest bit. "You need house paint, but painting will have to wait for better weather."

I listened until he finished. "It sounds as if we'll need lumber, and some fencing. I would like, later on, to have one of the outbuildings prepared for use as a henhouse. Perhaps then, I can buy some nice hens."

"I can get all the white leghorn chicks you want, won't cost you much," he volunteered with the first hint of eagerness I had seen.

"Yes, please! At least, as soon as we have the more pressing chores in hand and can make a good place for them. But you will have to advise me how many I need."

We discussed poultry with a kind of wary friendliness until Mrs. Potter bustled back into the room.

"Oh, Miss Livingston," she said, as she came in. "Whatever shall I do with this old coat of my brother's? I hate to throw it away. It's still good, see how thick the goods is? But I've missed the charity drive at the church. I brung it over to ask what you think."

"Why, I—" I began uncertainly, trying to follow her lead.

"Oh, maybe Mr. Brock there knows someone who could use it." She held up the coat for his inspection, and then pretended to be examining it for moth holes.

Mr. Brock looked from one to the other of us with sudden

suspicion naked and painful on his face. I felt that I had'
erred in having Mrs. Potter look out a coat for him, for I
was a stranger. If he suspected that we were pitying him
in any way, the good we were trying to accomplish would
be destroyed by damage to the man's already injured pride.

But perhaps Mr. Brock found too little evidence on which
to base his suspicion of charity. He stood, holding out an
indifferent hand. "I might find a use for it!" he said shortly.

"Well, praise the Lord for that," exclaimed Mrs. Potter.
"If there is anything I do hate, it's waste of a perfectly
good garment. Now, then, did you see about the duck, Miss
Livingston? I'd better check if it's cooking too fast."

With minute attention to her precious fowl that could not
possibly have been simulated, she turned from us, clucking
over the oven temperature and placing a tin pan of water
inside to cool it a bit.

I ignored the coat in Brock's hands, and returned to the
subject of the repair work.

"Can you tell me how to order the glass for the windows?
I fear I'm very ignorant. And I must meet the two o'clock
train. Do we have a buggy, or must I walk to the station?
A friend of mine is coming from Pittsburgh."

"There's a buggy. Want me to hitch up and go get your
friend?"

"Could you? It would be such a help." I described Eileen
to him, and soberly he went his way. He merely carried
the coat until he was out of doors, but I was pleased to see
him shrug into it on his way to the stable.

I turned from the window to find Mrs. Potter with her
chin almost on my shoulder, peering out also.

She surprised me with her first smile, a vinegary but
approving one. "Well, ma'am, I guess we did it. That poor
man!"

I returned her grin of congratulation, and from that moment on felt that I had found an ally in crusty Mrs. Potter.

It occurred to me that I had not prepared a room for
Eileen. Mrs. Potter, with another look at her precious cooking, and a judicious poke with a long fork at the duck, took
me into a back part of the house I had not yet seen. There
she had her rooms near other servant's quarters. I chose the

best and largest room for Eileen, and set to work sweeping and dusting it.

It was there Eileen found me an hour later, calling my name from down the hall.

"Here!" I cried, and stepped gladly to the door.

"Ah, here you are! That prune-faced cook directed me. Katy, how can I ever, ever thank you for bringing me away from Blackwood's!" Her kind, honest blue eyes filled. She gulped. "I can never tell you how much I hated that place."

"You don't have to," I replied feelingly. "And don't thank me for sending for you. I need you here very badly."

"I'll work me fingers to the bone, and you needn't pay me a penny, just me board and room!" she promised recklessly.

I laughed. "I think we'll both be working as hard as ever, but you shall have a fair wage. And that won't be as much as you are worth." I sighed. "But I can't guarantee that we will live among a more comfortable group of people, Eileen."

She removed her wet coat and hat, made me sit down while she unpacked her things, and I told all I knew about the situation.

"An' that poor old Mrs. DeWitt truly gave you this big fine house?" she shook her head in awe.

"Yes, but—"

"Something bothers you, me girl. Whatever is it?"

I explained about the Horace DeWitts and their conviction that I had stolen the property from the rightful heirs.

"They'll niver think that when they know you," Eileen reassured me stoutly.

I shook my head. "Mrs. DeWitt hates me. I don't think her opinion will ever change."

"An' the others? The Marchands?" Eileen asked.

I hesitated. "I—don't know. Mrs. Marchand seems quite delightfully kind."

"The Saints be praised for that! How about the mister?"

"He's—I—" I shrugged. "Truly, I just don't know, Eileen. He urged me to accept the house, when I wanted to give it back."

Eileen swung about from tucking petticoats into a bureau

drawer. "What? You tried to be giving it back? Katy, I despair of you, sometimes! Don't you know that this is a chance sent from heaven for a working girl?"

"I didn't feel entitled to it. I still don't," I said.

"Ah, well, 'tis such a surprise, an' all. Give it all time. You'll be getting used to it, and then you'll be so much the grand lady that you won't be sitting about in the maid's chamber, looking like a maid yourself!" She giggled, and ruefully I noted my disheveled appearance in the mirror.

I stood and struck a pose. "You are quite right, Eileen. Tomorrow I must rush out and buy a diamond tiara, and a satin gown for housekeeping!"

We startled the old house with a sound that had been lost to it for a long time, by giggling as helplessly as schoolgirls plotting over the boy next door.

It is wonderful that laughter can, for a little while, banish shadows. My worries evaporated for the hour we visited. Eileen gave me the latest gossip about Sibyl Blackwood and Miss Spendquill, after which I described the Marchand family to her.

At last, remembering the time, I went back to my own apartment. Eileen went into the kitchen to offer her services to Mrs. Potter. I heard part of their exchange of amenities as I passed.

"Lord have mercy!" Eileen exclaimed. "Sure an' however can you work in this pigsty, Mrs. Potter? Why, them windows hardly let in the light of day, and the walls were last scrubbed on the seventh day of creation!"

Mrs. Potter let out a sound like an enraged bear. "Why, you listen here, Miss Snippet, I ain't hired to clean. That is for the likes of you. I'll have you know I do *my* job, and I advise you to tend to your own rat-killing, if you please!"

"Ah," sighed Eileen. " 'Tis surely a wonder to me that you haven't gone and poisoned the entire household, with last year's rubbish into everything. Why, you can't move without stirrin' up the dust, fit to choke a coal miner."

I stopped listening and moved on, hoping the two women would not come to blows before they had established their placed in the hierarchy of the staff. I hoped devoutly that Eileen's peppery tongue would not drive Mrs. Potter to the point of quitting. With a lamentable lack of courage, I decided against intervening, placed the altercation in the hands of the gods, and fled to the peace and quiet of my own rooms.

I was tired. Never had I worked so hard and so steadily, even at the Blackwood Home. Here I was driven only by my own desire to see the house at its best, and a proprietary dismay at the present state of affairs. But this was a difficult enough task and I found my back stiff from scrubbing and shifting heavy furniture.

Nevertheless, the improved appearance of my apartment was worth it. Even without the desired accomplishment of beaten and aired rugs, impossible in this inclement weather, my rooms were fresh in appearance. I beamed at the results of my labors until I was brought up short by another glimpse of myself in a mirror.

Sighing, for I had a longing to crawl into the high bed and rest, I started preparations for a bath.''

By the time I was ready for dinner, there was a new priority on my list. I simply must shop for dress fabrics without delay, and find time to sew at least two garments. The faded rose gown I was wearing, had long ago lost any claim to fashion, and had been mended and washed until the fabric was scarcely strong enough to hold new seams. I must move carefully lest I split the tight bodice or rip out a sleeve.

Thankfully there was no recurrence at dinner of yesterday's unpleasantness. Aside, that is, from Mrs. Horace DeWitt's chill toward me. That lady, dressed in black lace over purple, Lyons silk, looked me over with a disdainful sniff, and raised a significant eyebrow in communication with her elegantly-clad daughter.

Yolande, wearing black velvet and satin that gave her an exotically sombre look in direct contrast to her bright, curious eyes and pink cheeks, studied me also. It was annoying to be subjected to scrutiny by these people. There was little I could do about it. I tried to ignore their rude inspection.

Eileen served our meal very capably. Mr. Marchand seemed pleased at having an addition to the staff, and spoke courteously to her. Joanna gave her a vague smile, then seemed to dismiss her from consciousness. Undoubtedly she was so accustomed to having servants do her bidding that they were merely a necessary part of the furnishings. She was far more interested in questioning Sidney upon his day's activities at school. The boy answered quietly. I was again impressed by the adult quality of his manners.

"You have mastered the math problems that were giving

you difficulty?'' Charles Marchand asked him.

"Yes, sir,'' Sidney replied.

"That is fine. See that you continue to study diligently.''

Clearly fretting during a conversation that interested her not at all, Lily DeWitt broke in.

"Charles, have you heard when the season at the Southfork Club will commence?'' she asked piercingly.

He gave her a level glance. "It will begin, I presume, on the usual date, in late June.''

"That should give us ample time to be prepared,'' Lily exclaimed, her big face coloring with anticipation. She looked at her daughter, beaming. This time Yolande avoided her mother's gaze, as if embarrassed by it.

"I don't understand. Why should you prepare for the opening of the club?'' Joanna asked.

"Why, surely I mentioned that Mrs. Winston Bainbridge, who is a dear friend of the Pitcairns and Mellons and Phippses, has invited us to stay at the Phipps cottage for a week! That is, she has invited Yolande, Horace and myself.'' Mrs. DeWitt simpered with almost ludicrous smugness.

"I had understood that Mrs. Bainbridge was merely a minor connection of Henry Phipps, and scarcely more than tolerated in that set. I shouldn't think,'' Joanna said with raised eyebrows, "that Mrs. Bainbridge would be quite so free with her invitations.''

Affronted, Lily gasped and purpled, and Mr. Marchand stepped into the awkward gap in the conversation. "You will find it dull, I fear,'' he said dampeningly.

"Indeed we will not!'' Lily spluttered. "I cannot doubt but that there will be the usual camaraderie between our family and members of Pittsburgh's *creme de societé*. And there will be numerous eligible young men for Yolande to—''

"Oh, Mama!'' Yolande exclaimed with exasperation.

Lily seemed deeply injured. She reached in her sleeve for a handkerchief, which she touched to her eyes. "Ah, there is no gratitude in the younger generation. The endless trouble I went to to obtain the invitation from Mrs. Bainbridge doesn't matter to you, you unfeeling child. But you will thank me one day.''

She was interrupted when Yolande threw down her napkin, temper flaring in her round face, and fled the room.

Eileen, bringing the Nesselrode pudding, caught my eye with a little grimace that said, How right you were about these people!

Struggling not to smile, I applied myself to the delicious dessert—savoring the combination of chestnuts, grated pineapple, and French candied fruit.

After the meal, I started for my room, but was stopped by Charles Marchand, who left the dining room, cigar in hand.

"Miss Livingston, I'd like a word with you, if I may?"

"Yes of course," I replied. "What is it?"

He glanced about absently. The other women had disappeared into the parlor, and Horace DeWitt had not yet come from the table, where port and cigars had been set out for the gentlemen. "Let us step into my study, if you please," Mr. Marchand suggested.

Conscious of my rather shabby appearance, in contrast to Mr. Marchand's expensive attire—his gleaming shirtfront with gold cufflinks and ruby studs, his dinner jacket and perfectly pressed broadcloth trousers, I walked timidly at his side past the parlor door. There Joanna Marchand, restlessly fingering a stereopticon, caught sight of her husband, and called out to him.

"Oh, Charles—!" She came hurriedly to the doorway, and seemed to become belatedly aware of my presence.

"Yes, Joanna?" Marchand paused. I moved discretely further along the hallway, but could not help overhearing the brief conversation between husband and wife.

"Forgive me Charles! I didn't realize you were busy," Joanna said. Was there a slight edge to her voice?

"It is nothing of great importance. What did you wish?"

"I—oh, never mind! We shall discuss it another time." With a swish of her daffodil-yellow silk skirts, Mrs. Marchand turned back into the parlor, and Marchand came leisurely to join me.

He ushered me into the study. I made a mental note that I must see that this room received a thorough cleaning as soon as possible. It was obvious that Mr. Marchand made much use of the study, and apparently had furnished it to his own liking, with comfortable leather-covered chairs, and a great desk covered with books and papers. Paintings of trotting and running horses were hung about the walls—lovely, proud, aristocratic animals. I said as much, grateful to have a topic of conversation to fill the uneasy silence.

"Those are likenesses of my own horses," Marchand smiled. "I commissioned the paintings from an artist friend of mine."

"They are all yours?"

"Yes indeed, and they are representative of the finest stock in the world. For instance, this one—" He showed me a beautiful black filly with powerful quarters and a slim, intelligent head. "Her pedigree traces back to Hambletonian and Latourette's "Bellfounder." And that gelding has British ancestors with illustrious records. I wish that you might see a new stallion that I recently purchased in Ireland, a liver chestnut, not a blemish on him, and if he does not run like the fiends of—"

He stopped, shaking his head smilingly. "But you don't wish to hear me run on about my horses! I invited you in here to ask what you think of your house, and how matters are progressing?"

"It's very impressive. A good cleaning and some paint and repair will make it even better, of course."

"I see that you have already hired some help."

"Yes, sir. The new maid is a friend of mine, from the Blackwood Home. She is hardworking and conscientious, and I am sure—"

He waved his cigar impatiently. "You needn't give me her credentials. I am sure your judgement is good in the matter. However, I discovered this evening when I went to unharness my team that you have also hired John Brock. I confess I am a trifle concerned about your choice there. The man has a poor reputation."

"I am aware of that," I said stiffly, feeling a sudden urge to defend Johnny. "But Mr. Galbraith assured me that basically the man is decent and deserves a chance."

"Galbraith recommended him?"

When I nodded, he gave a rueful grin. "Ah, I should have guessed it. Joshua has a penchant for rescuing lame ducks. Well, give Brock a trial by all means, but if you have any trouble with him, I hope you'll have the sense to dismiss the fellow without a great deal of soul-rending pity.''

I found myself growing annoyed. ''I believe that I am capable of handling Mr. Brock!'' I snapped, and was angry when he raised those winging black eyebrows and studied me with his chill, blue eyes as if trying to identify some heretofore unknown species of creature.

He shrugged and changed the subject, which was just as well, for angry words were pressing upon my tongue.

''Did Galbraith give you instructions for drawing on the bank account I set up in Johnstown for your expenses?'' he asked curtly.

''He did.'' I remembered something else, and my temper died a bit in remorse because I had not thought of it earlier. ''I must thank you for giving me back the opal ring.''

''Nonsense, my dear girl! It was already your property, in spite of that very dramatic gesture of presenting it back to the estate.''

He smiled and it was the wicked grin that had transformed his face before. How bewildering this man was, with his cold, forbiddingly correct manner slipping without warning into the winsome charm of a mischievous boy. Carefully I did not smile in return, for I felt that he was laughing at me.

''You believe that my return of the ring was merely playacting?'' I asked through clenched teeth. ''In that case, Mr. Marchand,'' I started to draw the opal off my finger.

''Oh Lord, not again, please! Did I say I thought your gesture insincere? That was not my meaning. For God's sake keep the wretched ring! I have no use for it.''

''Perhaps Mrs. Marchand would like it,'' I muttered, nearly in tears. I knew I had handled the situation badly.

He seemed quite simply astonished. ''You think I would take the thing from you and give it to my wife?''

I saw with awful humiliation that I had blundered again. Of course he would never offer the exquisite Joanna a piece of jewelry that had been in the possession of a mere working girl who was without family or status of any kind!

''If that's—if that's all you wanted to say, may I go?''

I asked, hating the tremor in my low words, and the un-swallowable lump in my throat.

"One more thing. I see that you need some—personal things." His glance moved down my body and I felt as if his eyes lingered on every inch. I knew he was merely examining my shabby dress—and that was unwelcome enough. Yet his glance was like an exploring touch. I could have sworn I felt the physical warmth of it, and I could not decide if it was embarrassment or the swift rise of murderous indignation that choked me. Oblivious to my reaction, he continued. "I shall expect you to purchase whatever you desire for yourself, in addition to household needs."

Speechless, I left the room as swiftly as possible. Really, the man was insufferable. Was my appearance so intolerable that I shamed his family? I wanted to stamp my foot and slam doors.

Eileen met me as I crossed the hall, and fell back with hands lifted in mock terror.

"Saints preserve us! 'Tis surely the end of the world at the very least!"

I made my face assume its normal lines.

"Who's been ruffling your feathers?" grinned Eileen.

I opened my mouth to tell her, then realized that we might be overheard. "Come into my apartment where we can talk in peace," I sighed.

She followed me, and for a little while her interest in the rooms distracted her from my problems.

"Why, 'tis as fine as where Sibyl Blackwood lives, to be sure!" she exclaimed.

"Yes," I agreed. "Although I wish there was a second bedroom as well. I hated to put you in the back of the house."

She seemed astonished and affronted. "Why, don't be such a goose! The chamber you gave me is a palace compared to what I have been used to."

"I want you to feel that you can come here at any time, as if the apartment were your own. You might like to use the kitchen, or the sitting room, if you have a friend visiting, for instance."

Her round, freckled face lighted. "Now then, I *would* like to cook a bit on that darlin' stove. I could make us a meal, now and again."

"I'd like that very much," I smiled at her.

"I'll come in an' do a bit o' cleaning tomorrow—"

"I've already done all that!" I laughed.

She looked about with a kindly, condescending air, even ran her fingertip over the wainscot molding, seeming disappointed when she found no dust.

"See? I told you," I teased, but she only screwed up her face with menacing significance and narrowed her eyes. "Closet paper!" she said.

"What?"

"Did you pull out the closet paper, Katy?"

"Why, of course not! Why ever should I do such a thing?"

Eileen shook her head pityingly. "Moths," she explained.

I could only stare in bewilderment. "Moths?"

She nodded vigorously. "We must strip out the paper to the bare walls and wash every last corner down with boilin' water and vinegar to kill them moth's eggs. An' then we shall put up fresh paper, else there'll soon be holes in your woolens, or my name ain't Eileen O'Donnell."

With a sudden shift of subject, Eileen again asked who had made me so angry earlier. But I found I had no desire to talk and gave her a vague answer, although she tried mightily to pry the details from me.

"Did you enjoy your trip to Johnstown?" I asked hastily.

"Oh, 'twas so-so," she shrugged, and then looked up at me with bright eyes. "Who is the gentleman who brought me from the station?"

"Gentleman? Oh, you mean Johnny Brock. I have hired him to repair the house and tend the grounds."

"Now, he's a handsome lad," Eileen stated thoughtfully.

"Is he now?" I grinned, and was surprised to see her blush.

We talked for a bit longer, then she left, and I prepared for bed. After I had brushed my hair, I took up the old rose-colored muslin, to hang it away in the wardrobe. I frowned at it. The first thing tomorrow, I decided, I would have Johnny Brock drive me into town, to buy materials for a few dresses. But I would not use the bank drafts Mr. Calbraith had given me for renovation expenses and household supplies. I had a little money put by from my wages at the Blackwood Home, perhaps twenty dollars in all, plus what was left of the money Mrs. DeWitt had given me. I would also write to the Pittsburgh bank for my small savings. Meanwhile the other money would purchase some of what I needed.

The decision relieved me. I climbed into bed and fell asleep almost before my head sank into the pillow.

My sleep was troubled with vivid dreams in which Charles Marchand's eyes and hands caressed me. I knew it was wrong, but I was helpless to resist his touch. As his lips moved over my face, I shuddered with exquisite longing and moved my mouth to his, pressing closer, an urgency building within me.

A hard spatter of rain on my windows woke me. The images that had engrossed my sleeping mind faded slowly. Drowsily, I clung to the delicious sensation of being in the arms of . . . I jerked to full awareness, realizing the shameful content of my dreaming. It seemed incredible to me that I could have so vividly experienced such feelings.

Quickly I threw back the covers and slid my bare feet to the cold floor, almost welcoming the discomfort. At least this was real, I was awake and my true self, with no foolish, falsely beguiling emotions clouding my thoughts.

I had slept later than usual. Perhaps the darkly overcast skies were to blame. I found my slippers, pulled on a heavy flannel wrapper, and went to build a fire for my morning tea.

I dressed while I waited for the water to boil, and splashed icy water on my face, ruthlessly driving away the last remnants of my dreams. As I brushed my hair, I looked out at the dreary morning.

Would it never stop raining? Since January there had been snow and rain enough to last an entire year, and still the heavens wept, and the cold, dismal air made everything feel clammy. I sighed. There would certainly be mildew among the linens. All would have to be boiled in strong borax solution.

But soon, I comforted myself, the first of April would be here, and surely winter would give up and leave us be.

Chapter Seven

I made myself a light breakfast and dressed for town, in my green wool dress. Wondering if Johnny Brock had arrived at work yet, I thought about offering the man lodging in the servants' quarters. It would be easier for him, no doubt, than to walk from Kernville every morning.

Providentially I found him in the kitchen with a cup of coffee and a plate of breakfast, looking rather bewildered by Eileen's proprietary urging of ham slices, eggs, and muffins.

At the sight of me, he sprang up guiltily. "Yes ma'am, was you looking for me?"

"Yes, but sit down and finish eating," I smiled. "Then you may drive me to town. Perhaps we can buy some of the building materials you'll need, and you can show me a good place to shop for sewing goods."

"Borgmeister's store in Washington Street," volunteered Mrs. Potter, from the stove. "That's the best place, nor Mr. Borgmeister won't cheat you. Why, last week Eldridge's Emporium was asking five cents a spool for sewing cotton! It's robbery, that's what it is."

"Thank you, Mrs. Potter, I shall certainly shop at Borgmeister's. Why don't you give me a list of kitchen needs, also."

She looked at me speculatively. "No ma'am. Mr. Marchand told me particular just yesterday that I am to do my own marketing, all the food for the house, and charge the bills to his account."

So Charles Marchand had gotten ahead of me on this point! There was no use in arguing, especially since I knew Eileen's sharp ears and equally sharp wits would not miss any note of censure I might let slip.

"Well, then," I said. "Eileen, would you wish to go shopping? Or to send for something?"

She looked wistfully at Johnny Brock's bent head, with its tousled rough hair. "No ma'am," she muttered. "I'd best git started shoveling the muck out of this kitchen."

Predictably, this started an altercation between her and the cook, which was both loud and vociferous. I wondered if I should find a moment in private with Mrs. Potter, and explain that Eileen meant very little of what she said, and that she simply enjoyed a rousing argument? Well, perhaps Mrs. Potter would find it out for herself, in time.

"Mrs. Potter, may I have a cup of your excellent coffee?" I interrupted Eileen's graphic description of the rodents and vermin that, in her estimation, resided upon the pipes under the sink, and behind the fruit jars in the pantry. She had digressed to the absolute horrors one might expect to find in the cellars when I interrupted the conversation.

"Why yes, Miss Livingston, to be sure!" said Mrs. Potter, darting a furious glance at Eileen.

"I'll git it for you, Katy!"

"Don't you lay one finger on my coffee pot!" roared Mrs. Potter. "It's my coffee. I made it, an' *I'll* serve it to Miss Katherine, an' furthermore, I'll thank you not to touch my stove nor nothing on it!"

Eileen seemed a trifle daunted by this direct attack, and she subsided with a little snort. I gave her a look that I hoped was sufficient warning to quiet her for a time, but I hadn't much hope.

I had almost finished my coffee, when I remembered that the first thing I must purchase today was glass for the broken upstairs windows, and that the panes must be measured. I said as much to the hired man.

"I'll measure the window, if you'll lead me to the room," he said.

Sighing, I rose. "I suppose we must. But as yet I don't know this house well myself. I will have to ask Mrs. Marchand, I suppose. Will she be up by now, Mrs. Potter?"

"Miss Joanna? Not for hours. But I can tell you what you need to know. It's them rooms on the third floor, in the east end. They've been broken for a week or more now. Seen 'em myself, coming back from my afternoon off."

"I suppose the rooms are unoccupied, at least," I mur-

76

mured. "So we shan't have to disturb anyone."

"They're occupied, all right." said the cook, turning away to slam her oven door almost upon Eileen's fingers as the girl reached for Mr. Brock's hot muffins.

"Whose rooms are they?" I asked. "Perhaps I'd best wait until later in the day, when they'll be empty."

Mrs. Potter shrugged. " 'Twon't make any difference. Them is poor Miss Rebecca's rooms, and she has to stay there all the time."

I stared at her. She met my glance and looked away. "Must be mighty cold in there for that child. She breaks windows in her tantrums, so a body might say she brings it on herself. But she ain't responsible, to my way o' thinking."

I found myself in the position of having to ask very cautiously for advice. "I—see. Well, then, should I—should I ask permission of her mother before I go up?"

Mrs. Potter shook her head so sharply the knob of hair on top quivered. "Oh, no ma'am. I wouldn't do that. Best not say anything at all to Miss Joanna about Rebecca." She gave me a look that said more than her words, and I remembered Joanna's reaction when I had innocently mentioned her daughter. I certainly did not want to upset Mrs. Marchand again!

Reluctantly, I turned toward the door, and Johnny Brock came silently behind me. I could not avoid the duty, for in this cold, damp weather, a definite health hazard existed for the girl. I wondered why her parents had not done something about the problem before now.

Nervously, I climbed the back stairs, with the hired man at my heels. I was not overly surprised to find dust and neglect in the corridor. The window at the far end of the second floor hall was so dirty it would scarcely have admitted light upon a sunny day. On this dark morning it might as well not have been there at all.

In the corridor we met young Sidney Marchand, dressed for school.

"Good morning, Sidney," I said.

"Good morning," he replied, looking at me with surprise.

"We are just going up to measure the broken glass in the third floor windows," I explained, then wished I hadn't, as his sensitive face went hard.

"*She* broke them out. She'll only do it again, when you fix 'em."

"Perhaps you're right, but it's far too cold not to replace the panes. Are you on your way to school?"

He nodded.

"Well, then, have a pleasant day," I said.

Without a smile, or another word, he hurried past us.

We found the stairway to the upper floor, and started to climb. I glanced at Mr. Brock, and found his black eyes on me curiously. I knew my face reflected my dislike of the situation—my discomfort at trespassing in the private portions of the house. I tried to smile.

"This is all very new to me. I am not quite sure what is expected of me, as yet," I confided impulsively.

He nodded kindly. I found myself liking this man, even though his weakness for liquor had damaged his worth in his own eyes and the eyes of the world.

"Miss Livingston—" he began, then hesitated.

"Yes?"

"You'd ought to be—careful when you go in where that girl is. I've heard she can be a mean one."

"But she's only a little girl!" Then I remembered that indeed she was not little but large, heavy and doubtless strong.

"Maybe so," he said soberly, "but I'd rather tangle with a wild animal than a human that ain't got the sense the good Lord gave a goose. I've heard that if the child don't like you, or she gits mad with you, she's apt to throw a chair at your head. Have you seen her?"

I nodded.

"Sure couldn't tell it to look at 'em, could you?"

I stared at him. "What do you mean?"

"Why—they say Miss Rebecca is the boy's twin."

Sidney's twin? That poor misshapen, near-mindless creature?

There was the sound of a door slamming, and the turn of a key in a lock. Around a corner came Mrs. Marchand's maid, Lottie Dilby, carrying a tray. She stopped short at

78

sight of us. I introduced myself, and explained our errand.

"You want to go in there?" she gasped.

"We must repair those windows." I said quietly. "I assume we may go in?"

"No—no, that is, it's locked, miss. Mrs. Marchand wants it that way. I'd best come back and see that it gets locked after you."

She seemed extremely reluctant to return to the room, but slowly walked with us.

"You've been feeding Miss Rebecca?" I asked, for something to say.

She nodded shortly. "I left her food with her, an' she'll have it slopped all over herself in five minutes."

"Then I imagine she will need to be washed," I said mildly.

"Well, it ain't up to me to be washing that screaming, half-witted pig all the day long!" she snapped, tossing her head on her thick neck. "I got my own duties with Mrs. Marchand, and I'm telling you right now, if someone ain't found in a day or two to take over, I'll be handing in my notice!"

Not knowing how to answer this, I said nothing as she set the tray upon a hall table and went to unlock the door, swinging it open to let us through. She herself stayed in the hall.

I could see why she did. The stench of the place was enough to drive a strong man back. It was evident that drastic cleaning measures were needed here. There was food—dried or rotting, under the chairs and in corners, and places soiled with vomit, and worse.

I gagged, then got hold of myself. I was used to the smells of sickness. This was somehow worse, but it must be borne for the moment.

I looked about for Rebecca, and found her on the floor near the far side of her bed. Her tray of food was in front of her, being messily and greedily consumed. She glanced up as we came in, and I thought of some bewildered animal in a display of caged beasts, eyeing us with dimly reasoning suspicion. She continued to cram food into her mouth, even as she watched us.

The room was icy! There was no fire in the hearth or

heater, and I supposed it could not be safely allowed if no one stayed with the girl. The air was almost as wet as outdoors, in spite of the blanket that someone had thrust into the broken panes of the window.

Mr. Brock, grimacing and being careful where he stepped, moved hurriedly to get his measurements, while I watched the child.

Something must be done, I thought, deeply dismayed. Something *must* be done! No human should live like this. It was beyond the limits of conscience. Surely the child's mother could not know the conditions in which Rebecca existed. Probably, since she was sensitive about the girl's affliction, she simply never came up here, unable to bear the reminders. The servants she hired had doubtless failed in their duty.

Within a few minutes, John Brock and I were outside again, but I knew the scene I had left behind would haunt me. My mind seethed with questions. Who had allowed such a dreadful state of affairs to develop? And what could be done to alleviate them?

Mentally I added a new errand to my list. I would talk to Joshua Galbraith. He would know what I should do.

And then I realized on what treacherous ground I walked. I was about to meddle in the private matters of the Marchand family, without the least suggestion that I take any such responsibility. It would almost surely lead to resentment and bad feeling toward me.

I am ashamed to say that I hesitated, for I dreaded causing Joanna Marchand, who had been kind to me under trying circumstances, to regret that kindness.

But a mental picture of the ten-year-old locked in that evil-smelling, cold room, strengthened my resolve. Something must be done, and I was going to see to it, come what may.

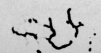

Chapter Eight

Johnny Brock and I purchased the necessary panes of window glass at a store on Main Street, along with various other things to be be delivered at the house later. Lumber for repair of the barn, a quantity of white paint, some brushes, and the like. They would be ready at hand when the weather permitted the job of painting the house.

Then my hired man let me off in front of Borgmeister's store. The rain drummed upon my umbrella as I hurried inside the doorway. Pausing, I carefully counted my money—then made my way to a counter at the side of the building where bolts of dress goods were displayed.

What a delight it was to examine the stock of fabrics with the actual intention of purchasing! The choice was difficult. There was French calico at eight cents per yard, chintz organdy in delicate pastel colors, satin, moire, and silk from Italy that I dared not even touch lest my rough fingertips mar the sheen. There was a lovely worsted *mousseline de lain* in jewel-like colors—emerald, ruby and rich sapphire-blue.

I was sorely tempted to buy the prettiest summer-flowered muslin, or silk and lace, even though I knew I must confine myself to more serviceable cloths.

At last I bought enough wine-colored double-fold alpaca to make a day dress, at ten yards for three dollars some Irish poplin for skirts, and white Victoria lawn for blouses. When I toted up what I owed the genial proprietor, I found I could still spend two dollars. Before my iron conscience could grip me, I recklessly pointed out a bolt of soft fine wool the color of new-blown lilacs. I would need a dress for evening, I told myself guiltily, and I would be sure to make it last for years to come! Already anticipating her delight, I also purchased enough moiré taffeta to make Eileen a fine Sunday dress.

Only another woman long-deprived of new dresses can imagine the soul-deep satisfaction I had in the bulky bundle Mr. Borgmeister carried to the waiting buggy.

But I had to lay aside my thoughts of sewing, and consider what I should say to Mr. Galbraith concerning Rebecca Marchand. I was by no means certain that I had the right to take the poor child's problems upon myself. Certainly no one would thank me for meddling. But if I did not do it, who would? I simply could not wash my hands of the matter, now that I was aware of the appalling conditions of the girl's life.

Fortunately Mr. Galbraith was free, and I was not required to wait, else I might have lost my courage. He ushered me into his office with a welcoming smile, and begged me to be seated.

"You are about bright and early!" he commented. "I hope it doesn't mean you are having problems with your new venture."

"Not personally," I assured him. "My friend Eileen O'Donnell has arrived to take a job as maid, and Mr. Brock is about to begin the house repairs."

"Good, good!" he said, and leaned back in his chair. "But something is wrong. I can see it in your eyes. They should be dancing with excitement, yet they are very sober indeed!"

I sighed. "You're right. I have come for urgently needed advice. But when I've told you, I shan't be surprised if you tell me to stay out of the entire business. And I cannot do that. It would be beneath the commonest human mercy."

"Suppose you begin at the beginning, Katherine. I may call you that, may I not, since we are practically old friends now?"

I smiled. "Yes of course."

But in spite of his encouragement, I found myself hesitating, until he warmly urged me once again to speak out, assuring me that he would treat the matter as confidential. So, haltingly at first, but made eloquent by indignation, I told him about Rebecca Marchand's room, and what I had learned about the quality of care she was receiving.

"You would not believe it, sir!" I cried, twisting my

hands. "The child is surrounded by filth—*old* filth! She is kept locked away like a wild animal, and as best I can ascertain, is left alone most of the time, except when it is necessary to bring food to her. No one has made any effort to teach her how to eat properly—you saw that yourself the evening you dined with us. Why, even the worst criminal would not be treated so!"

I finally halted, in the face of his continued silence, fully expecting a lecture upon minding my own business.

But he said nothing at all for a moment, and when he did I was instantly reassured.

"Katherine, I am glad you came to me with this. I had no idea—"

"But Charles Marchand is your friend," I blurted. "Surely *he* knows."

"If you mean that he has discussed Rebecca with me, you are perfectly correct," he admitted dryly. "The last time was only yesterday. You will be relieved to know that the gist of his conversation was on the necessity of finding a woman who would care adequately for the girl. But I do not believe he has any notion of the conditions you describe. He would never allow it, if only for reasons of health—not only for Rebecca, but for the rest of the family."

"Well sir, that is admirable, I am sure," I said icily, picturing the high-handed, domineering Charles Marchand, with something less than admiration. "But why does he not know of the appalling situation in which his daughter lives? Why does he not?"

Galbraith hesitated. "There is more here than you can be expected to understand, Katherine, and more than I am at liberty to explain to you. Suffice it to say that Charles is a very busy man. His horse farm in Kentucky is at a rather critical stage financially. If his horses make the desired reputation on the track, he will be over the hump. Otherwise his investment may prove a misguided one. And I assure you that his liability is a very heavy one, indeed. He will be satisfied with only the very best breeding stock, although I have cautioned him—"

I raised an impertinent hand. "I'm afraid I do not see what Mr. Marchand's horses have to do with his daughter.

·'I would venture to guess that those animals receive far better care than does that poor, helpless child!''

My tart remark caused Mr. Galbraith to wince. He sighed. ''I won't argue that, Katherine. The point is, Charles can have no idea of the problems you have described. To my certain knowledge, he seldom sees Rebecca, and would never think it necessary to visit her quarters.''

''That is inhuman, Mr. Galbraith. You may say that I have no right to pass judgement, but any Christian can see that it is wrong to—to abandon one's flesh and blood as Mr. and Mrs. Marchand have apparently done, relying upon the dubious consciences of subordinates to give her proper care. Why, she is not even bathed thoroughly, nor her clothing kept in repair!''

Mr. Galbraith frowned. ''Katherine, please. Have a care what you say about the Marchands, my dear. There are—factors there that you, as an outsider, cannot know. However, I grant you that something must be done for the child. You will be happy to know that I have located a woman who will live in and care for Rebecca, a Mrs. Martha Pinkham. She is a woman of excellent character, and she has had experience with a person with a handicap similar to Rebecca's. Her own brother was of—unteachable intellect, and she cared for him as long as he lived, to the age of thirty. Perhaps you are aware that the feeble-minded sometimes have an abbreviated life span?''

''If all are treated as Rebecca is, I do not wonder,'' was my muffled comment.

He smiled suddenly. ''Where did you get that temper, Katherine? I hope it doesn't land you in hot water.''

I found myself responding reluctantly to his smile. ''It continually does, sir. When will Mrs. Pinkham arrive at the house?''

''She had matters to attend to that will require a day or two. She has been recently widowed, and will have to make some arrangement to rent her house, or have it looked after by neighbors. She is from Southfork. That is about fifteen miles from here, up near the lake.''

''I see.'' Standing, I adjusted my hat. ''Thank you for listening to me so patiently, Mr. Galbraith.''

"You must call me Joshua," he said.

"Very well—Joshua." I felt suddenly a bit shy, and more than a little embarrassed at the too-forthright tone of my complaints about the child. "I shall see to it that Rebecca's rooms are thoroughly cleaned before Mrs. Pinkham comes."

"I am sure that is a good idea. Oh, by the way, I believe the Watson girls were to report for work this morning. What did you think of them?"

"I suppose I left before they arrived. But Miss O'Donnell will have taken over in my absence, and set them to work. I only hope they can bear her Irish tongue!"

Thanking him once more, I left. Back in the buggy, I rode in silence, busy with my thoughts. I blessed Joshua Galbraith for having dealt with the problem of Rebecca even before I had voiced it. But I gave little credit to Charles Marchand for having commissioned the attorney to do so. I told myself rather self-righteously that he should have personally seen to it that his daughter had at least simple basic care. Ignorance of her living conditions was no excuse, in my opinion, for I felt that as a parent he should not have *been* ignorant.

Oddly, I blamed him more than Joanna, who had been equally negligent. I can only explain the seeming inequity of my judgement by my feeling that Joanna was inordinately sensitive and refined. I could imagine that she was simply unable to face up to reality. Obviously she had been shielded since childhood from the ugliness of life. She was totally unprepared to cope with something as soul-wrenching as having borne a less-than-perfect child.

My mind was busy with plans as we arrived at the front door of the house. John Brock offered to bring in my bundles, but Eileen was already flying down the steps to meet me.

"Thank you, Mr. Brock," I said, "we can manage."

"Shall I get to those windows right away?" he asked.

I considered for a moment, as Eileen dimpled at him, and began to pick up the packages. "No," I decided. "I am going to move Miss Rebecca temporarily into other rooms while her own are being cleaned. You may as well wait until we have made it more bearable up there. But you might bring up coal so that we can heat the rooms a bit."

He agreed, touched the fat mare with the buggy whip, and drove away toward the stables.

Eileen and I carried my purchases inside. "What did you buy, Katy! Let me see at once," she begged, as eager as a child.

She followed me to my apartment, where I opened the packages and spread the contents upon my bed.

Eileen fingered the wine alpaca and the lilac wool, and her judicious nod was high commendation of the quality of the materials. "Them's nice goods," she said. "Very nice."

"I bought enough of the poplin for a skirt for you, too, and we shall both have new blouses."

"No, there, you didn't!" she breathed, her face lighting. "Thank you, Katy. Sure, your heart is too big for your own good."

"The moiré taffeta is yours too," I said casually.

She would not believe me, at first, and then argued vigorously that she would not take it. Laughing, I overrode her protests.

"You'll look a picture in your new Sunday dress, Eileen, and you know you've earned it already. But you shall have it, whether or no! After all, there's many a likely young man in this town who will have an eye for a handsome girl like yourself."

She seemed near tears. Quickly I changed the subject.

"Did the new maids come?" I asked, removing my hatpins.

She sniffled. "Yes. That they did."

"What do you think of them?"

She was holding the changeable taffeta, the color of a pigeon's throat, stroking it tenderly. "We'll have to see how they work out," she answered absently. "But I will say for them that they went right willingly to work redding out the parlor, and I ain't caught them slacking yet."

"That's good. I'm sure you will direct them to what we need done."

"Sure and I will, Katy!" she grinned. I had rueful visions

of her cracking a verbal whip over the hapless maids, and gave her a word of caution.

"But please don't offend them, if you can help it, or Mrs. Potter either! We need them too much."

That brought a look of hurt to her round face, and I felt remorseful. "Never mind, Eileen. I know I can rely on your good sense. Now, then. We have a very difficult chore ahead of us. I hesitate even to ask you to assist me, but—"

"Katherine Livingston," she said stoutly, "here's good advice. You had best learn that you are the boss. The other girls and me are here to do your bidding." She gave a mock curtsy, grinning, and I was relieved that she was already over her moment of pique.

Taking her at her word, I described the state of Rebecca's rooms, and the need for immediate and drastic measures.

"Saints above!" she breathed. "Locked in there untended and unwashed? Wait until I get hold of that Lottie Dilby!"

I shook my head. "She is employed by Joanna, and caring for Rebecca is not her responsibility. The poor child would dismay stouter hearts than Miss Dilby's, I assure you. There is another woman coming tomorrow or the next day, who will do a better job, I hope. But we simply must clean that room."

"So be it," said Eileen. "There's never a lick o' sense in waiting for dirt to clean itself. I'll start water heating, and bring the carbolic and soap and scrub rags. Why don't you and one of the new girls see to bathing that poor child, an' I'll take the other maid to help me."

"Such a task right at first may drive the maids away," I worried.

"Not if I explain that we shan't let matters come to such a pass again. Nor shall we!" Eileen nodded grimly. "Anyway, if these girls can't take orders, I'll go out meself into town and find willin' girls who can."

She hurried out, seemingly undismayed by the unpleasant task before us. I changed into my oldest dress, rolled up the sleeves, put on my biggest apron, and followed her.

My first chore would be the hardest, I felt, for I could scarcely move Rebecca, even briefly, without consulting her mother. It would not be an easy conversation, but it must be done.

Mrs. Potter advised me that Joanna would be waking about now. I offered to carry up the breakfast tray she was preparing, instead of waiting for Lottie Dilby to do so.

Holding the attractively prepared breakfast, and taking a deep breath, I tapped on the door I had been told was Joanna's. I had to knock twice before a sleepy voice answered.

"Yes, Lottie, come in."

"It is Katherine Livingston," I called, entering the room and closing the door behind me. I crossed the sitting room into the bedroom. It was so dim within that I was forced to allow my eyes to adjust before I could see the bed. Joanna's slight form was still upon it.

"Katherine? Oh. Open the drapes, will you?" she muttered.

I set the breakfast down and obeyed, letting in the dull light of the rainy day. Then I placed the tray for Joanna, automatically taking up the satin bed jacket that lay on a chair and helping her into it, as if she had been one of my charges at the Blackwood Home.

Someone had been in earlier and built a fire in the coal heater, so the chill was off the room. At Joanna's request I added coal and poked up the fire. She sipped her hot chocolate, complaining a bit about the taste. "Mrs. Potter will *never* learn how I like it," she sighed.

"You'll be wondering why I am bothering you," I began, as she began to look more awake.

"I supposed you came to bring up my tray. Nice of you."

"You are welcome. But there is another matter, most pressing."

As quietly as I could, putting it as a simple housecleaning problem, I told her that I would like to move Rebecca for part of the day.

She stiffened at the first mention of her daughter's name, and I thought she was going to refuse permission.

After a moment she asked, "Why is it necessary to take her from her own room?"

"Because the windows are broken, and the place is cold."

"We cannot allow her to have a fire, she would burn the place down about us!" she said bitterly, and with a defensive note. I was careful not to appear critical.

"I understand the problem, but we can scarcely work in there without warming the place."

"And of course she would be in the way, and hindering your efforts. Oh, well," Joanna shrugged petulantly. "Do anything you like. Only do not forget to lock her in. I can't have her wandering about."

I had some thoughts about that, but I felt it wiser to accept the small victory I had won, and save other matters for later.

"Thank you, Mrs. Marchand. I am sorry to have disturbed you with the problem, but I felt I should have your permission."

She looked at me and smiled crookedly. "If you can make some kind of order in this house, you have my permission to do whatever you wish. Well, after all it is *your* house, is it not?"

"But you are in possession, because of the rent," I said quickly. "I certainly would not like to intrude upon nor disturb you and your family."

"Disturb away!" she said, with a return of her airy laugh. "I only wish you were beginning your cleaning with this room. I am sure it has not been done properly in months."

"I shall make it my next priority," I promised. "If you or Mr. Marchand have any further suggestions—"

"No, no, I have no suggestions." Please be good enough to handle it yourself. As to Charles's rooms, you will have to ask him about that yourself."

I excused myself, and was halfway down the hall before I realized what she had let slip. Joanna's rooms were hers, alone. She and her husband had separate apartments.

Ashamed of my instant curiosity, I could not help the thought that slyly insinuated itself into my mind. *Why?*

Chapter Nine

Waiting for me outside Rebecca's door were Eileen and two young women who flushed nervously as I approached.

"Girls, this is Miss Katy. Katy, here are Lena and Marie," Eileen said by way of introduction.

Lena appeared the older, a very tall, rawboned girl with a long and mournfully-constructed face in which the eyes, a bright and merry brown, were the most appealing feature. Marie was somewhat shorter, yet both girls towered over me, tall as I am! Marie was rather pretty, her face strongly-boned and lightly freckled, her hair a carrot-red riot of sternly, pinned-down curls. Lena's hair was mouse brown, pulled back hard into a knot at the neck.

"Good morning," I said. "I'm so glad you've come to help us, particularly today. Has Eileen told you what a difficult job we have ahead of us?"

Lena nodded. "Yes ma'am.

It was a trifle disconcerting to be called ma'am by a girl older than I. I tried to look accustomed to the title. "I hope it will never be quite so—bad in future. There is a woman coming to care for the child. I am told that she understands the feeble-minded and will be fully responsible for her care. I would dislike, however, for her to be greeted by such a pigsty in my house. It was only yesterday that I myself knew Miss Rebecca had not been well cared-for."

They nodded their understanding. I felt as I imagined a general might, deploying his officers and men into the field.

I explained that I intended moving the girl to other rooms, and first must choose a suitable one.

"I've done that, Katy," Eileen spoke up. "The chamber across the hall has a locking door. 'Tis dusty but not so bad. I've built a fire to warm it for you, and I've brought a tub in there for the bath. We'll go down and bring up the hot water before we begin with Rebecca's room.''

I felt pleased at her initiative, and told her so. ''Which of you would prefer helping me bathe Rebecca, and which will begin work with Eileen?'' I asked the new girls.

They settled it between them, a bit doubtfully, and Marie was elected to assist me.

''We'll stand by to help until you have her settled in t'other room,'' Eileen offered.

''I think two of us can surely manage one child,'' I smiled. ''If you'll begin bringing up the water, that would be good enough. I'll need towels and—''

''Sure, an' I can guess you'll need soap!'' Eileen snorted.

I realized that I need not make my directions quite so detailed.

Perhaps I had merely been putting off the opening of the door in front of us. I sighed, fished the key I had gotten from Joanna from my pocket, and fitted it into the keyhole.

We advanced into the room. There were horrified exclamations from Lena and Marie as the smell of the room hit them. Eileen muttered prayerfully, ''Saints perserve us!''

I wasted no time, but hurried to the girl huddled in a rocking chair in the corner. She shrank back against the torn cushions as I approached. Her dingy yellow hair hung in matted hanks. Her clothes were filthy, smeared with food, and her hem was torn into fringes, as if she had systematically ripped it for fun.

''Rebecca,'' I said quietly. ''I am Katy. I have come to help you.''

She stared dully at me. I felt that she was afraid. Her eyes darted past me to the three women in the doorway, and I wondered if it had been a mistake for all of us to enter at once. I motioned for them to leave me alone in the room with her.

They did so, although Eileen frowned mightily.

''They are here to clean your room, would you like that?'' I asked the uncomprehending child. ''We'll make it clean and sweet-smelling for you, Rebecca, and I am going to help you take a bath.''

If she understood one word of what I said I could not tell it. It was like making conversation with a wooden doll.

"Where are your clean dresses, Rebecca?" I went to the wardrobe to find something for her to wear. In spite of the cold in the room, I found myself grateful for the broken windows that let in fresh air. Rebecca had pulled the wadded blankets away from the windows, and damp air poured in.

There were only two dresses in the wardrobe, both old and in poor repair. I managed to find a few items of underwear in the battered bureau drawer, but there were no stockings. Nor did Rebecca have on stockings now. My heart twisted with pity as I saw her feet, dirty and blue with cold.

Making a bundle of such clothing as I could find, I went back to Rebecca and held out my hand almost commandingly, but with a smile.

"Come now, dear. You must come with me, and you shall have a lovely hot bath."

She remained immovable. My heart sank. Would I be forced to call in the other girls and force Rebecca to accompany me? I disliked doing so.

Putting more force behind my words, remembering Charles Marchand's manner with his daughter that first night in the dining room, I tried again.

"Come, Rebecca!"

To my relief, she obeyed, putting her cold, rough hand in mine. Holding her fingers was like holding so many lifeless twigs. There was no response to the pressure of my hand. The girl came with me to the door, and then balked.

"Naw!" she squawked. "Naw!"

"What's wrong?" I asked. "Don't be afraid. We are just going over there." At my gesture, Eileen opened the door to the other room. I could not understand Rebecca's reaction, but I could see that she was badly frightened. It came to me that she feared breaking the rule about leaving her room. She probably had been punished for her last escapade which had so embarrassed her family.

But if she had wits enough to remember the rule—was there hope that she could learn a little about caring for herself?

I hadn't time then to follow that thought to a conclusion, for she was pulling back, and I thought she meant to break from my grip and run back into her room.

"It's all right, Rebecca," I said quietly, as one might soothe a very small child, or an animal. "It is all right this time. You may leave your room this once, while it is being cleaned. Come!"

Again she hesitated, but at last she lumbered over the threshold and came with me across the hall.

We entered a plainly-furnished bedroom, dusty and small. But it was such an improvement over the filthy environment we had just left that I felt like a freed prisoner. If only a few minutes in there left me with that feeling, what would it be like to spend all one's time in that place?

I shuddered. Releasing Rebecca's hand and closing the door, I took her clean clothing to the bed. The smallness of the room was a blessing, for the coal heater was already bringing the temperature to a comfortable level. There was more coal ready at hand. I added some to the stove. If I had to bathe the shy, wild, suspicious creature behind me, I was determined that she should not be chilled.

The door opened and Marie came in with brass cans of water. "Hello, Miss Rebecca," she said, and turned to me. "Eileen and Lena have run down for more water, ma'am."

I looked at our bedraggled charge thoughtfully. "Well, let us use some of this water to wash Rebecca's hair. I venture to guess it hasn't been done in a month or more."

"That may be harder than the bath," she giggled. "Shall I pour water into the basin?"

"Yes, please." I took Rebecca's hand and led her to the washstand and the china bowl. "Now dear, I am going to wash your hair, do you understand?" I picked up a thick lock of it and showed it to her. "It is dirty, Rebecca, see? I am going to wash it."

She allowed me to bend her forward over the bowl, and I had even gotten half her hair wet, before she reacted. She flung out her arm and shoved me back with a blow that took my breath away, then swept bowl and water onto the floor. The basin broke, and water soaked into the carpet.

"Think you'd best give up on that, miss?" asked Marie, obviously alarmed.

"No!" I said, my stubborn nature aroused. "Please go

and get me a basin from one of the other rooms."

When the fresh bowl of water was ready, I went to Rebecca. The child was cowering, huddled down on the floor with her dripping head in her hands. She was shaking. I caught one hand and patted it gently. After a moment, she looked up with a small, wary eye.

"It's all right, Rebecca. Come over here and watch for a moment. I will show you what we're going to do. I won't hurt you. Come, dear."

I coaxed her back to the washstand, but not near enough to put her head down to it. Then I slipped pins and combs from my own hair, and chattering to the girl all the while, proceeded to get my own head thoroughly wet. Thankfully, by this time Eileen and Lena, eyes round with astonishment, were back with more hot water and towels. I took one and wrapped it around my head.

"See, Rebecca? That was fun. It didn't hurt me at all. Come now, let's wash your pretty hair!"

"Lord have mercy!" exclaimed Eileen. "Next she'll be making all of us take a bath to show the poor lassie t'won't do lasting harm."

Ignoring the girls' giggles, I led Rebecca to the basin again, and bent her over it, patting her back. Her body was so stiff that I was sure she meant to duplicate her performance of a few minutes ago. Nevertheless I began to soak her hair, astonished at the dirt that stained the water even before I began to rub the hair with soap.

Quivering, she allowed me to continue. I worked as gently as I could, careful not to let the strong soap get into her eyes. Now that her hair was soaped, somehow I must get her rinsed.

Mumbling and shaking their heads, Eileen and Lena left to tackle their own unpleasant task. Marie came to take the dirty water and replace it with fresh. Hurrying as best I could, uncertain of the amount of time Rebecca would allow me, I managed to get a tolerably adequate job done, and wrapped a warm towel about her head.

She straightened, staring at me. In my memory, the most daunting thing about Rebecca wss that feral, frightened gaze she had. It made one think that any moment she might spring; clawing and biting.

"Now, the bath!" I said briskly, trying to ignore the tremors of nervousness. With Marie's help I undressed the girl. Her body was a pathetic sight, far too fat, pallid and quite dreadfully filthy. This child should have excercise, such as a brisk walk outdoors at least once a day, even if she had to be smuggled out past her parents' disapproving eyes!

Apparently bathing was not quite so unfamiliar as the hairwash. Almost docilely Rebecca sat in the warm water as Marie and I soaped and rinsed her thoroughly. Soon we had her out by the heater, wrapped in big towels. Dressing her was harder. Her limbs seemed stiff and resistant, and she grabbed almost automatically at every fold of cloth that came near her fingers. Again and again I must gently release her grip.

But finally the job was done.

"Thank you, Marie." I said. "I believe we have worked some improvement. Now, if I can only comb her hair."

"If you take my advice, ma'am, you'll do part of the combing with shears! She has too much hair ever to be nicely taken care of."

"I haven't permission to go that far—" I murmured doubtfully. Then I took a deep breath and nodded with decision. "You are perfectly right. Go and find a pair of scissors. Ask Mrs. Potter. We'll trim Rebecca's wild mane and give the new woman, Mrs. Pinkham, a fighting chance to keep our girl curried!"

Grinning, Marie obeyed, taking with her some of the dirty bath water to be discarded.

I found a straight chair, brought it to the heater, and got Rebecca seated on it. There was a set of combs and brushes upon the dusty dresser scarf, left there by some long ago tenant or guest. Doggedly I went to work upon the mass of wet hair. If Rebecca was tender-headed, I would be in for an impossible chore. But she seemed not to notice the tugging, and I began to breathe easier.

When Marie came with the shears, we went to work in earnest. Almost an hour later a good half of the matted length of Rebecca's hair lay on the floor, and the rest, reaching to approximately mid-back, was combed and beginning to dry. It was coarse hair, without a bit of curl. I braided it down the girl's back in one plait, then led Rebecca to a mirror to see the effect.

Short yellow tendrils lay upon her forehead in a fringe. She was, though no beauty, much tidier of appearance. There was nothing anyone but God could have done with that pitiful, slack, thick-lipped mouth, or the formless, doughy face.

"Why, how pretty you look, Miss Rebecca!" said Marie kindly, and I watched to see if there was the slightest spark of response in Rebecca. To my delight, she seemed to catch the meaning of the compliment, and put a hand on her head as if to feel the change.

"Pri—pr'ee—" she mumbled.

"Well, I think we've finished here," I told Marie. "If you will sit with Becky for awhile, I'll go across and help the other girls with that awful room."

"No ma'am," Marie spoke up stoutly. "You stay with her. It's more fitting for me to do cleaning."

She slipped out before I could protest.

I had a sudden impulse, and went to the door of the other room to call in to Eileen.

"I think I'll take our little friend for a short walk in the gardens. Is there a coat of some kind in the wardrobe?"

Eileen found a hooded cloak, evidently someone's hand-me-down. It was ripping out under each sleeve, and when I put it on Rebecca, I saw that it was too small. But it would do for a short time.

We went down the back stairs. Rebecca seemed almost to stop breathing, as if she knew what we were doing was forbidden. Yet she followed, her hand woodenly in mine.

In the kitchen, Mrs. Potter glanced up, astonished.

"Why—it's Miss Rebecca, all clean and pretty!" she said, after a moment's recovery.

"Yes indeed! We are going out, just for a few minutes," I informed her.

She opened her mouth, and I knew what words she bit back. She longed to warn me that I would be in difficulty with Mrs. Marchand if I allowed Rebecca to be out of confinement. But I felt that the cook's sympathies were with the girl, for she said nothing, merely gave a slight nod. "I'll call out if—if there's need!" she said almost grumpily, and turned away.

I led the child outside into the gray day. The rain had stopped and the air, though wet, was less cold. There was no wind to chill us. Nevertheless, conscious that I had not yet found stockings for Rebecca, and that her bare feet would soon be cold within her boots, I only took her for the briefest tour of the backyard.

She looked about her as if she had seldom seen anything so fascinating as leafless trees and winter-sodden earth. She gave me no trouble at all, merely followed like a puppy on a leash, and went back inside with only a wordless cry of protest and a momentary pulling back.

"Come," I said gently, "that's enough for today. But I will take you out again tomorrow. Do you understand, Becky? Tomorrow we shall go out again, after you have proper stockings and some rubber boots. Tomorrow."

She stared at me, mouth open and drooling. Her expressionless, glaring eyes blinked a few times, and her forehead wrinkled as if she labored under mighty thought. She meekly let me lead her up the back stairway to her freshly-cleaned room upon the third floor.

The girls had finished, and John Brock had repaired the windows in my absence. The room was a different place. It had been thoroughly disinfected with carbolic and lye soap. The odor was much pleasanter now than that of a few hours earlier. The maids had found better blankets for the bed, and clean linens, and had even hung faded but clean curtains. A comfortable fire warmed the room.

I could not disobey Mrs. Marchand's orders to lock the girl in her room, but I did ask Marie and Lena to take turns staying with Rebecca until Mrs. Pinkham arrived.

"We must have a fire in this room during the day, and I suppose it is dangerous to leave it unattended."

"An' cruel it is to leave the poor child unattended from one end of the day to t'other," Eileen said. "I'll come up and help her eat, if it's agreeable to you, Katy, so's we won't have the mess we had before."

So temporary measures were arranged, and with a lighter heart I went downstairs, already planning my next move in Rebecca's behalf.

Boldly I went to the phone in the hall and asked the

operator to ring Mr. Borgmeister's store. When he was on the line, I recklessly ordered a full wardrobe of serviceable clothing—including stockings, shoes, plus coat and hat—explaining that it would be needed for a girl of ten years, who was somewhat large for her age.

"Select them for—perhaps a heavy fourteen-year-old," I hazarded. "If they are overlarge I shall alter them. And would you please charge them to the Marchand account, and send the bill around to Mr. Joshua Galbraith's office."

I felt rather pleased with myself as I hung up the phone and turned away. There was scarcely any protest that Charles Marchand would feel free to make, since the expenditure was for his own neglected child.

My pleasure turned to trepidation when I saw that my phone conversation had been overheard. Joanna Marchand stood in the corridor leading to the parlor. Her face was white—rigid with an emotion I could not name, and I knew that I had seriously overstepped my bounds.

Chapter Ten

I was certain that Joanna was about to reprimand me severely for meddling. As I stood braced to receive her words, Mrs. Potter came from the kitchen.

"Mrs. Smith is here for the laundry," she announced. "Is there more to go?"

Joanna stared at me for a moment longer, then turned to the cook. "I believe there is some in my room. I will send Lottie down with it. Ask Mrs. Smith to wait."

She left, head high. Involuntarily, I gave a sigh of relief. Mrs. Potter went back to her kitchen, and I followed.

A woman with slightly-bowed shoulders who might have been in her forties stood near the porch door. She was thin, with graying brown hair, and a sharp, curious expression.

"This here's Mrs. Smith," Mrs. Potter waved a hand. "Mrs. Smith, Miss Livingston." The cook took up her coat from a kitchen chair, and uncompromisingly secured a hat upon her head with an enormous jet hatpin.

"I gotta do the marketing. Be back in a hour. Tell them maids I left their lunch warming in the ovens. See that you eat too, Miss Katherine." With this command, she vanished through the back door.

"Miss Livingston, I'm that pleased to make your acquaintance," said Mrs. Smith. "I heard the house had a new owner, but you coulda knocked me over with a feather, I surely thought you'd be much older."

I smiled at her. "I confess I'm a little surprised too."

She gave a birdlike nod. "I suppose you know the family well," she said, and I knew she was hoping for gossip.

"Well enough," I replied, and asked a question of my own. "I understood that your son would be coming for the laundry. I hope you haven't far to take it. There'll be a considerable amount.'

"Jakey is still at school. That is, if he ever went at all. Time and again he sneaks off to go fishing. That boy is the trial of my life."

"I suppose boys often worry their parents," I smiled. "How on earth do you dry the laundry in this wet weather?"

She seemed pleased at being able to enlighten me. "Why, there's a big old barn on my place—just up the river at Kernville. It ain't been used for animals in years. Made my boy clean it out and string a mess o' lines up. In bad weather I just hang everything in there."

"What a clever idea."

As we stood discussing the linens I wished boiled and bleached, Lottie Dilby came into the kitchen with Joanna's laundry, tied up in a sheet. She dumped it on the floor at Mrs. Smith's feet and went out with nothing save the barest nod of greeting for either of us.

"Now, there's a right poisonous snob," Mrs. Smith remarked, quite careless that the maid might still be within hearing distance. "Thinks she's too good to hobnob with the likes of me!"

"Perhaps she's only shy and retiring." I made excuses, yet thought Mrs. Smith was probably right. Miss Dilby was not friendly with me, either.

The washerwoman picked up the bundle. As she turned toward the door, she gave me a quick, brightly curious look. "Guess it didn't do 'em a lot of good, after all," she commented with a sly meaning that escaped me.

"I beg your pardon?"

"Poor old Miss Bertha's relatives. Guess she outwitted the lot of 'em, leaving the house an' all to you."

"Outwitted? I'm afraid I don't—"

She chuckled softly. "They thought it was in the bag, I expect, Mr. and Mrs. Hoity-toity Marchand and them DeWitts. An' so did everone else. Why, you coulda knocked me over with a feather when I heard none of 'em wasn't to inherit after all, but it was all going to a stranger!"

"Mrs. Smith, I don't think you quite understand the situation," I began, embarrassed by the conversation.

She shook her head sharply. "No, dearie, it's plain to me that *you* don't understand, or you wouldn't be living here amid the lot of 'em. I think Miss Bertha understood, but this here was her home, and she loved it. 'Twas all she had left. Why she didn't send the whole kit and caboodle of 'em packing before it was too late, I'll never know.''

I stared at her, confused. "Too late? What do you mean?"

But her eyes flickered past me for the tiniest instant and she closed her mouth upon whatever else she might have said.

"These things will be done and ironed by Wednesday morning, Miss Livingston. I'll send 'em over by my boy, Jakey, as usual. Shall I make the bills separate?"

"Yes, please," I answered absently, still all at sea over her cryptic remarks.

She left, with one final, darting glance at me, and a muttered sentence I wasn't sure I heard correctly. "Was I you, miss, I'd be careful!"

"What did you say?"

But she was gone. I turned just in time to see the door between kitchen and dining room move gently shut.

Instinctively I rushed to pull it open. But I was too late. I saw no one, and there was only the patter of hurrying footsteps to assure me that someone had been listening to my conversation with the laundress.

It was long past lunchtime. I found a large tray and started to place food upon it for Rebecca and Lena. Eileen and Marie came in while I was at it, and with a sharp scold, Eileen took the job from my hand, and ordered Marie to set me a place at the table. The red-haired maid served me with richly-scented stew and feathery biscuits that Mrs. Potter had left.

I submitted, but insisted that Marie sit down with me to eat, and reminded Eileen that she must also come back down and join us.

Already on her way out with the tray, she shook her head, grinning. "Ah, we'll never ever make a fine lady of you, Kate!"

"I devoutly hope you are right," I replied.

As we ate, I considered what I should tackle during the afternoon. There were dozens of jobs; it was a matter of setting priorities. Eileen relieved me of that decision when she returned.

"Where's that sourpuss, Mrs. Potter?" she asked.

"Gone marketing."

Eileen's eyes lighted wickedly. "Good! Then this is the time to clean this pesthole of a kitchen."

I shook my head. "I don't think it would be wise to take liberties with Mrs. Potter's territory."

"The place clean enough to suit you, is it then?" she demanded.

I looked around, and sighed.

Eileen chuckled. " 'Tis a mess, and you can't deny it. I'm itching to make some order of it."

"All right." I gave in. "But see that you leave the stove alone, and I'll have no squabbling with Mrs. Potter when she returns."

"Sure, an' I'll be meek as a little downy dove, Katy!" promised Eileen. "But I *will* scrub this kitchen. Why, I would wager it hasn't been properly cleaned for a year."

"I'll help you. No, don't argue!" I said. "Many hands make lighter work, and the sooner we finish, the sooner Mrs. Potter's feelings will heal."

Laughing, Eileen agreed. Accordingly, we hastily finished our meal as water heated on the range, and then the three of us began.

We were perhaps half done when Mrs. Potter came back. I saw that Eileen, an anticipatory smirk on her face, was only awaiting the first protest from the cook. She was all set to lambaste the poor woman with a list of her shortcomings in the cleaning department.

Hastily I got down from my perch on a stepladder, where I had been scrubbing out a cupboard. "Mrs. Potter, do you need help bringing in your bundles?" I asked.

She was staring at the bustle and unheaval of her kitchen, her cheeks mottling with temper. When she did not answer my question—indeed I doubt is she had heard it—I tried again.

"You are just in time to tell us what you want done in here. We have made a beginning so that things will be back in order in the shortest time and not disrupt your supper routine."

102

"Hmph!" she snorted. "I suppose you couldn't wait—"

"Not with *this* much rubbish and filth," began Eileen stridently.

I interrupted loudly. "What do you think, Mrs. Potter? Should we replace the shelf paper, or have Mr. Brock paint the cupboards?"

She set down an armload of purchases and turned to me. "Well now, paint would be nice. Since you've already got things in an uproar, soon's I get my hat and coat off, I'll lend a hand. Eileen O'Donnell," she screeched so suddenly that I jumped, "I was saving them biscuit tins!"

I sent Eileen a warning look, and she sighed with heavy disapproval and returned the collection of empty tins to a lower cabinet.

In spite of the strain of keeping Eileen and Mrs. Potter from open hostility, the afternoon passed profitably, with a great improvement to the kitchen. Mrs. Potter even seemed secretly pleased with the gleaming windows and the newly-ordered cupboards.

"We'll try to get to the pantry tomorrow," I told her. "And I shall tell John Brock to get whatever color of paint you prefer."

Majestically, she nodded.

I was pleasantly tired, and went to my rooms to rest. The quiet apartment comforted me. I brewed tea, and sat making a list of staples I needed so that I could prepare some of my own meals here. Potatoes, flour, tea, yeast and perhaps a box of bacon—that would be more than sufficient. When I had put down everything I could think of for the moment, I went to my bedroom to lie down for a luxurious half-hour, happily conscious that such a thing would have been grounds for instant dismissal at the Blackwood Home.

I did not mean to sleep, but the dim, cloudy light, the sigh of the wind against the trees outside, lulled me into a doze.

The nightmare came up like a thundercloud blown ahead of a fierce wind. I dreamt I stood at the telephone, trying desperately to reach the operator, who was my Aunt Betsy. And then Joanna Marchand came into the hall and confronted me, her beautiful eyes filled with hurt and anger. I was sick at heart that I had displeased her. She gripped my arm and told me, "You don't understand. You don't understand, or you wouldn't be living here. Be careful. Be careful, Katherine Livingston!"

I woke with a whimper, realizing that the room had gone pitch-dark, and I was cold.

Drugged with sleep, I staggered to my feet and clung to the bedpost for a moment to stop the swirl of dizziness.

There was someone knocking at the outer door, and then the quick thud of feet across the sitting room.

"Katy? Katy, where are you?"

Eileen swung the bedroom door open, starting when she saw me in the darkness.

"Katy?" she squeaked.

"Yes, Eileen. What is it?" I asked, rubbing my face and trying to wake up.

"Merciful Saints, how you scared me, standing there like a statue! Whatever are you doing in the dark? When you weren't at the dinner table, soon's I could, I came to see about you."

"I'm all right, Eileen. I just went to sleep, and haven't quite waked up yet."

She lit the gaslight and studied me worriedly. " 'Tisn't that you're ill, is it Katy? You've been working too hard, an' I said so not an hour past to Lena."

"No, no. I'm perfectly all right. I just dozed off—"

"An' you haven't had a bit of supper! Well, I can fix that. Come into the kitchen. I'll start a fire and get you warm. Why, Saints preserve us, you're shaking."

I realized that she was right, but it was not the cold that so affected me. It was the shreds of my dream, clinging like cobwebs to the rafters of my mind. The meaningless nightmare had infected me with a chill of unreasoning dread.

I did not argue with Eileen. Her brisk comfort was welcome. She made me sit at the table while she built a fire, and with a running description of events at the dinner table, she removed any need for me to make conversation.

"Mr. Marchand wasn't to home. They said as how he'd gone to Kentucky for a few days. But a man came to dinner. Asked about you, too."

"A man?" I could not think. Whatever was wrong with

104

me? I shook my head to clear it.

"A Mister Galbraith. Fine-looking gentleman."

"Oh, yes."

She grinned over her shoulder as she energetically pumped water into the kettle. "Marie tells me Mr. Galbraith is a bachelor, *an'* has a up-and-coming business as a lawyer as well. Maybe you'd ought to set your cap for him!"

"What?" The notion made me laugh, and that won a frown from Eileen.

"Well, an' what would be so bad about that? He's a fine gentleman, an he asked about you, didn't he now?"

"He's only interested in me as owner of the house, Eileen. He handled legal matters for Mrs. DeWitt, and has been most helpful to me. But it is only business."

Eileen sniffed and tossed her head. "Then maybe it's up to you to make it somethin' *more* than business, Katy me girl! You don't want to waste your life away without a good man o' your own, do ye now?"

"I suppose I'd like to marry some day, but—"

"Someday is as far as the Irish Sea! And' it just keeps gettin' further and further," Eileen said warningly. "You'd better be thinking about finding your man now."

I looked down at the crumpled and mussed clothing I had worn all day. "I hardly think a gentleman like Mr. Galbraith would be having thoughts about me, Eileen," I smiled. "I'm not exactly a great beauty."

"Feathered fiends of Hades!" she snorted. "You've looks and to spare, but for the clothes on your back. An' I intend to spread some o' that nice lilac woolen goods out on this very table soon's you've eaten and cut you a dress. I'll begin to sew it tomorrow."

"Why, Eileen, I didn't know you could sew."

"I grew up in a house with seven sisters! Me Mother could sew fine enough to make the ball gowns o' the ladies in the town, and I take after her. I'll sew you a dress as fine as any Mrs. Joanna owns, wait and see."

I shook my head. "You're a dear, Eileen, but I can't ask you to use your spare time on me. I think you should make up the cloth I brought you. I can manage to put together a simple dress, I believe."

"The dress I make will be better than simple," she promised, pouring fragrant tea into a cup for me.

It seemed to please her tremendously to be planning the gown for me. I couldn't find the heart to refuse her offer. True to her word, after she had cooked some eggs (which she filched from Mrs. Potter's larder), and toasted bread which I had with butter and jam (all likewise borrowed from the main kitchen), she allowed me to wash my own dishes. She brought the roll of fine wool from the bedroom and spread it upon the table. In less time than I would have thought possible, she had constructed a paper pattern, fitted me, and was pinning it upon the cloth. She mumbled as she worked, but refused to give me an idea of what the dress would be like, only ordering me to send for jet fringes and buttons and lace to trim it.

I admit remorsefully that I entertained fearful doubts as to her skill as a seamstress and winced a bit at she first cut into the lovely cloth.

It was very late when she cut out the last piece and straightened, a hand to her back.

"Eileen," I pleaded for the tenth time, "you're exhausted. Please go to bed."

To my relief, she obeyed me, promising to find time tomorrow to begin the actual stitching.

I made my own preparations for bed, turned out the lights, and crawled between the sheets. As usual, they felt damp and cold. I sighed, longing for summer warmth. Ah well, true spring weather would surely come soon. Already willow trees along the river were beginning to show green. It had been a long and difficult winter, and an unusually wet spring. The rains showed no signs of letting up yet, but surely it was only a matter of time.

My earlier sleep kept me from feeling drowsy. For a long time I lay awake, thinking about the things that needed to be done about the house, and how attractive the place would be when all was set to rights once more.

I realized that I was growing fond of the house, although I could not yet accept that it might be my own. There were many problems to be solved, but I felt that everything could be managed, given time. I pictured the house clad in its new coat of paint, raising a proud head once more in the neighborhood. I could hardly wait for good weather to allow Johnny to start the job.

I don't know what time it was when I heard the footsteps in my sitting room. It was a stealthy sound, and had I been asleep, as I normally would have been, I would not have detected it at all.

I listened for a moment before I felt the first prickle of alarm. At the Blackwood Home there was no such thing as a quiet night. Some patient or other always had to be tended during the late hours, and the night attendants would be briskly moving about. Thus the sounds in the other room did not at first frighten me.

Then I realized that there could be no possible reason for anyone in the house to enter my private quarters, except possibly Eileen. If she had returned for something, then she would probably tap upon my door in a moment.

But no one came to the bedroom door. I heard muffled sounds which I could not identify, and I became aware that I was afraid.

It was a new and unpleasant sensation. Of course I had been fearful when Aunt Betsy died, uncertain about my future, wondering if I could provide for myself. Nor had the Blackwood Home been conducive to serenity or a sense of security. Yet never had I known the onset of this kind of primitive terror, caused by nothing more than a series of unexplained thumps in a room where all should have been quiet and deserted.

The fright quite paralyzed me for a few moments. I could scarcely breathe, and I strained my ears for new sounds.

My eyes fastened on the rectangle that was the doorway leading into the sitting room—a dim glow of light showed there, and I realized that the door was open. I had not bothered to close it when I retired. How easy it would be for the intruder to step into the bedroom!

The thought broke my spell. I threw back the covers and slid my bare feet to the floor, then hesitated. What should I do? If I paused to light the gas chandelier, I would warn the prowler that I was awake and aware. Perhaps that would be unwise. My instincts were to keep the concealing darkness about me.

It seems very foolish now, but the thought crossed my

agitated mind that perhaps the noises I heard were not made by any human activity. I thought of the woman who had lived here, and then died. Had she died in these very rooms? Perhaps she resented a newcomer, perhaps she had returned to the place she felt was her own!

I got hold of my racing imagination and gave my mind a stern shake. What utter nonsense! I was scaring myself like a child, listening to tales of headless horsemen and chains dragged about at midnight!

Very likely what I was hearing was nothing more harmful or frightening than mice. It would be very strange, considering the way this old house had been neglected, if there were not whole colonies of the dreadful little beasts scurrying about. I suddenly became very conscious of my bare toes. If something were to cross my shivering instep at that moment—!

I was shaking now from more than the cold, but I made myself walk over to the open doorway. What was that dim, flickering light?

I don't know which I noted first; the innocent sound of the hall door closing, or the quick flaring burst of the light that had been so low and dim.

Like a badly managed marionette, I turned my head with jerky movements, seeking the source of that dreadful light. My indrawn breath was like a dried, thistle barb in my throat.

The color of the light was gold and red and quite beautiful. Even as I stared, it leaped and swelled and grew, moving up the sides of the windows, biting into the dry wood of sills and frames. God help me, the entire side of the room was ablaze.

Chapter Eleven

I was screaming even as I raced toward my kitchen and the pitcher pump.

But would anyone hear me? I pumped frantically until I had filled a pail, calling for help all the while.

"Fire!" I shrieked, as I rushed back along the narrow hallway, sloshing icy water through my gown and onto my legs. "Help, someone, please! Fire!"

Fortunately, I have strong lungs. My cries must have pierced the sleeping house like the mill whistle of the Cambria Iron Works at the changing of work shifts. In moments the door to my sitting room was thrown open and Eileen and Johnny Brock hurried inside. John had slept tonight for the first time in the servants' quarters. He had yanked on a pair of trousers over his long johns, but Eileen, hair flying, had not even paused for a wrapper.

Her screeches soon mingled with mine. The smoke was making us cough, searing my throat. I ran for more water. Johnny found the bedroom and snatched up a blanket. When I returned he was beating frantically at the curtains and blazing window frames.

"More water!" I yelled to Eileen. She ran, her flannel-clad body looking like a plump ghost as she disappeared toward the kitchen. I was dimly aware that Joanna Marchand appeared in the doorway. She was soon pushed aside roughly, first by Sidney, his eyes wide and his hair all on end, and then by the maids, Lena and Lottie Dilby. Marie was with Rebecca for the night.

"Get the children out of the house!" I cried. Lena vanished to warn her sister and get Rebecca out. Joanna grasped her son's arm. He shook her off.

"Leave me alone, Mother! I can help."

"Here, then!" Eileen, returning with a pan of water,

thrust it into the boy's hands. "Pour it on the walls near the windows."

As the boy obeyed, even haughty Lottie went into action, flailing at the flames with a small rug.

I followed Eileen back to the kitchen. She began pumping water furiously into a large pitcher, the only receptacle she had been able to put her hands on quickly. I brought my empty mop-pail.

"Katy, in God's name how did this happen?" She panted.

"I don't know. Here, fill the pitcher. I'll take this."

It must have been only minutes later that the fire was controlled, the curtains jerked off their rods by Mr. Brock and the walls thoroughly drenched. But it seemed hours, a nightmarish time of panicky, choking effort, before we all stood quiet, looking at the blackened, still-smoking wall. Someone, Joanna, I think, had thought to put on the gas-lights, and somehow the illumination made the whole scene more frightening.

I was shaking, but I forced myself to breathe deeply and cling to calm. The emergency was over. But the shock of it was still to be faced.

I saw that wondering surprise in every face. Eileen was standing with a protective arm about me. John Brock had taken the bundle of blackened drapes, laid them in the hearth, and was examining the floor for sparks. His glance at me was darkly questioning.

The same questions, in my mind, were beginning to force their way past the numbing barricade of the emergency.

How had the fire started? Who had come into my rooms—or had that been imagination? Yet, if no one had been there, how had the curtains ignited? There were lamps in the room, but none had been in use since the gaslights had been installed. There had been a fire in the sitting-room hearth early in the day, with the possibility of coals left in the ashes. Even if the firescreen had not been properly in place, it would have required a very hard draft down the chimney to blown sparks across the width of the room. I could not say with absolute certainty that I had so placed the screen, but I could not believe I would have neglected so elementary a precaution.

110

"Mr. Brock," I had to pause and steady my voice. "Mr. Brock, just now when you put the curtains in the fireplace, was the screen in place?"

He nodded shortly. "Yes ma'am it was. I set it aside when I put them drapes in."

"Then how could?" I couldn't go on.

"Yes ma'am," the hired man muttered. "I was askin' myself the same thing. How did that fire git started?"

I looked around at the blank faces. Only Sidney was not looking at me. He was crawling beneath the wide windows, intently examining the floor. His mother held her clasped hands stiffly at the waist of her blue, brocaded robe. Her corn-silk hair was floating unbound about her face, and her eyes were wide and shocked as they met mine. I thought the experience had frightened her badly. There was a pale line about her mouth, and her clenched fingers spoke of extreme tension.

Lena came back into the room. "Is it all out?" she asked. "I sent everyone out front."

She had her flannel wrapper half-on, the tail of it dragging out behind her. The sight of it reminded me that I was hardly dressed modestly myself, and I turned away to fetch my robe.

There was a buzz of talk from the sitting room as I left. "Merciful Saints!" I heard Eileen exclaim, "if that blaze had gone undiscovered, we'd all have been done to a turn in our beds, with Katy the first!"

I picked up my faded robe, dropped it because my hands were shaking, and retrieved it. Knotting it about my waist, I found my knees so unsteady that I was forced to sit for a moment, glad to be alone within my bedroom.

I heard Sidney, voice squeaking with excitement, cry out, "Look! Look here behind this chair. There's some paper twisted into a spill. Part of it's burnt."

There was a hard silence, then Johnny Brock uttered a crude oath that must have scorched every feminine ear in the sitting room. "This fire was set!" he said. "I'd stake my life on it. Somebody held this spill to them curtains until they caught. Prob'ly splashed kerosene on to begin with, from one o' them lamps."

His words made real the pushed-back thing I already

111

knew. The terror rose up in me until I felt that I must suffocate. Someone had tried this night to kill me, careless of the fact that other lives might have been lost as well. And I could not deceive myself that the person who had come into my rooms had simply meant to fire the house—that would have been more easily and safely accomplished in one of the unoccupied rooms. The primary intent must have been to take my life.

A coldness stole through my very being. I sat rigid, hearing Eileen shooing everyone back to their beds. John Brock left last of all, and Eileen spoke warmly to him.

"Sure an' you've saved every life here, tonight," she told him.

He cleared his throat as if with embarrassment. "I couldn't have done anything if Miss Livingston hadn't raised the alarm."

"Without your help we might not have been able to stop the fire in time," she insisted stoutly. "We owe you our lives, and we'll not be forgettin' it, John Brock!"

He went away, and Eileen came in to take my cold hands in her own warm ones. I looked at her without speaking, and saw the knowledge in her face. She had come to the same conclusions as I.

"Who was it did this thing, Katy?" she asked.

"I don't know," I whispered. "Someone was moving about very quietly. I heard, and went to see. But I was too late."

"The Saints be praised that you awoke at all!"

"I wasn't asleep. If I had been, I don't think the sounds would have alerted me."

"Katy, Katy," she said softly, her face white. "What have we gotten into here?"

I shook my head wearily. "I don't know. I'm sorry now that I sent for you, my friend. I think you should leave, first thing in the morning."

At once she bristled. "Ah, an' do ye now? Do you truly think you can send me away as easy as all that, Katy Livingston? Do you think I'll be leavin' you to face a bloody murderer all alone?"

"Eileen, whoever did this might try again!"

112

"Then, we'd both better be packing our things."

I shook my head. "I can't. I won't run away. I've taken on something here that I want to finish."

She studied me soberly. "Then I stay as well. Now that we know someone has evil designs on you, we'll watch night and day."

"Where were the DeWitts during the excitement?" I heard myself blurt. "Everyone else—except of course Marie and Rebecca, came running. But not one member of the DeWitt family came to see what the disturbance was. If Mrs. Marchand heard me, from her room, so should the DeWitts. They're on the same floor."

Eileen nodded, her eyes bright with conjecture. "I did see them just now, filing back up the stairs after Marie and Rebecca."

"Then they did get out of the house."

She met my look. "So it ain't that they slept through it all. But—they could have heard your screams, or Lena may have warned 'em on her way to Rebecca's room. It would be just like them to flee for their lives, not thinking of anyone else at all."

"Yes," I agreed reluctantly.

"On the other hand," Eileen voiced my thoughts. "Who has been against your being in this house, your owning it, from the first? Them DeWitts, that's who!"

"Still, I can't quite imagine Mrs. DeWitt sneaking down in the night to—"

Eileen snorted. "I wouldn't put nothing past that old witch! She's set on having as big a share of the inheritance as she can steal back from you. Mark me words, Katy."

"But—to try to kill me? Would she?"

Apparently even Eileen had a little difficulty casting the venomous Lily DeWitt in that role. She screwed up her face in hard thought.

"Maybe she thought—just to scare you?" she said doubtfully.

I shook my head. "This old house would have gone up like paper in another few minutes. If the walls had caught any more than they did, I don't think anything could have stopped it. She'd have to be very stupid indeed not to know that. And then how would she benefit?''

Eileen raised her hands in exasperation. ''There's no answering it, but for my money 'twas Lily DeWitt, an' I'll always believe it! Now, then, you get back into bed. You're looking ready for your coffin! I'll put a blanket on the sitting-room sofa and sleep there the rest of the night.''

I argued that the room smelled of smoke, and that she was welcome to share my big bed, but she would not listen.

''If anyone, including Satan himself, comes through that door again tonight, I'll be waitin', poker in hand.''

So it was arranged, and the rest of that uneasy night was passed. Not that either of us slept. I could not stop shuddering with reaction, nor shut off my demanding mind, and I heard Eileen toss and turn restlessly until dawn.

As the morning arrived, I did fall into exhausted slumber, and woke at the scandalous hour of ten. There were sounds from the kitchen as I rose. Hastily I found robe and slippers, and went out into the little hall. I had no desire to go into the sitting room just yet. Last night's happenings seemed unreal and far away. I would gladly leave them at a distance for the moment.

As I expected, I found Eileen bustling about, preparing breakfast. She seemed little the worse for wear after the harrowing night, and greeted me with a cheerful smile.

''Why didn't you wake me?'' I scolded. ''You mustn't do my chores as well as your own.''

''It will do you good to rest extra, this once. Come, sit down. I'll pour your coffee. I've breakfast cooking.''

I ate as quickly as possible, and was only just finished dressing, when someone tapped on my sitting-room door. I crossed that room, flinching at the ugliness of blackened walls and the wet and sooty floor. Opening the door, I found Mr. Brock standing there.

''Good morning,'' I greeted him. ''I'm sorry, I rose very late this morning, and I have not thought where we should begin today.''

''I've come to start repairing this room.'' he said, as if surprised that I hadn't requested it at once. ''I'll strip off what's left of the old paper, and build new window frames.

114

Mrs. Potter says there's some of the same pattern paper stored in the attic.''

I was touched that he had already thought it all out. ''I certainly would like to see the effects of the fire erased,'' I admitted with a sigh. ''I'll have to make new curtains, but that's a simple matter.''

''I'll start right away,'' he said. ''Oh, Mrs. Potter says to tell you there's a lady waiting to see you, a Mrs. Pinkham, I think she said.''

''She's come then! I'll go at once.'' Letting him into the sitting room, I hurried to the entrance hall. Waiting patiently in a chair against the wall sat a gray-haired woman, modestly dressed and clutching her worn, black purse in veined hands.

''Mrs. Pinkham?'' I asked.

''Are you Mrs. Marchand?'' she stood, nervously.

''No, no. I am Miss Livingston. You have come to care for Rebecca Marchand, I believe?''

''Yes. I was told the child is simple-minded, and needs someone who understands that kind of person. I raised and took care of my brother, until he died two years ago. As I told Mr. Galbraith, I am somewhat experienced.''

''Miss Rebecca is—undisciplined, and may be very difficult,'' I warned. ''But I hope that you can get along with her, and help her to have a happier life.''

''Been shut away all her life like a wild animal, would be my guess,'' she said quite matter-of-factly. ''It's the usual thing, I expect, in monied families.''

Her frankness startled me. But her statement had been made without rancor or hint of criticism, merely as a known fact of life. Nevertheless, I did not wish to be in the position of passing judgement on the Marchand family. I had already said more than was prudent to Joshua Galbraith.

''Should I speak with the girl's mother?'' asked Mrs. Pinkham.

''No—no, I don't think that will be necessary. I shall tell her that you are beginning your job, and if she wishes to give you any instructions, I'm sure she will ask to see you.''

She accepted this without surprise. ''Would you want me to begin at once, then?''

"Could you? It would be very helpful."

I showed her up to Rebecca's room, and gave her the adjoining one, with a connecting door. Marie, relieved of her watch over Rebecca, cheerfully took on the task of preparing the room for Mrs. Pinkham.

On my way down the corridor, I was intercepted by Mrs. Horace DeWitt. I felt that she must have been watching as I brought Mrs. Pinkham past, for she plainly meant to stop me.

"Miss Livingston!" she beckoned imperiously from her door. "Come in, please. I wish to talk with you."

I hesitated. There was literally nothing I wanted less at that moment than a conversation with Lily DeWitt. "I am very busy this morning—" I began.

She placed a demanding hand on my wrist and drew me into her sitting room. "I am sure you can spare a few moments for civil conversation, miss!"

"What is it you wish?" I asked, resigning myself to the inevitable.

She drew the tie of her silk wrapper closer about her flabby, uncorseted body and gave a little toss of her head. She had not taken time to dress nor to arrange her hair, and it was astonishing how much older she looked without her usual adornments.

"I understand that you are to see to the cleaning and renovation of our house," she said slyly.

"Of *my* house," I corrected calmly. "Yes. I am trying to make some improvements."

Temper mottled her cheeks at my refusal to let her verbal claim go unprotested. She chewed her lips, and worried her rings with plump pink fingers. "When my attorney proves—"

"Mrs. DeWitt," I interrupted strongly, turning toward the door. "I am very much occupied this morning, and I have no time to engage in useless argument. If you will excuse me now—"

"Wait!" She followed me across the floor. "I want to show you how much needs to be done to these rooms. They are a positive disgrace. No one has cleaned them in weeks, and I must demand that they be attended to at once!"

I wanted to suggest that if she, as an uninvited guest,

desired cleanliness, she must do some work herself. But I bit my tongue, remembering that Joanna Marchand would not be best pleased if I antagonized and further stirred up the DeWitts. I had no wish to upset Joanna, for I sincerely admired her, and wanted to promote a friendly relationship with her, if possible.

I sighed. "I have just hired some help, and we have begun to clean. There are priorities, as you will surely appreciate, Mrs. DeWitt. We will get to your rooms when we can."

"I shan't stand for poor service, just because you would like nothing better than to drive me and my family out of this house!" she said shrilly. "If someone isn't here today to clean these rooms thoroughly, I warn you I will speak to Mrs. Marchand, and you will—"

"Will what?" I asked, at the end of my patience. "I am not a servant here, Mrs. DeWitt, and you appear to have forgotten that fact. You may complain to whomever you like. Now I must go."

Without waiting to hear the vituperative remarks she doubtless had on the tip of her tongue, I left her. Hurrying down the hallway, I made a conscious effort to subdue the anger she always aroused in me. She was a silly, greedy person. I must take Joshua Galbraith's good advice and refuse to be disturbed by her accusations and criticisms.

I turned a corner and almost ran into Horace DeWitt. I had not seen much of the dapper little man since his arrival—nor was that any deprivation. Inwardly I sighed as he blocked my path. One member of his family had been more than enough for this morning.

"Ah, it is our lovely Miss Livingston!" he said, smiling. I thought the tips of his pale moustache quivered eagerly. "Where are you bound in such a flurry?"

"Excuse me, sir. I have to consult with the new maids and arrange the day's work," I said, edging past him.

Casually he placed the tip of his malacca cane against the wall, barring my way. I saw that I must engage in a childish shoving game with him, or give in and stand still for whatever he had to say.

"Surely all that can wait a moment, my dear!" he said,

and his pale, brown eyes slid along my body in such a way that I flushed with embarrassment and indignation. "I had hoped," he smoothed his moustache with a fingertip, "to become better acquainted with you."

"I am surprised, for I am certain *Mrs.* DeWitt has no such hopes," I said tartly.

"Ah. Ah—yes. Well, you see, my dear, Lily and I do not always see eye to eye on every matter! I shall not insult your intelligence by pretending that my wife has no suspicions and resentments toward yourself. But—that does not necessarily mean that I—agree with her conclusions."

"Am I to take that to mean that you have no part in the suit Mrs. DeWitt has instituted against me?" I asked quite pointedly.

He gave a small, husky chuckle. "Now, now, sweetheart, a man cannot always do as he likes, as you will have guessed. Not when a determined woman has the bit in her teeth! But I have not—let us say—quite made up my mind about you. If, in getting to—to know you, I find that your, ah, integrity is without question, who knows how I might be able to influence my wife." He touched my cheek with his forefinger.

Regarding him with astonishment, I flinched away. He smiled, his small gleaming teeth giving his sharp face a very hungry look. "Come now, don't be so skittish, Miss Livingston," he coaxed softly. "If you and I were to become good friends, then you have much to gain. I might even persuade my wife to abandon the legal actions she has undertaken."

We were near the head of the stairs. There was a sound like someone climbing up to this floor. Hastily Mr. DeWitt lowered his cane. I hurried past, my nostrils flaring with utter distaste—and in my agitation ran full tilt into the person who emerged at that moment from the stairwell.

Chapter Twelve

I can only blame our collision on the fact that I had my head turned toward the odious Mr. DeWitt, lest he attempt to touch me again. And because the newcomer could have had no notion that anyone was so near, he was not watching, either. We bumped together very solidly.

"Oh—forgive me!" I cried, held close in arms that had automatically caught me, and looked up into Charles Marchand's face. He viewed me with such an unguarded look of total surprise that it occurred to me that I was seeing the real man, unmasked, for the very first time. The coldness and the wicked charm were absent. Here was the face of a strong man, with lines of anxiety about the eyes, and winging black brows lifted over eyes full of the obvious question.

His nearness inevitably reminded me of the ridiculous dream I'd had. I hoped he took the burning flush of my face to be natural embarrassment at my awkward accident. But the touch of his hands were causing a helpless trembling to spread throughout my body. Desperately I told myself anyone would feel so, caught in such close and unexpected contact with a veritable stranger.

As he set me upright, his glance flickered past me, toward Horace DeWitt, who was now striding hurriedly away along the hall, and instant conjecture replaced the inquiry in Mr. Marchand's expression.

"Horace was annoying you?"

"He—I—that is—" I stuttered senselessly.

"Never mind. The situation speaks for itself."

I stepped back and took a deep breath. "Please excuse my awkwardness. I should have been watching my step."

"No harm done. Although," his lips quirked with wry amusement, "you have scattered my mail rather thoroughly."

119

"Oh, sir! I'll gather it up at once!" There was a regular snow of papers and envelopes on the hall carpet. I was even standing on some of them. Mr. Marchand must have been looking over his mail at the moment he stepped into the corridor and I ran into him.

I bent and began scooping up papers with agitated hands. Mr. Marchand caught my arm and pulled me up.

"I'll get them, Miss Livingston. You're making a jumble of everything."

"Yes sir. Excuse me!" I said, fighting tears, and started past him. But he still held my elbow, his fingers warm through the fabric of my sleeve. I caught the scent of tobacco and some spicy lotion.

"Wait a moment. I have something I wish to discuss with you."

He released me and quickly picked up the remainder of his letters. I was grateful for the opportunity to recover myself, unobserved, to blink away the tears that had almost brimmed over. By the time he had things gathered up, I was dry-eyed.

"Please come with me," he said with quiet authority. "Step into my sitting room for a moment, Miss Livingston."

At any other moment I should not have dreamed of going into a gentleman's private quarters alone with him. I can only defend my questionable action by pleading that I was agitated and confused by the events of the past few minutes. Also, Charles Marchand was a man one found it difficult to argue with.

I found myself seated on the edge of a leather-covered chair near a fireplace; Mr. Marchand kneeling to build a fire. The room had been unoccupied for several days, and was filled with the eternal damp and chill that Johnstown and the surrounding boroughs seemed never to escape these days.

I found myself studying Marchand's back. It was a strong, broad one, the shoulders wide within the beautifully-fitted, finely woven suit. His black hair lay thick and waving over his collar. There was something about the neatly-molded curve of his ear that made him seem younger—an effect that vanished like smoke when he turned suddenly

120

to me. Then I was like an insect upon a pin, those wintry, blue eyes holding me ruthlessly captive. The aggressive slant of strong cheekbones under weather-darkened skin, the commanding ridge of his nose, the stern, uncompromising line of his mouth made me feel like a child about to be questioned and reprimanded. I think I squirmed under his unmoving gaze, and bit my lip.

"Why do you look at me so?" he demanded abruptly. "Those great, gray eyes are pleading, as if you feared me!"

I blinked, ashamed that my face had revealed my thoughts so clearly. I made an effort to put on a look of serene indifference.

Perhaps I overdid it. Mr. Marchand laughed, and I knew my careful arrangement of features was lost in the sudden flash of temper I felt.

"Mr. Marchand, what is it you want to say to me?" I demanded, rising to my feet with an instinctive need to remove myself from a vulnerable position. I stood at my tallest, my height for once welcome.

He smothered his unkind amusement. "Forgive me, Miss Livingston. I am a rude man, I know. Please sit down again. I have serious questions to ask."

"If it is about Rebecca," I took the offensive, "I suppose that I owe you an explanation of my order, and of my conversation with Mr. Galbraith. I assure you I had only the child's welfare at heart, and now that Mrs. Pinkham has come, I will certainly leave everything up to . . . "

I saw that he was totally uncomprehending. I had assumed that he had spoken with Mr. Galbraith, and learned of my meddling—or perhaps Mrs. Marchand had already told him how I had highhandedly ordered clothing for Rebecca without permission, charging them to his account. Now I realized he knew nothing of this.

"Mrs. Pinkham?" he asked.

"Yes sir. The lady who has come to care for Rebecca. I spoke with her this morning. She seems capable and—concerned. I think she will work out very well, or at least I hope so, for she is much needed, as you must know."

I realized I was babbling inanely when he held up a hand, palm outward.

"Wait, if you please. Let me understand all this. You

spoke with Joshua about Rebecca?''

"I know I have overstepped my—''

He shook his head impatiently. "Nonsense. Are you trying to tell me Joshua has located someone to stay with Rebecca? That's excellent news. I hadn't expected he would find anyone so soon. But I didn't wish to speak to you about Rebecca.''

"What then?''

"About the fire in your apartment last night, Miss Livingston. I find that very serious indeed. What can you tell me about it?''

"How—how did you hear about it so quickly? You can't have been home very long.''

"Johnny Brock met me with the news, as was entirely proper! Surely you did not plan to neglect mentioning it to me? According to Brock, someone deliberately set the fire in that room.''

"We put it out very quickly.'' Why did I feel accused and defensive?

"Yes indeed, fortunately. But I am much disturbed that such a thing could happen in this house, as you can surely understand.''

Of course he was. I had not been thinking clearly. It had not been merely my rooms nor only my welfare at stake. The Marchand family, as well as the DeWitts and the servants lived under this roof. The fire could well have spread and cost them their lives.

"Yes, naturally. Forgive me.'' I wondered, in a corner of my mind, why I continually seemed to be contrite with this man—when I was not enraged with him! I sighed.

"What happened? Tell me precisely,'' he demanded.

I did so, and he listened with close attention, not even voicing a question until I finished. Then he took me back over the story, step-by-step.

"You say you heard someone in your sitting room. Why did you not call out at that moment?''

"I—I don't know. I was frightened, I suppose, and I felt that I did not want the—the person who had come in, to know I was awake. I admit that was very silly.''

"Not at all. Perhaps it was the wisest thing you could have done. It encouraged the devil to complete his preparations, yet allowed you to defeat his purposes. Had you frightened him away, he might simply have waited until another time, when you were *not* awake to defend yourself.''

I saw by the look he gave me that he had reached the same conclusion I had, that the fire was a personal attack upon me, or at the very least an attempt to frighten me.

"Have you any enemies, Katherine?" he probed.

"Well, of course there are some who are unfriendly. Mrs. DeWitt quite naturally despises me. But I cannot believe she would do something like this. And Mrs. Sibyl Blackwood was very angry at me before I left the Home. But she is in Pittsburgh, and I hardly think she would have anything to gain by persecuting me now.''

His gaze fell, as if his thoughts went inward to consider something. He had seated himself in a chair opposite my seat, and near enough so that he could have touched me if he wished, and could closely observe my expression. Although what that would have told him, I do not know, except that the memory of last night frightened me.

An ugly thought passed through my mind. I had assumed that Charles Marchand was far away, at the time of the fire. Yet he was here this morning. How could I be sure he had not been nearby last night? Near enough to let himself into this house, to come into my rooms, and—

I stopped my runaway thoughts sternly. What unutterable foolishness! Yet I couldn't quite put from my mind the thought that the only possible reason someone could want me to—to die, was this house, and my unexpected inheritance. Charles Marchand was Bertha DeWitt's next of kin. He was still first in line to inherit, I supposed, since I had no family that I knew of, not even distant connections.

But why should he go to such preposterous lengths to be rid of me, when I would gladly have signed away any and every claim to the property that first day in Mr. Galbraith's office? Of course it was unimaginable that he should.

I felt oddly relieved after thinking that through, and I suddenly realized that the man upon whom I had been speculating these past moments was looking at me somewhat peculiarly.

"What are you thinking?" he asked. "Has something

123

occurred to you?"

I felt annoyed. Did he assume he could demand that my very thoughts be voiced for his enlightenment or amusement, and I would obey, willy-nilly?

I straightened my shoulders and made my face unreadable. "Nothing at all, Mr. Marchand. I assure you I have no notion who would do such a dangerous thing as deliberately setting a fire in this house. The action seems to have been directed at me—although that seems laughable, when I speak it aloud. Nevertheless, in future, I shall carefully lock my door."

Before I was aware of his intention, he gently took hold of my hand. Holding it palm up, he studied it as if he had never seen such an object before. He placed the forefinger of his other hand gently on a callus, then began, as if absentmindedly, to trace a slow line along the base of each finger. This seemingly innocent touch gave me an indescribable sensation.

I tried to jerk my hand away. He held it fast and with a smile inherited from Lucifer himself, a smile that could have charmed a bird into a snare, he lifted my hand to his mouth. My breath caught in my throat as, lingeringly, he kissed my work-roughened palm, then put my hand gently back in my lap.

Enraged at myself because I had allowed such an improper situation to continue, even for those brief seconds, I sprang to my feet and rushed toward the door.

Calmly, as if nothing at all had happened, his voice followed me. "I have directed John Brock to buy and install a stout new lock for your door, Katherine."

I did not even look back. Hurrying away, I came face to face with Yolande DeWitt and her mother. Knowing my face was hot and red, I brushed past them hurriedly.

"Why—why that is Charles's room!" Mrs. DeWitt spluttered, behind me.

"So it is, mama!" Yolande giggled.

"Well, I never!" gasped Lily.

With horror I realized that there was no way I could explain my presence in Mr. Marchand's suite, and little hope that the DeWitt women would not spread their version of what they had seen. The worst of it was, they would not be quite completely mistaken.

My hand tingled in the spot where Charles Marchand's lips had touched it. Involuntarily I closed my fingers over the palm, and held my clenched hand hidden in a fold of my skirt, as if its very presence might accuse me to the world.

Chapter Thirteen

My hands were shaking as I burst into my own sitting room. I muttered something in passing to John Brock, who gave me a curious look, and rushed down the hall to the kitchen.

Eileen was not there, which blessedly gave me a brief time to myself. But I could not hide forever. There was all this enormous house to be cleaned. After a cup of tea, I sought Eileen and the other girls, and found them just finishing the parlor.

"Let's do Mr. Marchand's rooms next," I suggested. If it was an act to salve my conscience for my earlier blunder, one which might conceivably embarrass Joanna as much as myself, so be it.

The next days passed in a bustle of activity. Working with the maids, and glad to do so, I exhausted myself day after day.

Eileen begged me to slow down, to rest more, and warned me that I was not eating enough. Probably I should have heeded her cautions. But I was addicted to the work. It blocked out unpleasant and frightening thoughts and anxieties.

Beyond that, it gave me satisfaction to see the neglected house begin to approach a respectable appearance again. After working swiftly to clean Joanna's rooms, and working an improvement there that brought forth her delighted smiles, we settled down to cleaning, floor by floor, beginning with the first. (This in spite of Lily DeWitt's continual demands that we attend to her domain at once.)

Many of the rooms had been little used for years, and were thick with dust. The thick, furry rime on books, pictures, shelves, and knick-knacks became a personal enemy which I attacked with vigor.

I believe that it bothered Lena and Marie, at least to begin with, for me to scrub windows along with them. I rubbed beeswax and lemon oil into fine old furniture, and washed and ironed great stacks of draperies at their side. To them I was the mistress and owner of the house, and I imagine that they would have been more comfortable if I had only orgainzed the work and issued orders. I wonder if they ever became used to the sight of me in a stained apron, with my hair tied up in a cloth, wringing out mops without thought of my hands.

Thinking back, those hours of endless, backbreaking work were among the most pleasant I spent in that house. One might say, in light of the horror that was to come, that it was all for nothing. Yet I cannot feel that any honest work is quite wasted, and I am not sorry that all through those rainy spring days I happily followed my maids onto succeeding floors of the big house, crusading against dirt and disarray.

I awoke one April morning to the sound of sleet against my windows. Cold invaded the room as the wind swirled and buffeted the house. The day before, I had worked long hours in spite of a queasy stomach and various aches I attributed to the constant moving of heavy furniture. My throat had become painfully sore during the night, keeping me awake, and as I crept from my bed, I felt very reluctant to leave the warmth.

But it was time to be up and about. I set my feet on the floor and stood. The room abruptly turned a cartwheel about me and I fainted.

I must have been unconscious for only a brief time, rousing to find myself aching with cold, lying upon the floor near my bed. I heard Eileen's voice as she came across the sitting room. "Katy, are ye awake?"

She stepped into the room just as I was lifting my spinning head off the floor.

"Why, Katy!" she gasped. "What's happened?"

She ran to lift me to my feet, and laid a cool hand to my face. "Why, you're burning up, me girl! Here, now, get you back into the bed this minute. Merciful Saints, why ever didn't you call me?"

I was shaking now with an uncontrollable chill. I tried

to answer, but it seemed to require a very great effort, and by the time I framed the words, Eileen was gone from the room. I wondered with sudden anxiety if I had dreamed her entrance. Had she been here at all?

My throat burned and my head had begun to ache intolerably. I had just told myself that I must get up and see about making tea, when Eileen, followed by both Lena and Marie, burst into the room.

"Here," Eileen told Lena, without a word of greeting to me, "put those hot bricks to her feet and take care the towels are securely fixed. We mustn't burn her toes. I'll find some warm stockings for her. Marie, see if she can take some of that tea."

"Well, of course I can, that's what I've been wanting," I started to say crossly, and found that my voice did not exist, save for a weak, mewing croak.

I could not hold my cup, either. My teeth chattered from the chill until I could not sip from it, and my failure brought ridiculous tears running down my face. Murmuring soothingly, Marie held my heavy head and spooned the hot liquid into my mouth.

As Eileen wiped my tears, I tried to tell her I was perfectly all right, that they needn't fuss over me. But it was comforting to have the attention, and eventually I saw that I was going to have it in spite of any protests I might make. The tea eased my throat a bit. I grew warmer, and drifted off to sleep.

The comfort did not last. I woke from troubled, frightening dreams to nausea that wracked my body and kept Eileen running with basins. She had dispatched Lena and Marie to other duties, but she stayed faithfully at my side during my illness, which lasted several very trying days.

I recall little about those days. They were broken and confused by pain, nausea and faver dreams. I woke at odd hours to see snow piling up on the window sills, and I remember thinking fretfully that I was sure it was spring. Why was it snowing?

Several times an elderly physician came. I dimly recall his gruff instructions to Eileen, and his kindly, bearded face.

128

It was perhaps a week until I was able to sit up, feed myself, and feel my mind clear in spite of a very weak body. I had an unexpected visitor on that day.

Fortunately Eileen had bathed me and brushed my hair and helped me put on a clean, cambric gown. Otherwise I might have been even more discomfited when Charles Marchand strode into my room almost before he received reluctant permission from Eileen.

"Well, well, Miss Livingston," he said gently. "What have we here?"

He looked very tall and handsome in his white, tieless shirt and fawn trousers. I thought he must have been riding. His tall boots shone as though wet. I thought with maddening irrelevance that they would require a good polishing.

"I hear that you have been ill," he said. "This is the first time that little Irish dragon of yours would let me in to offer my sympathies."

"I—I am recovered now," I said, holding the counterpane up under my chin, certain that my sickness-whitened cheeks had become pink with consternation at his unexpected and disturbing presence.

"Hmm!" He studied me with embarrassingly probing blue eyes. "Well, I regret the necessity of contradicting you, but I think you are not at all recovered, and that it will take much more time to see you back in health. Nevertheless, I suppose that tomorrow we shall have to endure the sight of your stubborn attention to floors and laundry and such."

Really, it was amazing how quickly this man could anger me. "It was your idea that I should oversee the renovation and cleaning of this house, Mr. Marchand," I snapped.

"Ah yes, you have said it yourself. I wished you to *oversee* the work. I certainly had no notion that you would foolishly undertake the entire job yourself!"

"That is an exaggeration of the grossest proportions, sir," I remarked with careful calmness.

"Is it? Then how is it that you have exhausted yourself to the point of serious illness?"

"Have you ever heard of microbes, Mr. Marchand?" I asked sweetly. "It is said that they are the cause of illness, and may strike down the most stalwart at any moment."

His mouth quirked. He turned quickly away from my view, but I suspected now that he was enjoying our argument. This gave me such pause that I forgot to keep my forces of wit on the battle line, and he was able to win the skirmish when he turned back with an abrupt question.

"I am told that Miss O'Donnell warned you, you were doing too much, is that not so?"

"Well, yes," I admitted, "but she fusses over me so—"

"And here you are, just barely escaped from death's door, unless my eyes have deceived me!" he accused.

"Oh—horsefeathers!" I protested inelegantly. "It was merely the grippe, I am sure, and I am quite well now. I was never in any danger of—"

He overrode my words like a cavalry regiment at full gallop. "I do not care to debate the point, Miss Livingston, nor do I care to see a healthy young woman reduced to invalidism because of obstinate behavior that amounts to pure mulishness."

"Mulishness!" I gasped, sitting up, dropping my covering and remembering in the same instant, to snatch it back and conceal the front of my modest gown.

"Yes, my dear Miss Livingston," the insufferable man drawled. "I repeat—mulishness! You have been told repeatedly that you should turn some of the work over to others, and confine your attentions to directing the repairs and such. If you would not accept *my* suggestions, one might think you would accept those of Miss O'Donnell, your trusted friend—"

"Charles, really!" came a lilting voice. "You're upsetting Miss Livingston."

We both turned bemused glances upon Joanna Marchand, who advanced into the room, shaking her head and smiling. "Why are you shouting at Katherine? I am sure you are causing her no end of distress."

Oddly, she was wrong. I had gotten so involved in our verbal war that I felt only the invigorating heat of battle. It seemed almost natural to be matching wits with Charles Marchand—he striding about my bedroom like a restless lion—while I huddled indecorously within my bedclothes.

130

But of course now I saw the irregularity of the situation. I was relieved when Mr. Marchand, with a rather abrupt nod in my direction, left the room.

"How are you feeling, Katherine dear?" Joanna asked, coming to lay a cool hand lightly upon my forehead.

"I'm much better, thank you. I shall be getting up, directly."

She laughed teasingly. "I'm told that you have been trying to get up ever since you became ill, insisting that you had too much to do to lie abed!"

I had no memory of this, and could not comment. She continued without noting my silence. "Have you seen your new dress?"

The switch of subject was too much for me to follow. I stared at her stupidly.

She laughed excitedly. How lovely she was. Her eyes sparkled, her slender hands gestured gracefully, and her body vibrated with that strange inner sense of intense vitality.

"Eileen, come bring the dress!" she called.

In a moment a scowling Eileen appeared in the doorway, and Joanna turned and snatched the bundle from her hands. She shook it out happily and held it up. I recognized the finished dress as the pale, lilac wool Eileen had cut out for me. It was complete with the lace trimming and jet fringe that I had never, I remembered ruefully, gone out to buy. I knew my friend must have taken money from her own wages for these. It touched me that she had done so, and spent hours fashioning the dress in addition to caring for me these past days. I could scarcely force words past the lump in my throat.

"Isn't it pretty?" Joanna was saying.

"It is! Oh, Eileen, it's beautiful. When did you find time to work on it?"

Eileen shrugged. "There was time an' to spare, sittin' at your bedside," she said, her tone disgruntled.

I gave her a questioning glance, but she turned away to give a twitch at a curtain as if to straighten it.

"She does beautiful work," Joanna said, and laid the dress upon the back of a chair. "Well, I must run. I am attending a luncheon of the Orphan's Charity Committee, and I fear I shall be late. Take care of yourself, Katherine, I hope to see you back on your feet very soon.''

With this, and a last brilliant smile, she went out of the room. I felt grateful that she still considered me in a friendly way, remembering the day that she had overheard me ordering clothing for Rebecca, and her resulting and natural annoyance.

Eileen had gathered up the dress again. She muttered something under her breath.

''What did you say?'' I asked.

''Mrs. High and Mighty!'' she cried, her cheeks red with temper. ''Acts as if it was *her* gift to you!''

''Oh, I'm sure she didn't mean it that way,'' I said. ''Why, she must realize how many hours you put into it, and that it was entirely your own idea—''

''Hmph!'' she snorted, giving me a look without much liking as I strove to defend Joanna. ''If you'll be excusin' me, I'd best finish the hem.'' She went out before I could tell her again how much I liked the dress, and assure her that she was wrong about Mrs. Marchand.

Chapter Fourteen

The next morning, after Dr. Minikin's visit, and satisfied nod of approval at my progress, I insisted upon getting out of bed. I was weak, but aside from a swimming head and the conviction that I looked like a rag doll left out over the winter, I was well enough.

With Eileen scolding under her breath as she assisted me, I accomplished a delightfully hot bath, and even managed to wash my neglected hair before I sank, trembling, into a chair by the sitting-room hearth. Eileen had made a fire fit for a December blizzard (and indeed the temperature, with heavy snow upon the ground, was not much warmer), and I basked in the heat like a lazy, tabby cat.

Although I protested that I could do it myself, Eileen brushed my hair dry and arranged it, then brought a late lunch and laid the tray across my knees.

"You'd best be back to bed for the afternoon," she said.

I shook my head firmly, finishing my meal of creamed chicken with the first appetite I had felt in days. "I'm sick of that bed. I think I shall stay up night and day for a month."

"Then sit here by the fire and get back your strength. You're white as a windin' sheet, and so thin the least breath o' air would carry you off!"

"I'll get back my strength sooner if I begin to move about," I said firmly. "I must see to the things I had meant to do before I was sick. I know I'm falling far behind."

Eileen grinned peculiarly. "Well, then, I can see there's no stopping you, so if you must wear yourself down, I suppose I'd best go along to help carry you back here when you sink in your tracks."

Accordingly, she took the tray to the kitchen, and returned to escort me. But first she smothered me in a heavy woolen shawl.

We went out into the hall. I felt stronger now, and scorned to lean upon Eileen's arm, ignoring the slight trembling of my knees.

The house was quiet, except for the delicate tinkle of a piano in the music room far down the hall, where Joanna must be amusing herself.

"I wonder what we had best tackle next?" I worried aloud. "Thank goodness the lower floor is in fair shape now, although we shall have to keep after it or it won't stay in decent condition. But I shudder to think of all the bedrooms on the second and third floor that we hadn't got to."

"What's the hurry?" Eileen asked testily. "Are we expecting a visit from Her Majesty, Queen Victoria?"

I sighed. "You're right, I suppose. But I feel driven to put everything in order."

"So that you'll be feelin' worthy to own the house?" she asked shrewdly.

I had not thought of it in just that way, but I glanced at her with a startled feeling that she had hit upon something very near the truth.

"Perhaps," I admitted slowly. "But surely that is natural. I am not a member of Bertha DeWitt's family. The legacy was so—unearned."

"Do you imagine them Horace DeWitts or Mr. and Mrs. Marchand has 'earned' it any more than you yourself?" she demanded, trudging sturdily at my side as we ascended the stairs.

"Well, but it's not the same thing!" I protested. "One expects an heir to be a . . . "

"Member of the family!" she mocked me cheerfully. "Well, then, if you was to ask me, Katy Livingston, caring enough to help poor Mrs. Bertha when she was in the Blackwood Home, an' her kin was nowhere about, nor even seemed to *care* to be, maybe that made you her family, in a manner o' speaking. You was willing to be your brother's keeper."

I shook my head as we entered the second floor corridor, and was preparing a new argument, when Eileen interrupted.

"Now then, make your inspection, Katy me girl! See what chambers need attention next."

134

I opened the door of a room that had been next on my schedule.

It was spotless. And the same was true of every chamber on that floor, even those belonging to the DeWitts. There was no clutter anywhere save a few tumbled garments in Yolande's room.

"Why, how on earth did you accomplish all this?"

"Did you think we wasn't capable of doing the job without you wearing yourself to a nub?" she chuckled. "Now, there's more to be done, mind you, when good weather lets us beat and air rugs and wash the outer windows. But things is in decent shape. Up on the third floor too," she finished. "Lena and Marie did most of it while I sat with you. I gave them today off, as we were so well caught up."

"They certainly deserve it." I hugged her. "Thank you, Eileen. I made no mistake in sending for you."

My praise brought tears to her honest eyes. She quickly changed the subject. "Do you feel like walking up to the next floor? I think you'd be interested in seeing how Mrs. Pinkham is faring with Rebecca."

I was more tired than I cared to admit, but I did want to visit the child, so I pretended I should like nothing better than a walk up another flight of stairs.

We had only just stepped into the corridor when we met Mrs. Pinkham in the hallway, with Rebecca. The older woman stopped, consternation on her face.

"Oh, Miss Livingston! We were just going back to the room—" she began, seeming to expect I would reprove her for bringing her charge out.

"No, no. It's good to see that you are giving Rebecca a bit of exercise!" I exclaimed. "As soon as the weather is warmer, perhaps you and I might take her out of doors. I promised her days ago that we should have an outing."

"That would be the best thing in the world for her, Miss Livingston."

"Call me Katherine, please, or Kate if you like. Hello, Rebecca," I turned to the young girl, impulsively holding out my hand to her. Somewhat to my surprise she grabbed it very strongly, babbling something and becoming quite excited.

"Why, she remembers you," Mrs. Pinkham smiled.

"How very nice you look today, Rebecca," I said.

She was wearing a pink and white candy-striped dress with a white pinafore apron over it. Her hair was neatly combed and braided, and she was clean from her head to the toes of her new, stout shoes.

"The clothing arrived at last, I see." Mr. Borgmeister had ordered most of it from Pittsburgh, and there had been a bothersome delay.

"Yes, Miss Kate, and a blessing it is. Why, the child hadn't enough underwear for a change, and I was at my wit's end what to do. I was about to ask her mother, when the delivery came and that nice Mr. Brock brought up the bundles. You'd ought to have seen Rebecca, opening everything. She nearly wore the dresses out the first day, admiring them."

Mrs. Pinkham gave Rebecca a fond pat on the shoulder. The girl was tugging at my hand. I looked questioningly at Mrs. Pinkham.

"I think she wants to show you something," she guessed.

She was right. I followed Rebecca into her room, the child bounding awkwardly ahead, yanking me roughly in her wake. She went to the armoire in the corner and opened it, breathing heavily with excitement. An array of neat garments, including a coat, hung there. Boots and shoes were arranged on the floor. Rebecca grasped one of the dresses by the skirt and pulled. It was in danger of being ripped in two. Mrs. Pinkham came forward and caught her hands.

"Wait, dear!" she admonished quietly. "You don't want to tear it. Let me show you. Take it down this way."

She slowly went through the act of lifting the dress out of the wardrobe, repeating it once or twice, and trying to keep Rebecca's attention long enough to teach her the correct way to do it.

I cannot say that the lesson had any discernable effect. Indeed, Rebecca's temper was turning ugly from frustration when at last Mrs. Pinkham laid the dress in the girl's hands.

At once Rebecca turned to me. "Pree!" she exclaimed. "Dress. Pree!"

"Yes, yes, It is very pretty."

She flung it aside and grabbed at another garment. I

winced as she again grabbed at the nearest material and pulled. This time it was a sleeve, and Mrs. Pinkham was barely quick enough to save it from destruction.

She stood by for the predictable recurrence, handing Becky each garment in turn for me to admire. This evidently gave the child great satisfaction. She took up one of the dresses and began to gallop heavily about the room with it, chanting some unintelligible singsong over and over. Quickly, with our help, Mrs. Pinkham gathered the other things up and put them away.

"I do hope she soon tires of the novelty of her new clothes," Mrs. Pinkham sighed.

"You have a difficult job, keeping an eye on her."

"Ah, well. She needs someone, and there is gratitude in these poor unknowing ones," she said philosophically. "The good Lord didn't see fit to give them much of a mind, but there *is* affection there, and gratitude."

"How fortunate we are to have you, Mrs. Pinkham," I said feelingly. "Just to see this child kept clean and amused is a miracle. If you need anything from me or the maids, you must ask at once."

"Well, Miss Katherine, what's most needed is occupation. When I can take her out, and she can work off some of her energy, it will help. Until then, would it be possible for her to have some simple toys? I know she is beyond the normal age for baby dolls and such, but we must remember that she is very young in her mind. Or perhaps I should ask her parents?"

"No—at least, not her mother," I said hastily. "That is—" I sought for words to explain what I did not myself truly understand. "You see, Mrs. Marchand is—very sensitive on the subject. You might ask Mr. Marchand. I am sure he would send for whatever you wish."

"Well, the truth is," she admitted, "I'm a bit nervous about approaching him. He is such an—overwhelming gentleman, isn't he?"

I visualized Charles Marchand's tall, big-shouldered form, his stern face and icily probing eyes. Yes, I could certainly understand how this unassuming little woman would be afraid to speak to him about his moronic daughter.

"Well, then, I shall talk to him," I said impulsively, and immediately regretted my words. I had made the resolve to avoid Mr. Marchand as much as possible. But someone had to see to Rebecca's needs.

Sighing inwardly, I bid Mrs. Pinkham good-day, complimenting her once more on her handling of Rebecca, and turned to go. There was a distraction when Rebecca, now at the window, let out a wailing cry, half joy, half desperation.

"Siddy! Siddy!"

She began to pound at the glass with her fists, as if to remove the barrier it represented.

As we ran to stop her, I saw Sidney Marchand far below, coming across the front lawn.

"Oh dear!" Mrs. Pinkham exclaimed, pulling Rebecca away from the window. "I forgot the time. Everyday it's the same thing. I've contrived to have her attention on something else at this hour. Who is the little boy?"

"It is her brother, Sidney."

Rebecca was transformed from the happy child of a few minutes ago into a raging whirlwind, struggling in our hands, striking out at all of us. I was too weak to hold her very effectively, and I felt myself firmly shoved out of harm's way as Eileen took my place.

It took long minutes of determined restraint, as well as Mrs. Pinkham's steadily droning voice, to calm Rebecca. But at last she stopped trying to fling herself at the window.

"Come, dear, we'll play with the yarn, shall we?" Mrs. Pinkham said over and over, and at last succeeded in interesting the girl in a workbag that contained bright skeins of yarn. From the pitiable condition of the thread, I guessed that Mrs. Pinkham had generously used it to distract Rebecca before now.

The big, shapeless girl sank on the floor—hands full of yarn—and began to pull at pieces of it with utter concentration. I drew a deep breath of relief.

"She'll play with the yarn for hours now," Mrs. Pinkham said, not at all upset by the struggle. "I think she needs a dolly or two and some clothes for them to amuse her. I'd be glad to make the outfits if some scraps of cloth could be found."

"I shall ask Mr. Marchand at once," I promised, as Eileen and I left the room. When Mrs. Pinkham did not lock the door behind us, I looked back in to remind her to do so, feeling a twinge of shame. But I had been alarmed by the wild tantrum Rebecca had thrown, and I could well imagine what effect such a scene would have upon Joanna should her daughter burst in upon the family again.

I was trembling, and Eileen noted it.

"Ah, 'twas all too much for you, Katy. I shouldn't have brought you up here," she mourned.

"No indeed," I reassured her. "I am so relieved to see how capable Mrs. Pinkham is. And I needed to know if anything was needed for Rebecca's care."

"It isn't your responsibility," she snapped. "If that selfish mother of hers would—"

"Eileen, hush!" I gasped.

She lowered her voice, but continued stubbornly. "Well, and 'tis true, isn't it? Mrs. Marchand can't bear to think about her own flesh and blood, and so *you* bear the burden of it all, and it ain't right."

"Someone has to do it," I defended myself.

She sighed, but her face was still rebellious. "Yes, Katy, but it puts you in a bad position. If anything goes wrong, maybe you'd be handiest to blame!"

I laughed. "What can go wrong, now that Mrs. Pinkham is on the job? She's a wonder with Rebecca."

Now, with those words long in the past, I remember, and I tremble. How trusting I was, and how ill-prepared to meet the fates I tempted!

Chapter Fifteen

Since Charles Marchand was out of the house and would not be back until evening, I could not approach him immediately upon the subject of toys for Rebecca. I wondered if it might be wisest to simply order the things myself, as I had done in the matter of clothing. But I was reluctant to do so, feeling that I had gone too far in that, regardless of the need or the excellent results.

"Come back to your bed, do!" Eileen urged, as I hesitated in the lower hall. "You've overdone. Let me make you a nice cup o' tea, and you can rest."

I laughed. "I believe I shall burst into tears if I have to spend another daylight hour in my bedroom, Eileen. Bring me tea in the parlor. I promise I shall sit and rest until dinnertime."

"You hadn't ought to stay up for dinner," Eileen warned predictably.

"I'm dying to wear the new dress you made me, and since I'm sure you won't let me go out—"

"Indeed I shan't!" She threw up her hands. "There's six inches of snow on the ground, and 'tis cold as midwinter. Why, you'd catch your death o' dampness in a minute."

"Well," I said cunningly, "if you won't let me go out, I must go in—to dinner."

With an exasperated snort, she gave in. But her displeased mutterings as she left the parlor did not augur particularly well for the sweetness of her temper.

I turned to go to the fire, and was surprised to find young Sidney engrossed in a book, his slight form hidden by the back of his chair.

He stood up with manners too impeccable for a child.

"Good afternoon, Miss Livingston," he said.

"Hello, Sidney. Am I disturbing you? I can go into another room."

"No ma'am. I've finished. I was studying my history lesson for tomorrow."

"I understand that you do very well in school."

"Yes ma'am," he said, without false modesty, "except in math, I am at the top of my class."

"That is something to be proud of," I said, and sat down with relief in a comfortable chair.

"You've been sick," he said, in his odd, abrupt way.

"Yes. But I am much better now."

"My mother said you might die."

Astonished, I looked at him. His round eyes were fixed on me with an unreadable expression, his sensitive young mouth grave.

"Why, I am sure you must have misunderstood your mama, Sidney. I was never that ill. It was on—"

"Mama said you had a very high fever, and we must not be surprised if you died," he insisted.

I laughed, the sound a little weak and uncertain. A shiver went down my spine at this matter-of-fact discussion about the possibility of my demise. Of course I was touched that Joanna had been so concerned about me.

"Well, at any rate, I didn't die, and I hope you are not surprised at that, either."

He gave a faint, flickering smile that made him a very much more attractive boy. Lena came in with a heavy tray. Her long, freckled face was beaming.

"Eileen sent me with your tea, Miss Kate. It's so good to see you up and about again."

"It's like heaven to be up. Thank you, Lena. I can pour. Sidney, would you care for tea?" I asked him, as I would have an adult. "I see that Lena has brought some lovely little cakes and sandwiches."

"I'll go and fetch another cup," Lena smiled at the boy when he nodded, as if stricken with shyness.

She brought the extra cup at once, poured tea for us both, then hurried away to other duties.

It was oddly agreeable to be having tea with the younster. He was a little difficult to converse with, but when the subject turned onto his butterfly collection, he began to talk more easily.

"I have fifty specimens already mounted," he said.

"That sounds a great many. I should enjoy seeing them if you would allow me, someday."

I thought I had trespassed when he did not answer at once. He considered the idea critically as one might some unorthodox proposal for elimination of worldwide poverty, and at last nodded soberly.

"I will show you my collection on Saturday. I can tell you their names."

"Thank you. I'll look forward to it."

He smiled again, and I found myself wishing that he did it more often. What a disturbingly adult child he was.

"Have you a lot of friends at your school?" I asked.

He shrugged. "I like Willy Meeks. And George Wisett."

"It's nice to have friends," I said with such inanity that I was annoyed with myself. Somehow I had run out of conversation and I was glad when Yolande, bringing a fresh breath from the out-of-doors with her, whirled into the room.

"Oh, is that hot tea?" she cried. "I'm dying for some."

"Let me ring for another cup," I said.

Yolande threw her black coat carelessly over a chair. She was wearing another of her mourning costumes, a black, crepe, walking gown made with coat and skirt and a black satin blouse. The gown was trimmed with dull jet passementerie and jet rain fringe. Her small, black silk hat was embroidered with bugles. When I admired the toque, she removed the hatpins, took it off, and twirled it upon her finger.

"Yes, it is effective, isn't it? It came from Mr. Henry Jackson's, on Broadway, New York City. So did all my gowns." She gave a sudden, girlish giggle, her eyes sparkling. "I *hate* all this black stuff!"

I regarded her with surprise. "Then why do you continue to wear it?"

She shrugged. "Mama insists mourning dress will make me stand out and give me the edge over the other girls when the season begins at the Southfork Fishing and Hunting Club. She says it makes me appear mysterious and fascinating."

I managed not to laugh, although the exasperated look

she gave her expensive bonnet was very comical.

"I—see," I said with careful gravity. "Is it cold out?"

"Is it ever! I cannot believe it is really April."

"You've been shopping?" I asked idly.

She gave me a sideways, secretive glance. "No. I went with my mama to the Ladies' Auxiliary Tea, but I felt ill and left early."

Somehow the way she was consuming the sandwiches on the tea tray made me doubt she could be seriously ill. Still, the possibility that she might me coming down with the ailment that had laid me low caused a spark of anxiety.

"Surely you didn't walk home!"

She blushed scarlet, arousing my instant curiosity. "No, no," she said, not looking at me. "Mr. Brock happened to be passing by with the buggy, and he brought me."

Intuition told me that it was very unlikely John Brock had merely been 'passing by' at the exact moment that Yolande left the Congregational church. And how had she managed to leave the meeting without her mother in tow? I knew that Lily DeWitt was extremely protective of her daughter, and certainly would not allow her to go out on such a cold day, with the possibility that she might have to walk home.

My questions were answered when a voice like a mill whistle sounded in the entrance hall, as the front door was slammed.

"Yolande? Yolande, are you here?"

In a split second Yolande had patted crumbs from her lips with a napkin, replaced a half-eaten sandwich upon the tray, and had draped her body lengthwise along a sofa. I could have sworn that the rosy light in her cheeks dimmed by three shades.

"Yes, mama?" she called in a faint voice.

I believe the entrance of Yolande's agitated mama might have been fairly likened to the charge of a maddened, water buffalo. She came through the parlor door at full gallop, creating a draft that stirred the heavy, plush drapes.

"Yolande, where did you vanish to, you naughty girl?" she roared aggrievedly. "I glanced round during the discussion of who should pledge to stitch pen wipers for orphans, and you were gone! I was obliged to miss the election of officers, and I was nearly certain to have been nominated for secretary and treasurer. *What* is the meaning of this?''

Yolande's only reply was a shuddering moan. Fascinated, I watched as Mrs. DeWitt rushed across the carpet to bend over her recumbent daughter.

''My darling child, are you ill?'' she screamed, in a voice that must have put severe strain upon Yolande's eardrums.

Another moan. ''Do please forgive me, mama dear. I felt so sick, and I didn't want you to leave your meeting. I made my way home by myself. I wish you had stayed until the end.''

''Oh, my poor, dear baby! As if I should allow you to come out alone in the cold. It was wrong of you not to have left word with one of the ladies where you had gone. I should have liked to stay for the election.''

With a vast effort she put aside selfish concerns, and begain a catechism of Yolande, bent on discovering her symptoms. These proved a rather mysterious accumulation ranging from faintness and headache, to an elusive, movable pain, plus nausea, and I gathered, weakness of the ankles.

I had thought that my presence had escaped notice. I was mistaken. With a face that purpled as swiftly as a summer thundercloud, Lily DeWitt turned on me.

''My darling child has contracted your evil disease!'' she shouted. ''You have brought a pestilence down upon us all, and we shall suffer for our Christian forbearance in allowing you to stay in this house. Well, miss, be certain I shall advise my attorney of this development without delay.'' She turned to Yolande and helped the drooping girl to her feet.

''Come, sweetest. Mama will help you up to your room, and call Dr. Minikin at once.''

''No, no!'' Yolande was suddenly petulant. ''Mama, you very well know I cannot stand Dr. Minikin. He is so old, and he pokes and prods one so embarrassingly. I am sure this is just a passing spell.''

''But surely there is a reason for it—and I have my ideas about that!'' She gave me a venomous glance.

''Mama, you are misjudging Miss Livingston this time,''

Yolande surprised me by saying firmly. "I was not in her presence during her illness."

"Plagues travel!" pronounced Lily, her hat plumes trembling like righteously pointed fingers. "There are germs."

"It was not germs at all," Yolande came up with an inspiration. "I was suddenly reminded of—of dear Gerald—" her voice broke convincingly.

As Mrs. DeWitt assisted Yolande from the room at this point, I did not hear the rest of the conversation, and I was left with a small mystery.

"Now who in the world is dear Gerald?" I murmured aloud.

Sidney, who had remained silent throughout the whole exchange, gave a sudden snort of laughter. "Gerald Crumblet. He was Yolande's sweetheart," the boy informed me.

"Oh yes, I had forgotten. Her betrothed, who recently died."

"Betrothed, my big toe!" he said with a momentary lapse into boyhood. "My mother says Gerald never came close to asking Yolande to marry him. It was after he died of consumption that cousin Lily announced they'd been engaged." Sidney snickered, and I found myself smiling too. ing too.

"Oh. I see. I think."

"It's all to make old Yolande more romantic, my mother says," Sidney confided.

I felt a pleasurable guilt in stumbling onto the gossip, but I knew it would be unwise for me to pursue matters that were clearly none of my business.

I stood and gathered up the tea things. "I'll take these back to the kitchen. Thank you for keeping me company," I told the boy.

Replacing his mask of adult gravity, he gave me a silent nod and returned to his book.

I felt a bit nervous about going in to dinner. The new dress bolstered my confidence, yet made me more self-conscious. It had been a very long time since I had anything this pretty to wear. I had no wish to call attention to myself, and almost took the dress off again, to put on my old, green wool.

But I had already told Eileen that I would wear her creation this evening. If I did not, her feelings would be hurt. Sighing, I looked into my mirror.

I was thinner than ever. My face had little color, and my eyes gave me the distressing look of a starving waif. Fortunately, my hair had not lost its sheen. I had taken pains to arrange it high on my head, with soft waves next to my face. I wished for stylish, tight curls, but my stubborn masses of hair would never hold a curl even after being tortured with irons and curl-papers.

I had to admit that the lilac gown was a delight. Eileen had spared no effort and it was meticulously fashioned. The overskirt draped gently to a center point near the floor, and the snug-fitting bodice was trimmed with Mechlin lace and rows of jet buttons. There was a high lace stock. The sleeves were full at the shoulder and fitted at the wrist, where deep lace cuffs fell over my hands. The underskirt had two rows of jet fringe.

I had never looked so well-dressed. I found my Aunt Betsy's good lace shawl to drape over my shoulders, and lifting my chin in anticipation, went out of my apartment.

The doorbell rang as I came to the entrance hall. I went to answer, and found Joshua Galbraith on the step.

"Well, upon my word!" he exclaimed, smiling at me, and studying me with friendly flattery. "Miss Livingston, I presume?"

I smiled. "Come in, Mr. Galbraith."

He did so, still looking me over. I felt my face warm.

"I must say, if you have been as ill as I have been hearing, I hope you transmit the contagion to us all. It has brought you out of your cocoon, and a lovelier butterfly I never hope to see."

"Thank you. Should I call Mr. and Mrs. Marchand for you?"

"No, no. I am expected. I have been invited to dinner. Is Charles back from Southfork?"

"I am returned!" came a voice from the stairs, and I saw Mr. Marchand descending, adjusting a cuff link as he smiled at his friend. Then his eyes moved to me and his eyebrows lifted in a look of approving surprise. He gave me a slight bow as he stepped into the hall.

"Can this be our invalid? Surely not!" he exclaimed.

"Charles, it's no use your trying to charm Katherine with compliments, for I am ahead of you, and I am certain nothing you can say will compare with my own bald statements of truth," chuckled Joshua.

"Nonsense!" asserted Marchand, with his wicked grin. "Volumes could be written on the subject of such charm and beauty!"

"I must," I said with some asperity, "have been a dismal sight indeed up to now, to occasion such astonishment simply by putting on a new dress!"

"Untrue!" protested Mr. Galbraith. "*I* at least, detected your beauty long since, and I have said so often. Is that not so, Charles?"

"I admit it," Mr. Marchand grinned. "But now you must act as my witness, Joshua. Is it not indisputably true that *I* brought up the subject myself on the first day we met Miss Livingston?"

"Such a frivolous argument!" Joanna Marchand called down gaily, as she descended to the hall.

I felt embarrassed to have been caught speaking so familiarly with the two gentlemen. I told myself I'd ought to have left them the moment Charles Marchand came down. Feeling my face redden, I started to move away from the group that now included Mrs. Marchand. Joanna, running lightly across the parquet floor, had clasped her husband's arm and laid her exquisite face against his shoulder in an intimate gesture.

Joshua would not allow my escape. He caught my arm and gave me a teasing look that dispelled some of my sudden misgivings. And Joanna was smiling, so apparently she had not read the scene amiss.

But a quick glance at Marchand's face brought new anxiety. His mouth had gone rigid with disapproval, and since he met my eyes at that moment, I knew that I must have done something to cause his change of mood. But what?

I cannot describe the childish hurt I felt. It is very foolish, I know, but I had let myself enjoy the compliments the men had been tossing back and forth. I knew they were only in fun, but for that brief moment I had felt myself liked, and among friends. Now I saw that it was only an illusion.

147

There was no liking, no real friendship, in Charles Marchand. It was simply a pretense. I had detected his play-acting before. Why did it surprise and distress me now?

But it did. The moments of pleasure were spoiled. I was glad when the Marchands went in to dinner, and Joshua drew my cold hand under his arm with gallant kindness.

I hoped he would not say anything to me for a moment, until the ridiculous lump that had closed up my throat and brought silly tears to my eyes was gone.

As if he sensed my problem, he talked about the metamorphosis of the house, looking everywhere but at my face.

"It's been ages since I saw it like this!" he praised. "Bertha would be so pleased with what you have accomplished. I wish you had been here when she was alive to enjoy your efforts. I know it caused her dismay and sorrow that her beloved home was falling into neglect. Charles wanted to attend to it for her, but she was so fiercely proud that she would not allow it."

He turned to me just before we entered the dining room, and it was well I had regained my composure, for his eyes were suddenly very probing. It occurred to me that this is how he must look to a witness being questioned in a court of law.

"You never *were* here before Mrs. DeWitt's death, were you Katherine?"

Puzzled, I gazed up at him. "Why, surely you know that I was not. I did not even know of the existence of this house, until you yourself told me, in your office."

"Ah, yes, that must have slipped my mind!" But he continued to observe my face intently, and he had drawn me to a stop behind the others, who had already gone in to table. "You knew nothing of the will, and Mrs. DeWitt had never discussed her home with you?"

The statement was somehow a sharp question. Bewildered at his manner, I thought back. "It is possible, I suppose, that during the time Mrs. DeWitt was at the home she may have said something about—there was the mention of her home, I recall."

"What precisely did she say about? Try to remember, Katherine."

"Why, only that she wished to come home. She was not able to speak very clearly, you understand, but she repeated the one phrase several times 'I must go home to die.' When she said this, she seemed in the greatest distress and agitation. That is why I took it upon myself to write to Mr. Marchand and apprise him of her situation."

"Yes, yes. But she did not describe her house, or who was living in it at the time?"

"I—can't remember that she did," I answered honestly. "She told me that distant kin—the Horace DeWitts, I presume—were the ones who had placed her in the Blackwood Home. But I have no idea whether they were here when she became ill. I don't understand why you want to know these things, Mr. Galbraith."

He smiled, and the keen look of inquiry vanished. He patted my hand. "It's nothing at all, Katherine. You must forgive a lawyer's mind. Sometimes we see mysteries and complications where there are none."

I allowed him to escort me into the dining room and he held my chair for me. But my mind was still puzzling over the questions he had asked. Had they something to do with the will? Was it possible that the attorney for the DeWitts had found a way to nullify the document?

As my soup was served, I sat bemused by the thought that perhaps the house was to be taken from me. If that should occur, how should I feel about it?

Chapter Sixteen

If I were to be completely honest with myself, I must admit that loss of the house and my new way of life would be at the very least a severe disappointment. Now that I had poured my thought and effort into the renovation of this place, and had seen it begin to recover its lost elegance and pride, I should be very sorry to leave it.

Yet, I told myself firmly, I would be no worse off than before the surprising legacy that had sent my life in a new direction. I would refuse to allow it to cause me undue heartache. What was to be, would be. Worrying would change nothing.

At that moment I was roused from my thoughts by the touch of someone's toe upon my ankle, and then came the startling sensation of that toe actually caressing my leg, under the hem of my skirt.

I looked up to find Horace DeWitt ogling me from across the table, a sickeningly meaningful smirk twitching up the corners of his pale moustache. I jerked my foot away and my eyes as well, wishing I dared fling my serving of fish into the man's face.

"—your opinion of the situation up at the dam, Charles?" I caught the last of Mr. Galbraith's question.

"I don't like it," was the terse reply. Mr. Marchand was frowning. He leaned earnestly toward Mr. Galbraith, who was seated next to me.

"I have been investigating the rumor of a report made to Morrell, then head of the Cambria Iron Works, by a certain John Fulton, back in the eighties. Fulton was an engineer, and he stated unequivocally that the dam was dangerous—even then."

"What were his specific allegations?" Joshua asked.

"First, the dam was never adequately repaired after the

break in Eighteen sixty-two. When Ben Ruff bought it for two thousand dollars from Congressman Reilly, he used practically anything he could find to fill the break, even hay. And he removed the cast-iron pipes that had been originally installed to carry off surplus water. The pipes were designed to allow water to flow down the Little Con-nemaugh. The wooden control tower burned, you may re-member, in sixty-two, leaving no way to open the valves. I suppose Ruff felt the relief pipes were useless, and so he took them out. Unfortunately, they were the only possible means of reducing excess water behind the dam.''

Joshua frowned, nodding, and Charles continued. ''Ful-ton pointed all this out in his report, plus the facts that Ruff had put in that damned metal fish screen across the spillway. It catches debris and retards the water, throwing more pres-sure on the dam. Fulton also said that the crest of the dam had been lowered to make a road across it.''

''Is there immediate danger?'' Joshua asked.

Charles picked moodily at his fish. ''I hope not. But if we continue to have snow in the amounts we've been seeing, the spring runoff will be considerable. Something should be done before a crisis develops, but those in charge of the club since Ruff's death have reportedly refused to listen to warnings.''

''Who is the logical one to take action?''

''Colonel Unger is president and manager.''

Lily DeWitt, who had been chattering with Joanna about the Ladies' Auxiliary Meeting she had been forced to leave, and recounting every minute symptom of Yolande's illness, which kept her daughter upstairs tonight, turned at the men-tion of the name Unger.

''Charles, I think it is wicked for you to spread gossip about Colonel Unger. I have met the gentleman, and I assure you, I for one have utmost confidence in his good judgement. All this scare talk about the Southfork dam is plainly put about by jealous people who resent the fact that they cannot crowd in at the private lake, and spoil the place!''

Charles gave her a sardonic grin. ''How well do you know Elias Unger, Lily? I was not aware that you were a member of that particular circle. At least, neither you nor Horace were present at any of the gatherings I've attended that included Southfork Club members.''

"Why," she bridled, "I met the Colonel at a fund-raising dinner. We shook hands with him in the reception line, did we not, Horace? Horace! You are not listening!" she nudged her unresponsive husband.

Horace, as far as I could ascertain, was engrossed in the fit of Eileen's dress as she bent to serve him. He blinked and started as his wife's elbow dug into his ribs.

"What? Oh, yes, assuredly. Anytime."

Perhaps it is a commentary upon Horace's status that no one appeared to notice his lack of understanding regarding the conversation. Lily went on triumphantly to extol the virtues of the members of the Southfork Hunting and Fishing Club, and the beauties of the bountiful nature that they preserved there.

Marchand gave a slight shake of his head, as if declining to waste energy on further argument with his cousin's wife, and turned the talk to mill production, reportedly growing monthly.

This was interrupted when Joanna, who had been gazing fixedly at her son, sprang up to circle the table and place a hand on his forehead.

"Sidney, I do believe you have a fever!" she said worriedly. "Look, Charles! The boy is quite hot."

Charles turned politely. "Do you fell unwell, Sidney?"

"I'm fine, sir."

"Come here."

Obediently Sidney went to let Charles touch his brow.

"You are imagining things," Charles said. "The boy is no warmer than he should be."

"No, no. I am certain he is flushed and feverish. He may be coming down with the sickness Miss Livingston has had."

Her wide eyes touched mine. I felt accused, but told myself that it was only natural that others in the household might feel apprehensive about possible contagion. I wished that I had not presumed to come to the family table quite so soon after my illness. As soon as I gracefully could, I excused myself from the group, leaving before the dessert.

I fancied that Charles Marchand's eyes followed me with curiosity, and I was entirely certain of the bright malice in Lily DeWitt's look as she stared my way.

I was fatigued, and lost no time in hanging away the lilac dress, and preparing for bed. Thus I was not dressed for visitors when the light tap sounded at my door. But supposing it to be Eileen or one of the maids, I merely slipped into my faded, wool-flannel robe and called, "Come in."

The visitor had interrupted my nightly hair-brushing. As I left my bedroom I was still working at a tangle in the end of my long hair.

The door swung open to reveal Mr. Marchand's large form. He stepped in. Seeing my attire, he came no further.

Startled, I made a move toward my bedroom. My unwelcome guest help up a hand, smiling.

"Don't be foolish, Katherine. You are quite modestly covered, after all."

Of course he was correct, but being modestly covered by one's night clothes was not quite the same thing as being covered by daytime wear, as he quite well knew. It was totally improper for me to entertain a gentleman in my rooms at all, unchaperoned, and our meeting would certainly be considered outrageous under the present circumstances.

I should have insisted that he leave at once. But the easiest course seemed to be to inquire what he had to say to me, and hurry him out.

"You left the meal early. Are you feeling ill again? Shall I ask Doctor Minikin to examine you?"

"Certainly not. I am quite well."

"Then why did you rush out? Was it perhaps because of Joanna's inconsiderate remark?"

His perspicacity caught me off guard, and I suppose my confused silence gave him his answer. He nodded shrewdly. "May I come in and sit down?" he asked.

"Indeed no. I am sure."

"You're sure that I should not be here with you, alone."

It sounded very crude and suggestive, put that way. Would he now imagine that I had conjured up some—some possible intimacy with him? I felt my face burning. To answer either yes or no would put me a worse position.

"I can mend the problem," he said with a sudden grin, and went to the bellpull. He gave it a tug, although my hand flew out in an involuntary gesture of warning. The last thing I wished was for one of the maids to find me inproperly clothed and alone with the master of the house!

"What?" he laughed at my gesture. "You *do* wish for us to be alone after all? Well, then I shall simply send the maid away when she . . ."

"No! Please, Mr. Marchand," I cried desperately. "You must go before . . ."

"Before Lena or Marie find me here, and start a scandal?"

Perhaps my trembling anxiety awakened a tiny remnant of pity, for he stopped laughing and reassured me. "Don't be concerned, Katherine. I spoke to your friend Eileen just now, and asked her to join us here when she had finished. Surely you can trust me if she is present?"

Eileen saved me the necessity of speech by bursting in. "What is it, sir? Is she sick again?" she gasped, skidding to a halt.

"I am perfectly all right, Eileen," I sighed.

"The Saints be praised, for I know you have overdone this day, in spite of all my pleas and warnings! Why are you not in bed?"

"She is not in bed, obviously, because I have delayed her," Mr. Marchand put in gravely. But there was mischief at the corners of his mouth, and I was not deceived. What an exasperating man he was!

Smoothly, thumbs hooked in his waistcoat pockets, he continued. "Eileen, I wished to speak with Miss Livingston on business matters. I thought you should be present also."

Eileen nodded vigorously. "Indeed, an' I should think so. Come Katy, I'll help you get dressed again."

"Isn't it a bit late for that?" inquired my tormentor. "As I have already—observed the lady's attire, surely no further damage can be done. And it would increase the length of my visit if Katherine takes time to dress, which might occasion some remark."

I threw up my hands in defeat. "Oh, let us just get on

154

with it! Eileen, stay here with me. I will hear out Mr. Marchand, and he can go quickly!'' I put some emphasis on the last two words, which again brought out his wicked grin, and a considering tilt of the head.

"Eileen will be bored with the conversation. Perhaps she could make us some tea in your kitchen while we discuss matters.''

I grabbed for Eileen's hand, but she was already rushing from the room. I felt meanly that she had betrayed me, but there was nothing I could do. I marched over to a chair as far away from Charles as possible and seated myself in it.

Casually he moved to the door which led into the hall and locked it. If Eileen had not been in the apartment, my alarm would have known no bounds.

"I do not wish our conversation to be interrupted,'' he explained easily.

I wondered whom he expected to walk in upon our meeting. Lena or Marie, probably. Disturbed as my conscience was by the mere physical fact of the locked door, I was glad to note that he was not entirely insensible to the possibility of ugly gossip.

He came and sat in a chair he deliberately pulled too near mine. "I asked,'' he reminded me, "if you were disturbed by my wife's remark at dinner?''

"Not at all,'' I lied. "I merely had little appetite, and felt fatigued.''

I could tell he did not believe me. "Don't let such remarks whether they originate with Joanna or Mrs. DeWitt give you distress,'' he advised.

"Mrs. Marchand has been most kind. I am sure she did not mean anything critical by what she said. She has every reason to feel nervous. The members of your family have been exposed, by my presence, to illness. I should have thought of that and stayed in these rooms a few days longer.''

I disliked the conversation, and sought a change of subject. Providentially I remembered Mrs. Pinkham's request for toys for Rebecca, and brought it up. Mr. Marchand shrugged indifferently.

"Toys for Rebecca? Has she none? Certainly, order whatever you like. I thought you had already adopted that method.''

Reference to the clothing I had ordered without permission flustered me again.

"Perhaps I should have consulted with you or Mrs. Marchand before sending for garments for Rebecca. Her need was so immediate, and so great, that I yielded to the impulse.''

"I am glad you did so, and you have permission to purchase anything you wish for the child, the house—or for yourself.''

The last words were added so quietly that it took a moment for me to react to them. He was again suggesting that I refurbish my wardrobe, at his expense!

"For myself? Certainly I will not.''

"You will not object to buying what you need from the rent fee, will you?''

"That is entirely different, sir!''

He grinned and I thought of a great dark cat teasing a hapless mouse. "Exactly what is the difference? It all comes from the same pocket, Katherine my dear.''

I tried to express a dozen indignant thoughts at once, informing him that I was *not* his 'dear', and that there was a great deal of difference between the funds I employed for my purchases; and the rent money I tried to earn. At least it was legally mine, if the house were found to be mine. I found myself floundering, took a deep breath, and finished icily. "I shall not put personal purchases to your account, Mr. Marchand.''

Laughing, he stood. Eileen came in with the tea tray, but he waved away the cup she offered him.

"I must go. I see that you are well enough, and so I may lay my fears to rest. Tomorrow I am off to Kentucky once more.''

He went to my writing desk, and scribbled something on a sheet of stationery. Bringing the paper across the room, he put it into my hand, catching and holding my unwilling fingers for a moment, with Eileen an interested witness. "Here is the address of my farm, Katherine. If there is any problem here, I want you to write me at once. Better yet, telegraph me, and I will return at once.''

"Why, what problem could arise that would necessitate your early return?" I asked, puzzled.

He hesitated, and now the face he turned to me was genuinely grave, with a deep concern that I could not understand. "Kate—" he began, and stopped. He shook his head, with a smile that looked forced. "Who knows what can occur? It is merely a precaution."

"But surely Mrs. Marchand would be the proper person to get in touch with you."

His look went cold. "I have given you the instruction to send for me if there is need. Please act upon that instruction if anything troubles you."

Without further explanation he went to the door, let himself out, and was gone.

I found myself staring rather stupidly at the door.

"Well, an' what was that all about?" Eileen asked softly.

I looked at the folded paper in my fingers, and felt again the hard warmth and strength of the hand that had captured mine a moment before.

"I wish I knew!" I replied

Judging by the days that followed, Mr. Marchand's anxiety seemed increasingly needless. We had a few days of pleasant weather. My strength returned rapidly, and things went fairly well otherwise. Except that I was forced continually to dodge Horace DeWitt, who had taken to pinching or patting me in the most embarassing and infuriating way. I had not been in the habit of wearing my wire-net bustle under my day-dresses. Now I grimly put it on each morning as armor.

On Saturday, true to his promise, Sidney showed me his butterfly collection, with an explanation of each specimen. I felt pleased that he granted me the privilege of entering his world and sharing his interest for a time. He was a fascinating boy, very intelligent, well-read, and articulate on this cherished subject.

The morning after my conversation with Charles Marchand, I found some brightly-colored picture books, a baby doll made of hard rubber, and some watercolors that Rebecca could splash onto paper. Recklessly I bought a set

157

of miniature china, with little teapot and cups and saucers. I admit that I chose the last, more because I fell in love with them, than because I thought Rebecca would be appreciative.

Mrs. Pinkham brought Rebecca down for a stroll each day. Often I accompanied them, taking advantage of the improved weather, and hoping that we were done with cold. We had received fourteen inches of snow in April alone, and the ground was like a saturated sponge.

We were careful not to let Rebecca be seen out of her room by her nervous mother, and we stayed, on our walks, in secluded areas where neighbors could not indulge their curiosity upon the slow-witted girl. We strolled along the pasture fence, near the river which ran muddy and swollen, or climbed about on the quiet hills back of the house, among the pines and sour gums and oaks.

I prayed nothing would happen to prevent these outings. They were doing Rebecca good. She had more color, and more energy. Her violent spells occurred less frequently, as if the excercise in the mild, damp air helped to dissipate any excess of nervous energy. Nevertheless, I was well aware that if Joanna knew we were taking her daughter out where she might be publicly observed and remarked upon, she would immediately put a stop to our walks.

I tactfully mentioned this probability to Mrs. Pinkham, and warned her that we must excercise every care to prevent any mishap that would draw attention to Rebecca's outings.

She understood at once, and I was impressed with her uncritical understanding of human nature.

"It's most always the way, Miss Kate," she said. "I've seen it more than once. You take a fine lady like Mrs. Marchand. She's had nothing but the best since she was born, doubtless, everything done up to a tee-wighty for her! Then cruel fate gives her a child like this one, imperfect. You can't expect her to see that flawed as Rebecca is, she is still a human soul, and has to be loved just like a normal child."

"I believe you are right I don't think Joanna can help her aversion to Rebecca. Mrs. Marchand is a delightful person, and very beautiful and kind, but she is just not strong enough to face up to her daughter's affliction."

"Rebecca is a reflection upon her *own* perfection, that's what it is," said Mrs. Pinkham, nodding her gray head sagely. "Now Sidney, he's bright as a button, and Mrs. Marchand can feel pride in him. So she tries not to remember that her son's twin is wrong in the mind."

I sighed. "There are so many tragedies about us. To look at Mrs. Marchand, one would think she had everything; wealth and looks—"

"And a handsome husband," Mrs. Pinkham interrupted, with a birdlike sidewise glance at me. "Only the world doesn't know that Mrs. Marchand's husband is not that devoted to her."

"Where did you hear that?" I asked, before I could stop myself. I was aware of the mysterious estrangement between the Marchands, although I did not think it could be very serious. Joanna obviously adored Charles, forever clinging to him, no matter who might be present, smiling and whispering to him in an intimate and flirtatious way on occasion. His coldness toward her was incomprehensible to me. I thought probably it was the result of some argument that would soon be resolved. Yet Mrs. Pinkham spoke as if it were more than a passing misunderstanding between the two.

"Oh, I see more things than you might think. The nights are not always as quiet on the second floor as downstairs, Miss Kate! Sometimes when I must be up and about tending to Rebecca, and coming down for something, I hear—things."

"What do you hear?" I hated myself for asking, but something in me was unbearably curious.

Mrs. Pinkham seemed eager to confide in someone. "Mrs. Marchand *cries*. I hear her in her room. And once, when I came along the corridor, she was pounding on her husband's door, and—begging. To be let in!"

My mouth was open in astonishment. I stared at her. She seemed to read disbelief in my look.

"It's God's truth, as I live and breathe!" she said emphatically. "I thought the poor woman had been drinking. She staggered when she came back along that hall, and never saw me standing there at all, which is a mercy. But

I saw and heard her with my own eyes and ears. She was pounding with her fists on Mr. Marchand's door, and calling out to him to let her in. She said things—'' Mrs. Pinkham stopped, as if she felt herself going too far, and my own sense of caution was now in control. I bit down the inevitable questions. This was none of my business, and I must forget that I had ever heard it.

Mrs. Pinkham said one more thing, disapproval thick in her voice. "Can you imagine it? Mr. Marchand never opened that door to his poor wife, nor said one word to her that I heard! Miss Kate, the man must be made of stone.''

I made an excuse then and left her, but I could not help thinking about what she had said. I felt sick at heart, picturing beautiful, confident Joanna reduced to pleading like a mendicant at her own husband's door, careless of what anyone might think. Indeed Joanna must have been under the influence of spirits, or she could never have abased herself so.

What kind of man was Charles Marchand, to turn a deaf ear to his wife's suffering?

He was not a man, I thought fiercely. Charles Marchand was a monster—an unfeeling, uncaring monster.

Chapter Seventeen

The peace was too pleasant to last. One afternoon I found time at last to work on my new poplin skirt, and was making admirable progress with the sewing machine I'd had brought from an upper room. It was agreeable work, soothing in spite of the fact that I had not Eileen's exquisite sewing skill, and made blunders that did some damage to my temper.

My door burst open without benefit of a knock, and I turned to find Eileen, red-faced and fuming, throwing down her coat and wet scarf. I knew she had been out marketing, Mrs. Potter had at last delegated this chore, albeit reluctantly, complaining that Eileen was a dunce at selecting a decent cut of meat, and had on one occasion brought home shriveled turnips.

I was not altogether sure I wanted to hear what had set Eileen into such a stew. The past days had been so comfortable, with no new crisis.

Nevertheless, I knew I was expected to commiserate. "What is it?" I asked. "Is Mrs. Potter disappointed in the butter? Or have you overspent the food budget?"

"Tis that hussy, Yolande!" Eileen was literally gritting her teeth, and I had the feeling that only monumental anger was holding back her tears.

"Yolande? Why, what has she said to you?"

"To me?" She snorted, "Nothing! 'Twould be beneath her to take notice o' the likes of me."

I groped for understanding. "You are upset because she *didn't* speak to you?"

"Katy, how can you be so dense?" she flashed at me.

Feeling wounded at this unjustified attack, I turned back to my sewing in silence. If Eileen wished to explain, she could do so. I would not again risk my feelings in extending unsolicited sympathy!

After a moment there was a pleading touch on my shoulder. "Ah, sure an' I'm sorry, Katy. 'Tisn't you I'm ready to murder. It is that spoiled wax doll, her an' her fake mournin'. I wish—I wish she would trod surely upon a poisonous serpent!"

I had a desire to grin, but wisely kept my face grave. "What has she done, then?"

Eileen plumped down in a chair and embarked on a long tale that included her own inveigling John Brock into leaving his work of painting the house walls long enough to drive Eileen into the town. The jaunt had been, at first, much to Eileen's liking, with Johnny even laughing at her jokes and seeming more friendly and approachable than his habitual shyness usually permitted.

He had even gone into the Mercantile with her, and helped her carry out the purchases like a 'regular gentleman'. Eileen had just opened her mouth to suggest that they take a little drive along the Connemaugh, it being such a fine day an' all, when who should come tripping along the street, twirling her black silk parasol, but Yolande DeWitt.

"She looked like a little black witch in one of them fancy gowns she wears, an' she had a hat trimmed with feathers and jet aigrettes!" Eileen stopped for a moment, as if that alluring hat was an added, unfair weapon that reduced her momentarily to speechless indignation.

"Well?" I prompted. "What did she do?"

Eileen snorted, her face reddening again. "Katy, as the Almighty is me witness, she had the nerve to come up and insist—oh sweet as cream—that Johnny drive *her* to the house of some friend or other—like as not there was never no friend at all! An' when Johnny mentioned he was about to take me and the goods home, she pouted with that baby face o' hers, an' coaxed tears into her wicked eyes quicker'n priming a pitcher pump, an' said how she started out to walk, but isn't feeling too well after all, an' don't see how she can make it so far."

"Yes," I assured her, laughing helplessly, "I can imagine her going all pale and wan. That girl ought to be on the stage. And did Mr. Brock give in and take her?"

"The stage isn't where I'd like to see her! O' course he

162

took her, dumping me out, an' saying he'd bring the things I'd bought as soon as he dropped off Miss Yolande. *Miss* Yolande!'' she mimicked the hired man's deference. ''You mark me words, Katy, it'll be a hour if not more before I see them groceries!''

I could not resist the temptation. ''Oh, now I understand. You're concerned about the groceries, and the time they will arrive here!''

She gaped at me. Then a reluctant, half-hearted grin undid her ill-humor.

.''Oh—you!'' She threw a small sofa pillow at me. Laughing, I dodged.

''I'm sorry, Eileen. But I wish you wouldn't let yourself be disturbed by Yolande's flirting. You must know her mama would skin John Brock alive if he allowed himself to show any interest in Mrs. Horace DeWitt's darling!''

''If that's true, it don't keep that little black snake from making eyes at him.''

''She's just playing, surely. She's very young, and she's been held in too much. She'll tire of the game. If John Brock makes the mistake of taking her seriously, he'll have a big chip out of his heart to show for it.''

She nodded, but gloomily. I pressed on to another consideration. ''Besides John has a problem with his drinking, as you must know. I like him too, but I wouldn't care to see you give your heart to someone with that weakness.''

She gave me an astonished look. ''Just because the man drinks a wee bit? Katy, if girls was to be put off by a man liking his whiskey, there'd be few babes born in Ireland!''

She picked up her coat and stamped from the room.

After her tumultuous visit I found I could not readily regain my concentration, and besides I had sewed a pucker into the waistband that would have to be picked out before I could continue.

Standing, I rubbed the ache in my back that bending over the machine had produced, and went to the window. The light drizzle appeared to have stopped. I decided that I would go out for a walk.

Taking up an old shawl, I let myself out a side door. I would walk along the river pasture, and strive to regain my serenity, disturbed by Eileen's disatisfaction. I was so fond of her that I could not really be unfeeling, even though I felt her growing affection for John Brock was misguided, and should not be encouraged.

As I went out the pasture gate to walk along the river bank, I saw Mrs. Pinkham and Rebecca ahead of me, out for a stroll also. The big, ungainly girl was wearing a straw sailor pinned squarely on top of her head, and her new, navy wool coat over a red skirt. Mrs. Pinkham was her usual neat, shabby self. Her face was turned attentively to her charge, and I thought that Rebecca was telling Mrs. Pinkham something. It was one of the things I marveled at in Mrs. Pinkham, that she never failed to listen, or respond to anything Rebecca attempted to communicate.

Later I wished that I hurried to catch up with them. But I was selfishly enjoying my solitude. Rebecca was always very demanding of one's attention. What I wanted at this moment was peace and quiet.

Rebecca's first croaking cry brought me out of my unheeding contentment. I looked up in time to see her break away from Mrs. Pinkham and rush down the bank toward the nearby waters of Stony Creek.

My heart lurched. What if she should fall into that rapid, swelling, muddy stream?

I ran, passing Mrs. Pinkham, who also followed hastily. As we took the slippery path toward the bank I could see Rebecca lumbering ahead with awkward swiftness, arms waving. Over the rushing waters I heard her bullhorn cry, "Siddy! Siddy!"

When I saw the knot of boys fishing by the river, I understood what had sparked her rebellion. She had caught sight of her brother, and with the strange, passionate fascination he always seemed to inspire in her, she had broken away to run to him.

Desperately I tried to catch her before she reached the boys, for even from here I could see the white, stunned face Sidney Marchand turned toward his sister, and his instinctive retreat along the bank.

It could hardly have been a less pleasant situation for the

boy. He made no secret of his revulsion for his sister. To him, she must have seemed a misshapen fiend sent to make his life miserable on every possible occasion. To rush so hungrily upon him when he was with his curious friends, her pendulous mouth stretched in a great grin which caused her eyes to be hidden in the folds of her poor face, was something out of his nightmares.

Rebecca seemed unaware of the other boys. They stared at her and at the way she caught Sidney, fishing pole and all, in a delighted embrace. Sidney made no outcry as he struggled to release himself, but his eyes were expressive of utmost horror.

I still had not quite reached the group when one of the boys picked up a rock and threw it in a flat arc—it struck Rebecca's back hard!

"Crazy Becky!" he started to chant. "Crazy, crazy, crazy Becky!" Immediately the other children joined in. They were loudly taunting and flinging whole handfuls of pebbles and rocks at her when I charged into their midst. Some of the stones caught me on the cheek, not hard enough to cut the skin, but stinging and narrowly missing my eyes. Rebecca's hat was knocked off by a large rock. Still clutching her brother, she began to scream.

"Stop that, you bad boys!" I heard someone say, and knew that Mrs. Pinkham had arrived. "Stop that at once, or I'll report you to your fathers this very day!"

The rocks stopped flying, but the hardest part was still to come. It took all my strength, assisted by Mrs. Pinkham, to wrest Rebecca away from her brother. She stopped her awful screaming and began to yelp Sidney's name, bawling hoarsely like a great baby.

As we pulled her away, Sidney was shaking. His mouth was helplessly open and his expression shocked. I feared he might in his agitation step over the bank of the creek, just behind him.

"Sidney, take care!" I cried, but I do not think he heard me. His eyes were on his twin sister, eyes hot now with anger and disgust.

"Get away from me!" he shouted, finding his voice at last. "I hate you! I hate you!" Tears rolled down his face, but he seemed not know that he wept. "I wish you were dead!" he screeched, and turned to pound away along the bank of the stream, dropping his fishing pole and not even looking back.

I looked around. The other boys had scattered and were running away as well.

And so the crisis was over. But I knew we had not heard the last of it. My eyes met Mrs. Pinkham's stricken ones. Both of us knew that this would spell the end of Rebecca's outings.

The confrontation was delayed until just before dinner, when I was called into the presence of Joanna Marchand, in her rooms.

I met Mrs Pinkham hurrying away from there, her face sombre. She gave me a silent nod. I sighed, dreading my turn at judgement, knowing that Joanna would not be best-pleased by what had happened to her cherished Sidney. I was angry at the boy for tattling on his poor sister. Yet I tried to be fair. The experience had been very difficult for him, and his mother had clearly led him to a dependency upon her. He was scarcely to be blamed for reporting the incident.

I tapped on Joanna's door, expecting a curt order to enter. Instead, her voice came softly muffled. "Come in."

I found her pacing the floor, already dressed for dinner in a gown of velour frappe, a mignight-blue design of ferns stamped on a pale, cream velvet background. Cream lace formed the high collar and fell in a jabot to Joanna's waist, then formed the train which began at the shoulder.

She had her face covered by a dainty handkerchief, and when she lifted those beautiful blue eyes to me, eyes swimming with tears, my heart smote me with remorse. I had only wanted to help Rebecca, not hurt anyone, certainly not Joanna.

"Oh, Katherine, thank you for coming. Please sit down. And—" she wiped her eyes, "please forgive my appearance. I am distraught. Do you know why I called you here?"

"I must assume it concerns Sidney and—Rebecca." She nodded, and sank limply into a chair near mine.

"I cannot expect you to understand—" she began.

166

"I believe I do, and I am very sorry the incident occurred." I had resolved to offer no excuses, and simply take the reprimand she would surely mete out, as amply deserved.

"You say you understand, yet I wonder if you do?" she met my eyes steadily. Oddly, her weeping had not diminished her beauty in the least. If anything, she was the more appealing for her helplessness under the lash of her emotion. "Katherine, if *only* I could explain what my son means to me, and how very difficult things have been for him!"

This was not what I had expected. I had steeled myself for accusations of meddling, of causing an unforgivable public scene that had disrupted the peace of the family. Instead Joanna was begging for my understanding. If anything it made my remorse sharper, and I wished miserably that I had used better judgement.

"Sidney is a sensitive boy," Joanna murmured. "The very existence of—of his sister—his *twin,* is devastating for him. You know how cruel children can be, and for Sidney's little friends to see that—that—" words failed her. She put her trembling, delicate hands over her face again.

I could scarcely have felt worse. I would have given almost anything I could name to undo the unfortunate events of the afternoon. Yet, even in that remorseful moment a tiny voice within questioned why this mother's heart was so tenderly responsive to the one child's problems, but seemingly had no concern for the other. Was not Rebecca much more to be pitied than Sidney?

Joanna made a visible effort to recover herself, and even smiled. "Well, I mustn't pour out my troubles to you, a veritable stranger. As I say, you can hardly understand the damage that has been done to Sidney. But I must ask you not to—interfere with arrangements that have been made at great cost to my peace of mind, and that of Mr. Marchand, of course."

"Arrangements?" I asked, knowing that she expected the question.

"Yes, Katherine. I know it must seem strange to you that doors are kept locked and restraints placed upon—upon—"

"Upon Rebecca," I offered helpfully, a tiny flicker of rebellion caused probably by the promptings of Satan making me supply a name apparently forgotten by the girl's own·mother.

Joanna favored me with a sharp glance, and I knew she had not missed the barb. She shamed me by holding onto her patience.

"Yes, of course," she said evenly. "I won't keep you longer, Miss Livingston, since you need to dress for dinner."

I *was* dressed for dinner, in one of my older garments. Having only one dress appropriate for dining in company was proving more of a curse than a blessing, since I could scarcely wear it night after night.

I flushed and stood. "I quite understand what you have been saying, Mrs. Marchand. Again I apologize for using poor judgement about Rebecca. I felt that she was in need of healthful exercise—"

"What earthly good can it do?" she asked gently. "Can it give her a mind?"

I wanted to defend my conviction that the girl's health was of importance, aside from her obvious mental deficiencies. I knew it would be useless, and merely seem to be the conjuring up of lame excuses.

Without further discussion, Joanna showed me to her door.

The next morning, still feeling depressed, I ventured forth to see what progress John Brock was making with the painting of the house. I was amazed to see how much he had done, in spite of interruptions caused by having to drive members of the family or staff into town. I watched him for a brief time, my thoughts not so much upon the paint as upon the man himself. What *was* it about him that had Eileen in a continual tizzy and apparently was proving attractive to the spoiled and pampered Yolande as well?

He was not a handsome man, to my eye. His face was too long and (I thought) lugubrious. I fancied I saw signs of his weakness for the drink there; in a mouth that was kind but without firmness, a lack of confidence in the overall expression, and little strength or determination apparent in chin and jaw.

Personally I preferred a face built on the immovable rocks of a man's inner spirit, even if it might at times make him seem stern and even cold. I preferred a mouth that was not afraid to smile with devilish humor—

Startled at the unbidden direction of my thoughts and the image that arose in my mind, I quickly picked up my skirt hem and hastened away, no doubt to the relief of poor Mr. Brock. No one likes to work with eyes boring into his back.

I walked through the neglected yard to the front of the house, toying with the idea of finding tools and beginning to cut and rake away dead growth.

I rounded the corner of the house just in time to see Joshua Galbraith on the front walk. He was looking upward with a smile on his face, his hand lifted in a greeting. Naturally I too glanced up, and saw a curtain falling back into place.

Why is curiosity always so near the surface of the human mind? The question sprang into being at once. To whom was Mr. Galbraith waving? I looked to see what suite those windows occupied. They were Joanna Marchand's of course. The little mystery was solved, and how insignificant it was, after all. Mr. Galbraith had arrived and alighted from his buggy. Mrs. Marchand had happened to be looking down upon the lawns, and had greeted her husband's friend.

Joshua had not yet seen me. I spoke, and was unprepared for his swift, startled turn.

"Why—Katherine! I did not see you standing there, my dear! Surely you were not there when I drove up, or else I shall have to have eyeglasses right away."

Puzzled, I studied him. The man seemed nervous, a tendency I had never before noticed in him.

"I was looking over the grounds. Will you come in?"

"Er—no! Not since I have found you. I came to—ask you out for a drive."

Pleasure erased other thoughts. "Truly? I would like that very much."

"Getting a bit tired of being a landlady?" he asked, smiling.

"Yes," I admitted, and I suppose I sighed, for he looked

at me more sharply.

"Something is bothering you. Come, get into the buggy, and you can tell me all about."

I let him hand me into the vehicle, and moments later he was beside me, clucking his horse into motion. I had the sensation of eyes upon me, and turned my head, as if compelled, to look again at Mrs. Marchand's windows. Joanna was standing there, staring down at us. Of course I could not make out her expression, and there was no reason for the uneasiness that attacked my spirit, or the feeling that perhaps I was doing something that I should not do. Nevertheless I was forced to remind myself quite sharply that I was *not* a servant in that house, nor accountable for my time to any person.

"Now, then, Katherine," Mr. Galbraith smiled at me as we rocked down the street. "What has put you in the doldrums?"

It was a relief to tell him about my mistake with Rebecca, and the trouble it had caused.

"I know I should have asked permission before encouraging Mrs. Pinkham to take her out of the house," I said miserably.

"Permission that would certainly have been refused," he commented.

"Yes. Of course I knew that. I am guilty of taking matters into my own hands."

"I believe you often tend to do so." His voice held mock gravity.

I had to laugh, albeit ruefully. "I stand convicted, sir."

"Well, were I your judge you should receive a commendation instead of a sentence."

"But you are not." I returned to sobriety and sober reflection. "I realize that I have caused embarrassment and a disruption of peace in the household. I had no right to do so."

"Yet you wonder at Joanna Marchand's—unconcern for her daughter," he said shrewdly.

I hesitated. "Please do not misunderstand me, Mr. Galbraith. I—admire Mrs. Marchand, in most ways. She has been kindness itself to me. She is very beautiful, a very charming lady, and I would give much to be like her. But—I must confess that I don't understand why she seems to have no pity for Rebecca."

"It is not that Joanna has no pity," Mr. Galbraith explained. "It is simply that she is so sensitive in nature that she cannot face the cruel fact that she is the mother of that poor, pathetic creature. Each of us has emotions that are simply beyond our powers to—to control."

His voice fell away. I studied the side of his face surreptitiously. His large jaw was knotted with some inner tension, and his gaze seemed far away, not even focusing on the roadway ahead of us. He seemed to feel my puzzled look, and roused himself to a heartiness that did not seem entirely natural.

"Ah, Johnstown grows busier every day! The business at the mills is booming, They are turning out steel rails and barbed wire in great quantities. If this keeps up we'll be a real city one day!"

I nodded. Indeed, it was a bustling scene all about us as we passed through the main business district of the town. Great wagons pulled by patient draft horses transported goods along the cobblestoned streets. There were carriages, buggies, light wagons, and pedestrians hurrying in and out of stores. Perhaps it was the return of mild weather that brought so many out. I remarked as much to Mr. Galbraith.

"Doubtless you are right. I have lived here for several years, and I do not recall a winter so wet or so enduring. Here's hoping the rains and snows will cease and leave us to enjoy the springtime soon."

It brought to mind the conversation between Joshua and Charles Marchand, concerning the dam far up the river at Southfork.

"Is there really danger of serious flooding later in the spring?" I asked. "I feel quite frightened when I think of the lake."

"Would you like to see the lake and the dam?" he asked impulsively. "Why don't we drive up there?"

"But—won't it take too much of your time?"

"I shall award myself a day of leisure—and pleasure in such lovely company."

I smiled at the teasing gallantry. He took that as an assent, and urged his horse to a trot along the road upriver.

Chapter Eighteen

It was a very pleasant drive. We rolled along next to the horsecar line, past the enormous factory Mr. Galbraith told me was the Gautier plant where barbed, fence wire was made, and into the pretty little town called Woodvale. A mile or so beyond here were the towns of Franklin and Connemaugh. Passing through these, Mr. Galbraith received friendly hails from several people. Evidently he was well-known and liked.

Perhaps an hour later the road through the cramped, steep-sided valley led us to Mineral Point, north of the river. It consisted of twenty or more houses in a lovely setting at the base of the hills. From there we moved on at a brisk pace along the wet, narrow road, and sometime after noon we entered the quiet town of Southfork, where over a thousand people lived. Mr. Galbraith insisted that we must have our lunch.

"Oh, please, I am not dressed to go into a public place," I protested.

"Then we shall have a picnic."

He stopped the horse before a small general store, went in and purchased a loaf of fresh-baked bread, cheese, and great mustard pickles. At a saloon along the street he found a bottle of wine, and sarsaparilla for me.

So provisioned, we drove on, along two miles of pine-flanked muddy road next to a rushing creek. The path grew much steeper, and at last we neared the dam itself.

From below, this man-made mountain did not appear unnatural but rather some great landslide of boulders set here and there with young saplings, brush and weeds of various sorts. The spillway carried a loud torrent of water frighteningly down at the eastern end. Here a bridge crossed the turbulent falls. Beyond, the road rose to the top of the dam, there to divide—one branch crossing a second structure that bridged the spillway, the other going along the top of the dam itself.

As we drove out onto the narrow breast of the dam, I gasped at the body of water spread out before us.

The bank to our left seemed to drop straight down to the water. The lake curved away southward, and on the western shore were the summer houses of the wealthy who congregated here in the hot months.

The expanse of water seemed very awesome, to me. Joshua volunteered the information that it covered some 450 acres, with perhaps five miles of shoreline.

At the center of the dam the road dipped slightly, and then rose again. I felt relieved when we had passed over the fragile-seeming barrier that held back all that water, and began to circle the lake itself.

We passed several private houses, and the big lodge that had been built for the wealthy summer guests of the club. Mr. Galbraith stopped the buggy in a secluded nook out of sight of the buildings.

"Is anyone living here now?" I asked, feeling like an intruder.

"Only the resident engineer and a few others. They will not mind our little picnic."

We got down and searched for a place to sit. But the earth was wet and cold, saturated with the snows that were even now melting on the slope above us. It was cold up here, in spite of the watery sunlight.

Nevertheless, I liked the feeling of being so close to nature. The dark trunks of hardwood trees only now beginning to leaf out, the Christmas scent of the evergreens, the calls of birds come back for spring nesting, all excited and pleased me. I found a stump large enough to set out our food and drink. A log lay nearby. Its bark was damp, but it would harm my old serge skirt but little if I sat upon it. I was not so sure about Mr. Galbraith's broadcloth suit.

"Shall I cut you a sandwich?" I asked.

There was no answer. I glanced round to find Mr. Galbraith staring at a nearby stream that tumbled muddily into the lake. The attorney was studying the roiling water with sombre face and drawn brow.

173

"Mr. Galbraith?" I called.

He turned at once, and smiled, but it seemed merely a polite cover for the trouble in that broad, strong face. "I beg·your pardon, Katherine?"

I repeated my question.

"Yes, yes. We'd best have our lunch and start back. I do believe the clouds are coming in again, and we may be rained upon if we don't hurry."

He came to take the bread and cheese I had cut, but I saw him glance away at the stream again, very thoughtfully.

I settled myself upon the log and ate with good appetite, looking out over the lake. From here I could see other streams like the one that so fascinated Joshua, and all were funneling torrents of water into the lake.

"Do these streams flow year-round?" I asked idly.

He shook his head. "Some will be dust-dry in late summer. Some run minimally. It's the melting snow and this infernal rainy spring that has them bank-full now."

"Surely that is a great deal of excess water to come in behind the dam," I remarked.

"Yes," he replied quietly. "It is, indeed."

But he changed the subject abruptly, and rather hurried our meal, somewhat to my disappointment. Was he finding my company so unappealing?

It was not that I felt more than a passing interest in this gentleman, in spite of Eileen's stringent advice on the topic of the 'lawyer-gentleman'. But it was a minor blow to my pride that I had failed to interest him even enough for conversation.

Inwardly derisive of myself, I gathered the crumbs of our lunch and flung them about for the birds. The remaining wine and my sarsaparilla bottle I put in the basket to take home, for it would be a shame to leave rubbish in this landscape.

The ride home was mostly a silent one, although at intervals Mr. Galbraith seemed to rouse himself to the courtesies of pointing out things along the way, or to make the beginnings of polite conversation. These starts invariably fizzled, through no·lack of effort on my part, and when we came into the street in front of my house, I felt a bit discouraged with the day.

Joshua handed me down and gave me a wry smile. "Forgive me, Katherine. I know I have been poor company. There is much on my mind."

"That is quite all right. I'm sure I hadn't noticed," I answered with a certain forgivable stiffness, and took leave of him.

I was scarcely within the front door when Eileen came hurrying from the back of the house.

"There you are! Why, I've asked high and low for the whereabouts of ye!" she exclaimed.

"Oh—I'm sorry, Eileen. I should have told you. Quite on impulse, I went for a ride with Mr. Galbraith. But surely someone saw me leave?"

"If anyone did, there's not been a word said!"

Sighing, I apologized again.

"Well, no matter dearie, I'm sure, but Mr. Marchand is asking for you, and has been these past two hours."

Something quivered convulsively in my breast, a leap of gladness, hastily quelled.

"When did he return home?" I asked.

"About the noon hour. He spoke with Mrs. Marchand—" her voice dropped to a whisper, and she looked nervously about to see if there was a possibility of being overheard. "Then he came to me, asking for you, and sure I've been looking for you ever since."

"Well, I'd best freshen up before I see him. I imagine I am about to be taken to task for Rebecca's scene," I muttered with some resentment.

"He said you was to come to the study the minute you stepped in," Eileen warned doubtfully.

"Nonsense. He's waited this long, I think he may endure another fifteen minutes."

"Ah! And is that your considered opinion, Miss Livingston?" barked Charles Marchand, who had just turned the corner into the entrance hall, and plainly had overheard my rebellious remark.

"I have been out all afternoon, sir, and would like to—"

"And *I* have been waiting to speak with you about a

175

matter of importance all the afternoon. Please come into my study at once!''

There was nothing to be gained by wrangling where we might be overheard by any of the servants. I followed him, inwardly fuming. Really, the man treated me like a recalcitrant child. He would soon learn that I had my pride and independence, and would not tolerate his highhanded ways.

I became angrier with every step. By the time we went into the study, and he had firmly shut the door behind us, I felt my face quite hot with indignation.

"Your outing has given you a lovely color!" he said, and there was sarcasm in every word.

"Are you attempting to imply, sir, that I should not have taken a drive? I was not aware that I must ask permission of anyone before accepting an invitation, nor that my time was the rightful property of any other soul!"

"My, my, such temper!" he mocked. "I thought you the gentlest of women, and I discover you possess the tongue of the adder."

I gasped. "Sir, I must inform you that I have no intention of placidly listening to such abuse. What earthly right have you to question my activities?"

"None!" he almost shouted. "None," he repeated more quietly jerking rigid fingers through his black hair. "You are perfectly correct. Please forgive me. It is just that I have had a trying day, met at the door with tales of woe about Sidney and Rebecca—"

"Mr. Marchand," I interrupted, "about that, may I say—"

"No, you may not! I am sick of the subject. Joanna has. . . " He stopped as if he had ventured too near a forbidden thought.

"Please Katherine. I am sincere in asking your pardon. Of course I have no right to question anything you do. Nor the friends you may choose."

"Are you referring to Mr. Galbraith?" I asked incredulously. "Why, he is *your* friend, Mr. Marchand, not mine. Of course he has been most kind to me, and naturally, I am very grateful."

"Oh, I am quite certain he has been *kind* to you!" he

raised his voice. "Of course he has! He'd have to be blind not to see how lovely you are, how desirable—"

He halted in mid-sentence, his eyes blazing into mine. I could not believe I had heard the last words. The entire conversation had taken on a nightmarish quality.

Charles was standing very near. In my confusion and anger I had not realized that we were almost face-to-face. Now we were motionless as statuary, words vanished, only our eyes speaking.

"Katherine!" he groaned at last, and caught me tightly against him. My face was pressed in the hollow of his shoulder, the wool of his coat rasping against my cheek.

I stood trembling and paralyzed as his hard fingers slid into my hair, loosening it. He bent his head, lifted my unresisting face and kissed my eyelids, my mouth, my throat.

Somewhere deep in my inner being, something wild and flaring with light broke its bonds, and went sizzling along every nerve of my body. I felt Charles's hands slide along my shoulders and back, gentle, yet demanding, pulling me deeper into the whirlpool of feeling he had set in motion.

A warning sounded in my brain. With a great effort, I jerked free of his arms and stumbled backwards. Charles too stepped hastily away, turning to face the far wall. But I had seen his face, tormented, angry.

Angry at me? Doubtless my own features told a story in that moment that I would prefer not to be known. Fortune was with me in that I was not facing the door when Joanna opened it.

"Charles? Oh—forgive me, you are not alone! Shall I come back later?"

I fashioned a blank look from sheer desperation and turned quite calmly. "No need, Mrs. Marchand. I was just on the point of leaving. Mr. Marchand has been telling me that I mustn't take Rebecca out again. I have assured him I will not. I am so—so sorry to—to have caused a difficulty."

My nerve gave way then. The past tumultuous moments dissolved into shock that made my eyes fill, and I brushed past Joanna and fled to my own rooms.

For obvious reasons, I did not dine with the family that night. How could I have met the gaze of Charles Marchand without betraying my confusion and dismay?

Had it happened? Had it actually happened? Had Joanna Marchand's husband taken me—*me* into his arms?

I sat shivering in the dusk for an hour, living over and over that incredible, shaming scene. What on earth had I said to give Mr. Marchand the notion that he could make such advances?

I whipped my indignation hard, but it was useless. At last honesty forced its cool, clean way into the muddy thinking that desperately sought to obscure unpalatable truth. I was forced to admit that whether or not I had somehow enticed Mr. Marchand, I had not found his touch unpleasant. For a wild instant I had wished for that embrace to go on and on.

I shuttered the thought away quickly, for it was producing a leaping warmth, a longing to remember that instant, and worse, to cherish it.

How could I have strayed so far from what I knew of right and wrong? Perhaps I had harbored this sweet poison unknowingly from the very first, and my unschooled face had given him the signal that I would not be averse to—

Self-loathing flooded my soul. There was no way to put a better color on the situation. I had been close to at least a mental acceptance of adultery. And with a man I had thought I hated!

Ah, but perhaps that was a trick of my starved senses. Ruthlessly I lacerated my self-respect. Perhaps I had been alone and unloved too long. Perhaps any man who offered me the least attention could occasion a runaway response in me. Hadn't I even been piqued at Mr. Galbraith's lack of interest?

Oddly, that gave me the first stepping stone back to a practical and clear look at the truth. I was reacting much too strongly to the whole incident. I was *not*, at twenty-one, the desperate spinster of ugly jokes. My disappointment with Joshua Galbraith's long silences today had been simply—natural disappointment. I could not imagine myself wishing to be embraced by the bear-like Joshua as Mr. Marchand had embraced me!

I gave a tearful laugh in the darkened room, and resolutely got to my feet. I'd best gain control of my emotions before Eileen came in and noticed that I was out of sorts, for she would ferret out the reason or die trying.

And so I did the sensible thing. I washed my face in cold water and made myself a cup of tea and some supper, putting Charles Marchand's actions, and my own dismaying reaction, out of my mind. Or—almost.

Chapter Nineteen

The next day I found an opportunity to go up and visit with Mrs. Pinkham. She had been given a comfortable room adjoining Rebecca's. I intercepted Lena, who had Mrs. Pinkham's breakfast tray, and took it up myself.

She called for me to come in when I knocked. I found her already dressed and busily cleaning her bedroom.

"Mrs. Pinkham, one of the maids will do that for you," I scolded. "You have quite enough to do with watching over Rebecca."

She turned with a welcoming smile. "I like to keep busy, my dear. Becky sleeps very late. I am accustomed to early rising. How good of you to bring my breakfast!"

"I brought an extra cup so that I might have coffee with you, if that is all right."

She seemed pleased. At once she found me a comfortable chair, and poured out my coffee herself before settling down to her poached egg and muffins.

"How is the child?" I asked.

She looked up at me gravely. "Poor Becky! She was very upset after we took her away from her brother. She raged—simply *raged* for hours. I had great trouble getting her to sleep that night, and she would not eat at all, not even sweets, and you know how she likes them. She flung her food at the walls and floor, something she had not done for days."

"I am so sorry, Mrs. Pinkham. I should have come to help you. I had no idea." New guilt lowered my spirits.

"Why, Miss Kate," she said briskly. "I accepted this position knowing that I must meet the challenges myself. And for that matter, the presence of another person might only have made the situation worse. I have often noticed that *any* child, normal or otherwise, once committed to naughtiness, is worse with an audience."

"I am afraid I know very little of children," I admitted.

She smiled. "You have a kind heart, my dear, and good instincts for child-rearing. You will make a fine young mother, one day."

The compliment cheered me a bit. "Thank you. But I feel that I made a serious mistake in suggesting that Becky be allowed out of the confines of the house."

"It depends on whose viewpoint you go by," she replied with a hint of bitterness. "If you are thinking of Rebecca's good—then it is only common sense to let the poor girl feel the sun once in awhile! On the other hand, if it is Mrs. Marchand's pride that is most important—"

I disliked criticism of Joanna, yet I could not truthfully say that I did not feel the same.

"What can be done for Rebecca now that she will not be allowed out of doors?"

She shook her head wearily. "She enjoyed getting out very much, and she expects to continue—to the extent that her limited mind will let her remember from day-to-day. Several times she has asked for her walk, and she grows more restless hourly."

"It's cruel to keep her penned up within those four walls!" I burst out.

"So it is. But we have no choice. At least she has her toys now. I am so grateful to you for bringing those things to her. She spends hours over her doll—she seems to adore it, dressing and undressing it. And she has been so touchingly careful with the little tea set. After she broke the first piece, she seemed to realize she must be more gentle."

"Yet she is still ill at ease?"

"She needs more exercise, I believe. There is too little space in that room."

I had a sudden thought. "If she has been forbidden to go out—perhaps we can find her a place to run and play indoors."

"Yes, but—" Mrs. Pinkham began doubtfully. "But where, Miss Kate? And what would Mrs. Marchand say? She was—quite harsh in ordering me never to allow Rebecca out of her locked room. I must tell you, I haven't the courage to defy her!"

I sighed. "Let me think about it. Perhaps I can get permission from Mr. Marchand.''

Mrs. Pinkham set down her cup and glanced at me with sharp concern. "Katherine, may I speak my mind, dear? I don't wish to offend you, but—"

"Certainly. Say whatever you like."

"I think it would be unwise to—to go over Mrs. Marchand's head in this matter."

"I have already done so repeatedly," I frankly admitted. "In fact, I bypassed both parents when I ordered Rebecca's clothing."

"You are very brave," Mrs. Pinkham said, "and I know that you have merely wished to spare Mrs. Marchand distress. But—"

"She wouldn't thank me for bringing up the subject of her daughter, particularly so soon after the incident with Sidney," I replied. "It has been my impression that she would prefer her husband—or indeed anyone else at all—take the responsibility of any decisions concerning Rebecca."

"That may be true. Yes, I am sure it is. But should *you* be the one to speak with Mr. Marchand about such matters?"

Mrs. Pinkham finished her surprising statement very quickly and nervously, then awaited my reaction.

I could hardly believe that I correctly understood her implication. But a study of her face convinced me that she had meant exactly what her words seemed to imply. I stared, completely astonished.

"Are you trying to say that—that Joanna may believe there is something improper between me and—and—" I could not bring myself to say his name. Unbidden, the memory of Charles Marchand's arms about me slid into my mind, and I felt my face flame.

Mrs. Pinkham took my flush for a sign of anger.

"Oh, there, I knew I shouldn't say it! Do forgive me, Miss Kate. I know I shouldn't be repeating gossip."

"Gossip? There has been gossip on the subject?" I felt sick with shame.

"Oh, not to any extent at all, I am sure!" she frantically sought to retrace her steps. "Oh, Katherine, I am so very sorry that I brought it up. Please do forget what I said."

"No, indeed. You must tell me at once who has been spreading gossip, and exactly what that gossip consists of," I demanded. "I have the right to know, Mrs. Pinkham!"

It took me some minutes to persuade the deeply distressed woman to give me the entire story. But at last the ugly truth was out in the open.

"It was—that maid of Mrs. Marchand's, that Lottie Dilby," she said reluctantly. "Oh, she made no remarks to me, you understand. She wouldn't dare, for she knows I am fond of you. But I overheard her filling Mrs. DeWitt's ear one afternoon. I assume that anything Miss Dilby knows, Mrs. Marchand knows as well."

"What did she say, exactly?" I probed.

Mrs. Pinkham sighed and squeezed her hands together. "She said—now mind you dear, I know there isn't a word of truth in it—she said as how you were always making excuses to see Mr. Marchand, on one pretext or another, and that she had seen him coming from your apartment one evening. And Mrs. DeWitt chimed in—oh that absolute *cow* of a woman! She said that she had seen you coming out of Mr. Marchand's rooms, with your hair mussed, and—"

"Oh!" I gasped. "Oh, that is a lie!"

"I knew it was. I knew you wouldn't be in a gentleman's rooms—"

"No, no," I stopped her ruefully. "I *was* there, but very briefly. Mr. Marchand called me in on a matter of business. But there is not a *word* of truth to the statement that my hair was—"

I felt my eyes fill with indignant, helpless tears, and I had to swallow the rest of my sentence to be rid of the obstruction in my throat. Sympathetically Mrs. Pinkham came and patted my cold, clenched hands.

"Now, don't let it assume a greater importance than it should, dear! Forewarned is forearmed. If you are very careful in future, I am sure the silly talk will die down for want of fuel."

I assured her that I was grateful for the warning, and would see to it that there would be no basis, ever again, for such ugly rumors. But that resolution was cold comfort as I left her and went about my morning duties.

That day I felt that my face was permanently red with shame and humiliation. The worst of it was the knowledge that I had almost deserved the talk that was being viciously circulated. Unwittingly I had neglected to be circumspect in my meetings with Mr. Marchand. He had initiated these meetings, and there had been nothing of an improper nature in them—at least until the last meeting. But I had not avoided the appearance of evil, and I was fast learning that there is always someone ready and willing to believe the very worst.

I believe my temper was very close to the surface for some hours, and after I snapped at Eileen twice and at least once at Lena, I went to my room for a good cry. Would I never cease to make foolish mistakes? I despaired of it. But as I bathed my swollen eyes, I vowed I would live down the loathsome speculations. I would be so cautious that I would never see *any* gentleman alone, as long as I lived, if necessary to rebuild my reputation!

That being the best I could do with the situation at the moment, I turned my mind to Rebecca's problem, finding it a distinct relief to think of someone other than myself.

The main obstacle was the finding of a large space, far enough removed from the family's quarters to prevent any kind of disturbance, and yet within the bounds of the house.

The solution was not difficult, it was merely a process of elimination as I mentally reviewed the many rooms. There was only one possibility. The attic!

It was already late in the day. The shadows were lengthening outside the big windows of my sitting room. But now that the idea of a playroom for Rebecca had solidified within my head, I wanted to see if it indeed had possibilities. I had not ventured into the attic as yet, but I assured myself that there was no time like the present.

Foresightedly, I supplied myself with a lamp and matches, and went on my journey of exploration. On the stairs I met Joanna, with Lily DeWitt. Horace was a few steps behind. Almost absently I dodged his inevitable pinch. Lily DeWitt had apparently glanced back in time to see her husband's outreached fingers. "Brazen, wanton hussy!" she hissed.

Sighing, I forebore even to reply. I hurried on, moving

184

hurriedly up the stairs to the third floor. In the corridor I could hear Becky's guttural voice, from behind her locked door.

At the far end of the hallway the narrow stair rose to the attic door.

It was growing dark up here, and darker still as I turned at the landing for the final steps. The meagre light from below was quite shut away. For a silly moment I imagined, as the shadows closed about me, that I heard something behind me. I glanced back. A footstep, carefully and quietly placed, but betrayed by a creak from the staircase. Of course there was nothing. It could only have been the echo of my own passage.

Shrugging off my fancies, I approached the door, wondering if I would find it locked. I think that I almost at that last moment, wished that I might be denied admittance—at least until a nice, sunny day!

But having come this far, it would be very silly to retreat without even trying the door. Accordingly I put my hand on the knob, and turned it. It seemed still with rust or disuse, but was not locked. With a squeal that did nothing pleasant for my nerves, the door grudgingly gave way.

It was dim and dusty within. Before going further, I paused to light my lamp, then carried it within the vast, cavernous area at the very top of the house.

My light was a mere firefly glow in this great space. There was an uneasy feeling moving along my spine as I peered inside—the dark was scarcely shoved away by the glowing lamp.

What is it about an old attic? Is there any logical reason why an uninhabited storage space can assume such a frightening atmosphere? I knew very well there could be nothing very alarming here, only discarded pieces of furniture, trunks, boxes of clothes, books and papers. At the worst there might be a bat or a few spiders.

I wished I had not thought of spiders as I made myself explore more deeply into the lonely darkness, and look about the place that might become a playroom for an unhappy child. A cobweb stuck to my face, draping itself over my brow, and I immediately pictured busy legs walking about in my hair.

I gasped and rubbed the web away, bending over to brush at my head in the hopes of dislodging any uninvited stroller.

After a few minutes I set the lamp atop an old chest of drawers. It would not do to frighten myself into dropping it and igniting the house.

I was becoming less nervous. There were windows up here, if very dirty ones. Properly cleaned, they would let in at least a limited amount of daylight. The maids would think I had taken leave of my senses when I proposed putting this place in order, but I knew their capacity for work. Together, we could transform a portion of the attic. We would, I planned eagerly, move out all the unused junk that might be a hazard to running feet. However, I would leave some of the trunks of old clothing. Rebecca might have fun playing with discarded gowns and hats long outmoded. No one would mind if she tore them, or dragged them about the floor to her heart's content.

It was not very warm up here this time of year. Perhaps John Brock could install a small wood-and-coal heater. We might even partition off the further reaches of the attic, as it would not be desirable to have Rebecca vanishing into the dark depths. I could find a used carpet to lay on the floor, and bring lamps to hang high out of her reach.

I went to a dust-furred window pane, rubbed it cleaner and looked out. The panes were small. There was no danger that Rebecca could break them and fall from this great height, a possibility that worried me about her own room.

Well, I had seen all that I needed to for today. Probably it was time to dress for dinner—unless I decided once more to prepare my own in my rooms. Would that be the coward's way out, I wondered wistfully? Probably it would. Sooner or later someone would wonder why I had discontinued my custom of having dinner with the family. Not that anyone especially *wanted* me there, I thought with unusual bitterness and a deep, aching surge of loneliness.

Sighing, I turned from the window, and started toward my light. Something slammed hard, and a draft blew out the flame just as I reached to grasp the lamp.

"What is it! Who's there?" I cried.

Chapter Twenty

There was no answer. I stood in the dark, for an eternity, too frightened to move, or even to breathe.

The door. Someone—or something—had caused the door to close. Probably it was only a stray draft of air, I told myself, trying frantically to calm my shattered nerves. Yes of course, only a draft, and it had blown out my lamp.

The first thing to do was to get the lamp going once more. But that thought brought increased dismay. I had brought only two matches, and had used both earlier.

It was so dark! I felt a whimper of despair swelling in my throat. The sun had set while I lingered up here, and storm clouds gathering over the ridges had soaked up any lingering illumination from outside. The windows were still visible from where I stood, but only very dimly.

I knew I must grope my way to the door. With a shuddering breath, I closed my eyes for a few moments, hoping to make my vision adjust to the darkness. It did little good. I could discern shapes within the blackness, but only from the corners of my eyes. I could see barely enough to enable me to find my way across the big space I had ventured over. How easy it had been then, with the cheerful lamplight making a path for me among the debris of many years that cluttered the floor.

I thought I knew the direction of the door, but even as I made my first tentative step, I felt confusion settle upon me. Was it this way? Or further to my left? No, I had been correct at first, unless—

I wanted to scream, and only the most desperately enforced resolution prevented it.

I fancied that I heard furtive rustlings and movements in the area about me. My former anxieties about spiders were nothing to compare with what I now imagined might be advancing on me, unseen. Mightn't there be large rats up here, never disturbed for years, growing and fattening on scraps foraged from the kitchen and pantries?

A shudder racked me. I found myself gasping, as if there were not sufficient air, and I realized that I must get a healthy grip upon my nerves, at once.

"Nonsense!" I almost shouted. "It's the same room I crossed safely before. There is nothing to be afraid of, *nothing!* Only children are afraid of the dark."

I cannot say that the sound of my own voice was reassuring, but perhaps my determination not to panic was useful. I made myself set one shaking foot ahead of the other in what I hoped was the right direction. Almost immediately I stumbled against something. Gingerly I bent and touched it. A trunk lid. There were other boxes and a discarded highboy to the left, but clear space to the right.

Stepping to my right, holding both hands out, I moved forward carefully. Slowly, slowly I felt my way through the crowd of miscellaneous castoffs.

But I had not realized that it was so far across the space to the door! I walked for what seemed an endless time, groping before me, and found only more space. Had I wandered too far off my course, and begun a black journey along the attics in one of the long wings of the house?

The thought so terrified me that I cried out before I knew the sound was forming in my throat. My heart seemed to cause my whole body to vibrate and suddenly I longed just to sink to the floor and cower there. This uncertain search in darkness was doing awful things to my imagination.

It was harder this time to rein in my racing fears. But, shivering, I made myself walk, a bit faster now, bumping painfully into whatever lay in my path.

And at last my hands made a bruising, blessed contact with something flat and solid. Thank God, the door at last!

I felt downward to where the knob should be. My mind felt near bursting when I realized that it was not a door at all, but merely a section of wall. The door could be to either side. But which? And how far?

Before the terror could make me helpless again, I moved ten sidelong paces to the right, patting at the planking of the wall. I tried not to think how many spiders I might be disturbing.

When I had gone as far as I could bear, I reversed my steps, ten, and then ten more. On the nineteenth step I found what I was seeking, and nothing ever felt better to human touch than that stout door.

Eagerly I found the knob and turned it, already tasting the end of my captivity in the darkness.

But the knob would not turn. Again I tried. It must have jammed—it had been stiff with disuse earlier. Surely a bit more effort.

It required an incredulous moment or two of frantic twisting of the brass knob before I realized that I was locked in. And if the door was locked, someone had deliberately done it. Someone wanted me to be caught in here like an animal in a trap!

All my control shattered. I began to scream and pound at the unyielding door. When I had exhausted myself, and still no one heard or came, I laid my wet cheek against that barrier and wept. Never in my life had I been so frightened! Even today I do not like to remember the hours I spent in the attic. I was not missed until dinner, and then everyone assumed that I was merely having my meal in my own quarters. My absence from the apartment was discovered by Eileen at ten o'clock that evening, when she came to speak with me before retiring to bed. Had she not had been ironing pillow slips in the kitchen after supper, she would have sought for me sooner.

Eileen is not a shrinking violet. I believe she speedily alerted the entire household with her Klaxon shouts of alarm, begun after she had checked every room on the first floor, and inquired of Mrs. Pinkham if she had seen me.

At the top of the house, I heard none of this. I had fallen asleep, worn out with fright and anxiety. The first I knew of the search was when feet thudded on the landing outside my door.

Someone tried the knob as I came groggily awake. "No, it is securely locked. She cannot be in there," I heard Joanna Marchand say. "But where on earth has she gone? Could she have gone out this evening, without telling anyone?"

Heavier footsteps approached. "Did you look in the attic?" Charles's deep voice inquired; and received the news that the door was locked. Some instinct had made me listen quietly before betraying my presence, but now I rose to my knees and called out, pounding at the door with sore hands.

"Please, I am here. Let me out, please!" I cried.

There were exclamations from outside. Someone yanked hard at the knob, and the door trembled.

"Where is the key to this door? Does anyone know?" Mr. Marchand demanded harshly.

"I never knew there was a key," Joanna gasped.

I heard Eileen's shrill tones. "I'll run down and ask Mrs. Potter. She'll be knowing, if anyone does!"

"No, that will take too long." He must have leaned closer to the door. "Be calm, Katherine. We'll have you out in a few minutes. I'll be back in a moment."

His running feet went away, and Eileen took his place near the door. "Katy?" she shrieked. "Are ye all right, dearie?"

"I'm—I'm fine," I called, forced to clear my throat first, for weak tears were flowing again. Quickly I wiped my face on my skirt hem, knowing that I must look a mess.

It was only a short time until Charles came back, directing me to move to my left and well away from the door. A shot rang out, the sound stunning my befuddled mind further. A second shot was required to break the lock, and then the door was flung open. Charles's tall body sprang into the dark attic.

"Katherine, where are you?"

I stumbled toward him. His hand caught mine hard, and he led me out into the blessed light of a lamp held by Eileen, who was blubbering into a large handkerchief. She almost dropped her lamp as she clutched me.

"Katy, have you been here in the dark all the while? What notion made you go in there? And why did you lock the door?"

"I didn't. I didn't lock the door." A shudder moved down my spine.

"Why, what nonsense, Katherine dear!" Joanna patted my cheek gently. "You must have locked it, for we were quite helpless to turn the knob in any direction. I am certain it was locked!"

"Oh yes. It was locked," Charles agreed, and the quietness of his statement fell startlingly amidst the excited chattering of the women. The group now included: Lena, Marie, Mrs. Pinkham, Mrs. Potter, Mrs. DeWitt, and even Yolande. They had apparently heard the shots and were now clustered like starlings on the stairs below the attic door.

"There, you see? Of course you locked it," Joanna said soothingly, "and then I suppose you lost the key, and are embarrassed to admit your mistake." She laughed, a fondly chiding sound.

I shook my head and dizziness made me sway. Charles grasped my upper arm strongly. Joanna's eyes flickered to her husband's hand. Quickly I pulled away. "No. Please. I had no key. You must believe me. The door was unlocked when I went in. Someone—someone locked it from out here."

There was sudden absolute silence as everyone took in my statement, and stared at me with varying expressions. Eileen's eyes were round with alarm, her mouth open, yet I detected no doubt in her honest face. I could not read Charles Marchand's probing look at all. Joanna was a picture of incredulity.

"Why, whatever are you saying, Katherine?" she said. "Do I understand you correctly? Dare you imply that —one of us would stoop to such a childish trick as to lock you into a dark attic? Why, what *can* you be thinking?"

"The girl is exhausted. She's had no supper and is undoubtedly cold. Leave the explanations and questions for later. Eileen, take Katherine downstairs."

Charles's order was not to be disobeyed. With alacrity Eileen tugged me along down the narrow stair, one arm supportively about my waist. I was grateful for her aid—my knees trembled and I was still dazed. Behind us, I heard the argument resume.

"Why, it stands to reason, my darling," Joanna insisted to Charles. "For some reason Katherine wanted to go into the attic. She *must* have had a key, else how did she get in?"

"She said the door was unlocked," was his indifferent reply.

We went out of hearing, and I was grateful, feeling I

could endure nothing more this night.

But I had to bear the avidly curious scrutiny of the DeWitt women as we passed them, and hear their whispering speculations.

"What an utterly mad thing to do!" Mrs. DeWitt's hissing voice was clearly audible.

"Perhaps she had a reason," Yolande began.

"Probably she thinks poor Bertha secreted money somewhere in the house, and is bent on getting her thieving fingers on it."

Beside me, Eileen stiffened and came to a stop, turning to stare at the pudding-faced, overdressed Lily, who bulged unpleasantly out of her ciel blue gown.

"Mrs. DeWitt, I have known pickpockets, common tramps, and ladies of the evening with more breeding than you!" she said, and whirled to march me out of the line of fire.

"Well! Well I never!" gasped poor Mrs. DeWitt.

I found that I had just enough strength to giggle. Eileen joined in, roaring with laughter, as she swept me along the halls and down the stairs.

It was bliss to be in my own rooms. Dear Eileen made me tea and asked Lena and Marie to bring hot water for a bath. She brushed the cobwebs and dust out of my hair and tucked me into bed in a soft flannel gown, then made French toast for my supper.

"Tomorrow," she promised as she left me to sleep, "I'm having a little bed brought into your sitting room where I can stay nights."

"If you wish, but you mustn't think I'll submit to being nursed like an invalid, nor waited on hand and foot like a lady!" I teased her drowsily.

She did not return my smile. "Katy, 'tis the second time someone in this house has tried to harm you—or frighten you to death, at the very least! I'm thinkin' you need a bit of watching over and 'twill be over my own dead body that anyone reaches you with murdering intentions in the future!"

Without waiting for a reply, she closed the door and left me to my thoughts—but they were not peaceful or reassuring ones. And when I slept at last, I dreamt of the dark, menacing attic, and myself stuck fast in the web of an enormous spider, with the absurdly affronted face of Lily DeWitt.

Oddly enough, for days after that things settled into a quiet routine. We were into May now, with hope of better weather. Yet still the spring held off, not deigning to grant us her ardently longed-for presence. Much of April's snow still lay on the upper slopes of the valley. Sporadic rains continued. It had made it difficult for John Brock to finish the house painting, but now he was nearly done.

I enjoyed standing away from the place and admiring it. It seemed a different, prouder house with its glistening white paint and neat, green trim.

John had begun work on the attic. Joanna, somewhat to my astonishment, had given permission for the project, so there had been no need to approach Charles on the subject at all.

There was another surprising, if minor, incident. The day after my shuddering experience in the attic, I was examining the flower beds, weed-grown and in very sad shape, when Sidney came up behind me and nervously spoke.

"Miss Livingston?"

He startled me, for I had been absorbed in the emerging tips of tulips and narcissus, and had not heard his quiet step.

I jerked around at the sound of his voice, and my face must have whitened, for he held out a hand in an odd gesture. "Oh! I didn't mean to scare you, Miss Livingston."

I recovered myself and smiled at him. "No, it's quite all right. I didn't hear you."

"Can I talk to you a minute?"

He seemed disturbed about something, and with his stout boot-toe traced a line in the wet grass. He did not meet my inquiring eyes.

"Surely. What did you wish to say?" I turned back to the flower bed, pulling up last year's weeds that choked more desirable growth.

"I—" He hesitated so long that I glanced around at him.

"What is it, Sidney?" I prompted.

"I'm sorry!" he blurted, his face going red.

"I don't understand."

"I'm sorry, Miss Livingston," he said, hurriedly, as if he was afraid he could not get rid of all the words quickly enough. "I never meant to get you or Mrs. Pinkham in trouble."

I began to see what was worrying him. It was the unfortunate scene with Rebecca that had resulted in Joanna's displeasure toward Mrs. Pinkham and myself.

"I am sure you didn't," I said. "I wish you hadn't tattled on your sister, but perhaps it was for the best in some ways."

His head snapped up in surprise. "But I didn't tell!" he cried.

I was disinclined to believe him at first, but as I studied his young, sensitive face, something there convinced me. "But how did your mama find out about it?"

"She saw it happen, from her windows, and she asked me about it. I was—was mad as hops, and I—"

"You told her that Rebecca had embarrassed you in front of your friends?" I asked.

He nodded. "But I didn't know mama would be mad at you!"

"It was my idea that Rebecca be taken out for walks, and I had not asked your mother's permission," I explained. "I was responsible for your sister's being out that day. So I owe you an apology too, Sidney. I certainly did not want such a thing to happen, or to make you angry or unhappy."

He stared at me as if an apology from an adult to a child was something he had never heard of and could not take in.

"Anyway, it is all past now. We are making a place for Rebecca to play, up in the attic, and she will not be out again. Of course, that is sad, for she loved the sunshine and the fresh air," I could not resist adding.

"I don't care!" he said with sudden vehemence. "I hate her. I hate Rebecca!"

Chapter Twenty-one

"Surely you don't mean that," I said calmly, moving further along the flower bed. "Your sister is to be pitied. She does not have a good mind, like yours, and will never have a happy life like other people. She is not to blamed for her mischief, for she cannot understand that it is wrong."

"I—I know that," he admitted, and his look held misery. "But—she never learns. I would help her, if I could. We used to play together, when we were little kids. Only, she never learns, and never changes, and all the fellows I know make fun of me for having a twin sister like that! They say, maybe I am really like that too, that someday I will wake up and I will be just like—like Rebecca!"

He seemed too horror-stricken to say more. Abruptly he whirled and ran away.

I found myself feeling a new sympathy for the boy, and seeing him in a new light. It was true that he had been spoiled. It was wrong that he should detest his poor sister. Yet he was not incapable of some pity for her. The crux of the problem seemed to be that she was his twin, and therefore almost a part of him. How he must question his own body and mind, with Rebecca as a mirror held up before him!

John Brock quickly and skillfully finished the partitions needed to convert part of the rambling attics into a playroom. He made a ceiling to hide the rafters and shadowy reaches of the roof peak. It was while working on this that he found a trapdoor leading out onto the roof, and a ladder for getting up to it. It was present at the time.

"Now that's handy," he commented. "Ill leave a hole in the ceiling to get to that trap, if you don't mind, Miss Katherine. No doubt I'll be needing to git out on them roofs and replace shingles sometime."

He laid the ladder against a partition, out of the way, yet ready for use in case of need.

It was Mr. Brock's suggestion that he construct an additional small window or two, to add to the light, and paint the playroom walls a bright yellow, so their roughness was not unattractive. With the maids' help I laid carpet on the floor, with bright, small throw rugs here and there, for color. We affixed lamps high on the walls, and moved a few chairs upstairs. John even made shelves which we filled with books and toys. He repaired the door and installed a new lock—and that was the single distressing bit of equipment. Poor Rebecca must still be caged.

Nevertheless, the attic was transformed. With little cost, we had made a spacious, airy place where Rebecca could romp and not disturb anyone.

On the day we first took her to the attic, Mrs. Pinkham was fairly humming with pleasant anticipation. She had told Rebecca about the playroom, and while no one could be sure how much the girl understood, I believe she absorbed some of our pleasure. Certainly she displayed symptoms of excitement.

The maids and Eileen wished to see how Rebecca responded to the room we had all labored to complete, and so it was quite a congregation of us who softly crept up the stairs, following Mrs. Pinkham. From the doorway, we watched as the elderly woman showed Rebecca the new toys; colorful balls and more dolls, bright hanks of yarn in many colors, a rocking horse—outsize, to accommodate Rebecca's weight.

At first the child seemed puzzled, not understanding that the things were for her, until Mrs. Pinkham placed them in her hands one by one, and coaxed her into a game with a giant rubber ball.

Soon, with wordless shrieks, Rebecca was scrambling about the big room, darting from one object to another. I hoped we had not provoked her to a dangerous level of excitement.

"The poor dear lassie!" Eileen mumbled tearfully, as we closed the door and went quietly away.

"I wonder if we could not build a sandbox up there?"

I mused. "She could have a little pail and shovel, and make sand castles. It would be more like being out-of-doors."

"I thought," Lena spoke up, "that it might be nice if she had a few potted plants at her windows. Mightn't Mrs. Pinkham teach her to water them?"

"And she must have a dear little kitten," Marie said with finality. "I'll bring her one myself, tomorrow. Mrs. Billings on our street has some. I'll help her take care of it, myself."

"Those are wonderful ideas!" I pronounced. Feeling happier that I had in days, I went downstairs, leaving the maids to their upstairs dusting.

I myself intended to do some ironing, and had left sad-irons heating on the kitchen range for this purpose. My new skirt, finished after supper the night before, was in need of a pressing, and there was a capacious basket filled with linens that I was determined Eileen should not exhaust herself doing up.

But I hesitated outside the kitchen. There were voices raised in argument, I could not help overhearing them when I entered the kitchen passage. I stopped with my hand on the swinging door.

"*I* say somebody oughta tell her!" a woman said. I did not recognize the voice for a moment, then realized that it was Mrs. Smith, the washerwoman.

"Then you do it, an' no thanks you'll likely get fer your trouble, Mary Smith!" snapped Mrs. Potter. "Miss Katy don't like to hear no one slandered, nor a lot o' wicked rumors spread about—"

"I ain't about to slander a living soul!" cried Mrs. Smith. "But if you had one Christian bone in your body, you'd warn that sweet girl!"

"Warn her about what? That you think Miss Bertha DeWitt was pushed down them stairs? What could Miss Katy do about it, even if it was gospel truth, and I ain't saying for one minute that it is!"

"Maybe you ain't saying it, but that don't mean that you don't know in your soul it *is* true. You know Miss Bertha would never have tried those stairs all by herself, them last weeks! She told me that herself. She said very plain, last time I run up to sit with her a minute; she says 'Mary, I'm past going up and down them long stairs, unless I got somebody to hold onto me real good'!''

"Yes, but—!''

"Don't you 'yes but' me!'' said Mrs. Smith triumphantly. "Can you tell me of one time she took it in her head to come down by herself after that? No ma'am, you can't for she would always ring for what she needed. She told me she had no need to come down at all, as she had a pleasant sitting room an' all she needed upstairs.''

"That doesn't mean she couldn't have done it on a impulse, though,'' Mrs. Potter said rather weakly. "I was off, visiting my sister Agnes that day. Maybe she needed something before I got back.''

"Didn't you tell me you went up to see that she had all she wanted before you left, an' that you told her you would be back at three, an' she told you she was going to have a good nap?''

Evidently the two women had been over the story before, and often, for Mrs. Smith recited the details very precisely. I realized that I was shamelessly eavesdropping, but I could not for the life of me back away until I had heard it all. No one had ever told me the circumstances of Mrs. Bertha DeWitt's death. The hints I had already caught of her demise being somehow irregular had been pushed to the back of my mind, where they occupied an uneasy, seldom-visited corner. Now, with mounting anxiety, I questioned whether those hints might have been based on solid truth.

Mrs. Potter was speaking again. "Yes, I told you all that, and I shouldn't ever have, Mary! You and your wild imagination, you see spooks and murderers in every corner.''

"I don't see one ounce more murderers than *you* do, Franny Potter!'' She lowered her voice a fraction. "You're scared to let on what you really think, ain't you? You work here, an' maybe you're thinking that what happened to Bertha DeWitt could happen to you!''

"Mary!'' gasped Mrs. Potter. "For the Lord's sake watch your babbling tongue!''

"See!'' came the triumphant accusation. "I'm right. An' if I'm right about you being nervous, then I'm right that whoever pushed Mrs. DeWitt to her death, poor soul, did it for the property the old lady had. But then, who got the house? Not the murderer at all, for Miss DeWitt had been too smart fer 'em and made a new will. So the murderer still ain't got what he wants, an' *who* stands in the way?''

There was a pregnant silence. I felt stunned at the things Mrs. Smith was implying. Belatedly I turned and went away from the door, not stopping until I was alone in my own apartment, my ironing forgotten.

I was still there when someone tapped at the door sometime later. I had been vainly trying to regain my serenity and common sense, arguing against myself from every conceivable position.

Surely Mrs. Smith's suspicions were, as Mrs. Potter said, merely the wildest imaginings. I could not (could I?) seriously believe that someone had actually murdered Mrs. DeWitt, my gentle little friend, for this old house and whatever small sum of money she might have had. The murderer could not still reside in this place. I did not stand between him and his insane goal.

Nonsense! Utter, childish melodrama. And yet—there was the fire that someone had set in my rooms. and there were the long hours I had spent cowering in the attic, locked away there in the dark. I had come to the conclusion that the last action, at least, was a stupid attempt to frighten me. It had certainly succeeded in that! I felt that Sidney probably had done it. Perhaps this conclusion had been reached, unfairly, because he was at the age for such foolishness, and because I knew he connected me with Rebecca's embarrassing scene down by the river.

But the boy had come to me and apologized for his part in provoking Joanna's anger toward me. Would he have shown such remorse if it were he who had, the night before, made me a captive at the top of the house, there to suffer agonies of fright?

Perhaps the revenge he had thus taken upon me had been a bit more than he planned, and he had regretted his impulse in locking me in.

At this point in my thinking, my visitor knocked at the

sitting-room door. Absently, I murmured an invitation to enter.

"Don't you ever come to see who is waiting outside before you invite him within?" asked Charles Marchand, stepping in with a smile.

I sprang to my feet. He was the last person I had expected to see, and the last I wanted to visit. I had been very carefully avoiding him, since Mrs. Pinkham had given me her kind warning.

"Mr. Marchand!" I said faintly.

"The same!" He bowed from the waist, laughing at my very obvious discomfiture. "What disturbs you this time? Somehow every time we meet, I have the impression that you are minded to flee."

I regained a bit of my equilibrium. "You cannot blame me, surely, after what occurred in your study."

"Ah, you remembered!" He nodded with odious satisfaction. "I am delighted. I feared that you would banish that moment from your mind as thoroughly as you clearly intended to."

"I do *not remember*," I responded furiously and foolishly.

"No? Then I shall have to remember it long enough for both of us," Charles said with a sudden gravity. He was no longer teasing me. I knew, somehow, that now he was perfectly serious, and this alarmed me as nothing else could have.

"Mr. Marchand, this is an improper conversation. I must ask you to leave, at once."

He thrust both hands into his trouser pockets, hunching his shoulders almost miserably within the fine blue wool of his suit coat as he turned away. I thought he meant to obey me and go. Why did I feel a pang of regret?

However, he swung back to face me. "You are perfectly right, Katherine. I hope you will accept my apologies for inexcusable behavior. I know that I have no right to—to tell you how I have come to feel about you."

"Mr. Marchand, please!" I said desperately, and he waved me to silence.

"I know you must despise me. I am behaving like a cad."

200

"I could never despise you!" I knew at once I should not have said it. His blue eyes moved to my face, and the question that flew wordless between us showed that I had made a most serious mistake.

He made a step toward me, holding out his hands. May God be my judge, I wanted terribly to run into his arms. In another moment I would have cast self-restraint to the winds. I would have been held close, touching him again, the forbidden delight of it blinding me to the wrongness.

I suppose he realized in time that he must not come any nearer. Deliberately he stepped back, and dropped his hands. But he kept his eyes steadily on mine, and with anguish and shame I knew that my expression was betraying me.

"Katherine!" he murmured—"sweet, lovely, innocent. How I wish you and I might—but it is impossible. God, I know it is impossible, and I dare not cause the grief it would inevitably bring!"

He forced a smile and shrugged, hands lifted palms out. "You must forgive me, my dear. I did not come to distress or embarrass you. May I stay one more moment? There is something I must discuss with you."

"If—if you insist," I said with difficulty. "But will you leave the door open, please? Then no one will have more to say about—"

I faltered to a stop, but he had caught my meaning. "About us? There is talk about us?"

Miserably, I nodded. "Mrs. DeWitt and—Mrs. Marchand's maid Lottie were overheard—speculating."

His face went rigid. "Katherine, can you ever forgive me? I promise you I will never expose you to such a hateful thing again! But I think you needn't worry just at present. Mrs. DeWitt and Yolande are gone to Pittsburgh, shopping, and Horace accompanied them. I can't say where that weasel Miss Dilby might be, but there was no one about when I came in. I shall be very careful not be seen leaving."

I swallowed. "What is it you wished to say?"

"I have been thinking about the evening you spent locked in the attic. The more I think about it the less I like it. Have you any idea who might have confined you there?"

"Are you saying you don't think I did it myself?" I

asked with a hint of bitterness.

"Of course I never believed any such nonsense," he replied quietly. "I know you would not lie about it."

"Thank you." Stiffly I inclined my head. "But I cannot tell you who locked me in. I was at the far side of the attic. I had a lamp, but when the door slammed, my light was blown out. I have no idea who was out there. I only know that *someone* was."

"But why?" he mused, frowning. "Why would anyone wish to do such a thing?"

"I can only surmise that someone did it as a prank. Or to frighten me."

"Again, why?" He seemed to be speaking more to himself than to me.

"Not everyone in this house is glad that I am here," I reminded him. I could not bring myself to share my own thoughts, that Sidney might have been the culprit.

He shook his head, and his look was determined. Again he was the cold, stern Charles I had thought I disliked. "I promise you that I won't rest until I get to the bottom of this. If someone is harrassing you—Lily DeWitt for instance, I will not stand for it! Meanwhile, I want you to be on your guard. Probably you are right, and someone is merely playing vicious jokes, hoping to scare you into leaving. Nevertheless, I wish you would be cautious. Try never to be alone even in this apartment, unless you lock yourself in. And don't, for God's sake, invite in everyone who knocks at your door."

He smiled, and I smiled back, suddenly feeling warmed and comforted. It was so good to know that someone else besides faithful Eileen (who would not have doubted me had I reported a purple giraffe under my bed) had faith in me, and cared about my welfare.

"Eileen has been sleeping in my sitting room," I said.

"Excellent. You are certain she is to be trusted?"

"Yes," I said simply.

He nodded. "I think you are right. She is an honest soul. Now, I'd best go."

"Wait!" I said impulsively. "May I ask you something?"

202

"Anything."

"I have heard a—tale about your aunt, Bertha DeWitt," I began rather uncertainly.

"Yes? What tale?" He waited patiently, his hand upon the doorknob.

"That she—that she was murdered," I finished, and waited for him to stare at me with scorn.

Instead he merely studied the rug at his feet for a long moment. My heart slowed its nervous racing.

"Who told you this?" he asked.

"I would prefer not to say."

He nodded. "Very well, I won't insist that you tell me. What did you wish to ask me on the subject?"

"Why—if you think there is any—truth in it?" I fumbled.

"I—" he hesitated. "Let us say that I don't see how it could be true," he replied carefully. Then he opened the door a crack, peered out to see if he would be observed, and swiftly was gone from my presence.

Only after the silence—the suddenly very lonely silence—had settled about me again, did I realize that he had answered my question in a peculiar way. He had stated that he did not *see* how the rumors could be true. He had not definitely said that they were untrue, nor that they were utterly impossible. He had not said that at all.

Chapter Twenty-two

The next morning, a drizzly Sunday, Eileen and I made our breakfast in my little kitchen. She had been up for some hours, and had gone out to early mass. I, conversely, had allowed myself an extra half-hour of sleep. My night had been restless, filled with frightening dreams when at last I slept. Now I was heavy-eyed and not in the best of spirits.

"I give ye no sympathy, Katy." Eileen shook her head with mock sternness. "If you would go to church instead o' lyin' abed, you would feel better, body *and* soul."

I was in no mood for a lecture, and it was on the tip of my tongue to speak sharply to my friend. I restrained myself with an effort. Probably she was right. I had been brought up by my staunch Presbyterian aunt to attend services regularly, and I had vaguely intended to do so once I was settled in this town. But somehow the weeks had gone past while I made one excuse after the other.

"Well, then, I shall go this morning. There is still time," I said on impulse. Eileen stared at me as if she could not believe this capitulation.

"Do ye mean it Katy? Why, that's fine! I tell you what. I'll go along too. I suppose they will allow a good Catholic girl through their doors, will they not?"

"Not if they know what's good for them," I sighed. "You've already been to one service. Do you really want to go to another?"

"Why not? Sure an' I've nothing else to do. The girls and me cleaned very thorough yesterday, so there's little to tend this mornin'. I'd hoped Johnny Brock might take me for a picnic. But he's gone off somewhere."

"Well, then." I set down my teacup and rose. "I'll wash the dishes and get dressed. I suppose we must walk if John Brock is not here to drive us."

"I'll just run out and see if he might be back yet," she said.

By ten-thirty we were prepared to leave, Eileen having located the missing Mr. Brock to drive us. I wore my serviceable green wool, which should have been too warm for this time of year. But spring still played a will-o'-the-wisp game with us, and the temperatures were more like those of March. I pinned on my old Neopolitan braid hat, and took up my new gloves. These were a luxury I had rather guiltily allowed myself. With Aunt Betsy's black cameo brooch pinned at the neck of my new white blouse, and Mrs. DeWitt's opal ring on my right hand, I felt that I looked presentable.

Emerging into the hall, I found Eileen and Mrs. Potter there ahead of me, both in their modest best, and wearing a dignity of expression and bearing that I felt had been unconsciously put on with their Sunday clothing.

"Johnny will be round with the carriage in a minute," Eileen said. "The DeWitts have already been drove to the Congregationalist church, so he has time to take us," she finished rather maliciously.

"Well, well! Am I to be all on my own this morning?" Joanna called gaily down to us from the stairs.

"Why, Mrs. Marchand, ain't Sidney going to stay with you?" asked Mrs. Potter.

Joanna laughed and waved a slender hand. She was not yet dressed. Her silk wrapper clung to her slender body, and her thistledown hair was all about her face like a child's. She looked very innocent and very beautiful.

"Oh, I asked Charles to take Sidney to Pittsburgh with him this morning. It will do my son a world of good to be away from those common ruffians he plays with! Charles will not be home until tonight."

"Would you care to come to church with us, Joanna?" I asked impulsively. "I don't know where you usually attend, but of course we could drop you off wherever you like."

Again she laughed. "What a pious group you look! No, thank you very much, Katherine dear. I am not feeling very well today, and I believe that I will stay quietly at home and rest.''

"If you are ill I'll stay with you!" I said, beginning to draw off my gloves.

"No, no!" Her voice was quite sharp, and I felt that she disliked being offered even so small a favor. "I can manage very well on my own," she assured me. "Besides, Mrs. Pinkham is on the third floor, if I should need her. Oh, I hear John coming with the carriage. Do go along, and have a pleasant morning, all of you."

Reluctantly, we left her. She did not look ill. In fact, her color was quite good. But might that be the result, perhaps, of fever? Almost I turned back before getting into the carriage. Eileen gripped my elbow and firmly forced me to step in.

"Don't be a goose, Katy! She can take care of herself."

I obeyed, but I thought Eileen might have shown a bit more concern for Joanna. I had long been aware that my friend had no particular liking for Mrs. Marchand, and was not very sympathetic to her.

Also, as we drove down into the town, I remembered that Mrs. Pinkham would not be available, as Joanna had said, for she had arranged to take Rebecca to her own home for the day. She had gotten permission from Joanna, who must have let it slip her mind. The arrangement had been made early in the week. Obviously Joanna had forgotten.

I felt increasingly uneasy. Joanna would be entirely alone in the house. Even her maid Lottie was away on a brief visit to family in the Altoona area.

But of course we would be away only an hour or so. There was no real cause for alarm. Joanna had been well enough to get up and come downstairs, after all.

I tried to put the whole thing out of my mind and concentrate on the order of service.

I found it soothing to be again in a place of worship. The minister was young and not an eloquent speaker, but his message reminded one of old and time-honored truths. He preached upon the Ten Commandments, taking each in order.

When he came to 'Thou shalt not commit adultery!' I felt absurdly that for an instant he looked directly at me, as if he could read the forbidden thoughts I kept trying to sweep out of my mind—thoughts of Charles Marchand. The minister's sermon abruptly ceased to be soothing.

Remorse gripped me that I had allowed such notions about a married man to take root even for the briefest instant. Why had I permitted myself such dangerous mental liberties?

Feverishly I clasped my gloved fingers about my small Bible, and vowed that I would not be lured so close to unspeakable temptation again! Whatever it cost to fight off my own sinful nature, that price I would gladly pay.

"What's the matter?" Eileen nudged me and whispered. "Are you sick, Katy? You're white as a tame duck!"

"Thou shalt not bear false witness!" the minister shouted. I had completely lost the thread of his discourse, and I realized that I did feel ill, quite nauseated, and I must get out of the crowded sanctuary before something disastrous resulted.

Hand pressed to my mouth, I rose and scurried along the aisle. Outside in the raw, wet air, I saw that Eileen had followed me.

"What is it, what ails you, Katy?" she asked anxiously, her sailor hat askew over her round face.

Oh, if only you knew! I thought miserably. But if anyone had told Eileen that I might be guilty of looking with—with *lust* upon another woman's husband, she would not believe it of me!

"It—must be something I ate," I lied.

"I must get you home. But how?"

"I can walk. I think the fresh air will do me good."

She was doubtful, but there seemed little choice. We started along the muddy boardwalk toward Main Street. There was little traffic today. Most folks were still in church, or at home preparing to enjoy the heavy Sunday meal. We passed a bank, stores, and approached the empty park with its great trees and its chain fence. The trees were budding with tender, pale green leaves, and birds fluttered and chirped in the branches despite the wet weather.

"Do ye want to sit on a bench for awhile?" Eileen inquired.

"No, no. I feel better now." And it was true. The physical sensation brought about by guilt and self-hatred had passed, although I still felt cast down and uneasy in my mind.

We hurried along the streets, Eileen loudly wishing we had brought umbrellas The rain was light, but steady, and it was beginning to penetrate our clothing. I felt a strand of wet hair slip out from under my hat and plaster itself to my cheek.

"Merciful holy angels!" Eileen muttered, "I've never seen the like of this rain, not even in Ireland. We shall surely be dead of mildew and mould before the sun comes out a full day!"

I could only shiver and hurry a bit faster. We were not far from the house now. I saw that there was a horse and buggy before it, and I was glad that Joanna was not all alone, after all. I imagined that she was not the type to enjoy the big house standing silent all about her.

Eileen hesitated, halfway to the front door. "I believe I'll just trot around to the stable and see if John Brock is there," she said casually, but her cheeks flamed at my sharp look.

"Oh, all right," I sighed. "Go ahead. But I wish you would rid yourself of your infatuation for that man, Eileen."

"I thought you liked Johnny!" she said.

"Of course I do. He has been a good worker and a great deal of help here. But—there is this thing with Yolande, and his reputation as a drinking man, and I don't see how anything good for you can come of it."

"I think I can handle my own affairs, Katy Livingston!" Eileen tossed her head. "When I need your advice, I'll ask for it."

Angrily she whirled and disappeared around the side of the house. Sighing, I walked up to the porch.

"Maybe she's right," I muttered dispiritedly. "I can't say that all my choices have been so wise."

Quietly I let myself into the dim entrance hall, pausing to remove my wet coat and gloves. I would make myself a nice, hot cup of tea.

Voices broke into my thoughts. They came from overhead, just out of sight, around the turn of the staircase.

"I must go now, my darling," a man murmured, his voice throbbing with feeling. "It's been heaven to be with you again. I was beginning to think you would never send for me."

"I had to wait, you must see that! I feared that Charles was growing suspicious. And there were the new people in the house—"

She did not finish her sentence, for the two of them had come down far enough to see me, and to be seen. There had been no time for me to retreat. I stared at Joanna Marchand and Joshua Galbraith, shocked to my toes.

My dismay must have been minor compared to theirs. There they stood, arms about each other's waists, frozen with surprise as unpleasant as could be imagined.

Joanna still wore her silk wrapper, only now it was plain that beneath it she wore nothing else at all. Joshua was fully dressed, but his tie was crooked, his abundant ginger hair rumpled as if by playful fingers.

Joanna raised a hand in a curious gesture, her delicate fingers curbed almost like claws, and she started down the stairs, face contorted.

Involuntarily, I stepped back. Joshua caught Joanna's elbow and swung her about.

"Joanna, wait!" he said sharply. "Listen to me. Go up to your room, quickly. I'll explain to Katherine. I am sure I can make her see that I dropped by purely by accident."

I think he knew from the sound of his own words what a pathetic attempt at an excuse it was. He gave Joanna a shove up the stairs. To my relief she went, running as if from demons. Distractedly he watched her go, then came heavily down the stairs to me. His face was tortured.

"Katherine, this isn't what—" he began.

"No, it isn't," I said cooly. "You needn't fear. This is none of my business. I am sorry to have blundered in at an awkward time. Now, if you will excuse me." I started past him.

"Katherine, please!" Sweat sprang out on his forehead. "Wait, let me talk to you. Won't you please let me talk to you?"

In spite of myself, I felt pity at his deep distress. I could not respect this man again, but I had liked him. I had leaned on his advice. Perhaps I owed him the chance to say what he thought he must.

He must have seen his victory in my face. Eagerly he came and took my arm. "Come. I'll take you for a ride in my buggy, and we'll talk."

"I don't wish to go for a ride," was my stiff reply. "If you have something you insist upon saying, let us go into the study. No one will disturb us there, as Mr. Marchand is away."

I saw him wince at the mention of Charles's name, but he followed as I marched down the hall.

I went into the study and turned to face him. He shut the door firmly. "Katherine, please sit down," he begged.

"I'll stand, thank you. I haven't much time I can spare at present."

It was a lie and we both knew it, but he nodded understandingly.

"I realize how this must look, Katherine, and how—disappointed you must be in me."

"I have no opinion," I lied again. "What you do, or Mrs. Marchand does, is of no consequence to me."

"But what you think *is* of consequence to me," he said gently. "I don't want you to imagine that I am the kind of man to seek to—seduce my friend's wife in his own home."

"Then what kind of man should I think you are?" I said somewhat cruelly.

He met my scathing look in silence, then sighed. "It wasn't quite like that. I can't expect you to understand, nor to believe me, but I never intended to become—involved in this sort of thing! It happened. It was not—planned," he finished with difficulty.

I wished desperately that my sympathy was not always stirring so near the surface! Was it possible that I was beginning to feel sorry for Joshua and Joanna?

"There is no need for you to explain anything to me," I said. "I am a stranger here, ignorant of your private lives. I have no wish to pry into secrets that have nothing at all to do with me."

"Katy, please!" The words were low, almost tremulous,

and the last of my self-righteous comdemnation was shattered. I sighed and rubbed my eyes.

"Mr. Galbraith, I shan't pass judgement. But you needn't tell me more."

"It is important to me that you know the whole story, and not just the ugly bit you saw," he insisted. "Will you do me the great favor of listening, just for a few minutes?"

Reluctantly, I agreed. He made me sit, pulling over a chair from next the wall to bring near mine. He leaned forward, his square face haggard and anxious. He ran freckled, blunt fingers through his red hair.

"First, I want you to know this is the first time I have been—alone with Joanna for months."

"But it *has* happened before," I blurted, and wished I had not.

"Yes. I have to admit that my love for Joanna is not new. It began two years ago, although it was some time before we . . . we . . ."

"I understand," I inserted hastily, feeling extremely embarrassed. I heartily wished myself transported to Australia!

"Katherine," he gazed at me earnestly. "Haven't you ever felt something you knew you shouldn't feel? Ah, well, perhaps not. You are very young and innocent."

I felt my face warm, and hoped he would not read the guilty facts in my eyes. He seemed not to notice my discomfort.

"I first met Joanna and Charles when they moved here from Pittsburgh two and a half years ago. I was Mrs. Bertha DeWitt's attorney, as you know, and we met through her.

"At first," Joshua said, "at first Joanna was only someone to be admired from a distance. Incredibly lovely—a fairytale princess come to life! But she belonged to another man, and I have always avoided involvements with married women, believe me!

"As time went on, I was invited often to the house, and I came to know both the Marchands well. I saw that Joanna was bitterly unhappy. She did not want to settle here. She missed the city; the balls, the theater, the gaiety. I have always wondered why Charles insisted that they come here to live with his old aunt. I assumed at first that it was for

Bertha's benefit, but later I was not certain of that."

His gaze went past me. He told the story as if it had happened to someone else, his voice taking on a dry, legal flavor as if he summed up, before a jury, a case involving a client.

"One day I came to see Mrs. DeWitt on business. When I had finished, and left the house, I encountered Joanna walking on the grounds. She told me that Charles was away in Kentucky and asked if I had time to take her for a short drive.

"It was a hot, August day, I remember. We drove down-river, and I learned that Joanna had been almost nowhere except in the business district of the town. She was wistfully grateful that I took the time to escort her. It gradually became a regular thing when Charles was away and she had no one to drive her about—not that Charles ever bothered to do so when he was here!"

He shook his head bitterly. "You may take this for a very lame excuse if you will, Katherine, but if Charles Marchand had given his wife a tenth of the attention she needed and deserved, she would never have turned to me. The poor girl was desperate for simple kindness and consideration. And I could not be with her and fail to love her. So in time—one thing led to another."

"Please don't go on," I interjected hurriedly. "I really do not wish to hear."

"She was in my blood, Katherine!" he persisted, his face agonized. "I could never describe my guilt, my shame at what I had done. It's been hell to face Charles as if nothing had happened. We had become good friends—don't ask me how I could be so insensitive as to go through the motions of friendship with the man I was betraying. I don't know. It just—was! But I tried to stop. I told Joanna that we mustn't see each other again, shortly after—the first time."

"Did she agree?" I asked.

A curious shudder moved over his big frame. "She went wild, Katherine. She was hysterical! She pleaded with me not to abandon her to a life of loneliness and neglect. She threatened to kill herself. What could I do? I told her that we would continue as before. God help me. I have not had an easy night or day, since.''

''Yet—something caused you to stay away from her for awhile.''

''Several things happened. Mrs. DeWitt died. You came. And something frightened Joanna. She feared that Charles was growing suspicious.''

Joshua laid his face in his hands, his bulky shoulders hunched. ''It has been torture for us both, until today. She called me and said that everyone was gone for an hour or so. I can't tell you how I felt. I had just begun to think that I could find the strength to sever the relationship, that I could straighten out the mess I've made of things. I knew that I would always love her, but I felt that if I gave her up once and for all, I might be able to face my own conscience again.''

He raised his head, and his eyes were so unhappy that I could not fail to believe him.

''Then,'' he said huskily, ''she called. She summoned me, and all my good resolutions vanished. I wanted to tell her that I would not see her alone again. I tried to say that it was best we not meet. But I couldn't. The old fascination is too strong, Katherine.''

''What will you do now?'' I asked, sorry for him in spite of myself.

He groaned and rubbed a hand over his eyes. ''I don't know! It depends—'' he took his hand away and gave me a penetrating look. ''It depends in some measure upon what you do, I suppose.''

Some of my sympathy vanished in indignation. ''I beg your pardon! *I* have no part in any of this. I would rather a hundred times not even to know of it. You cannot be more distressed than I at the turn of events that brought me home early today!''

''Yes, but—will you report to Charles?'' he asked quietly.

Chapter Twenty-three

Aghast, I stared at him. "How can you ask such a thing? What do you take me for, a common backyard gossip? Of course I shall not carry a tale like this to Mr. Marchand—nor to anyone else!"

He stood and paced about the room. "Forgive me, Katherine. I should have known you wouldn't. Yet—Charles has a right to know."

"Certainly he has. However, it is not my place to tell him." I studied him, still indignant. "But you must know, Mr. Galbraith, he is sure to find it out in time. Someone will notice something, and there will be talk, and it will get round to Mr. Marchand. I am surprised he has not already found out."

"So am I," he admitted. "I believe it is only his indifference to his wife that has preserved the secret thus far. Well, thank you for hearing me out, and I promise you that I will find a way to rectify matters."

"If Mr. Marchand no longer cares for his wife—that is—" I floundered, out of my depth.

"Yes?" he asked, pathetically eager for advice, even from me.

"Why doesn't Joanna ask him for a divorce?" I finished uncertainly.

He turned sharply away, and I saw that I had touched some raw nerve. "She will not do that," he said.

"For—religious reasons?"

"I don't know her reasons! I only know that I have repeatedly begged her to come away with me, with or without a divorce, and she refuses."

"Because of the children, perhaps."

"No. I would of course take Sidney—or even both, if Joanna so desired, and I don't believe Charles would object. He has no more interest in the children than in Joanna."

The whole matter had somehow become simply a puzzle to me, losing its too-personal, embarrassing nature. I sat, turning solutions to Joshua's problem over in my mind. Why would Joanna not agree to leave her husband? She risked exactly what had happened today, and perhaps discovery next time by someone who would not stand clear of the situation as I desired to do. Was it because of Mr. Marchand's money? Yet I believed that Charles's business was on rather unsteady legs at present. His was only moderate wealth, his investments heavy and risky. Mr. Galbraith was comfortably well-off, and his law office might well make him well-known and even wealthy, one day. And then there was the possibility he and Charles had now and again discussed at dinner, that Joshua should go into politics.

I had almost forgotten the lawyer's presence. His sudden expletive, as he smacked his fist into his open hand, startled me. "Damn it all! Why do I try to fool myself, and you? I know very well why Joanna will not leave Charles. She adores him! She always has, and his neglect has not altered it. She would let him walk upon her body with hobnailed boots and still she would fawn upon him! Sometimes I would like to—"

His face was white, and I felt sick at the intensity of his fury. What had he been about to say?

I was never to know, for without another word, he whirled and left the room.

I sat there for a long time, trying to understand what I had heard, and endeavoring to arrive at some sensible conclusion about it in my own mind.

In a way I was glad that I had heard Joshua's story. I thought now that I understood his emotional trap, and my first righteous shock at his behavior had softened. I could see, at least partially, why Joanna had strayed into the arms of another man. It was undeniably true that Charles stood always aloof from her. If she loved him, and I believed she did, that must have been unending agony and frustration for a woman who all her life had needed only to wave a hand and indicate what she wished, to have it placed at her disposal.

Sighing, I rose and walked about the room. I told myself

I had no right to sit in judgement on either Joanna or Mr. Galbraith. Yet I hoped that Joshua meant what he said, and that he would indeed do something to bring the relationship to an end—or out in the open to be resolved. I disliked very much being the possessor of such an unsavory secret. And I had no doubt that it would make it much harder to keep things running smoothly in the household. Joanna would certainly fear and distrust me, knowing what I had seen and heard although Joshua would tell her that I had no intention of carrying tales. But would she be able to believe it? Would I, in her position?

I feared things in future were going to be much more complicated and difficult, all round. And who could guess where it all would lead?

Abruptly, a racking sensation of cold shook me from head to toe, and I felt a deep, inexplicable dread, as if something awful, some unseen, cataclysmic event, inexorably approached. I knew for that insane instant that I was being driven into its path, and I would be crushed by it!

I clenched my hands and inhaled a deep, trembling breath. What utter, superstitious nonsense! What ailed me? Surely there was enough uncertainty and trouble in this house, without imagining more!

I heard Eileen calling me. Taking another steadying breath, I arranged my features into a mask of serenity, and went out.

If I thought that day difficult, the next easily eclipsed it in unpleasantness. Mrs. Pinkham came down with a very bad chest cold, and was unable to leave her bed in the morning. The maids and I took turns seeing to Rebecca, but during the change of guards in the afternoon, the girl once more glimpsed her brother returning from school. She escaped from her room through a door someone had forgotten to lock, and was cunning enough to run down the back stairs where she was not likely to be intercepted. She went like a whirlwind through the lower house, bursting in upon Joanna, Mrs. DeWitt and Yolande, who were entertaining two Cambria Company wives in the parlor. There Rebecca wreaked utter havoc, and fled before anyone could act to save the tea tray with its elegant collection of little sandwiches and cakes.

I heard the screaming and commotion even from Mrs. Pinkham's bedside. I had just brought her tea. When the yelling commenced, she met my eyes with horror.

"Merciful heavens, it's Becky!" she gasped. "Katherine, run!"

I did so, but I was not in time to prevent Rebecca from finding Sidney, who was reading in the library. When I followed her hoarse shouts of delight, I found her dragging him by the hand toward the door. He was pulling back with all his might, face set and furious.

"Leggo!" he roared. "Let me go. Leave me alone, go away!"

I don't know where Rebecca intended taking her brother. Perhaps she wanted to go outside and play. I believe that she had never forgotten the pleasure of being out of the house. Wheatever her motives, I had to control her somehow before she brought further trouble upon her own hapless self.

"Rebecca!" I caught her and tried to loosen her grasp upon Sidney. This seemed to enrage the child, and she got one hand loose, and smacked me so hard I fell back and would have have hit the floor, had not someone caught me. Strong hands set me safely aside, and I saw Charles Marchand go to his daughter. I was filled with sudden terror. What would he do to Rebecca, who had redoubled her efforts to pull Sidney from the room? To add to the confusion, she was fairly howling her brother's name amid garbled, unintelligible speech.

"Oh, don't hurt her, please!" I cried.

I don't know whether he heard me. At least he did nothing to his daughter save wrench her clutching hands from Sidney's wrist, and hold her big, furious body still. She was squalling now, and never had she looked so dreadfully ugly, nor to me, so pathetic.

"Siddy!" she screeched, over and over. "Wan' Siddy!"

Her brother stood as if fixed in his tracks. I saw that there was blood on his wrist, where Rebecca's nails had cut him. He looked sick. I went to him and touched his arm.

"Sidney, come and let me bandage that for you," I said. He leaped away from me as if my touch burned. "It's your fault!" he yelled. "You let her out again, after you promised you wouldn't. I hate you both! I hate you!''

"That will be enough!'' Charles Marchand's voice cut
like sharpened steel. "You will apologize to Miss Livingston for that stupid outburst.''

"No, it's all right, really,'' I said. "He has a right to be
upset.''

"He has no right so speak in such a disrespectful manner
to a lady. Sidney, apologize at once to Miss Livingston,
then go to your room. You will do without supper tonight.''

Sullenly obedient, Sidney mumbled an apology, and fled.
Rebecca was still sobbing. It was difficult to hear anything else, yet I caught Charles's low question. "Katherine
my dear, are you hurt?''

I fear I was not the only one who heard it, for at that
moment I became aware of Joanna Marchand in the open
doorway just behind us. Her beautifully-dressed friends,
and the DeWitts were clustered behind her. Joanna's eyes
were on me, still, utterly expressionless.

I had not come face-to-face with her since I had interrupted her meeting with Joshua Galbraith. What was she
thinking? Was she hating me, conscious that I knew the
deepest, most carefully concealed secret of her heart?

There was no time to think about such matters. "Please
bring Rebecca back upstairs, Mr. Marchand,'' I suggested.
"Mrs. Pinkham is ill, and we forgot to lock the child's
door. It is entirely my fault. If you will take her to her
room, I shall try to calm her.''

At that moment Eileen shouldered her way through the
cluster of women at the door, and if every one of them had
not been so obviously dumbfounded by the events of the
hours, they would heartily have resented her lack of courtesy. As it was, they moved obediently aside like so many
sheep.

I was relieved to see Eileen there, and at once gave her
instructions to bring up hot water so that I could attempt
to bathe Rebecca. I sent one of the other maids up with hot,
sweet tea, cookies and cakes. Rebecca was a glutton for
sweets; I thought that the food would help to distract her.

Weary hours later, Eileen and I tucked a clean and exhausted Rebecca into her bed. I hesitated before leaving her alone in the room, with the door locked. Eileen made up my mind for me. If I had not been so very tired I would not have given in and gone to my own rooms, and I often wonder now how events might have been altered, had I only stayed in that room all night.

"Come away, now. She'll sleep like a baby. You know she seldom stirs in the night," Eileen said. "I'll have Lena come in early tomorrow."

"No, I'll do that myself, and feed her. I blame myself for all this trouble."

"That's foolishness!" Eileen bristled. "Do ye think you're the only one who was too worried about Mrs. Pinkham to think of the door? And none of us likes locking this poor child in like a criminal. It isn't at all right, and maybe that feelin' makes us forget on purpose." She sighed, looking down at Rebecca's slack, sleeping face. "But sure none o' us will forget again! It only makes things worse for poor Becky when we try to give her a bit of freedom."

"I really think I'd best stay—" I began.

"You'll do nothing of the kind. You're ready to drop, and you've had no dinner. You'll come down this minute an' I'll give you the supper I had Mrs. Potter leave in the warming oven."

"First, I must see to Mrs. Pinkham."

"You brought her meal and hot chocolate not half an hour past!"

"Yes, but she ate very little."

"I looked in on her a few minutes ago. She said she'd be fine 'til mornin', and wants only to rest. Come away now!"

So I allowed myself to be persuaded. I was really very tired. I could hardly eat any of the supper Eileen brought, and would not even have tried it if she had not stood over me. I wanted only to crawl into my bed. When I did, I was asleep almost instantly. Not even old anxieties and new questions kept me from a deep, almost dreamless slumber.

Fortunately, I woke very early, even before Eileen. I felt remorseful at having left Rebecca and Mrs. Pinkham unattended all night. Swiftly I rose and dressed, taking time only to splash water on my face and brush my hair smooth. I did not even pause to pin it up, simply tying it back with a ribbon for the moment.

Then I slipped past Eileen, still snoring in her small bed in the sitting room. Mrs. Potter was already up, as I had hoped, and in the main kitchen. The big range was nice and hot and she prepared a quick breakfast for Rebecca, giving me a cup of coffee as it was cooking.

Then I took the tray and went up the stairs, hoping I would find Rebecca still asleep, and thus not into any mischief. The chances were very good that she would not have waked just yet, for she usually slept very late.

Yet there were odd sounds from within her room. I hurriedly set the tray on the table by the door and searched for the key that was habitually laid there. It was missing.

Perplexed, I looked about on the floor upon my knees to search. I could not find it. Now, what had I done when I left the room last night? Had I absentmindedly placed it in the pocket of my skirt, or . . .?

There came another indefinable noise from within the room, and a sudden wailing cry. Alarmed, I grasped the doorknob. Something was wrong, and I would not be able to get in until I found the key.

But the knob turned easily, and that gave me new worry. Had we again left the door unlocked, even after the troubles of the day before?

I shoved the door back, and looked anxiously in to see what Rebecca was up to. She was not in the rumpled bed, nor was she anywhere in the room, within range of my vision. Hastily I looked under the bed, behind chairs, and within the armoire. Where could she be? Had she slipped out through the unlocked door before I came? But no, I had heard sounds of her movements a moment ago. I had heard her voice. She *must* be nearby.

I thought that she must have gone into Mrs. Pinkham's room. Trying the connecting door, I found it locked. A pulse of growing anxiety was beating in my throat. *Where* had the child got to?

And then I heard her again, crying out hoarsely as if in fear. And I knew, with a tingling horror, where she was.

I should have realized at once. The window, always kept securely locked, was fully open. Rebecca's cries were coming from *outside it*!

I ran over. Yes, there she was, lying full length upon the narrow ledge that lay beneath. Her support could not have been more than eighteen inches in width. Below it the house walls fell sheerly some thirty feet to the ground. Rebecca had crawled perhaps five feet to the right of the window.

I sucked in my breath sharply. The girl heard me and looked round, her face red with weeping, her dull eyes filled with wondering terror.

I clutched the windowsill, trying to think without panic. How could I possibly get Rebecca back into the room? Even if I could have reached her, she was far heavier that I, and awkward of movement at best. If she tried to turn around on the ledge—or even rise from her prone position, she would surely overbalance. The result could only be her death.

Still staring at me pitiously, she made a sudden, jerking movement. My heart lurched. "No, Becky!" I said quickly. "Stay where you are, dear. I will help, but you must lie very, very still. Do you understand me? Lie quite still, and wait for me just a moment, Becky."

Praying that she understood, and would not take my departure as a signal to try and raise herself upright, I fled across the room and out into the hall. I wanted to shriek for help, but I knew my cries might not be heard immediately on the second floor, and they might alarm the child on the ledge. I must not further frighten her.

Heart pounding, I ran down the stairs as fast as I could. As I came into the corridor, a door opened, and Joanna Marchand stepped out into the hall.

"Why Katherine!" she said. "Whatever is the matter? I heard you running—my dear, what is wrong?"

"Where is Mr. Marchand?" I gasped.

Her face cooled. "Why do you wish to know?"

"Mrs. Marchand, please. It is most urgent. Rebecca is . . ."

"What's happened to Rebecca?" she interrupted sharply. "Tell me at once. I can see by your face it is something dreadful. Katherine, for the love of mercy, tell me!''

Pale and wide-eyed, she clutched at my arm with painfully strong fingers.

''She is all right—for the moment!'' I cried. ''But I must have help. She is on the ledge outside her window, and someone strong must help me lift her back in, or she will fall. Where is Mr. Marchand?''

''Dear God!'' gasped Joanna. Her hand fell nervelessly away. ''I'll go and call Charles at once. Go back to Rebecca. Try to get her back in, please, please!''

She sped away down the hall toward her husband's rooms. I think that I liked Joanna better in that moment than I ever had. At last she was behaving as a mother to her daughter, forgetting Rebecca's defects in the press of concern for her welfare.

I hurried back upstairs, wondering belatedly why Mrs. Pinkham had not heard the noises of Rebecca climbing out onto the ledge, and the cries of the frightened child. She would not have been able to help Rebecca. Yet it was strange that she had failed even to hear. If I had not happened into the room when I did, that failure might well have meant doom for the girl.

I rushed to the window, almost afraid to look out. Thank God, Rebecca lay as I had left her.

''I'm here, dear,'' I said, as calmly as I could. ''Lie very still. Your father is coming to help you. Just be still until he comes.''

I continued to talk quietly to her, leaning out of the window as far as I dared, trying to see a way of getting hold of her hands. But even had I stepped out upon the ledge, only the child's bare feet would have been within reach.

Heavy steps pounded along the corridor. Charles, still knotting the belt of his dressing gown about his waist, ran into the room.

''What in the name of God has happened here?'' he demanded harshly. Quickly I held up a cautioning hand.

''Don't startle her, please!'' I whispered. ''She is very frightened. I think the least movement could send her off the ledge.''

222

"Let me see," he said more quietly, and took my place at the window.

"Well, Rebecca," he spoke to the whimpering girl below. "You have gotten yourself into a fine pickle, haven't you? Never mind, child. We'll soon have you back in. Stay where you are. Don't move."

He turned back. "Go and see if John Brock is coming with the rope. I sent Joanna to find him. Tell him to hurry!"

I ran to do his bidding, and almost collided with Mr. Brock and Eileen, with Joanna hurrying behind them.

It seemed a lifetime, during which we suffered the most horrifying imaginings, but I suppose it was not more than a quarter of an hour before the men—with Charles climbing perilously out upon the ledge himself to affix the rope to his daughter's waist—had the child safe in her room. I was trembling in every limb as they helped her over the sill and Charles, after a heart-stopping pause, followed. Gently John Brock set the girl down upon her bed. She was bawling noisily, and seemed even further frightened by all the faces in the room. She stared from one to the other of us, babbling something I could not for a moment understand. It sounded like "Dah! Dah!"

Finally I realized that she meant her beloved largest doll, the one she kept with her almost constantly. I looked about for it.

I could not find it. Rebecca's cries became more frantic. I went to her and put my arms about her shoulders. "Becky, I cannot find the doll, but I will look for it after you have had your breakfast and your bath. Please don't cry."

To my surprise, I was pushed aside by Joanna, who gathered the loudly sobbing girl into her arms and began to pet and comfort her. I had never thought to see that sight. It was very touching. If Rebecca's near-fatal accident had wrought this miracle in her mother's heart, then perhaps all her suffering was not for naught.

"Is that what she's crying for?" Mr. Brock asked, pointing outside the window. I went to look. There lay the doll, just beyond the point where Rebecca had been. Even as I watched, a gust of wind lifted the baby doll and swept it down, down! I felt such a thrill of horror that I had to bite down upon a sharp cry. It might so easily have been Rebecca, tumbling through space to the mud below!

It was at that moment I first asked myself the question that would haunt me for days. Why had Rebecca climbed from her window? Why had she taken the doll with her?

"Where is Mrs. Pinkham?" Charles was querying sharply. "She is paid to attend to Rebecca!"

"She has been ill. Did we not mention it yesterday?" I hastily explained.

He scraped his hand over his unshaven face and sighed. "Yes, yes, of course you did. I had forgotten. John, will you make arrangements to put bars over that window, please? I want every window in the attic securely barred, as soon as possible."

"Someone should have been with her, even if Mrs. Pinkham is ill!" Joanna cried, moving away from Rebecca. The sobbing child sat upon the bed in her torn and dirtied gown, shaking with cold and shock. I wrapped a blanket about her shoulders and kneeled down to find her carpet slippers.

"Do you hear me, Katherine?" Joanna said shrilly. "I demand to know why one of the maids was not assigned to stay with Rebecca until Mrs. Pinkham was well."

"Joanna," Charles intervened. "Miss Livingston is not our servant, remember, nor has she any responsibility for Rebecca."

"It seems to me that she has *taken* a great deal of responsibility!" Joanna commented acidly.

I was stung by Joanna's attack, and it crossed my mind that her critical remarks might have more to do with her bitter knowledge that I was the possessor—however unwillingly—of her guilty secret, than with Rebecca's care. Certainly Joanna had never before taken an interest in the girl.

But arguing about who was to blame for this morning's emergency would only waste time and cause further friction. Ignoring Joanna, I turned to Eileen. "Would you help Rebecca with her breakfast? I fear the one I brought will be stone cold. We'll need another from the kitchen. I think I'd better go and see if Mrs. Pinkham is in need of anything. I cannot understand why all this commotion has not roused her?"

Eileen nodded and I went out and tapped on Mrs. Pinkham's hall door. There was no answer. I called to her.

"Mrs. Pinkham? It's Katherine. May I come in?"

Still no answer. I tried the door. To my relief, it was unlocked.

I stepped into the dim room. I could see the older woman's form in the bed. "Mrs. Pinkham? Are you awake?"

The silence was suddenly alarming. I hurried, drawing back the drapes to admit the pale morning light. It was another cloudy, wet morning. The gray illumination was barely sufficient to show me the still face of Mrs. Pinkham, mouth slackly open, eyes closed.

I thought for a moment that she was dead! I hope that I may be forgiven the ragged nerves that caused me to scream. I hurried to touch her face.

My heart resumed its interrupted beating. The flesh was not cold. And Mrs. Pinkham was breathing, although her respiration seemed very shallow and inefficient.

"What is it?" Joanna and Charles came in, Joanna's face disapproving at this new alarm. I felt very silly indeed.

"Oh, forgive me for crying out," I said. "For a moment I thought—"

"What's wrong with Mrs. Pinkham?" Charles stepped past his wife and came to bend over the elderly woman. Gently he shook her shoulder. When she did not respond, he shook her more roughly.

"Mrs. Pinkham, wake up!" he demanded. Her head lolled, and she mumbled something, but did not waken.

"Is she ill?" I asked, frightened by the blue look on her lips. "She had a bothersome chest cold yesterday, but she seemed much improved last night."

"I think we had better call a doctor, at once," Charles said. "Katherine, will you go and do that, please?"

I lost no time in running downstairs to follow his instructions.

Dr. Minikin was not at home. Fortunately his assistant, a Dr. Wardlow, was available. As I turned away from the phone, Mrs. Potter came along the hall from the back of the house.

"Is anything wrong?" she asked.

"Rebecca almost fell off the ledge outside her window," I told her quickly. "And Mrs. Pinkham is much worse. Dr. Wardlow is coming."

"Well, I'd best make more coffee," she said with comforting practicality, "and heat water for the doctor's instruments. Come, Katy. I'll give you a cup of coffee. You look as if you need it!"

"Can you give me a pot of it on a tray? I'll take it up to the others. Everyone is upset, I'm afraid."

"Surely. Now don't fret, the doctor will be here soon. His house is just over Stony Creek, not more'n half a mile."

She was right. The doorbell rang even as I started up with my tray, and I went back to open the door for the doctor.

The physician followed me up the stairs with swift steps. He was a man of perhaps thirty-five, and I felt that he eyed me with curiosity. "You are the Miss Livingston I keep hearing about, are you not?" he asked.

"Why, yes sir. But I can't imagine how you have heard of me? I have been here only a short time."

"One of my patients spoke of you. A Mrs. Smith."

"Oh yes, Mary. She is your patient? I didn't realize she had been ill."

"She has a chronic heart condition that I have been warning her about for years. I wish she would give up heavy work, but she is a very strong-willed woman. She is a widow, and raising a young son."

"I had no idea she was not well. I wish that we had not given her so much wash to do!"

She needs the money, Miss Livingston, and if she thought that my mention of her heart caused you to hold back on work she badly needs, I'd have the sharp edge of her tongue, let me assure you!"

He smiled and shook his head. He was a pleasantly plain man with a lantern-jaw, and a kind and humorous mouth.

"Perhaps you have also met Mrs. Pinkham?" I asked, midway up the last flight of stairs. "It is she who is ill."

"Oh yes, indeed I know Mrs. Pinkham. What seems to be her trouble?"

I told him all I knew. "I am very puzzled, Dr. Wardlow. She'd been suffering from a cold, but seemed much improved last night, and said a good sleep would make her right again. But this morning we cannot wake her.''

By now, we were at Mrs. Pinkham's door. I opened it and gestured the doctor in. Joanna and Charles were waiting near the bed.

Taking my leave I carried my tray into Rebecca's room. John Brock was still there, measuring the window for bars. Eileen was helping Rebecca with her breakfast. ''Would either of you like some coffee?'' I asked.

''I would indeed,'' said Eileen, ''and so would John, I am sure.'' She came to take a cup of the steaming liquid for him and one for herself.

''Doctor Wardlow's asking for some of that coffee for Mrs. Pinkham,'' Charles said, stepping in the doorway. He studied me with concern. ''Are you all right, my dear?'' he asked, very softly.

Carefully I concentrated on an unneeded rearrangement of the service. ''Yes, of course,'' I said. But my voice shook. I cleared my throat and picked up the tray.

''I'll bring it at once. Is she awake then?''

''Barely. The doctor managed to rouse her just a bit.''

I took a cup of the coffee to the doctor, then retreated to the open door of Mrs. Pinkham's room.

My elderly friend had been propped partially upright in her bed. It was sad to see her head wobble on her thin neck as she struggled to wake. The doctor was forcing black coffee down her throat a spoonful at a time.

''This woman has taken a very heavy dosage of morphine,'' he said sternly. ''Where did she get it?''

''Why, I don't know anything about her personal habits!'' Joanna sniffed. ''Nor does my husband. We had no idea at all that she was taking anything. But I would assume she had the drug from another illness.''

''She never had a prescription for any such medication from me, nor, I'd stake my reputation on it, from Dr. Minikin,'' stated the doctor flatly. ''I've never known Mrs. Pinkham to take more of medicine than she ought. She is a very sensible and dependable woman. I've known her for years.''

Doctor Wardlow turned from his patient and looked about the room. He found what he was seeking upon the dressing

227

table, and went to pick up a small bottle, reading the label aloud. "Dr. Fahrney's Pepsin Anodyne Compound." Sternly he said, "This is ofttimes given to infants and hailed as a 'mother's friend' by the manufacturers." He set the bottle sharply down. "The damned stuff will dope a baby into insensibility, and ignorant mothers are relieved of the child's fretting." He shook his head. "It would require a heavy dosage to produce these effects in an adult."

Joanna threw up her hands as if shocked. "You say Mrs. Pinkham is a reliable person! This is scarcely the action of a responsible person, to dose herself with a potent drug so that she failed to wake when my daughter needed her! I assure you that if such a thing happens again, I shall dismiss her at once!"

Charles said calmly, "Joanna, the woman is not well. This is not the time for accusations and recriminations. I think we'd best leave the doctor alone with her." He took his wife's elbow, and led her from the room.

Her face was flushed with emotion, her eyes filled with tears. Apparently not noticing my presence at the side of the doorway, she turned suddenly to Charles and flung herself into his arms, pressing the length of her body against his.

"Oh, Charles, I am so frightened!" she cried.

He set her away from him gently. "You needn't be. Rebecca has suffered no harm."

"But it might so easily have—she might have been killed!" She placed both dainty hands over her face and began to weep. Embarrassed, I closed Mrs. Pinkham's door softly. But even from within the room, I could hear Joanna's sobbing.

Chapter twenty-four

From the day of Rebecca's brush with death, the sprouting seeds of anxiety, uneasiness and dread I had felt in this house swiftly became full-blown, an evil-smelling flower of fear that tainted the very air about me.

Oddly, what most plagued my mind was Rebecca's doll.

I cannot recall the exact moment when I became certain that Rebecca had not taken the doll out upon the ledge with her. She had, I believed, gone out *after* it.

Yet to my knowledge the doll was never mentioned in the family as the reason for Rebecca's being on the ledge. Why I myself did not suggest this, I cannot quite say. Was it because I knew what the response would be? I could hear Mrs. DeWitt saying, "Nonsense! The poor idiot threw out the doll, on a stupid whim, and then witlessly followed it."

Or perhaps it would be Joanna herself who would give me a pitying glance for my ignorance. Rebecca was a thing to them, without reasoning power, acting on mad impulse. True, after the frightening event, Joanna had shown a commendable (if very short-lived) fear and concern for the girl. Yet she would laugh at the idea of Rebecca having any sensible reason for her action.

But *I* knew that Rebecca would not have thrown the doll out. I knew that she was touchingly, stubbornly, protective of it, as if it called upon some wisp of human instinct deep within her undeveloped mind. In her most violent moods, when she might attack walls or chairs or even one of us, she had never touched the doll with any but the gentlest fingers. And when, after the doll's fall from the ledge, I had rescued it, and bathed the mud from its hard-rubber body, and washed its white batiste dress, Rebecca had received it from my hands with a gasp of delight. For days after she scarcely let it out of her grasp.

Beyond the doll, there were other considerations. Why was Rebecca awake at that early hour? Habitually she slept very late, until mid-morning or past, and then was made to wake only with some effort.

And what about the drug that had caused Mrs. Pinkham to sleep through the entire sequence of events?

It was the day after the near-tragedy that I spoke with Mrs. Pinkham on that subject.

No one had as yet told her about the thing that had happened to Rebecca, out of deference to her weakness. She listened to my version of it with obvious horror.

"I cannot believe it, Katherine!" she gasped. "That child out upon the ledge! Ah, if she had not held fast until help came! How long was she trapped out there?"

" I have no way of knowing. I came up, heard sounds, and found her."

"I can't think why I never woke."

I regarded her with surprise. "Has no one told you? It was, according to Dr. Wardlow, the morphine in the Fahrney's Pepsin Anodyne Compound that you had taken."

She wore a perfectly blank look. "Morphine? What are you talking about? I have never taken morphine in my life."

"Why, here is the bottle, Mrs. Pinkham." I got up and found it upon the bureau top.

"Let me see that!" she said sharply. Puzzled, I handed it to her. She unstoppered the bottle, smelled and tasted the contents gingerly, and reclosed it with a quick and almost violent twist of her fingers.

"This stuff is not mine, Katherine. I have no idea how it came to be among my things."

"Not yours?"

"I suppose you will not believe me. It is only the word of an old woman, isn't it?"

"Why, of course I believe you!" I said, and took her trembling hand. "If you say you know nothing of the morphine, then you know nothing of it, and there's an end to it!"

"Thank you, my dear." Her eyes filled. "But if I had morphine in my system, how did it get there? I swear I took no medication that night. I do recall that I ate the poached egg, and drank the hot chocolate you brought me.''

She stared at me suddenly, and I bit my lip. There was no way for either of us to prove it, but in that moment we both knew that the cocoa Mrs. Pinkham had taken from my hand had contained a large amount of Dr. Fahrney's Compound.

"How—how could it have gotten into the chocolate?'' I found that my voice quavered slightly.

She shook her head. "I don't know, dearie, but it was there when I drank it, I would wager my soul!''

"Yes.'' I drew a deep breath. "So would I. Let me think. I had been working with Rebecca, who was so terribly distraught after being taken away from Sidney again. Eileen stayed with her while I ran down to fetch your supper. I had asked Mrs. Potter to prepare it as the family sat at dinner. When I went down, I found everything prepared and warming. I had only to place it on the tray and poor the chocolate from the pan at the back of the range.''

"Ah,'' Mrs. Pinkham said grimly. "Someone knew the chocolate was for me. Someone slipped into the kitchen and poured the Fahrney's syrup into the chocolate, and later set the bottle into my room, after I was asleep. But who heard you order my meal?''

I thought, and shrugged helplessly. "Everyone at dinner, I suppose. I gave the order to Lena, who was serving the family, and she told Mrs. Potter.''

"Then anyone might have planned it. But why, Katherine?'' her voice rose frantically.

"I can think of only one reason,'' I said, shivering. "Someone wanted to be sure you would sleep very deeply. Someone did not want to be disturbed when—''

"Rebecca?'' she breathed, and her face went a shade whiter. "Whoever dosed my chocolate wanted to harm Rebecca!''

I took a deep breath. "I believe that person wanted Rebecca dead.''

"That's insane! What harm is she to anyone, poor child? What possible benefit would her death bring?''

I shook my head, but I was seeing Sidney's blue, innocent eyes, and the panic and revulsion they had reflected when he screamed at his sister on the riverbank, "I hate you. I wish you were dead!"

I felt a sudden compelling need to look in on Rebecca, and I left Mrs. Pinkham with a falsely comforting word or two. I do not think she was fooled for a minute, for my fear and suspicions must have been written on my features.

However, when I went up to the attic playroom, I found Rebecca in perfect security, with Marie. They were both down upon the carpet, romping with a calico kitten. I beckoned Marie to me.

"Is—everything all right?" I asked.

"Why yes, Miss Katy." She frowned as some of my anxiety reached her. "Why, whatever's wrong? You look as if you seen a ghost!"

I tried to smile. "No, it is nothing. Only I want to be very sure . . . Are you keeping the door locked carefully? We must be certain that Rebecca doesn't take it in her head to get out again."

"Or," the young woman said slowly, watching my face, "that somebody gets in?"

I met her eyes, and saw complete comprehension there. She gave a brisk little nod. "Never you mind, Miss Katy. None of us below stairs thinks Miss Becky tried to climb out on that ledge without—help."

I hesitated. It would never do to let such gossip get started about the town. Yet Rebecca must be protected. I decided to trust Marie's good sense. "You have grasped the problem perfectly," I said with quiet emphasis. "From now on I think we must never leave Rebecca unattended. Mrs. Pinkham will soon be able to take over in daytime. Perhaps you and Lena would not mind taking turns staying with her at night. I shall have another bed moved into her room."

Marie nodded her agreement. Feeling much like someone who has barred a door against unknown terrors, I went downstairs.

There, I was just in time to overhear a remark made by Lily DeWitt to Joshua Galbraith. The two were in the entrance hall. Apparently Mrs. DeWitt had just admitted the attorney, or more likely, he was just leaving, since I had not heard the bell. She was regaling him with her version, slightly garbled, of Rebecca's misadventure, and as usual she made no effort to keep her voice under a shout.

"—saved her, scratching and snarling like an animal at her rescuers! Though what was the good of them risking their lives to pull her in, I couldn't say. If you ask me, it might have been a blessing all 'round if—"

"If what, Mrs. DeWitt?" I asked coldly, from behind her. "If an innocent and helpless child had fallen to her death, and thus relieved everyone of her care? If she had died horribly and in anguish?"

She swung around, her face purpling, like mouldy clabber. Her mouth drew up as if pulled by drawstrings. "Well! It's Miss High and Mighty Livingston, sneaking about and listening to private conversations!"

"It would be difficult not to hear, when you are airing your cold-blooded views loudly enough to be enjoyed by the entire household," I snapped.

Quickly Joshua came forward. "Ah, Katherine. I am glad you came down. May I speak with you a moment on business? In private, if you please."

I turned my back on Mrs. DeWitt. "Certainly, Mr. Galbraith. Come into my sitting room." As we walked away, I distinctly heard Mrs. DeWitt hiss, "Shameless, brazen hussy!"

In spite of my much-altered opinion of Joshua Galbraith, his rumbling chuckle and wink did much to restore my good humor. I heaved a large sigh, and smiled.

"That woman may make a murderess of me yet," I murmured.

"You would be amply justified. I promise to defend you in court should the occasion arise!"

He bowed me into my sitting room. I asked him to be seated, and then shut the door with a firm little click, in case Lily DeWitt was still lingering curiously about.

"Speaking of court," Joshua began at once, "I regret to tell you that the DeWitts have made more progress in contesting Bertha DeWitt's will than I would have thought possible."

"Then they may yet take the house?"

He shook his head. "No, I hardly think that could happen. In any case, Charles is the next of kin, not the DeWitts. But they seem bent on embarrassing you if they can. They

233

have enlisted the assistance of Sibyl Blackwood, owner of the Blackwood Home.''

"I can guess what her testimony will be!" I bit my lip in distress. "I've already heard it from her own lips. She will say that I schemed and cajoled and somehow influenced an elderly, ailing woman into making me her heir.''

"Do not be overly concerned, Katherine," he reassured me. "There are plenty of people who can refute that. The fact that you came nowhere near Bertha for months after you had helped effect her release from the Home would, I should think, satisfactorily spike any such accusations. It would be difficult to believe that you or anyone could exert much in the way of influence from that distance, with no more contact that one letter.''

I glanced at him in sharp surprise. "Yes, I did write her once, a day or two after she left the Home. But how did you know that? It was only a thank-you note for the ring.'' I glanced at the opal glowing on my finger. "And it was never answered. I often wondered why.''

"Charles and I found your note among Mrs. DeWitt's personal papers after her death. As to why she did not reply, I cannot say. Perhaps she meant to, and forgot. Perhaps it would not be too far-fetched to guess that when she received the letter, she had already contemplated changing her will, and felt that any contact with you might lead someone to the assumption that you did have some influence upon her. She knew her kin very well, I assure you," he said rather grimly, and glanced at me with sudden keenness.

"Tell me, Katherine, what would you feel if this house *were* taken from you? I see no likelihood of such an event, but I am curious. Merely as—as a friend.''

I considered the question. "I replied at last, "I think my feelings would be a confusing mixture. I would be less than honest if I were to tell you that I have not enjoyed my change—in status. Being a property owner does quite amazing things for one's self-esteem!" I smiled, and he grinned understandingly.

"And I like the house, of course. It is very attractive now, with the new paint and the repairs. I cannot help feeling proud of it. But—" I hesitated.

"Yes?" he prompted gently.

"I—so many things have happened since I came! Unpleasant, even frightening things. Like this latest episode with Rebecca."

"Ah, yes. I wanted to hear your version of that. Even allowing for Lily DeWitt's exaggerations, it sounded a very serious situation indeed."

"Yes. Yes it was. I think it might just as easily have become a tragedy." Involuntarily I shuddered.

He asked very penetrating questions for the next few minutes, and again I caught a glimpse of the clever attorney's mind behind his genial, friendly-bear pose. I felt no hesitation in relating to him everything I knew, and some of what I suspected. Of course I did not mention Sidney's name. Not that I thought I was wrong in suspecting the child. He was the only one I could think of who hated Rebecca so violently as to be tempted to do her bodily harm. Yet he was a child himself, and not for the life of me would I take the chance of falsely accusing him. If he was guilty, I profoundly hoped that either he would never do such a thing again, or that others would find him out and take proper measures. Certainly to some extent he was to be pitied, and there was much good potential in that intelligent child! What a dreadful waste it would be if the existence of Rebecca, and his terrible resentment—almost fear, of his twin—should negate all that potential.

When I had finished speaking, Joshua sat quietly, one leg crossed over the other, booted foot swinging gently. His thoughts plainly absorbed all his attention. I did not disturb them, leaving him to speak, or not, as he chose.

It was several minutes before he stirred and turned to me again.

"You definitely believe someone deliberately put Rebecca's doll on that ledge, to entice her out—and to her death?"

"Yes," I said simply.

Calmly he nodded. "Sidney?"

I sighed. "If you please, I don't wish to speculate on that, without any proof at all."

"Still, it had to be Sidney. No one else would have any reason."

I shook my head, feeling very helpless. A sudden thought

235

struck me.

"Mr. Galbraith. Perhaps this is totally unrelated to what we have been discussing. But I have a question or two I wish you would answer for me. I have been hearing rumors that Bertha DeWitt did not die naturally."

"It was a fall. An accident."

"Was it?" I looked at him steadily. "There are those who quite sincerely believe it was not."

He spread his hands out. "Katherine, I can only say this much. I—we—have certain suspicions."

"Against whom?"

He smiled. "You are intelligent. You must know that even if I had an answer for that, I could not give it to you. But the fact is, there *is* no answer. Probably there never will be. There are suspicions, or shall we say, suspicious circumstances, but no evidence that points to anyone at all. Except," he gave me a sly look, "you, of course."

I am sure my mouth fell open. "What did you say?"

He grinned and shrugged his bulky shoulders. "Well, you are the only one who has so far benefited from her death, simply by being the heir."

"But that—that is outrageous!" I rose and stood before him, quivering with indignation. "How dare you suggest such a—a monstrous thing? I was not even in this town until I received your letter, notifying me of Mrs. DeWitt's death!"

He leaned forward and grasped my hand strongly. "Calm down, Katherine. I shouldn't have teased you. Forgive me. I only meant to point out that usually when someone dies, and there is a feeling that someone had a hand in it, usually we look first for the one who would gain. Of course we are satisfied now that you were nowhere near the scene."

"What do you mean," I interruped. "What do you mean, you are satisfied *now*?"

He gave a little whistle of admiration. "You're too bright and quick for me, Katy! You caught me on that one. Shall I tell you the truth, or will you be so angry at me that I will lose a valued friend? I know that I have already strained our friendship sadly."

"Tell me, please."

"All right. The day you appeared, rather belatedly, in

236

my office in response to my letter—"

"I could not have come sooner. The letter was given first to Mrs. Blackwood!"

"Yes, yes, I understand that. But you arrived at a rather interesting moment. Charles and I were actually discussing you—and Mrs. DeWitt's death—when you were announced. We were both curious about you, for the reasons I have already stated. You must realize, we did not know you, and were searching for any motive for Bertha DeWitt's death. You had the most obvious one."

"But—I didn't know about the legazy until you yourself told me!" I repeated rather desperately.

"I know that now. And after we carefully checked your assertion that you had never been in Johnstown before the day you came to my office, and found it to be perfectly accurate, we knew you had to be completely innocent."

"How could you check on such a statement?" I asked, astonished, and not liking the feeling that for a time I had been under investigation by this man and Charles Marchand. The thought made me quite ill. How trusting I had been! Doubtless this was the reason Charles had urged me to accept the legacy, with the proviso that he and his family would stay on. What better way to have me in a position to be watched—and judged!

"It was quite simple," Joshua explained. "Under pretext of investigating the circumstances of the will, I questioned the staff you had worked with, and even Mrs. Blackwood, about your activities in months past. I learned, among other things, that you had not taken a day off in weeks, because the Home was shorthanded, and you were receiving a small extra sum for this. There simply was no opportunity for you to have caught the train, come to Johnstown, and murdered Bertha DeWitt."

"I suppose," I remarked waspishly, "that I should be grateful for your prying into my life, since you have absolved me of heinous crime!"

He grinned. "Indeed you should, my girl! But I do not blame you in the least for being distressed at such sly digging into your private affairs. If it gives you any comfort, Charles ridiculed the notion of your possible guilt, even before I investigated your life at the Blackwood Home. He

237

simply believed your eyes were too innocent—and other remarks to the effect that one could not be with you for an hour and not believe in your good character. I believe I gave him a list of convicted murderers with the faces of angels!" He gave a bark of laughter, and I found myself smiling, reluctantly.

"But if I am no longer suspected, then—who is?"

"I have already told you. There is no evidence pointing to anyone."

"Well, who was in the house that day?" I asked.

"Have you ambitions to take up sleuthing?" he teased.

"I am serious. Please answer my question."

Joshua shrugged. "We are not precisely sure. The DeWitts were staying here at the time, also Charles, Joanna and the children, although Charles was in Kentucky that week."

"I suppose you have investigated *him*?" I asked rather tartly.

"Yes indeed, and he knows I have." Briskly Joshua continued, "as a matter of established fact, at the moment of his aunt's demise, Charles was assisting a doctor of veterinary medicine in the difficult foaling of a very expensive and promising brood mare. They saved the mare, but lost the foal, and our Charles went out and got himself roaring drunk."

I felt myself flushing at the graphic lot of information I had uncorked. "Well, then, the others? The ones who were in Johnstown and perhaps in the house at the time?"

"You are very persistent. I assure you that I have, with Charles's help, quietly attempted to trace the activities of everyone. Mr. and Mrs. Horace DeWitt say that they were off on separate activities that afternoon—Horace to purchase a box of cigars, his wife went to a charity luncheon. I have been unable to corroborate either of their stories. Horace cannot seem to recall where he bought his cigars, and no storekeeper to whom I have casually mentioned Mr. DeWitt's excursion can quite remember serving him. Personally I believe Horace spent the afternoon in a certain—house of ill repute. I even went so far as to question the proprietor of that unsavory establishment, but she is an old hand at keeping what she knows to herself.

"As for deal Lily, I interviewed two of the women on the membership list of the Assistance of Orphans Society. One feather-headed lady says she is not sure Lily attended the luncheon that day. But then she cannot quite remember whether she herself was present! The other thinks Lily was there, but whether Mrs. DeWitt was with the group, a rather large one, for the entire length of the meeting, she could not say. I had to leave the investigation at that point. I could hardly question every woman on the list without raising some very speculative gossip."

"I can see that one would need to be very discreet with such inquiries," I admitted.

"Particularly," he emphasized, "when the official explanation for Bertha DeWitt's death was that she lost her footing upon the stairs; very understandable for an elderly woman who had only recently recovered from the paralysis of a stroke."

He rubbed his sizable nose thoughtfully. "I asked all the questions I dared, however. I even attempted to trace young Sidney's movements that day—gone fishing all by himself, he says. And I went so far as to interrogate the servants. But I came up with nothing really helpful. Even Joanna was unable to give me much information. She had one of her severe headaches that day and spent most of the afternoon in bed. She was asleep and heard nothing. It was a dreadful shock to her when she rose, started downstairs late in the afternoon, and found Bertha at the foot of the stairway. Mrs. DeWitt had apparently been dead for up to an hour."

"Then it seems," I sighed, "the truth about her death will never be known."

"That is my conclusion. Charles still insists he will get to the bottom of it, but I doubt he ever will know more than we know today."

He stood abruptly. "I must go. But I have been invited to dinner tonight. Will you be present also?"

I shook my head. "I don't think so."

"I understand that you feel uncomfortable in our company, so much has happened, so much—ugliness has been bared.'' He met my eyes gravely. ''But I wish that you would dine with the family tonight. I believe that it will probably be the last time I shall sit at Charles's table.''

''Surely not! Why do you say that?'' I asked, startled.

''Because—'' he hesitated. ''Because today I made an arrangement with Joanna to meet her later tonight. I intend to tell her that for her sake and for my own I can never see her—in an intimate situation—again. I can't face myself any longer, pretending to be a friend to a man who trusts me, and now seeing myself through your clear, honest eyes.''

His expression was so bleak that impulsively I touched his coat sleeve. ''You are doing the right thing, Joshua. I admire you for it, for I know it must be very hard.''

He patted my fingers, and sighed. ''You are very understanding, Katherine. And very lovely. I wish that I had met someone like you before I made so many mistakes.''

He lifted my hand, kissed it, and went away. I sat for awhile, thinking of the sad waste of it all. Joshua was a good man at heart. He had simply been tempted past his endurance. The same was doubtless true of Joanna, and I felt pity for her and the parting that was to come. What she had done was very wrong, but there had been provocation. *Why* had Charles held himself so aloof and cold? I wondered how she would take Joshua's declaration, and if she would blame me. It was not my fault—I had never wished to become involved in her secrets! But I knew that it was inadvertently stumbling into their assignation that had brought the matter to a head. Would she hate me for it?

Chapter Twenty-five

After some hesitation, I decided to honor Joshua's request and join the others at dinner. There were several reasons, some of which I would rather not have admitted to myself. I had not seen Charles since he had saved Rebecca from the ledge, except for a distant glimpse of him riding his tall chestnut stallion. This was, of course, as it should be—as it must be. Yet, foolishly, I felt a deep need to see him, just to be in the same room for a time, and quietly watch his face.

Also, I was eager to know what was being said about Rebecca's mishap. I wondered if anything at all was being done to find the cause of it.

But the talk that night never touched upon Rebecca, at all. Both Charles and Joshua were soon deep into a discussion of the local controversy over the Southfork dam.

"There are some twenty million tons of water behind that unsafe structure!" Charles was saying.

"Now, Charles, earthen dams have been used for centuries, and we've had scares about the dam every year since it was built," Joshua temporized. "Maybe our concern is not fully justified. I've seen statements by men who should know, that even if the dam breaks, little harm could result."

Charles stared. "Good God, man, you've seen the valley! Those fourteen miles are as steep as nature could make them, and there is no possible place in that narrow sluice where water could spread out. If the water ever breaks through that flimsy, badly-tended barrier, the mountain slopes will squeeze it into a wall sixty or seventy feet high, at who can guess what awful speed. And then, God help us all!"

Lily DeWitt took the conversation forcibly away, in her loud, whinnying voice.

"Is it not exciting? In only two weeks the season will begin at the club! I have ordered new clothes for myself and Yolande. She will be the prettiest girl there, won't you, my dearest pet?"

Strangely, Yolande showed little interest. She had sat picking at her food, her head thoughtfully bowed throughout the meal. I wondered what lay so heavily upon her mind that even the promise of new dresses would not divert her.

"I said, isn't that so, Yolande?" Lily insisted more loudly.

Her daughter looked up as if she had not heard any of what went before. "What mama?"

"Haven't you heard a word I've said? Are you daydreaming about the swathe of hearts you will reap among the eligible young men at the club?" Lily simpered and glanced about the table for approval of her wit. For some reason I felt rather sorry for the woman—there was so little appreciation shown, even by her daughter, for all the devious machinations and planning that had doubtless gone into the girl's debut into upper-crust society. I smiled at both women. "I think you are right. Yolande will indeed be the belle of the crowd."

There was quite an audible sniff from Eileen, who was serving the dessert, and I knew I would be chastised by my friend for befriending the enemy.

Eileen's dislike for Yolande had abated not one whit in the past days. Often she complained to me of seeing the girl slip from the house on one pretext or another, and hurry down to the stables or wherever John Brock might be found. Eileen threatened daily to tell Yolande's fond mama.

Even I wondered uneasily if it might be best, for the secret little romance did not seem to be dying on the vine as I had blithely predicted. I myself had seen John with Yolande, driving through the town, ostensibly on some errand or other, all perfectly respectable. But the look in the man's eyes as he gazed at his pretty little passenger said enough to be disturbing. Was it possible that Mr. Brock was letting himself be drawn to the unobtainable?

With sudden bitterness I told myself that I was hardly the one to cast stones, since I could so little control my own heart. Even now, sitting far down the table from Charles Marchand, I trembled at his presence as if there was none other in the room with us. Once he met my eyes—so tenderly! It warmed me—frightened me—because of the intensity of my own inner response. Something leaped wildly in my heart, a longing I was wholly unprepared for, something I had never experienced before, bittersweet and aching.

My little compliment to Yolande seemed to spur Lily on to greater conversational efforts. Throughout the rest of the meal she endlessly praised the families who would be coming up to Southfork for the season, speaking of the Mellons and Fricks with a warm familiarity as if she were quite close to them.

Since I knew this to be untrue, my brief spasm of compassion soon died, and I wished that the woman would have sense enough to curb her tongue. It was a relief to rise with Joanna and the other women and leave the room. I did not follow them into the parlor, however, but went upstairs to check upon Mrs. Pinkham and Rebecca.

I found Mrs. Pinkham had left her bed and was again in attendance upon the youngster, who was clinging to the elderly woman as if she had missed her. It was touching to see Rebecca's awkward, patting embraces of Mrs. Pinkham, and her repeated offerings of picture books and other treasures.

"I think you should have rested longer, Mrs. Pinkham," I said severely. "You are scacely well enough to begin work again."

"I'm fine," she said. "I want to be back at my duties, and I am sure Lena and Marie are needed elsewhere."

"One of the girls will sleep here in Rebecca's room each night," I told her. "I think it best."

She nodded somberly, pausing to make some admiring remark to Rebecca, who had brought the kitten and put it in Mrs. Pinkham's lap. The beautiful little cat curled itself into a contented ball and purred throbbingly. Rebecca put her ear on the little animal's body, grinning with delight.

"You are right, but I will take that duty, Katherine," Mrs. Pinkham said. "It is my responsibility. And I assure you that neither Rebecca nor I shall drink or eat anything that hasn't been made by my own hands or yours or one of the maids."

"I don't mind staying with Becky," Lena remarked. She was doing a bit of tidying in the room, hanging up garments that Rebecca had flung about.

"I know you don't dear, and it's very good of you, but I feel it is my place." Mrs. Pinkham was firm on the subject.

When I left, Rebecca had taken the kitten back and was rolling a ball for it to pursue, roaring with hoarse laughter as it cavorted gracefully about. I noticed that the window had been fitted with bars. Ugly as they were, I was glad of them.

Thoughtfully I went along the hall and started down the stairs. I met Charles coming up. He smiled at sight of me.

"Ah," he said softly. "I hoped I might find you. I must talk to you."

Hating the furtiveness of my own involuntary gesture, I glanced about. "I mustn't be seen with you," I said softly.

"The women are all in the parlor. I left Horace and Joshua arguing politics. They think I went to speak with John Brock."

"Nevertheless—"

"Only for a few minutes," he begged. "It's important. I promise you I shall say nothing—prsonal. Where can we talk undisturbed?"

"I'm sure this is unwise, Mr. Marchand."

"Charles, Katherine. Let me hear you say it." His low, vibrant words touched me as surely as if he had reached his fingertips to my face.

"No. I am not—"

"Say it!" he insisted, with that wicked, devil-may-care amusement on his face.

Nervous of being discovered here, I gave in. "Charles," I breathed, and was unprepared for the look in his eyes. I found myself trembling, and clasped my hands tightly.

He cleared his throat. "I have it," he said. "Let us go up to Rebecca's attic. I have not seen it, after all. I shall kecp you for only a few minutes, I promise.''

And so, knowing the folly of it, I went with him, praying like any miscreant that we should not be observed. After all, I told myself unconvincingly, we had no purpose in mind that was in the least improper, merely a few words of discussion.

But I knew even as I reassured myself, that the compelling emotion that pulsed between us was reason enough why we should not be together, alone, anywhere.

However, Charles was true to his word. When we had closed the attic door behind us and he had lighted lamps to banish the shadows of the big room created for Rebecca, he gestured me to a seat and took one nearby.

''I want your opinion of something,'' he began.

''Certainly. If I have one, and if it is worth anything.''

''Your opinion is worth more than a king's ransom to me,'' he said, so tenderly that I interrupted with haste.

''What do you want to know?''

''Why did Rebecca go out upon that ledge?''

''I thought everyone was agreed that she is so woolyminded that she might do any foolish or dangerous thing!'' I said rather bitterly.

''Sometimes it is best to seem to agree with the opinion of the majority,'' he said.

''All right,'' I sighed. ''I will tell you what I have been imagining. But you won't like it, and I have no proof of any kind, of course.''

''Tell me.''

.I hesitated, groping for words. ''I think—someone drugged Mrs. Pinkham with the morphine preparation we found in her room. Then that person entered Rebecca's chamber very early in the morning and woke your daughter. I think that he or she then took Rebecca's doll, and threw it out upon the ledge to entice the child out the window. And I think if Rebecca had not gone of her own accord, she would have been pushed out, with much worse results. As it was, with Rebecca clinging to the ledge, the assumption must have been that shortly she would fall. But it gave the intruder time to be safely away from the scene.''

''I—'' It was impossible to go on. How could I accuse

Sidney to his father, with no reason except the feeling that only the boy had been made so miserable by his sister's existence that he might have plotted her harm?

"Come, Katherine," Charles said impatiently. "You must have some suspicion!"

"No," I lied calmly. "I cannot imagine anyone in the household deliberately attempting to lure poor Rebecca to a cruel death. Yet, I still firmly believe that murder *was* attempted!"

"What is this you say about Mrs. Pinkham being drugged? I know that she took too much of the Fahrney syrup, the night before the mishap."

"She did not knowingly do so," I interrupted eagerly. "She says she has never taken any such preparation—in fact would never have purchased the stuff for any reason."

"I myself saw the bottle in her room," he said.

"She says it was not hers, and that she has no knowledge of how it could have gotten there. I think she is telling the truth."

But I was not at all sure Charles believed me. "If Mrs. Pinkham lied," I asked, "why did she not tell you or Mrs. Marchand this tale? What good would it do her to disclaim responsibility only to me? I did not hire her, nor pay her wages, nor have the power to dismiss her."

He nodded acceptance of my argument, and I felt encouraged. "I shall discuss it with her," he said.

"I think I must go now, Mr.—Charles," I said. "It isn't wise for my absence and yours to be remarked upon. And the longer we wait, the more likely it is that someone will be about on the second floor when we go down."

He had to agree with me. "You go first, Katherine. Go down the back stair."

He must have seen the distress I felt at such clandestine sneaking about, for he touched my hand lightly.

"Please forgive me, my dear. I know it goes against your principles to be secretive. I can only say that I had to see you—talk to you. And it does seem necessary at this point to quell certain vicious speculation. I cannot even pause in the hallway to give you greeting now without someone twisting it into a—rendezvous!" He smiled crookedly.

246

"Would that it could be! Yet, I would not do that to you. I know it is not possible for me to—follow my heart where you are concerned."

"Charles, you have a beautiful wife. She is surely all any man could wish for!" I said desperately.

"Appearances can be deceiving," was his only reply. Then he led me to the door and let me out, whispering that he would wait here for fifteen or twenty minutes before going down.

Heart pounding, feeling like a thief, I made my way downstairs without mishap, and went to my own rooms. Only when I closed my own door behind me did I feel the painful tension in my chest dissolve, and I again made the resolution that I would not be alone with Charles Marchand in future. I was not made for secret meetings and hiding from prying eyes.

I suppose it was only the disruption of my nerves that made me fall across my bed in tears.

Chapter Twenty-six

I do not know what occurred when Joshua Galbraith had his final meeting with Joanna, but I realized he had indeed ended their relationship, for Johanna's behavior altered radically.

She at first secluded herself in her room for two days, and I wondered if she had become ill. After that she emerged to walk restlessly about the house, silent and abstracted, her lovely face still and white. I knew that she was suffering, and I longed to help her. But there was nothing I could do. The very sight of me must have been a painful reminder, and I could only wish with all my heart that I had never known about Mrs. Marchand and Joshua Galbraith.

Joshua came no more to the house. I found I missed his impromptu visits. He had been my first friend in Johnstown. His advice had been sound and heartening. Even though I could not condone all that had taken place between he and Joanna, I had not lost my respect for him, nor my concern.

I half expected Joanna to call me to her and treat me to a tongue-lashing. At the very least I felt that her manner toward me would be one of cold dislike. Once again I found I had misjudged her, for after a time of silent absorption that no one, not even young Sidney, seemed able to penetrate, she appeared to achieve a firm grip upon her emotions. And toward me she became kinder than in prior weeks.

It had the effect of making me feel very guilty, although I told myself that my involvement in the distressing situation was nothing but the worst possible bad luck. I felt that I had escaped a just punishment by the leniency of my judge, and my gratitude was tinged with uneasiness and a longing to atone.

She came to me in my sitting room on a dank, wet afternoon, tapping at the open door and entering with a smile. I glanced up from a petticoat I was mending. I suppose I started at sight of her, expecting trouble.

"May I come in, Katherine?" she asked.

"Why—certainly, Mrs. Marchand." Awkward with surprise, I stood and made as if to put away my sewing.

"No, please, do go on with what you are doing. How industrious you are! I quite envy you your boundless energy."

She sank gracefully onto the sofa. She was dressed today in lustrous flowered silk, and her long pale hair was brushed down her back, tied back with a pink ribbon. I was glad to see that she was looking more herself. For days after Joshua's renunciation she had seemed a decade older, with all her lightness of spirit and laughter vanished.

Nor was she quite returned to normal, as yet. There were new lines visible at the corners of her round blue eyes, and at the sides of her mouth. She used some of the old, extravagant gestures, but her hands were clenched whenever they lay at rest.

"Sit down, do, Katherine!" she protested with a little laugh. "And pray do not look at me so—so sorrowfully. I see that you know there has been an—upheaval in my life, but I assure you that I shall survive.

"I am—I wish I could tell you how sorry I am that . . . "
I came to an uncertain, embarrassed stop. How could I say it, after all? I'm so sorry that your illicit love affair has come to an end, but I am sure it is all for the best, when all is said and done.

She came to my rescue. "I know that you are sorry, Katherine dear, and I imagine that you are foolishly blaming yourself that my arrangement with Joshua Galbraith is a thing of the past, simply because you happened to see us together that day."

I was amazed at her candor, but much relieved. This was the first time that fateful and distressing day had been mentioned between us. Perhaps now I could explain how dismaying it had been for me, and that I did not presume to judge her, nor Mr. Galbraith.

"I hope you know that I—I would never wish to pry into your private—matters, Mrs. Marchand," I said earnestly. "What happened that day upset me, too."

"What, no deep, dark joy that you had stumbled onto such a tasty morsel of gossip?" she laughed.

I shook my head hard. "There has been no gossip that I am aware of, and if there had been, it would not have issued from me. You have my word."

"Don't look so solemn, I believe you. Forgive my teasing. You must admit that most women would have delighted in such a revelation of another's shortcomings!"

"Even when it could only bring hurt to everyone involved? I hope I am never prepared to sacrifice the peace of mind of another for a moment's sensation."

Her small face became almost querulous. "How very tiresomely upright you are! You cannot but cause an ordinary mortal to feel inadequate!"

I opened my mouth to protest that I had not meant it that way, and certainly had no wish to seem sanctimonious, but she waved me to silence. "No, no. Let us not argue. I came to tell you that I bear you no ill will. Probably I am fortunate that you were the witness, instead of—some other."

I knew she referred to her husband. I kept silent, waiting for whatever she wanted to say. I was puzzled by this visit. Something about it did not ring true. But perhaps that was only because we felt uneasy with one another, after all that had happened.

She seemed to read my thought. She leaned forward and took my hand warmly between hers. "We have had our misunderstandings, Katherine, but I think it is time the breach was mended. I was, I confess it now, very angry when you took it in your head to let Rebecca out in public, and poor Sidney was so distressed. But I see now that, though misguided, you meant well. And it *was* through your quick action that Rebecca was saved." She shuddered delicately. "Come," she said with a courageous attempt at lightness. "Let us be friends. Bygones must be bygones. We have both made mistakes. If you will not judge me for mine, I will gladly forgive yours!"

"Yes of course," I said. "I know that things will be

better for you in future!'' I said impulsively.

"*Do* you know that?'' she smiled with faint bitterness, then seemed to shake it off with determination. She rose with a fluid motion. ''I wonder if anyone has told you about the Memorial Day Parade next Thursday? I should like you to join Sidney and myself, and Charles as well, if he is home. John Brock will take us all in the carriage.''

''Why, thank you, Mrs. Marchand. I shall be delighted, of course.''

''Then stop calling me Mrs. Marchand!'' she mocked gaily.

''Very well, Joanna. Thank you.''

''And I want you to come shopping with me this very afternoon. As soon as you can pin your hat on.''

I protested that I had planned to do some cleaning, but she was insistent. It was so good to see her laughing again that even if it were only the simulation of happiness, I did not want to mar it. So I changed into my newest skirt and a white, lace-trimmed blouse, put on my hat and a shawl, and off we went to town.

Even now I look back on that afternoon as one of unexpected pleasure. Joanna in this mood was excellent company. She kept even shy John Brock smiling on the way to the business district, and when we alighted on Main Street, she led me in and out of stores for two hours. She was careless of money, spending recklessly on anything that caught her fancy. I suspected that some of her purchases were unwise and would prove unusable. She bought cheap silk petticoats along with fine, embroidered muslin underwear, sleazy striped taffeta, and expensive velvet, without discrimination as to quality.

Her extravagance did cause me some anxiety, yet I could not remain disapproving in the face of her childlike display of excitement over every novelty she encountered.

Nor could I dissuade her from buying me a dress. It was elaborately fashioned of lace and crimsom satin, and I felt it was far more suited to her way of life than mine. But when I protested that I should have no occasion to wear such a garment, she was undeterred, thrusting it into the clerk's hands with an order to wrap it up.

"But of course you shall wear it, Katherine! Perhaps I shall give a soiree, myself, and we shall even invite some of the prestigious people Lily is forever eulogizing. Charles is well acquainted with that set. We shall see for ourselves how close our Lily's friendship is with Andrew Carnegie."

There was only one unpleasant moment in that afternoon. This occurred as we were placing our packages in the buggy, in preparation to go home. I caught a glimpse of Joshua Galbraith, striding along the street. He saw us too, but did not seem pleased. He turned abruptly into a tobacconist's shop, but not before Joanna had seen him.

"Joshua!" she called out, quite shrilly, so that to my embarrassment, passersby looked around.

Joshua did not look back, nor stop. His broad, blue-suited back disappeared into the shop. Joanna stood for a frozen moment with one hand upraised, staring after him, Then she turned her head stiffly and stepped into the buggy. I followed, and John clucked to the horse, even as he gave me a puzzled glance. I knew he was wondering why Mr. Galbraith had so rudely snubbed Mrs. Marchand. There was no way John could know that the attorney could not bear to come face-to-face with the lovely woman he adored and had given up.

Stricken, and aching with pity for Joanna, I sat biting my lip. She, however, lifted her chin proudly and began to chatter about the Saturday night band concerts in the park, and how pleasant it was to have arc streetlights on Main and Franklin, and how she expected that one day the entire city would be lighted at night.

I tried to match her nonchalance. But I knew that the day had been spoiled for Joanna. She had not yet forgotten Joshua. I wondered if she ever would.

It was even more certain of her continuing infatuation with him when I overheard Joanna speaking into the telephone that evening. I was reading, with my sitting-room door open, in the quiet hour before dressing for dinner. At first I thought Mrs. Marchand was arguing with someone who had arrived at the door.

"—I know he's there!" she cried almost hysterically. "I spoke with his landlady, and she said he was returning to his office. He has given you instructions not to put me through, don't you dare lie to me! I demand that you call him to the phone."

There was a brief silence, and then further vituperations for Joshua's hapless secretary, and I rose and gently closed my door.

It was a good thing that Charles was absent from home again, I reflected. He would surely see that something was badly amiss with Joanna if he were here.

How I pitied her. She had no one to turn to. She must feel totally abandoned now, without even the solace of a lover's affection to compensate for her husband's neglect.

I wondered how she could continue to love Charles? But I was convinced that she did, desperately, and if he had been the husband she needed, she would never have become involved with another man. So I reasoned, with my limited experience.

It was quite clear to me that Charles was to blame for most of this sad entanglement. And yet—I also loved him, God help me! I admitted to myself for the first time, and it was like biting down with bitter, inverted satisfaction upon a swollen wisdom tooth. My misplaced adoration of Charles Marchand was more to be scorned than Joanna's! At least she had a legal and moral right to his love and loyalty.

Feeling very depressed and discouraged, I made a light supper for myself, and prepared to retire early.

I was brushing my hair when Eileen came in. I saw at once that something was bothering her mightily. Inwardly I sighed. I was in no mood to hear about Yolande's latest sly trip to the library—by way of the stable.

But I had guessed wrong this time. It was not John Brock on Eileen's mind, but her sister Laura, in Pittsburgh.

"Her husband has been killed in an accident at the mill where he worked, and him not a day over twenty-five!" Eileen said tearfully, unfolding a letter to show me. "Sure, and dear Laura is expecting her third babe any day now, and the shock has been too much for her. She wasn't even able to send for me. 'Twas her neighbor, Mrs. Bronowski, who was kind enough to write. But I hate to go and leave you, Katy!"

"What nonsense!" I said, hugging her. "Laura needs you much more than I do just now. Things are in much better condition here. I can manage quite easily with Lena and Marie's help."

"Tisn't the work I'm worried about," Eileen sniffled into a wet handkerchief. "I know you refuse to take it seriously, but there's been so many strange things goin' on in this house that I fear for you."

"But we have seen that it is not I, but Rebecca, who is in danger, and we have set a watch over her," I reminded gently.

She snorted and frowned at me. "An' have you forgotten about the fire set in your own sittin' room, and you thought to be asleep, and easily burned in your bed? And the time somebody locked you in the attic?" she cried.

I sighed. "Of course I haven't fortotten. But you know I will be very cautious. I'll even have one of the girls sleep in here if it will make you feel better."

She brightened at once. "Would you, Katy dear? I'd feel ever so much easier in me mind if you will do that. Only, make sure 'tis Lena. Marie would snore through Armageddon, I do believe!"

I smiled. "Whatever you say. Now then, go and pack your grip and be ready to leave on the first train in the morning. And give your sister my best. I am sure with you to help her through this, she will be fine, and her baby as well. She couldn't have a better nurse, or a more staunch helper. I know that well."

Eileen burst into loud sobs at the praise, and with her apron over her face, rushed from the room.

I saw her off, tearfully, I must admit, in the early dawn of another cold, rainy day. There was even some frost along the swollen river's grassy banks, and standing in the shivery air, I wondered pessimistically if we were ever to have a proper summer this year!

It was Wednesday, I remember, the twenty-ninth day of May, but still the winter cold and the almost unceasing rains held sway. It was difficult to be cheerful, in such weather.

Sighing, I turned back into the house, knowing I would miss Eileen. What was needed, I decided over my morning tea, was a good, hard job of work. There were several chores still to be done in the renovation of the house. I wanted, for instance, to examine and clean out the cellars. Not, however, on a dark day like this! There were still the flower beds to be dug out and cleared of weeds. That would have to wait until better weather as well. And there were a few rooms on the second and third floor that would benefit by new wallpaper and paint. But that hardly seemed worth the expense, since no one was likely to be using them soon, and with Mrs. DeWitt's will still being argued in court, it would be foolish to expend more effort in that direction.

Still, I longed to sweep and scrub and dust away the doldrums. All at once I knew what I would tackle. We had never done the apartment that had belonged to Bertha DeWitt. No one wanted the suite, and so we had not as yet taken time to put away her belongings and thoroughly clean the rooms.

As I finished my breakfast, I made up my mind that I would begin that job. The maids would cheerfully help, but I wanted to be alone, to work and think and try to sort out my uncertainties. I gathered up a broom, mop, and pail of hot water, and went up to Bertha's rooms.

They were musty, cold and dark. The drapes had not been opened in weeks. This was my first action, although the watery gray light was not especially cheering. On second thought I climbed upon a chair and took them down entirely, rolling them into a bundle to be laundered. The dust was thick upon the wine, damask cloth.

I tied cloth about my hair and began to sweep down cobwebs. Then I busied myself folding Bertha's clothing into a large trunk, with fond thoughts of the elderly lady who had worn them.

Very few of the garments were of a style more recent than ten years past. Apparently in her last years, the old lady had been satisfied with dresses that were familiar and comfortable.

I folded away a dark flannel robe that I recognized, one Mrs. DeWitt had worn at the Home. It brought back the kind, aging face, beautiful with its accumulation of experience and wisdom. I remembered how desperately she had longed to come home, and how elated I felt then at being able to help grant that wish for her. But had it been a kindness, after all? If the talk I had been hearing was true, even here she had been at the mercy of some cruel hand. Still fingering the soft flannel of the robe, I sighed.

"I'm sorry if I did wrong to help you come home," I whispered.

A sudden jarring thump behind made me jerk around in fright. A book I had noticed earlier slid off the small desk by the far wall. It was a volume of Whitman's *Leaves of Grass,* and it lay open upon its back. What had made it fall?

I found myself crouching over the open trunk, staring at the fallen book, and—listening!

It was not rational, and I don't know exactly what I expected to hear, but I was in the grip of a compulsion. It was as if someone had called my name from a distance, and I must now concentrate with every one of my senses to hear what was being said to me.

Of course, I heard nothing at all, and after a long moment, knees trembling, I stood and moved to pick up the book. When I did so, a paper fell from it. I bent to retrieve it from the carpet. It was a carelessly folded sheet of stationery.

I almost threw it away without unfolding it. What instinct stopped me I cannot say, only that in the very act of tossing the paper into a wastepaper basket, I felt a frightening sensation all about me as if static electricity was lifting the hair at the base of my skull—tingling urgently along my arms and hands.

And I knew, quite simply, that I must examine this missive.

Chapter Twenty-seven

I opened the paper and held it to the uncertain, cloudy light at a window. It was a letter, but unfinished. I knew I should not read it, yet was sure in some unexplainable way that I must, even when I saw that it was meant for Charles Marchand.

> My Dear Nephew:
>
> It causes me great distress to be the bearer of what I must tell you. I hope you will believe I mean it for the best for all concerned, and it is written with the prayer that something you can say or do will mend a very sad and unsavory situation.
>
> I realize that I may be accused by some of being foolish and old-fashioned. Perhaps I do not see things in as broad a light as I ought. But I cannot countenance the things that have been taking place under my very roof—

Provokingly, it ended there. I stared at the note, perplexed. There was no doubt in my mind that it had been written by Bertha DeWitt, although this handwriting was better than the uncertain scrawl her stroke had left with her. It was dated March first of this year.

I wondered what I should do with the letter? Should I throw it away? Yes, for what good was it to anyone now, written almost three months ago, and never finished. And yet—?

It was not mine to destroy. Perhaps the best thing would be to give it to Charles, for whom it had been intended. When he returned, I must find an opportunity to pass it on to him.

I thrust it into my skirt pocket and went on about my work. But it kept sliding back into my thoughts. Why had it been in the book that fell—had Bertha been using it as a bookmark? It hardly seemed possible, because the content of the letter was of such a private nature that one would be unlikely to leave it lying about. I wondered if there had been another, a completed copy that had been sent on to Charles. And what had Bertha meant by a 'sad and unsavory' problem? Could it, just possibly, have something to do with Bertha's death?

My hands stilled in the act of packing away a winter cloak, cut in a long-obsolete style. The question echoed urgently in my mind. But of course there was no answer for it, none at all.

I skipped lunch in order to finish cleaning Bertha's suite of rooms, and when I went down, I found Lena looking for me with a worried look on her long face.

"Oh, Miss Katy, there you are! I was beginning to get anxious. Eileen told me to keep an eye on you, and I couldn't find you anywhere."

I explained what I had been doing, and received meekly the inevitable reproaches for not having allowed the maids to help.

"I needed a good, hard morning's work," I said, and she nodded understandingly.

"It does do wonders for the megrims, don't it, Miss Katy?"

I remembered that I had promised to have Lena sleep in Eileen's daybed in my sitting room, and I asked if she had any objections.

"It's not that I am nervous," I assured her, "but I did say I would allow someone to stand guard over me, and I dread to break a promise to Eileen."

"I'd be *scared* to break a promise to Eileen!" Lena exclaimed. "I'll be glad to move into your sitting room. It pays to be safe rather than sorry, I always say."

That settled, she took my cleaning equipment and told me to have a good lunch and then to rest. She sounded so much like Eileen that I felt cheered and comforted, and obeyed her to the letter.

After lunch I mended a rip in a blouse, then lay down for a short nap. Rain spattered sharply on my windows.

Sighing, I made a fervent wish for sunshine and bright days that I could spend out-of-doors among the flower beds. The mental choice of seeds that I would like to plant occupied my mind pleasantly until I fell asleep.

It was after four when I woke. My room seemed very cold and the whole house dark and lonely. I wished for Eileen's cheerful, scolding monologues. Or even her daily complaints about Yolande!

Rising, I went to build a fire in my range and heated water for bathing and a bracing cup of tea. Later, dressed in one of the warmest dresses, my hair wound up neatly into a chignon, I went out to look for human company.

The house was very quiet. I wondered if Charles had yet returned from Pittsburgh. He had gone there to speak with the owners of the Southfork Fishing and Hunting Club about the condition of the dam. I had no idea of the expected date of his return.

Restlessly I walked through the lower rooms of the house—all were empty. Suddenly I felt that this would never be a happy dwelling. It was a handsome house, but now it was too much like my own life, full of empty, echoing and joyless rooms, where there should have been light and laughter.

Impulsively I stepped into the study, hoping shamelessly to find Charles there, to kindle that wicked, amused sparkle in his eyes, to hear his outrageous, provoking remarks, to argue spiritedly—

The room was dark, and as someone stirred in the high-backed leather chair by the hearth, I thought for a glad moment that Charles indeed waited there.

But the figure that stood and stared across the room at me was not Charles, but his son, Sidney.

Swallowing disappointment, I spoke lightly. "Why, Sidney, I thought no one was in here. I seem always to be disturbing you!"

"No ma'am," he said politely.

"It's getting quite dark, isn't it?"

He made no answer as I lighted the gas chandelier and the room flared into comfortable brightness. "I think I shall make a nice fire, too, don't you think? I have never seen it so very cold for this time of year. Why, we are almost into June.''

"I can do that,'' he offered, and got down on his knees to lay kindling on the hearth, doing the job with meticulous concentration. Soon flames were leaping in the pine logs, and I drew a chair gratefully nearer to the fire.

"You do that very well,'' I said, and Sidney flushed with pleasure. With the dignity of a young prince he sat down again in the big leather chair. What a handsome child he was. He had inherited his mother's delicate beauty, and his glance was intelligent and probing.

"How is school, Sidney?'' I asked.

"All right, I guess. We are let out for tomorrow,'' he said.

"Tomorrow? Oh yes, Memorial Day! There will be a parade, I am told. That will be fun, won't it?''

He shrugged with such a lack of normal, childlike enthusiasm for a holiday, that I felt rebuffed. The boy's eyes clung moodily to the glow of the fire, as if I were no longer in the room. It was difficult to know how to converse with this boy. One could not think of him as an adult, yet there was so little of childhood about him that one scarcely knew what approach to use.

A sudden impulse, perhaps unwise, took hold of me. Had anyone asked this boy what he might know of the day Rebecca had been found clinging outside her window?

"Sidney,'' I began carefully, "do you remember the day we spoke of Rebecca, and how you feel about her?''

"Yes ma'am.'' The reply was indifferent.

"Did you know that she came very close to falling from the third-story ledge a few days ago?''

His eyes darted swiftly to meet mine, and I was reminded of a wary, cornered little animal, ready to spring in any direction to safety—or to attack.

"Everybody knows that,'' he said with scorn.

"What would you have felt—if she had fallen?'' I dared to ask.

He stared at me in silence for such a long time that I wondered if he had heard me at all. At last he stirred. A shadow of some distasteful emotion passed over his face.

"I don't know, exactly."

"But—you would be sorry if she were hurt, of course," I prompted.

"Yes. No—yes, of course I would, but—" he stopped as if in confusion, then tried again. "She—she can't ever be well, can she?"

"No, but she has a right to enjoy what life she is able to have, don't you think?"

He shrugged, and I felt he was losing interest in the conversation. "I guess so. As long—" He stood and put both hands in his pockets in what seemed a defiant gesture.

"As long as as what, Sidney?"

'As long as she leaves me alone!" he said sharply. "I've got to go now." He was already in motion as he announced this, and had run from the room and shut the door before I could say anything more to him.

Something icy coiled in my chest. Had he meant his statement to be as threatening as it had sounded?

From sheer loneliness I went in to the family dining room at the usual dinner hour. I might as well have stayed in my rooms. Only Sidney appeared, to bolt his dinner in silence and disappear again. The DeWitts were dining out. Joanna did not come down. I wished that I dared to go up and talk to her. She had come in from somewhere just before dinner, exquisitely dressed in a matching skirt and long jacket of blue silesian cotton with a satin ruffled collar. Her designer hat was straw and lace in a deeper shade of blue, with a bird's wing at one side of the crown. She looked, as always, exquisite, golden hair gleaming in puffs and ringlets under the charming hat. But her face was set and cold. I wondered if she had tried to see Joshua Galbraith, and been refused.

Perhaps it was illogical of me, but I questioned whether it was necessary for Mr. Galbraith to be so cruelly final about the parting. She had depended upon him for a long time, and now she had no one.

After dinner, I wandered into the kitchen, and in that more comfortable atmosphere, some of my tension and loneliness eased. I enjoyed the maids' chatter with dour Mrs. Potter as they washed dishes. I took up a tea towel to help. They all tried to include me in their conversation, even as I made an effort to join in naturally. But my mind was too full of unanswered questions and anxieties. I was poor company, at best.

At last I excused myself, saying I wanted to get to bed early.

"Sleep late tomorrow, Miss Katy, it's a holiday!" Mrs. Potter said kindly.

"I'll be in later," Lena promised, and I was glad of her words, for the uneasy atmosphere of the house was beginning to work upon my nerves in an unpleasant way. I was not half so contemptuous, now that darkness had fallen, of Eileen's insistence that Lena take her place.

But there was no disturbance that night, and my lack of sleep could only be attributed to the uncertainties roiling about in my mind. It must have been very near dawn when I fell into an exhausted slumber.

Sunlight woke me—the first I had seen for days. But I had scarcely gotten up from my bed and washed my face in the cold water that had stood the night in my china pitcher, when clouds rolled in from the southeast. The light became fitful and threatening, and I sighed. Another rainy day! *When* would the weather give us some respite?

I dressed warmly and went to build a fire. Lena had already left my apartment and gone about her duties. It was she who came in excitedly about nine o'clock and gave me the startling news.

I was pressing my green merino traveling dress to be worn later at the Memorial Day parade. It would be far too cold to wear the lilac Eileen had made for me. Lena burst into the kitchen, freckled face alight with unusual amusement.

"Miss Katy, you'll never guess!"

"Why, what has happened?"

"There's such an uproar, I wonder you didn't hear it."

"I did hear Mrs. DeWitt's voice a bit earlier, but I thought nothing of it."

"Oh, she's fit to be tied, she is!"

"What have I done now? I asked, only half joking.

262

Lena grinned and leaned closer. "You have encouraged her precious Yolande in an infatuation with a common hired man, namely Johnny Brock, and they've run off together!"

"What?" In my astonishment I forgot the iron resting on my green skirt. Lena smelled the incipient scorch and swiftly snatched the iron away and placed it upon the stove. I stood staring at her as she explained what had been happening that morning.

"You know how them pampered DeWitts almost always stay abed until near noon. But today Mrs. DeWitt was up early, worrying about which fancy mourning dress her darling lamb should wear to view the parade. It must be the *perfect* one, you know how she is! So she went into Yolande's room at eight, expecting to find her dear daughter tucked in her bed. But the bird had flown, bag and baggage. Except she'd left all her black feathers and finery behind." Lena giggled, and I had to restrain a smile myself at the image of Yolande kicking over the traces with this symbolic gesture, breaking free of the black draperies her mama thought so provocative to eligible bachelors.

But sobriety returned at once. "That poor, silly child!" I exclaimed. "Whatever will become of her? John Brock had had nothing, only his position here, and now that is lost to him."

Lena shrugged, obviously unconcerned about the welfare of Yolande. "She's made her bed," she said.

"Yes. Well, I suppose there's nothing to be done about it now. I never would have believed that John Brock would be so reckless! And what can Yolande have been thinking of? She has been used to every luxury, all her life."

"I expect she will learn her mistake before very long," Lena said comfortably.

One could scarcely blame Lena for her satisfaction at Yolande DeWitt's downfall. The young girl had been as condescending to the servants as possible, acting as if they were not humans at all, but faceless mechanical contrivances placed here for her convenience and comfort. She scarcely ever deigned to notice one of the maids, unless she fancied some chore had been left undone, and then her tongue was as sharp as her mother's. It made it even more difficult to understand her fascination with John Brock.

"Surely you were not serious in saying that Mrs. DeWitt blames me?"

The question was scacely out of my mouth before I had my answer, but not from Lena. Mrs. DeWitt herself came down the hall and into my kitchen like an elephant on a rampage. She was clothed in a girlish pink nightgown and negligee of sheerest chiffon. Her uncorseted bulk bounded about unpleasantly within the insecure confines of her night-clothes. Her graying hair was still up in curl papers, and there was evidence of some greasy preparation on her face. I knew that she must be in the ultimate throes of distraction, or she would never appear outside the privacy of her room in such a state. This thought was not reassuring, nor was the red glint in her eye. She advanced on me alarmingly, and even attempted to slap my face.

Forsaking dignity, I retreated. "Mrs. DeWitt!" I cried.

"You scheming strumpet!" she hissed. "You unmiti-gated bundle of wicked deceit! You Jezebel!"

"Please, Mrs. DeWitt," I begged, keeping the ironing table between us. "I have done nothing, truly. You must believe me! Lena has just this moment told me about Yo-lande. You have my most sincere sympathy, and I assure you—"

"You assure me? *You* assure me? I would as soon be-lieve a two-headed snake as trust one word from your mouth!"

My own temper got away from me. "I will not stand here and be insulted. You will either discuss this like a reasonable adult, or you will leave my rooms at once!" I thundered, somewhat surprising myself.

She seemed taken aback as well, for she stood with open mouth for a moment, and then, to my astonishment, burst into loud wails of grief.

Her sobs were gargantuan. But they were the most gen-uine expression I had ever heard from this silly, pretentious woman, and I felt suddenly moved to pity. I knew that she loved her daughter, and had harbored the greatest hopes for her. Now all was lost. To make matters worse, the cherished lamb was off somewhere, perhaps never to be found. I did not doubt that it was the most severe blow Lily DeWitt had ever faced.

I came round the ironing table and took her arm, leading her to a chair. "Come now, Mrs. DeWitt. Sit down and I'll pour you some tea."

Still sobbing as if her heart would break, Lily DeWitt obeyed me.

Chapter Twenty-eight

I caught a movement from the corner of my eye. It was Lena sidling toward the door, and some imp of mischief made me call out, "Oh, Lena, do help me make a nice breakfast for Mrs. DeWitt. I am sure she has not taken time to eat this morning."

The shake of the weeping woman's head could have been corroboration of my guess, or a refusal of my hospitality.

"You must keep up your strength," I told her firmly, and quickly brewed a fresh pot of tea as Lena, obviously gritting her teeth at being detained in the war zone, cracked eggs into an iron skillet. I buttered bread to toast on the oven's top rack, then poured tea and pressed the liberally-sugared brew into Mrs. DeWitt's hand. Still snuffling, she gulped at it. Encouraged, I found a clean tea towel and gently mopped her face. She endured my attention, drank more tea, and gradually ceased to cry.

Lena handed me a generously-filled plate, which I set before my guest with the injunction that she must not leave a bite.

"May I go now, Miss Katy?" Lena asked nervously.

I gave my permission. Hastily she left us.

Blowing her nose upon the napkin I handed her, Mrs. DeWitt attacked her breakfast. Don't think you've pulled the wool over my eyes!" she warned with a full mouth. "You'll never wheedle your way around me. Miss Meddlesome!"

"I have no such intention." I sank into the chair across the table from her. "But I beg you to believe that had I any inkling such an escapade was being planned by Mr. Brock I would have dismissed him at once. I understand your deep corcern for your daughter, and whether you believe me or not, I share it."

266

She glared at me with suspicion, but held out her cup for more tea. "Are you going to tell me you didn't know John Brock was cozying up to my little girl?" she demanded.

Fortunately, I had believed Yolande was the pursuer, and so I could truthfully shake my head. "I wouldn't have believed that he would be so foolish. Is it quite certain that they have gone away together?"

"There is no doubt," she said miserably. "The poor silly baby left a note saying that she loved the wretched man and was willing to give up all for him! I *cannot* believe it. My own child, carefully nurtured and prepared from birth for a fine marriage with some prosperous gentleman—"

She choked, whether on eggs or sorrow I could not tell. Quickly I intervened. "Did she say where they were going?" And does anyone know when they left, or how they traveled?"

"Pittsburgh, Yolande said in her note. John Brock intends to find work there. Oh!" she wailed, "my precious baby will be living in some dirty tenement, ruining her hands in dishwater."

The notion seemed to strike her speechless with ultimate horror. "And the time they left?" I prompted.

She shook her head and drank tea. "Sometime in the night. I suppose that they will have gone by train."

Perhaps they can be traced?" I said gently. "Yolande could be brought back. Cannot Mr. DeWitt attempt to catch up with them?"

"That helpless nothing of a man!" Purple rage rose in her quivering jowls. "He says there is nothing for it but to let them go, that she will beg to come home soon enough when she sees that that common—*hired* man cannot give her the things she is used to."

"He may be right," I ventured carefully.

"Doubtless he is right that my darling will beg her mama to come and save her!" shouted Lily. "But by then it will be too late, and her reputation—all the wonderful plans I have made for her—all, *all* will be ruined!"

"Well, if he will not go after her, why don't you do so, yourself?" I asked. "Perhaps in Pittsburgh you might hire a—detective, perhaps. I have read of the Pinkerton Agency with offices in New York and Philadelphia. You might wire them for help.''

She looked at me with dawning respect, a forkful of eggs halfway to her mouth. "You are right! Yes, of course." Hastily she rose and pushed back her chair. "Yes, yes. I shall go and dress at once. *I* shall bring my baby back, and I will have the law on that despoiler of innocent girls! I will see that he is locked away forever. I'll have the scoundrel hung!''

She was still breathing fire and threats as she left at a floor-shaking trot.

I felt a moment of remorse at having set her onto John Brock's trail. But she would have thought of it herself, soon, and it might very well be best for Yolande if she were prevented from consummating her folly.

Rather shaken by the encounter with the girl's maddened mama, I returned to pressing my skirt, wondering what else the day would have in store for us.

I was not certain that Joanna would remember her invitation to accompany the family to the parade. Charles was not yet home, so it would only be Joanna and Sidney, as the DeWitts were doubtless otherwise occupied. Lily seemed to be packing for her rescue mission. I resolved that if Joanna had forgotten, or was not feeling in the mood for the festivities, I would walk down into the town myself, or with the staff, to whom I had given the day off.

Only Mrs. Pinkham could not be spared, although I went up and asked if I might take her place for the afternoon while she enjoyed the parade.

"I've seen many and many such a celebration, my dear," she said. "And they are all the same. I'd much rather stay and finish the doll dress I am making for Rebecca."

"I wish that you could both come. How she would enjoy it!"

She nodded, sadly. "But it is out of the question, and we must accept that. Mrs. Marchand would never allow Rebecca out in the crowds."

And so I left her, cheerfully fitting a pink satin dress on Rebecca's baby doll, with the girl kneeling entranced at the older woman's knee.

268

As I descended the stairs, I heard Joanna calling me from below. "Ah, there you are! Are you ready? Yes, I see you are, and you look very nice indeed. But—" she tilted her head and smilingly studied me. I felt uncomfortable under scrutiny. But I found that it was kindly meant.

"I think you need a new hat!" she announced.

I winced. I knew that my old black Neopolitan braid was not in the latest style, but had hoped that it would pass. Surely not everyone would be as fashionably-attired as Joanna, in her lavender velvet gown, trimmed with a deep flounce of point-lace, and bordered by a band of sable fur. Her velvet toque was trimmed with two long ostrich plumes, satin rosettes and jeweled buckles. Her white gloves were of finest kid, and the gleaming black toes of her shoes were just visible under the sable-banded hem.

"Wait. I believe I know just the thing!" Like an excited child, she ran up the stairs. It was difficult to believe that this was the same woman whom I had seen come in last evening, rejected and defeated.

In moments she was back, holding a hatbox.

"Now," she laughed. "I see your pride girding up its loins for battle! But please don't be tiresome, Katherine. I have a hat I ordered from New York. It is just as lovely as I thought it would be, yet not quite right for me, somehow. I have never worn it, and I wish that you would do me the favor of at least trying it on. If you don't like it, you have only to say so, and I will not urge you to accept it. On the other hand, it is a small enough gesture of appreciation from me for all you have done to make us comfortable here!"

So, smilingly, she opened the hatbox and uncovered the creation within. It was, as promised, quite beautiful. No woman's heart could have gone untempted. Made of réséda-green straw, with a brim that turned up saucily over the left eye, it featured a delicious plume that followed the upper edge of the brim, and finely-worked jet passementerie around the softly-rounded crown. Providentially, it was a delicate shade that nicely complemented my old green merino dress.

Already ashamed of my longing, I allowed her to place

the hat on my piled-up hair. She muttered abstractedly to herself as she shifted it a bit, this way and that, and finally anchored it firmly in place with an expensive-looking jet hatpin.

"Now!" She stepped back. "Go and look at yourself in the parlor mirror."

I did so, and my downfall was complete. I think I would have entertained offers from Satan for the possession of that marvelous hat. I hope that I shall not appear hopelessly vain if I say that under that cleverly-designed, extravagant piece of millinery, I was suddenly a lady, a creature of elegance and poise. My eyes sparkled with sinful satisfaction, the wings of my upswept hair gleamed, and my chin had just that tiny bit of proud lift that removed me—like Cinderella—from the old status to the new.

Of course I knew that the clock would strike twelve, and the illusion would vanish like mist! But that was for later. For this moment, for an hour or two, I was the princess at the ball.

Joanna had followed me into the parlor, beaming. "That handbag is not right for the hat. I have one that you may borrow."

She brought it. My few belongings were transferred, and just like that, with a wave of Joanna's magic wand, I was impeccably dressed.

Even Sidney, bounding down the stairs and coming in search of his mother, widened his eyes in appreciation of the new Katherine.

"Why Miss Livingston, you look very pretty!" he blurted.

I thought just a tiny shadow passed over Joanna's face at her son's compliment. If so, it was gone in an instant. "And what of your mama, young man?" She pirouetted girlishly and curtseyed. I thought that she would have made a wonderful actress. I have never known anyone before or since who could compare with Joanna Marchand for perfection of face and form, for gracefulness of carriage and quicksilver charm of personality.

"You are beautiful, as always, mama," Sidney supplied.

Joanna laughed. "Well, then, shall we go? We shall have

to walk," she grimaced, "since Mr. Brock has chosen this time to desert his post. Well, never mind. But we had best take umbrellas, for it looks very threatening again."

I went to get my old one (rather regretting having to use it in close proximity with my new hat!) and the three of us left the house.

I thought the walk into the town pleasant, in spite of the dampness. It was not raining yet, and the nearer we came to Main Street the more people we saw, all converging upon the route. The celebration was to begin at two-thirty.

It was two when we found a place at the street edge, made for us by an admiring gentleman who tipped his derby first at Joanna and then at me.

"Why, Mr. Hopkins," Joanna trilled. "How nice to see you. Where are Mrs. Hopkins and young Gracie?"

"They will be coming soon," he said, flushing with pleasure that she remembered him and his family. "You know how it is with women, always some last minute prinking to do. I told them the crowd would begin gathering early, and I'd best come and hold a place for my women-folk."

"I do hope we have not taken their places!" Joanna exclaimed.

"Not at all," was the gallant reply. "There is room for all. Unless they delay much later," he amended. But at that moment the missing lady and her adolescent daughter arrived, and were suitably installed where they might have a good view, when the Grand Army veterans, the Odd Fellows and the Fire Department marched.

There was a considerable crowd, many more than I had thought possible. I had been told that within the ten boroughs of which Johnstown was the center, there were some thirty thousand souls. With the shouting and jostling multitude lining both sides of the flag-decorated street, it was not hard to believe that almost everyone had turned out for the parade!

I looked around with interest, infected by the gaiety of the people, particularly the children. After a few minutes, Sidney was encouraged by his mother to run and find his "little friends." The boy seemed more than eager to leave our company.

I saw Marie and Lena in the company of a burly fellow in painfully clean, working clothes. I wondered if he were a brother, or perhaps one of the girls had a beau. It was too bad, I smiled to myself, that Eileen was not in town. She would soon have had the answer to that interesting question.

There were many in the crowd who were immigrants. There was a knot of these folk nearby who seemed to be enjoying the occasion a good deal, even though the parade had not yet begun. Joanna glanced over at them and sniffed with audible displeasure. She nudged me in the ribs.

"Look at those Hungarians!" she hissed in my ear. "They should have to stand in a place reserved for them, away from decent folk!"

I did not agree with her, and was embarrassed by her remark. The little family consisted of a strong young father holding a fat, sleepy baby and a shy, wide-eyed wife firmly grasping two other young children. They were causing no one the least harm, and I felt that they had a right to enjoy the festivities as much as we.

This small unpleasantness, to which I had not the courage to respond, was overshadowed by what happened next.

Joanna grasped my arm, demanding attention. "Oh Katherine," she said sweetly, "I wonder if you would do a little favor for me?"

"Why yes, if I can," I replied absently, for the bass drums were beginning far up the street, and like everyone else I was craning my neck to see the start of the march.

"I have just realized that we are just in front of Mr. Galbraith's building. See, there he is at his office window. Please go up and invite him to come out and watch the parade with us."

She had my full attention now. I stared at her in dismay. Her bright smile did not alter in the least, nor her expression change, although she could not have missed the amazement I felt at her suggestion. It was as if she did not realize the enormity of what she was asking, as if the events of the past few days—Joshua's renunciation, and his determined avoidance of her—had vanished from her mind.

"Why—I can't do that!" I gasped. "You must know that he wouldn't wish—"

272

She interrupted as if I had not spoken. "Do hurry in and tell him we are out here, and unescorted. I am sure he will come down at once."

"Joanna, no! It would only embarrass him, and he would doubtless refuse me. Forgive me, but I simply cannot do it."

Her eyes flickered. How can I explain it? It was as if someone I had never met looked at me out of those round, innocent blue eyes, someone alien, and totally inimical.

"Oh," she laughed gaily, "I think you shall, Katherine my dear, or else I shall make a scene right here on the street, in front of all these people. I assure you, they will find it more exciting than an ordinary parade."

She smiled more widely as I took an instinctive step backward, and looked about for an avenue of escape.

"If you run, I shall scream that you have stolen my purse," she said fondly, even reasonably. "Oh, hello, Mrs. Dannette!" she broke off momentarily to wave and call to a lady a short distance away.

"Now then," she said, gripping my arm feverishly. "Do be a good girl, and go up and speak to Joshua. After all, it is a small favor I am asking of you!"

I shook my head helplessly. "Joanna, what are you thinking of? Do you really hear what you are saying?"

She unclenched her grasping fingers and gave my arm a little pat. "Do as I say, Katherine. Do you see that fat policeman over there? He is a special friend of mine, and he would—" she giggled with horrifying coquetry—"he would believe anything I told him, anything at all. If I say that you have stolen my purse, he won't hesitate to arrest you, no matter how much you protest. You will notice that I did not bring a handbag. You cannot deny that the one you are carrying *is* my property, now can you? And do not think you can simply ask Joshua to come to me, receive his refusal, and let it go at that. If you and Mr. Galbraith do not return in a very few minutes, I have other interesting stories I shall tell the police, and my husband, when he returns. Of course I should be most distressed to have to relate such ugly things about my—friends."

She smiled into my eyes brightly. The blood pulsed at my temples keeping time with the booming drums advancing along Main Street. I longed to run from the scene, but now I had no doubt that she would send the fat officer of the law pounding after me, and have me arrested.

Helplessly, I went to do her bidding, feeling her eyes upon my back with every step.

Chapter Twenty-nine

It was not difficult to predict Joshua Galbraith's reaction. I stood before him, trying to behave in a normal manner, and made my request. He stared at me as if I'd taken leave of my senses.

"Whose idea is this?" he barked.

"Why—" I tried to swallow the lump in my throat. "Mrs. Marchand suggested that you might like to join us."

"And you agreed to that?" he asked harshly. "You of all people must know what it has cost me to avoid contact with Joanna. Perhaps you don't realize that since I told her our relationship must end, she has hounded me by phone, has even come to this office, in spite of my continued refusal to see her. I don't know what's come over her. By all the gods, Katherine, she must stop it, or my reputation—and hers—will be totally destroyed! I never thought she was capable of this. You must see my position."

Miserably I nodded. "Yes, of course I do."

He ran his fingers through his crisply curling hair in agitation. "They why do you come to me with an idiotic request like this?"

The tears that had been forcing their way into my eyes in spite of all my efforts, spilled over. I turned away, but he had seen, and put his hands on my shoulders, spinning me around. "What did she do? What did she say to you, Katherine?"

I told him, wondering if he would believe such a tale. I should not have doubted him.

He gave a gusty sigh, shaking his head. "I didn't know her, Katherine," he muttered, releasing my shoulders. "I see now that I never knew her! I would never have believed that she would do such a thing. I thought her the gentlest of women."

I tried to find some excuse for Joanna. "Perhaps—she cares so much for you that she is driven to do things that she would not otherwise—"

He jerked his head up, meeting my eyes gravely. "I don't believe it. I may as well tell you that during the months when she and I were—closest, I knew deep in my soul that she did not really care for me. She—wanted me, and my attentions, yes. Almost greedily! But as for love—I loved *her*. God how I adored her, Katherine! But I guess I never really fooled myself that what she felt for me was love. And I do not believe it now, in spite of this embarrassing pursuit."

"She has seemed distraught these past days, desperate to communicate with you."

He shrugged grimly. "I have been a fool. Not that I ever doubted my stupidity, where Joanna was concerned. But I flattered myself that as an attorney and as a man I could read people better than that. It is my belief now that Joanna simply cannot tolerate any balking of her will. She believes I have rejected her, and she will not stand still for it. It is not love, Katherine, it is a kind of revenge. And, God help me, maybe I deserve it!"

"Whate will you do?" I asked.

He reached for his hat. "What can I do? She has involved you, and I cannot allow you to be distressed because of mistakes I have made, or because of the overweening pride of a woman I thought I loved. I shall let her have her way until I can find some way of persuading her that this is madness!"

"Then you will come down with me?"

He took my hand, gently. "Come, my dear. Don't look so upset. I promise you I'll find a way to protect you from Joanna's threats. But for now, I think she has us both backed into a corner."

When we emerged into the street we found that it had begun to rain, mistily, and that Joanna was waiting for us near the door. She met our eyes with a blazing smile that once I would have taken for innocent delight. Now I knew better. It was triumph, without a hint of compunction.

I tried to slip away, scarcely feeling the cold drops of rain on my face, nor did it occur to me to put up my umbrella.

Joanna caught my arm. "Oh now, stay, Katherine. I insist that you remain with us. You are my guarantee that Mr. Galbraith will not simply tip his hat to me and bid me a polite good day," she said, her voice low and gurgling with laughter.

"Please—" I began.

"Let her go, Joanna!" Joshua said. "She has nothing to do with us. Don't involve an innocent third party."

"Innocent?" Joanna's trilling laugh rang out. People near the curb, where the sound of band music was drawing tantalizingly nearer, turned curiously. I felt hot with embarrassment and despair.

"How protective you are of our Katherine!" Joanna said in a thoughtful tone. "Can it be that she is the reason you have been avoiding me, Joshua? Strange, I had not thought of that!" Her eyes flicked over me, and I felt foolishly frightened. Here we stood, three people in full view of hundreds, and I knew Joshua Galbraith would never allow Joanna to cause me any real harm. In fact he was already removing her clutching fingers from my arm. And yet a cold breath of terror moved over my spirit.

"Joanna, don't be foolish," he said gently. "You know that there is nothing between Katherine and me. She is not a part of this, and it is unkind to—"

"I do not know if you speak the truth about you and Katherine, and I do not care," Joanna whispered, her eyes suddenly filling, as if on cue. "But I promise you that if she does not stay right where she is, I will loudly accuse her of things she will never live down in this town!"

"All right, all right," Joshua replied placatingly. "She will stay, won't you, Katherine? It is just that I thought you would like to speak more privately."

Joanna put up her umbrella with a snap as the rain became a bit harder. "I have tried to reach you daily for a private talk, and you have evaded me at every turn," she said, too loudly for my comfort. Thank goodness for the brass band that was loudly playing a Sousa march, and for the cheering

277

of children as men in blue uniforms marched past. "I am sorry about that," Joshua said quietly. "Perhaps it was wrong of me. But this is neither the time nor the place—"

"It is the perfect time, cannot you see that?" she insisted. "What can be more innocent than three friends conversing on the street, watching the parade in each other's company?"

"All right," he gave in. "Say whatever you have to, Joanna."

Amazingly, she laughed, and I wondered how she could go from tearful helplessness to laughter and mockery almost in one breath. "I am glad to see that you cannot fight me, Joshua." She smoothed her glove with a satisfied gesture. "And I hope that Katherine has also learned that lesson. There are other matters I wish to discuss with her, and it is as well that she knows whom she deals with!"

I stared at her with a complete lack of comprehension, but she offered no explanation of her extraordinary statement. Instead she launched into a series of demands that Joshua must resume his visits to the house, and that she would expect him to show her every deference when and if she chose to visit his office, or ring him upon the telephone. He listened in helpless silence.

I stood in shock as she blatantly and explicitly demanded that every facet of their past relationship must be restored until the time that *she* saw fit to discontinue it.

"What about Charles?" he asked quietly, and I knew that he was trying to reason with her, giving her the most cogent reason why the affair should not continue. But I saw the growing distaste in his intelligent eyes, and I thought that he would be unable to give what she asked simply because with every word she was damaging his respect and his past love for her.

She shrugged. "What about him? What he does not know will not hurt him. And certainly none of us here will tell him, will we?" She gave me a smiling look. I could only gaze at her dumbly. Was she mad? Or was she, as Joshua had suggested, driven wild by pride and self-concern?

I do not know how much longer I could have endured my enforced participation in this unholy alliance, trying desperately not to let my face show the horror I was feeling.

Release came as someone shouted Joshua Galbraith's name. We turned, even Joanna, to see Charles come pushing urgently through the crowd, hatless, tie askew, with a day's unshaved stubble on his chin. As he reached us he took Joshua by the arm. "I'm glad I found you."

"When did you get back?" Joshua asked, and I saw the mixed relief and apprehension in his face. Surely Joanna would stop her cat-and-mouse game in the presence of her husband—or would she? How could one know, now, what might be in her thoughts or what incredible thing she might do?

However, she merely cooed a welcome to Charles, and reached up to kiss his cheek. Anyone in the crowd who happened to look away from the town band marching past would have thought it a touching scene. To me it was nauseating.

He suffered her embrace with an impatient glance, then turned to Joshua. "I have to talk to you."

"You talked to some of the Southfork Club members?"

"I tried to. The ones who would see me shrugged off the notion of any danger, and told me to talk to Colonel Unger."

"Did you see Pitcairn? As head of the Pittsburgh division of the railroad it seems to me he'd take an interest."

"He was in conference, or so I was told. I couldn't get in to see him. I think he knew why I was there, and didn't want to be bothered about the matter."

Charles seemed bitter and fatigued.

"I can't believe Robert Pitcairn would deliberately refuse to see you, Charles," Joshua protested. "I know he has a good deal of respect for you."

"I've considered him a friend. But none of them want to worry about the Southfork dam, Joshua! If we're right, and the infernal thing has a chance of failing, think of all the years they've ignored warnings!"

"I see your point. Come into my office, Charles. You look as if you could use a drink. Excuse us please, ladies." With a last unreadable glance at Joanna, Joshua led Charles into the building.

Abruptly thrusting Joanna's handbag into her hands, I rushed away from her into the crowd, my heart pounding as loud as the bass drum in the street.

Is it not odd that a personally devastating event can take place, and one will somehow expect the whole fabric of living to be changed, only to find that things stubbornly go along just as usual? Friendships may be crushed irrevocably—yet one will speak courteously to the estranged friend, hiding from him and from others the new enmity and distrust. Governments may fall, deaths and illness come to take away all one values most—yet one must brush one's teeth and meals must be served on time and coal fed into heating stoves.

So it was, that evening. I admit, I tried to hide in my room and avoid every member of the Marchand family. But Lena, flushed and excited from the fun of the day, brought me a message from Joshua that I was expected at dinner. I knew that between the lines of the innocuous little note he was saying appearances must be kept up, and a show of courage made, else the enemy had the battle by default.

Sighing, I put on the dress Eileen had made me, with the instinctive feeling that I needed now to look my best. When I lifted the lilac wool from the armoire, I touched the red satin ball gown Joanna had bought for me. The cold, smooth satin gave me an unpleasant sensation, and I thrust it roughly back behind my old, familiar garments. Already I had sent Marie up to Joanna's room with the borrowed hat I had so proudly worn today, and I felt a little better at having made that gesture. Yet it solved nothing.

I waited until the last minute to go in to dinner. Joshua was waiting for me, and he went with me into the dining room. Joanna, already seated, glanced up at us with a grin. I think I shuddered. Joshua patted my hand in reassurance.

Perhaps my preoccupation with the afternoon and its dismaying events saved me a certain amount of anxiety from a different source. I heard urgent talk between the men about the condition of the Southfork dam, but I could not truly fasten my mind upon it. I do recall that they spoke of growing anxiety among mill owners and townspeople who had been gravely concerned for weeks with the unusual amounts of rain. Now, more than ever, they questioned the safety of the earthen blockade that held back the swollen body of water high in the mountains. That water was being increased daily due to overflowing streams fed by the melting snow on the north slopes.

"It's madness!" Charles was saying. "I am going up there tomorrow and speak with Colonel Unger. Surely I can persuade him now to at least take down that damnable fish-screen, so more of the water can be released over the spill-way. If I cannot convince him, then I am going to ask the mayor to consider evacuating the town. Even so, God help the towns above us along the Connemaugh!"

Joshua shook his head. "I question the wisdom of such a move, Charles. And I doubt if many would agree to go."

"You are right!" Joanna broke in with a high laugh. Her cheeks were glowing with hectic color tonight, and I wondered if she had been drinking more than the white wine now being served at dinner. "I certainly would not leave the comfort of this house in such weather, with the certainty that when the house is abandoned the Hungarians would certainly rob us of every valuable!"

"What nonsense," Charles said irritably. "The immigrants have as much to lose as we. And certainly lives are more important than possessions. I intend to see to it that everyone in this household removes to higher ground until the rivers are past their crest. I will ride my stallion up to the dam in the morning. I advise you all to be packed and ready to leave in case the people in charge up there will do nothing to help the situation."

"What really *can* be done up there?" Joshua asked, with unaccustomed gloom. "Even if they pull the fish-screen out, would that prevent a disaster? There is no way to release the bulk of pressure on the dam itself, since the underground pipes were pulled out and never replaced."

Charles rubbed his chin, his eyes grave. "You may be right. But something must be done. If it should rain again in any quantity—I tell you, the situation could become extremely hazardous."

"Oh well, the dam has stood firm 'til now, in spite of

the alarms. Let us hope it continues to do so," Joshua said.

The rain that had begun in the afternoon had ceased sometime after darkness fell. Before I went to bed at ten o'clock I stood at my window looking out at a sky that seemed to be clearing. The wind was high, and clouds blew fitfully across, but I thought with relief that we were not to have the rain that earlier had threatened.

Nevertheless, now that my uneasy preoccupation with Joanna's inexcusable behavior had worn off a bit, I found myself thinking about what Charles had said at dinner.

The dam was in the mountains, some fourteen miles away. Could something so distant really reach out and harm us? Even if the water should somehow escape, it would dissipate its force long before it reached us, although the little town of Southfork, only two miles from the structure, would certainly be in great danger. So would the villages between Johnstown and the dam. But here—

Yet uneasily I remembered the drive I had taken to the Lake with Joshua. In my mind's eyes I saw again the miles of wooded, steep ridges that narrowly hemmed in the Connemaugh valley. I could only dimly imagine, God help me, what this signified, but I went to my bed that night filled with vague dread. Nor was it any reassurance when, late in the night, I waked to the pounding slash of rain against the windows. It was no gentle drizzle this time, but a rushing torrent that drummed savagely on roof and walls.

I slept very little, and rose at dawn.

It was well I did so. I was already dressed and pinning up my hair when the quiet knock came at my sitting-room door. Lena, asleep in that room, stirred and mumbled. I hurried to open it before the knocking would disturb her, and found Charles outside. I felt an instant delight—and instant dismay.

"Charles. What is it?" I asked softly.

"I'm glad you are up. I must talk to you. Please," he added urgently.

"What is it, Miss Katy?" Lena called drowsily. "If it's Marie, tell her I'm getting up now, and I'll be out to help her in a minute."

Charles took my hand and drew me outside in the hall. "Come, we must talk. Let's go into the study."

His expression was so grave that I couldn't argue with him. We hurried quietly along the corridor, and he shut the study door firmly behind us and turned to face me.

"There is something I have to tell you. I had a long talk last night with Joshua Galbraith, at his request. He has revealed—everything—about my wife's infidelity, and about her threats to you."

There was nothing I could say. I bit my lip and watched him. I could not have been the one to tell him, but I was glad he knew. There was something very reassuring in knowing that he was in full possession of the facts.

Steadily he continued. Only the lines of strain deepening about his eyes told me that he was disturbed. "I will have to make a change in my future plans because of what I now know. I have already spoken with Joanna, and told her that I intend to demand a legal separation."

"Charles," I found myself saying, "I don't think you fully understand. Joanna does love you. But you have not been—that is—I have noticed that you remain aloof from her. I think she was driven to seek Joshua's attentions. He can be so very charming, you see, and she was tempted—"

He stopped me, almost coldly. "I understand what you are trying to do. You simply do not know all the facts, Katherine. How could you? I brought Joanna and the children here two years ago, thus removing her from the city where she could not be prevented from carrying on her—liaisons with various men. I had warned her that if it did not stop, I would take her away from temptation. At first, she hated me for bringing her here, then appeared to adjust to the change. Fool that I am, I thought that she had finally realized that she could not continue as she had been."

I suppose that I was not as surprised at his revelation as I would have been a week ago. I had seen Joanna's other face.

"Still," I persisted uncertainly, "I have seen the way she looks at you. She loves you, Charles."

"No!" The word fell like an icy stone between us. "I

cannot expect you to understand. You are too honest, your own motives too sincere, ever to fathom the kind of mind, the kind of—soul Joanna has. You must simply accept what I tell you. Joanna does not love me. She only *wants* me. Physically. If that offends you, I am sorry. It is the only way I can say it. I was a fool to marry her. Only a month after our wedding I learned my folly, when she calmly told me that she was carrying a child the day we took our vows.''

I drew in my breath sharply. ''You cannot mean—''

He turned his eyes, darkly brooding, upon my face. ''The twins are not my children. Even so, like a fool, I forgave Joanna, and for a brief time we were—happy.'' A bitter smile lifted the corner of his mouth, but the eyes remained as bleak as winter. ''Then I learned that Joanna had become involved with one of my closest business colleagues shortly after the twins' birth. Nor was he the only man with whom she was initimate in those first years. That is when I removed my affection from my wife, Katherine. And if I were to list for you the number of men she subsequently took as lovers, you probably would not believe me.''

''Then why did you remain with her?'' I asked, stunned by what he was telling me.

He shrugged. ''Because of Rebecca. Joanna would not care for the child once she saw that Rebecca was handicapped. I could have provided money for her institutional care—Joanna would not agree to that. I suppose she saw Rebecca as her only hold over me.''

I could not doubt that he was telling me the truth. Everything fit together, even the lack of normal parental love between Charles and Sidney. He had accepted the responsibility for both children—although he had not always checked to see if the care he paid for, in Rebecca's case, was actually provided. But he could not consider the children as his own, and who was I to judge his refusal to go this extra mile?

''I know,'' he said gently,'' that this is embarrassing for you to hear. I would not burden you with it, except that I must ask you to make a choice. If you wish to remain here, I will take Joanna elsewhere and set up a household for her and Sidney. She can keep Rebecca with her, if she wishes, and I will pay for a nurse. Or I will find a suitable place for the child. But if you prefer to live somewhere else, I will help you find a place to stay. I will either buy this house from you, or continue to pay to rent it, and I will hire reliable people to maintain it in the excellent condition you have achieved.''

I shook my head slowly. "I—thought that I wanted to stay here. But—so much has happened. I think I'd best go. I will sign the house over to you. I know you'll argue with me, but I don't think you can actually prevent my giving back what was never rightfully mine. Joshua Galbraith will understand my reasoning.''

Charles sighed and clenched his hands as if he wanted to strike out at something. "You're right. I cannot stop you. But I hope that you will give me time to try and change your decision. There's so much I want to say to you, and there isn't time. I must be on my way to the lake. Will you promise me that you will await my return before you go to Joshua?''

He had so much on his mind, so many worries, that I could not bear to add to them at that moment.

"I will wait. But I won't change my mind. Please don't expect that.''

He came and took my hand in a hard grip. "There's one thing more. I want you to know that if it were possible, I would ask you to—wait for me, until I have straightened out my life. But the moment Joanna knew that you and I were together, no matter how long I might wait, she would go to any lengths to blacken your character. It was the worst mistake of my life to bring you here, to this house. Now she can always imply that there were illicit reasons for my having done so. I cannot allow her to hurt you more than she already has.''

"Why *did* you bring me here?'' I asked thickly, over the knot in my throat.

He studied my face for a moment. "I will not lie to you, my dear. I thought that you might have some knowledge of my aunt's death. Forgive me for that suspicion. I was grasping at straws. You had not been here a week before I knew that any suspicion directed to you was ludicrous.''

He touched my cheek with one finger. "Now I must go. Please take care while I am away. When I return I shall make arrangements for you to go wherever you wish. Although how I can give you up, I do not know."

With that, he was gone. Trembling, I realized that though the word had not been uttered, I had said my farewell to him. Charles Marchand was gone from my life as surely as if we had never met at all.

Chapter Thirty

The hard rain that kept me wakeful stopped by morning, but there was a heavy, cold fog filling the valley. After Charles left for the lake on his tall stallion, I stepped out onto the front porch for a moment, shivering in the dank chill. I was astonished at the roar of Stony Creek. It had never sounded like that before, and a finger of anxiety touched me. If the rivers came up much more, there would certainly be flooding in the lower parts of town.

At seven the mill whistles blew for the change of shift. I later learned that the men arriving for work were told to return home and prepare for a possible flood. When Mrs. Smith's boy, Jakey, came to bring a basket of finished laundry, he excitedly related to us that cellars in the lower parts of Johnstown were rapidly filling with water. He left us quickly, eager to go and play in the water in the streets. Under one arm he carried a little homemade boat. Sidney was in the kitchen at the time, and he had a longing expression on his face. I knew that he would have liked to join Jakey. The growing anxiety I felt made me order him, rather sharply I am afraid, not to leave the house. I had no authority over the child, and it is a wonder that he obeyed me. I suppose he knew that his mother would have echoed my sentiments, if she had known what he was planning.

I went upstairs to see if Mrs. Pinkham needed anything. She was just getting Rebecca dressed. The girl seemed listless, and did little to help in the process. Mrs. Pinkham was mildly worried.

"I hope she is not coming down with something," she said. "She's been coughing half the night. It's this awful damp weather. There's just no getting away from the wetness. It's in the bedclothes and the underthings and even the walls are damp to the touch!"

I sighed. "Surely it can't go on forever. If Rebecca isn't feeling better soon, I shall call the doctor to come and look at her."

I was about to leave, when Mrs. Pinkham called me back.

"Katherine, maybe I shouldn't ought to say it, but I don't feel easy in my mind about the river. The Connemaugh and Stony Creek are both up, and I can't remember when that ever happened before."

"Well, we are situated on higher ground than most of the houses," I said. "But perhaps I should have maids help me bring the more valuable furniture up to the second floor."

She shook her head. "Dearie, this house has so much stuff you could move furniture for a week and not make a proper dent. You'll only wear yourself out. Probably there's no danger, anyway. Forgive a nervous old woman's fancies."

Nevertheless, when I went downstairs, I asked Lena and Marie to go from room to room with me, deciding what paintings and books were of such value, that they should be removed from the lower floor. We all worked until nearly noon carrying things to the imagined safety of the second floor. From time to time I stepped out on the porch and looked out across the valley. I could see people leading cattle and horses to higher ground on Laurel Hill and other slopes, and whole families wading along the streets with bundles of belongings pushed on makeshift rafts.

I wondered if I ought to gather the family and servants and do likewise. Only the thought of the wet cold of the day and Rebecca's cough held me back. Also, I was very much in doubt that I could budge Joanna from her rooms to go out into the rain and the mud, even had we been on good terms. As things stood, I knew she would slam the door in my face if I ventured even to suggest such a thing. I could only hope that Charles would return soon and tell us what we must do.

Mrs. Potter, bless her, made a suggestion that I readily accepted. She said that we should be ready to climb out upon the roof in case the water came up into the house. I remembered the trapdoor onto the roof that I had noticed when John Brock was working on the playroom. I immediately went up to the attic, deserted today, and taking up the hooked pole left for the purpose, I pushed open the little door onto the roof. I set the ladder in place and left the playroom door standing open, feeling slightly better for having taken such a precaution.

Just past eleven o'clock we had a scare. Sidney called out excitedly from the front porch, bringing the maids and Mrs. Potter and me running. We saw a great many logs racing by in the turbulent water of the river below us.

"Must have been a log boom broke loose upstream," Mrs. Potter said.

We watched as they rolled and banged against each other and rushed like so many wet, dark animals down the overflowing little river, to jam up in the arches of the stone bridge.

"I don't suppose there's any reason to panic yet," I muttered, but I caught the anxious look in Mrs. Potter's eye. "Do you think we should go up the hill?" I asked.

She considered, deep in thought. "I don't know. I doubt if Mrs. Marchand will go, anyway, it being so muddy and all."

I made a sudden decision, based more on the mute, frightened expressions of the maids than anything else. "Nevertheless, I want all of you to go, at once. There's nothing more you can do here. If it gets worse I'll talk Joanna into leaving. I think that the more of us who are already out, the better. There will be less confusion in case of a definite emergency."

They looked at each other, and then they argued that their place was with the family. But I was adamant.

"I am ordering you to go. When Mr. Marchand comes, the rest of us will climb to safety. There will be fewer of us then to consider; only the children, Mrs. Marchand, Mrs. Pinkham and myself."

Lena giggled suddenly. "You're forgetting Mr. Horace."

"What? Is he here?"

I realized that I had not seen the man since Mrs. DeWitt left to find Yolande, but one of the girls had mentioned that he must have been spending a good deal of time in the saloons, as they had seen him come back to the house, almost too unsteady on his legs to climb the stairs. If I had thought of him at all today, I would have assumed that he was likewise occupied, in town.

"He's dead drunk, up in his room," Lena informed me. "I seen him when I went in to straighten things.

"Well, never mind him now," I said distractedly. "All of you get your boots and coats and be on your way."

They obeyed me, and I saw them out the back door. To my surprise, Mrs. Potter turned back to hug me warmly. "Please take care!" she begged. "If Joanna won't go, get the children and come away up the hill. Don't leave it 'til too late."

I watched them go, climbing over the pasture fence, and straggling up the slope. I had forgotten the deep gully that almost circled the property on its way to the river. Of course it was running strongly, and I held my breath with anxiety as the three women went into the muddy little stream. Lena's feet slipped out from under her, but with Marie's help she got up again. Even from here I could see she was dreadfully soaked. But all three climbed out, safely, and crawled on hands and knees up the slippery bank.

After they were out of sight in the woods, I restlessly walked about the house, joined by a very solemn Sidney. I was grateful for the child's presence.

At one o'clock the phone rang, and I rushed to answer it. It was Joshua Galbraith, asking if Charles had yet returned.

"No," I told him, tears almost too close to the surface to disguise in my voice. "Do you think he—he's all right?"

Joshua gave a bark of laughter. "Charles? Of course he is. Charles can ride like a wild Indian, Katherine, and a bit of river water won't faze that horse of his. How are things there?"

"I've sent the maids and Mrs. Potter to higher ground. Rebecca seems to be coming down with a cold, and I don't like to take her out unless it is necessary."

He told me that the eastbound railroad track up the valley had washed out,. and that the Poplar Street and Cambria

City bridges were gone as well. The water from the rivers was waist-high to a tall man on Main and Franklin.

My voice quavering a little, I asked if he thought there was any danger from the dam. Again he laughed. Sometimes in my dreams I still hear that deep, kindly laugh that Joshua Galbraith, my first friend in Johnstown, had.

"Now, pretty Katy, don't go letting your imagination run away with you! You've been listening too much to Charles's scarey stories."

A lifetime later I was to learn that even as Joshua spoke so reassuringly, one message of warning had already been received at East Connemaugh's dispatch tower. It was directed to the yardmaster there, and strongly suggested that the people of Johnstown be notified to prepare for a possible failure of the Southfork Dam.

The message was sent on to the Johnstown telegraph office. But the freight agent, a Mr. Frank Deckert, took no stock in the warning. Beyond mentioning it to a few others in the depot, he made no effort to spread the warning. Perhaps he thought it would result in a harmful panic.

But of course all of this was then unknown to us. We had no way of realizing that the work to try and remove the fish-screen at the main spillway of the dam, was not possible. The heavy metal screen was by now so jammed with debris that there was no dislodging it. The water was creeping inexorably up to the level of the dam, with its vulnerable, sunken area in the middle. On the outer face of the earthen bulwark, many serious leaks had become apparent. It was at this time that Charles, who had been laboring with the men trying to remove the screen, knew that it was useless. He mounted his stallion and galloped down to the valley in an effort to warn as many as he could. He then planned to come home to us.

A man was dispatched for help by Colonel Elias Unger, president and manager of the Southfork Club. He left the dam twenty minutes ahead of Charles, and headed for the telegraph tower at Southfork. It was this message that found its way to Mr. Deckert—and went no further.

But in my lack of knowledge, I was warmed and reassured by Joshua's words, at least for a time. I busied myself in preparing a lunch from food Mrs. Potter had left warming on the stove. I left Sidney in the kitchen with fresh bread and a bowl of soup, while I took trays up to Mrs. Pinkham and Rebecca. The child was fretful and would not eat, although we both coaxed her. I felt her forehead and thought that she was feverish.

"I believe that I should call the doctor."

Mrs. Pinkham shook her head. "He won't be able to come. I think the bridges will all have been washed out by now."

I looked at her in consternation. I had forgotten the bridges. And there was something else I had not thought of. If the doctor could not come to us, very likely Charles could not, either. I swallowed uneasily.

"I think—I think we had better make some preparations, Mrs. Pinkham, in case the water goes higher. Would you have Rebecca's warm coat ready and help her put on her boots, in case we have to leave?"

"I've been thinking the same thing. I'll get her boots at once. But I hope she won't have to go out in this cold fog and rain."

I left them, but first I gave Mrs. Pinkham instructions not to lock the door this time. I went down to prepare a tray for Joanna, who had not come out of her rooms at all, today. I dreaded seeing her. There was no forgetting her cruel use of me the day before. And it was impossible to guess what her mood would be this afternoon, since Charles had demanded a separation. Joanna was the last person I wished to seek out. But I felt responsible for all in the house during this frightening situation, and I felt that she ought to eat.

I needn't have worried about having to face her, for she neither came to the door at my knock, nor did she reply when I called to her that I had brought lunch. I knew she was awake, for I could hear the study, monotonous squeak of a rocking chair within. She must have heard me, yet she said nothing. At last I went away. If she wanted to sulk, so be it.

Time crept by. Charles did not return. Water swirled about the house, but it did not yet come in, thanks to our elevated site. I felt a heavy dread fall over my spirit, and I kept Sidney with me. The boy was silent, as if he too felt a fear too deep to express. I was glad to have his company. Yet when I felt compelled to desert the lower floor, with water from Stony Creek lapping into the front hallway, I sent the boy to Mrs. Pinkham.

Startled, he refused. The idea of being in Rebecca's presence was hateful to him.

I put my hand on his shoulder. "Sidney, listen to me. If the water rises much more, we shall have to leave the house very hurriedly, and I shall need your help with Rebecca and Mrs. Pinkham. I have no one else to turn to. You know it is what your father would expect of you."

I think it was the mention of Charles that convinced him. Reluctantly, he nodded.

"Thank you, Sidney. I was certain I could rely on you. Now get your rubber boots, and a coat and cap, and wait with Mrs. Pinkham."

Standing along in the second floor corridor, I tried to think clearly. There were six of us to be considered. I knew that there was little chance of Charles being able to get back to us before nightfall, and decisions would have to be made before then. It was up to me to take proper steps. Charles had said we must be ready to leave the house, but where could we go?

There was no question of walking from the house to the nearest hillside, now. The flooding was deep and strong about the house. We were already surrounded by water at least two-feet-deep. And I knew that even if Mrs. Pinkham and Rebecca could get through that, there was the deep gully back of the stables. It would take a strong man to help the elderly woman, and for that matter, Joanna, through the swift stream. It was useless to expect Horace DeWitt to help. Even sober, the man was probably as strong as *I* !

Stubbornly, I was only considering the possibility of river water driving us from our refuge. Yet in the back of my mind, like a distant death knell, tolled the threat that had so occupied Charles's mind—the dam!

Something drew me to Bertha DeWitt's rooms. As I went in and closed the door behind me, I had a mad impulse to stand in the center of the sitting room and ask aloud, 'What shall I do? Please help me.'

Of course I did nothing of the kind, and if anything, something about the atmosphere of the room heightened my anxiety. Very clearly in my mind I saw the man-made mountain of earth and boulders, but not as it had been the day Joshua and I had driven over it. I was caught in a kind of buzzing absorption with the image in my brain, a trance, if you will. It shut out every sensory distraction. I gazed at the dam, exactly as if I stood below it. I saw, paralyzed with horror, that there was now a stream of water some ten or twelve-feet-wide coming over the top, through a tear several feet deep in the fabric of the barrier. It seemed as if some giant's sand shovel had made a cut through the great bulk of the dam, and with a roar, the water gushed through. All those tons of rock and soil were shoved away. A wall of water seemed to mount to the sky and tower over me.

My scream echoed in the empty room. Blinking, I looked about me. Dear God, what had happened? Had I fallen asleep on my feet to dream that horrendous scene?

My eyes fell upon a clock that would not have been ticking, for who had an interest in keeping it going in an unoccupied room? But it was running. I shall never know who bothered to set the timepiece going. I only know that the hands stood at ten minutes past three.

I rushed to a window, for the thing I had seen so vividly in my imagination could not be shaken off.

The scene reassured me. There was yellow water in the streets, yes, overflow from the rivers. I saw people in row-boats evacuating those who were in the low-lying areas near the river, and people leaning out of the upper windows of their homes and buildings. But there was no great emergency; all was as it had been all day. I felt my heartbeat slow, and drew a deep, shaking breath.

The door opened quietly. I turned to see Joanna Marchand standing behind me. She was not yet dressed for the day, but had pulled a gauzy wrapper over her nightdress. Her beautiful, long, pale hair was uncombed and tangled about her frozen face.

And in her hand she held a pistol.

Chapter Thirty-one

Slowly my mind registered what I saw. Perhaps I was already so numb with anxiety that the shock was dulled.

"Here you are!" she said. "I have been looking for you."

Stupidly I replied, "I came to your door earlier."

"Oh yes, but I was not ready then. I was still planning what must be done with you." A tiny smile moved her pale lips.

"What do you mean? Why have you got that gun?"

"It must be obvious, my dear Katherine! Please don't pretend you can't understand. You have played your game, and you thought you had won it, didn't you? You thought that you taken my husband from me, but no one takes what is mine. No one!"

"How dare you accuse me of such—"

"Stay there! Turn away from me. I shall be merciful and not force you to look upon your death."

"Joanna, what are you saying?" I gasped.

"Turn around! Do as I say, and you will have a few minutes more to live. I could have killed you in your sleep last night, you and that silly maid you have guarding you. But I wanted you to know that I have not been fooled, not for one minute, by your clever little deceits! And I am quite pleased that I have found you here. It is so fitting, isn't it?"

"I don't know what you mean!" I cried, face turned toward the window, hands gripping the sill.

"Why—" she laughed unpleasantly, "here in Bertha's rooms. It is almost a repetition of what happened before, don't you see? Except that you have already told my husband your vicious little tale, and Bertha was only about to do it! I stopped her. It is too late to stop you, but I can administer a fitting punishment."

My head jerked. "Are you saying that—*you* killed Bertha?"

Her girlish peal of laughter sent chills down my spine. "But of course! That silly, dowdy old hag, always creeping about, spying. How I hated her! Charles set her to watch me, but I saw to it she would never report what she found out."

"She knew about you and Joshua!" I blurted. So that was the meaning of the note I'd found. I realized that I had forgotten to give the note to Charles, after all. Well, it could scarcely matter now.

Joanna snorted as if with disgust. "Don't be so stupid. Of course she never knew about Joshua. Do you imagine he'd have been fool enough to meet me here?"

"Then—I don't understand—"

She giggled. "It was Horace, you ninny! Bertha saw me with him that afternoon, just coming out of my room. Charles was in Kentucky, but I knew when I saw the look on her silly sheep's face that she'd lose no time telling him. So I sent Horace away, and I—did what had to be done. You're all alike!" she shouted suddenly, and the venom in her voice made my skin crawl. "You putty-faced, pious she-cats, meddling in things that are none of your business! Except that you're no better than me, sneaking about to be with Charles—"

I struggled for something, anything, to pacify her. "Joanna, I thought we were friends! You were so kind when I came here—"

"I made up my mind to disarm you, lest you suspect me of old Bertha's death. But I might have saved my efforts. You were determined to destroy my happiness from the very first. I knew Charles must have a mistress, but I could not find out who. But Bertha knew about you and Charles, didn't she? And she hated me, and would have done anything to hurt me, and that's why she left you the house. When Charles brought you here, I knew you were the one he'd been seeing. That's why I started the fire in your room. I hoped it would kill you, for turning Charles against me!"

The insane twistings of her mind were unbelievable. "How could I turn him against you?" I tried to reason with her. "He was disillusioned about you, years ago, long before I met him. If you had been faithful to him—"

"No!" she shouted. "It was because of Rebecca! Yes, that was it. I could see it in his eyes when she was little and she did not develop in her mind. I could see the disgust, and how her existence made *me* disgusting to him. If I could have been rid of her, if he had not had to look at her, he would have come back to me, I know he would have! I tried to be rid of her. Once I held her down in her bath, but the nurse came in and I had to explain that she had slipped under the water. And there were other times, until I could no longer bear to be near her, ugly, *ugly* thing! But I failed each time."

I felt frozen, sick. "It was you who lured Rebecca out upon the ledge, who drugged Mrs. Pinkham—" I whispered.

"Oh yes," she admitted quite calmly. "And if you had not come along when you did, it would have been ended, and Charles would have wanted me again. He would have forgotten that monster I birthed."

"You are mad!" I breathed, shaking.

Again she laughed. "Of course I am not! You are the one who is insane. Charles will see that when he finds that you have killed yourself with this gun."

"It is not my gun. It is yours. How will you explain that?" I grasped at any remark to detain her hoping that someone would come, would stop Joanna. But who was there to find us? I myself had sent the servants to safety. Lottie Dilby was still away on her visit. Sidney and Mrs. Pinkham were on the third floor with Rebecca. And Charles would not be able to reach the house until the water went down. Despair made my knees quiver and my stomach knot into a burning lump. I knew that in a few minutes I would die, as Bertha had died, at this woman's dainty, elegant hands.

The turmoil in my mind was pierced dimly by the sound of a locomotive whistle, a long, unbroken scream in the distance, but I could not take my attention from Joanna.

"No one knows I have a gun," she said with patient satisfaction, as if she enjoyed instructing me. "It was given me by—a man I knew—" she chuckled to herself. "Everyone will believe it is yours. I shall say that I have seen it

297

in your rooms, and that you have been strangely despondent all day. Oh, it is an excellent plan, as good as the one I devised for old Bertha, knocking on her door that afternoon, pleading with her to go downstairs and phone the doctor. I said I was feeling dizzy and ill—and then just one shove at the head of the stairs—"

"You are inhuman!"

"Perhaps. Well, it is time, Katherine."

I heard her cock the pistol.

"Who is going to believe that I shot myself in the back, with the bullet fired from that distance?" I inquired scornfully, heart in my throat.

"Why yes, how silly of me! Well, that is easily arranged. Stand where you are."

I heard her light steps across the carpet, my flesh crawled, my muscles cried out for me to whirl, to run, to do something to defend myself.

I turned my head. The clock on the mantel was striking four o'clock, and the scene is fixed in my mind forever. I saw my enemy's face, her usually pale cheeks red with excitement, eyes bright and tongue moving sensuously between her lips. She brought the gun up, and nearer, and I thought that there might be a tiny chance for me to grasp it and push it aside.

At that instant, with my murderer staring me in the face, we were both, incredibly, distracted.

It was a sound, so compelling that Joanna's eyes involuntarily left me and sought the source.

How can I describe it? I hear it in my dreams, and I shudder at it in conscious memory. Yet it almost defies words, perhaps because it was *more* than sound. Even through the closed window of the room it came, tremendous, compelling. First a deep, basso profundo grinding, and above that a hollow, rushing roar, accompanied by a barely perceptible trembling of the floor beneath our feet, as if the skin of the earth quivered with horror. There were screeching, rending overtones, and a sudden powerful wind that raced before the sound. Both Joanna and I, who had been a second before upon the brink of eternity, now stood side by side at the window, transfixed, staring out at the town.

First we saw small buildings and plank fences blown flat. This was alarming enough, but the sight that came on the heels of the wind brought paralyzing terror.

It was a brown, roiling cliff of water, carrying within its vast mass, great objects—trees and buildings and even freight cars, borne as easily as feathers upon a summer breeze. But the thing that sticks in my mind most clearly is the black heavy pall of smoke that hung over and accompanied the waters. Like the very breath of Satan it rolled and tumbled and fell greedily upon the helpless town. Later we learned that it was steam and smoke from the destruction of the Gautier works. But at that moment, it held a supernatural-appearing threat, like the embodiment of all one's worst nightmares.

Joanna let out a strangled cry, and I was released from my spell.

"The children!" I gasped, and ran for the door, forgetting the gun that still dangled from her hand. She stood as if never to move again. I screamed to her.

"Joanna! We must get Sidney and Rebecca out!"

I think it was the name of her son that stirred her to action. "Sidney?" she murmured, as if waking from a deep slumber, and as I ran along the hall toward the stairs, I heard her coming behind me.

A door was flung open ahead of me. Mr. DeWitt had roused and was coming out into the corridor. Drunkenly, he peered at me.

"Wha—Wha's it?"

"The dam! Come quickly."

He seemed not to understand. I grasped his arm and pulled him along with me. "Hurry!" I pleaded with him, as Joanna ran past us.

We ran to the third floor, wondering when the water would be upon us. I remember thinking that the house was nearly a mile from the railroad bridge, and set upon a slight rise. It might escape. But there would certainly be water in the lower floors, and we must get out upon the roof. Perhaps someone would come and get us, I thought feverishly, and then some cold, reasoning part of my mind told me that there would be few left to help those who survived that awful mountain of debris-filled water.

We found Mrs. Pinkham already in the hall, hustling Rebecca and Sidney to the attic stairs. Abandoning Mr. DeWitt, who seemed to be moving more alertly now, I grabbed Rebecca's hand and the elderly woman's arm, and helped them up the steep flight and through the door into Rebecca's playroom.

The next minutes are a blur. I recall my mind-tearing anxiety as the children were pushed up the ladder I had set ready—thank God for that foresight! Joanna scrambled after them. Mrs. Pinkham resisted fiercely when I attempted to shove her up next.

"No, you go! You are stronger. You can help the children more!"

"We are both going," I shouted in her ear, and bodily forced her up ahead of me.

We both made it out upon the roof, followed by Horace DeWitt, and were in time to see our worst imaginings achieve reality.

Clinging to the sobbing Rebecca, who could not have understood why she had been made to climb out on this frighteningly high place, I looked upon the devastation that had already swept away countless lives and would soon be upon us.

Washington Street, at the eastern end of town, was gone. The water had split, like greedy fingers growing each second longer, more grasping. One great, roaring stream flowed behind the Methodist church, another ploughed a howling path of destruction through the center of town, while the rest followed the bed of the Connemaugh. Landmarks were vanishing; smashed and swallowed up. I made out the park. East of it the water rushed thunderously to unite with our own swollen creek.

We saw large buildings strongly made of brick, bow and sink into the torrent as if they were children's paper toys. Wooden structures were torn loose from foundations to join the great masses of wreckage already clutched by the flood.

I knew, sickly, that it would be only moments until our fate was decided.

"Hold tight to each other and to the roof!" I screamed above the awful noise. "It is coming our way in a moment!"

Joanna, eyes blank and glazed, was shaking her head

dumbly. She clutched her son. I grasped Rebecca, who was screeching with fright. On the other side of the girl, Mrs. Pinkham did likewise, and my hands wound into her coat collar. If only I had kept that hold upon her!

We saw friends' houses being dashed to pieces, their inhabitants flung from roofs and upper windows to perish in moments, their screams unheard. The flood raced to challenge the hill back of Stony Creek, but it could not breast that bulwark, and with frustrated venom, it slammed back onto the demolished town and toward us.

I could not look away from the gulping, gluttonous water. Bodies were being carried on its crest, amid carcasses of animals, freight cars and tangled wire and lumber. All manner of debris combined into a giant club with which to smash our fragile refuge.

"The house cannot stand," I murmured. No one could have heard me. The clamor of wind and water and the groaning of mangled buildings was almost more than the mind could bear.

With a shattering blow the wave hit us. Instinctively I took one hand from Rebecca to grip the opening of the trapdoor, where Joanna, Sidney and Horace also clung. I now used the fingers I had wound into Mrs. Pinkham's collar to grasp Rebecca's coat. I felt the shock of impact throughout my body, and my left arm felt as if it were being wrenched from the socket. In desperation I held on, ignoring pain.

As the water surrounded and filled the house the pressure on my arm eased, but with my body I felt the death throes of the house Bertha DeWitt had loved and bequeathed to me. The structure cried out almost humanly as beams and joists and siding were twisted asunder. We were screaming too, I believe, but even my own voice was inaudible to me, so great was the cacophony of the fate that had come upon us. I closed my eyes with an instinctive wish to escape within myself when the water struck. When I opened them, I saw that Mrs. Pinkham was gone.

I believe she had been flung away from us when the flood hit, had fallen down the steeply-slanting roof and into the maelstrom below.

But there was no time for more than a stomach-wrenching

knowledge that my friend was lost. I saw that Joanna and the others were still safe—if one might use the word in such a situation.

The portion of the roofs where we clung, tilted sharply behind us so that it seemed we were nearly level. We were moving, being whirled along in the swift upstream current.

The roof dipped, turned and threatened to capsize as it went. All we could do was to cling to the trapdoor opening and pray for deliverance.

All about us, wreckage tumbled and rushed. Here and there in the broad stream were clusters of human survivors atop just such precarious refuges as our own. I saw some of them go under, their hands reaching up, grasping vainly for succor. Among the terrified victims was our laundress, poor Mrs. Smith, who stared at me without recognition as the board she clung to was sucked under, taking her to her death. I saw two little girls, scarcely more than babies, sitting on a bit of floor. Before our shocked eyes these little ones were smashed under the waves by a great tree trunk that reared over their unsteady raft and was flung down upon them.

I knew that at any moment our fate might be the same, and I prayed steadily, trying to prepare myself for what was to come.

I do not know how far the flood carried us up Stony Creek. My mind, subjected to one horrible sight after another, seemed at last to reduce the ordeal to hazy unreality.

I was jerked back to awareness as our roof whirled, bucking and scraping against other floor-borne objects, and started to move the other way, as the water lost its momentum and fell back toward Johnstown.

I had kept a tight grip on the now silent Rebecca. Her face had gone blank and still. She seemed stunned and totally uncomprehending. I let go of her for a moment to rub my very painful left arm. And then something happened that shall torment me all my days.

I had not realized that the simple-minded girl had put her beloved kitten inside her coat-front. Now the terrified little animal poked its head through a space where buttons had sprung loose, and wriggled free. With a yowl of complaint,

302

it skitted toward the edge of the roof.

The tragedy was slow and inexorable, like something seen in a bad dream. Rebecca turned toward her pet, seeming to belatedly realize its peril.

Something warned me—I grasped at Rebecca again, but she jerked free, leaped up and ran lumberingly for her cat, poised now on the edge of the roof.

"Becky, no!" I screamed. I got to my feet and scrambled toward her, but I was too late. The kitten leaped for a house that rumbled next to us. At that moment the gap widened. The cat made the jump safely, but Rebecca, following mindlessly, did not. She went into the water.

I managed to catch the end of her hair. As I braced myself to hang on, someone rushed past me. Sidney dived into the flood.

There was a shriek of protest from Joanna as her son vanished.

Chapter Thirty-two

Rebecca's body must have been caught from below by some wreckage. She was suddenly jerked from my grasp with a jolt that, horribly, left some of her hair in my hand. Sidney surfaced, spluttering. I grabbed his upflung hands.

"Where is she?" he yelled. "Let me go. I'll find her!"

But I knew it was useless. Becky was gone.

It was only the mercy of God that gave me strength to drag Sidney, sobbing and protesting, from the water. "We must get Rebecca out!" he kept pleading, and collapsed in my arms, weeping, when I would not let him go back to try again.

"It's too late," I said, tears choking me. I shuddered, seeing the grinding, surging tangle all about us. Rebecca's body would be down among that. There was no earthly way to find it.

I pulled Sidney back to the comparative safety of the attic opening. We were drifting, more slowly now, back toward the Connemaugh Valley. Silent and shivering, we huddled together, Sidney, Horace, Joanna and I. Our raft swung close to a still-standing building in the Kernville section. People who had taken refuge there, eagerly reached down with willing hands to lift us onto their roof. Joanna slipped and fell into the water. A burly mill worker who spoke only broken English saved her, but she had swallowed a quantity of the cold, muddy water. Wet and shaking, she lay with the rest of us upon the roof that felt like heaven's shores, for it stood stable and secure as the water thundered past.

Cold, and in pain both physical and mental, we and a half dozen other people stared out over the darkening scene of utter desolation. Where Johnstown had been, there was a lake, stoppered in place by the great mound of debris caught in the arches of the stone bridge, where barbed wire from the Gautier Works, railway cars, trees, houses, dead horses and cattle, were wedged inextricably.

Only a few buildings stood. Alma Hall, where Joshua's office was located, the Presbyterian and Methodist churches were still there, and a few other structures.

It would have seemed that we had endured all the fates could fling at us. But as darkness fell, there appeared a new horror.

At first it did not attract our attention, for it was only a pinpoint or two of light at the stone bridge. But soon someone let out a shout and pointed at the flames licking about in the pile. A fire had somehow started, there under the arches.

My heart twisted. There must be people, injured but still alive, in that twisted mess—people trapped by the fire that had, against all reason, begun there.

We heard the anguished screams from across the water very clearly. The fire grew with mad haste, fed perhaps by oil from tank cars. I buried my face in my hands and wept, praying for the poor, tortured captives of the bridge.

The night was dark, save for that awful fire, and freezing cold. All was made hideous by the moans of our suffering companions and pleading calls for help from out of the blackness. Dogs howled on the hillsides. Surely Hades could offer nothing worse.

We lay exposed upon that roof all the night, fearful of attempting to get down into the attic. We worried lest this building also collapse into the twenty feet or so of water that lay all about us. We learned later that the railroad embankment had at last broken beyond the stone bridge, letting out some of the water, and lowering the level across the valley. But there was still fearfully deep water below us, and in the darkness we dared not move about much.

And so we huddled together, shivering and exhausted, weeping as realization periodically flooded us with utter despair.

Strangely, it had gone completely out of my mind that only hours earlier, the woman who lay muttering feverishly next to me on the soaked shingles had sought to take my life, and had confessed herself a murderess..It was not until

305

near morning, after a brief and tormented sleep, that I remembered. With a frightened start, I wondered if she still had the gun, and if she would again try to harm me.

I think that it was the cessation of the dreadful sounds that woke me from my exhausted slumber. I had grown used to moaning, to the creaking of wreckage all about our building, and to distant screams that pled for mercy, or for death.

Silence came in the hour before dawn. Even the rain had stopped. The normal sounds of the town were gone, of course, and in that dark hour it seemed they were gone forever. Somehow the quiet was as frightening as the nightlong clamor had been.

It was then, waking, that I remembered about Joanna. I marveled that I had lain down to sleep near her, not even stopping to think that in the darkness, she could easily shove my exhausted body into the water, and probably no one would have known of her deed.

Even now she might be lying awake, tensing herself for just such an effort—

I jerked my sore and stiffened body into a sitting position, shaking with the chill, my wet clothes plastered to me. There was a slight movement from Joanna, and she muttered fretfully.

I drew away as if she had been a poisonous viper, and stared down at her form, just visible to my straining eyes. Again she moved and spoke, and this time I made out the words.

"Mama!" she said in a little-girl voice. "Mama, I am so cold—mama—mama?"

She was silent for a moment, then began to mumble again. Gingerly I reached to touch her face, and found it burning hot. Joanna was out of her head with fever.

My fear became hollow, and I even felt a tinge of pity for this strange, desperate woman. But there was nothing I could do for her. Nothing that I could do for any of us.

I wrapped my arms about my knees, trying to warm myself. There was a movement nearby and someone crawled over next to me. I felt a fumbling at my skirts. With a gasp I jerked away, and heard Horace DeWitt's sly whisper. "Come now, we might as well enjoy ourselves. Don't move!" He put an arm about my waist.

I found enough strength to hit him, an open-handed blow across the face, hard enough so that he toppled backwards and had to claw frantically at the shingles to right himself.

"Don't come near me again!" I hissed at him.

The big mill worker came then and sat beside me. He said nothing, but his presence was warning enough. Horace slunk away.

At last the daylight came, to show us desolation where our bustling, cheerful town had been. Almost everything had been destroyed, or was submerged under the filthy water. The fire at the stone bridge still burned. We could see men working there, apparently trying to free any survivors. On the hillsides, small groups of people stared dazedly, as did we. Some who had been caught out in the waters during the night, were trying to get to shore, picking their way over the rubble.

As it grew lighter, we moved also, each helping the other. The big young immigrant carried Joanna. Survivors from the hillsides came to our aid, and helped us to a place on higher ground where the mud was at least clear of debris. There were no dry clothes, nor blankets, but someone managed to build a fire.

Joanna was very ill. We made her as comfortable as we could. When farmers from the surrounding countryside started to bring food and spare clothing and other necessities—bless those kind people—things were a little better. Someone helped me tie up my wrenched and very painful left arm in a sling, and gave me coffee that warmed my very soul. As soon as I was able I set about helping to care for those among us who were injured and ill.

Much has been written on the suffering that was the aftermath of the flood. Truly, for a day or more, the dreadful situation of the living was indescribable. Then the trains started to arrive with medicines, volunteers, food and blankets. On Wednesday morning, Miss Clara Barton brought some of her newly organized Red Cross workers from Washington. Her headquarters were inside a railroad car, and she had tents set up for the injured. Those I had been

307

attending were moved to her hospital, and I went also.

It is impossible to praise Miss Barton too much. She achieved in a short time what seemed impossible. Many who lived through the days after the flood owe their lives to her, and the fifty doctors and nurses who accompanied her.

When I insisted that I was able to continue to help, she allowed me to stay with Joanna, who had pneumonia, and with Sidney, who had come down with chills and fever and was also seriously ill.

I was bending over Sidney's pallet, helping him to drink some boiled water, when I felt someone near me and I looked up to see Charles Marchand. He had one leg in a cast and was leaning on a makeshift crutch. There was a purple bruise on his temple.

He held out his free arm. Wordlessly I ran to him. He held me comfortingly for a few moments, careful of my injured arm.

"Thank God I've finally found you!" he murmured hoarsely against my hair. "I've been going mad, searching among the bodies, asking everyone—"

I stepped back and wiped at tears with the back of my hand, trying to recover my calm. In my deepest heart I had believed Charles was dead, swept away like so many others. Seeing him had cracked away an icy shell that had closed like a sealed coffin about my emotions. But I feared the awakening of feeling, feared that I would go mad from the awful events of the past days.

Charles moved past me with an exclamation, recognizing Sidney's feverish, wan face on the cot. Gently he touched the boy's face, turning to me with a fearful question in his eyes.

"He will be all right," I said. "The doctors say that he is a strong boy, and will recover."

"And the others?" Charles asked. "Where are they?"

I motioned him out of Sidney's hearing. As unemotionally as I could I told him of Rebecca's death, and that of Mrs. Pinkham. "Joanna is very ill," I said. "I will take you to her."

In the next tent, I left Charles alone with his wife. I did

not want to see how the awful change in Joanna would affect him.

Since that first night, she had never been in her right mind. Whether it was due to the high fever, or whether shock and fear had unhinged her mind, I could not guess. She had lost her beauty, as well. Her face was like a death's-head covered tautly with skin, eyes sunken into their sockets. Only her lovely hair remained as it had been.

The doctors had warned me that there was little chance of her recovery. Until last night she had seemed to be conscious, although never aware of the present reality. She mumbled endlessly of events long past, never mentioning Charles, nor even Sidney. Now, however, she lay in a coma, only barely breathing, and I felt in my heart that her hours were numbered.

Charles came out of the tent, his face rigid, older. We found a place where we would not be disturbed.

"She is dying, isn't she?" he asked.

"I—think so."

"I failed you—all of you! I should never have gone to the dam. I should have stayed to take you out of harm's way."

"You were considering the lives of thousands, Charles, not just a few. It was the right thing to do."

He groaned and took my hand between his.

"You've been hurt," I said. "Please tell me what happened.

When he described his experiences the day of the flood, I shuddered at the risks he had taken. Working side by side with the men who were striving to remove the fish screen, Charles had labored frantically with dwindling hope, through the afternoon. But when the water broke over the top of the dam, he knew it was only a matter of time. His only thought was to try to reach us and warn people along the Connemaugh.

He had mounted his stallion and urged him into a run. After riding only a short distance he looked back to see the dam disintegrate. With eyes that stared sightlessly at the memory, he described that disintegration.

I felt my body go tense and cold as he drew for me,

309

stroke by stroke, the scene I had imagined—no, had *lived,* standing in Bertha DeWitt's sitting room!

Had I somehow seen it all through Charles's stunned eyes? Perhaps his next words offered a kind of explanation.

"I thought, even as I turned the horse toward the hillside, that I was a dead man," he said softly. "I fixed my mind upon your face, Katherine, as the most precious thing on earth to me."

The stallion had tried the steep slope gallantly, struggling to find purchase for his scrambling hooves in the sliding mud and shale.

"We had almost made it to safety, when Beau fell," Charles said. "It was not his fault, he'd done his best. But it was too steep, the ground too muddy. He fell on my leg and it was pinned against a boulder. I felt it snap as he got to his feet, and climbed on up the mountain. I heard the water coming—the sound of it, my God! I knew I had to get higher. I crawled, dragging the bad leg, until I passed out, just a foot or two above the path of the flood."

I exclaimed with anguish at the thought of his brush with death. Quickly he finished the story.

"After the water had emptied from the lake—about half an hour, I was told, someone found Beau, riderless, and looked for me. Searchers took me back to the club buildings and did their best for me. But it was two days before they could find a doctor, and I was not able to move about until a day ago. I found a man who would help me get to Johnstown, dreading in my soul what I would find here."

Joanna died two days after Charles's return.

How can I explain that I grieved for her? Perhaps it was simply easier to think of her as I had first believed her to be—charming, beautiful, warmly hospitable to a stranger. Her attempt upon my life seemed unreal now.

I suppose that is why, in the days after Joanna's death, I never told Charles of the awful things she had confessed. I never disclosed the jealous and diseased imaginings that had driven Joanna to the brutal murder of an old woman, and the repeated attempts to murder her own daughter. I never mentioned her threats to me.

I don't know where Joanna is buried. There were so many

310

dead, you see, many thousands. Charles arranged for his wife's final resting place, and that of Joshua Galbraith, who was found in the charred ruins at the stone bridge. It is ironic to think that if Joshua had remained in his office building, he would be alive today. But he went out, we were told, to help others, and in so doing, lost his life.

I nursed Sidney until he was well enough to be moved. Charles then took us to his Kentucky farm, to the large mansion where Mr. Chester Swopes, Charles's partner, lived with his kind wife.

In that beautiful setting, Sidney recovered his health, and I some of my peace of mind. Eileen came to us there. She wept with joy to see me, and together we mourned good friends lost forever; Mrs. Pinkham, Rebecca, Mrs. Smith—countless others.

Eileen had news of the Horace DeWitts. After the flood, Horace joined his wife in Pittsburgh, where Lily had located their wayward daughter and Johnny Brock. The DeWitts were unable to coax Yolande away from her love, and to the surprise of all, later years proved the match a solid one. John Brock, set up in business by his reluctant father-in-law, made a success of his life. He and Yolande had three beautiful and very willful children, and lived in a comfortable house in Pittsburgh until John's death in 1895, of a liver disorder.

If Eileen grieved over Johnny's elopement with Yolande, she was too proud to show it. But she has never married, seeming content to stay with us, and I wonder if she still thinks of the time when she gave her honest heart to Mr. Brock.

As soon as my arm was completely recovered, I sought a position to make my own way. Charles was vigorously opposed, but gave way before my insistence. I used my nursing experience to gain employment with the village doctor, and moved into a rooming house near his office.

Eileen lived with me and worked for Mrs. Hempstead, our landlady. On Sunday afternoons, Charles would take Sidney and me driving, after we had all attended church. I looked forward to these hours each week. I tried to forget all that was past—all the horror of the flood. With my work

311

work to occupy my mind, the bad memories were softened.

Yet for months Charles and I avoided speaking seriously of the future. I suppose at first Charles was remembering a golden-haired girl whom he had once loved very much, who would never again be part of his life, tantalizing and tormenting him. I know that he missed Joshua Galbraith, too, as I did. I thought often of the man who had been unable to resist Joanna's wiles, yet was a kind and loyal friend to me.

On an April Sunday, eleven months after the tragedy that had struck Johnstown, Charles invited me to a picnic. This time, Sidney was left behind.

We rode in Charles's buggy behind a sleek black thoroughbred mare whose swift trot carried us merrily along roadways pleasantly lined with spring's tender green growth. Charles had chosen a hilltop place for our feast. We could look down upon the wide, white-fenced pastures of Charles's farm, where mares kept a jealous eye on their lovely new foals.

The day was warm and sunny, with only an occasional breeze that was cool enough to warrant the shawl I had brought. I wore a dress I had made in my spare time. It was a frivolous gown of pale green organza, with a wide skirt caught up at the hem with tiny, dark green velvet bows over lace flounces. Perhaps the dress was my declaration of a determination to begin the future without looking back, without useless regrets.

"Katherine, you are very lovely today," Charles said, as I set out the roast chicken and bread and cheese for our lunch.

I felt my face warm and suddenly felt unaccountably shy.

"Katherine, look at me," he demanded.

He stood a few feet away, arms folded over his white, tieless shirt, booted feet apart. Charles had changed. He seemed older than the man I had met in Joshua Galbraith's office. There was a sprinkling of silver at his temples, and lines at the corners of his blue eyes. The winging black brows were often thoughtfully drawn now. Yet, to me, he was more handsome than ever, with a new gentleness to his strength.

There was something new in the way he looked at me

today. It flustered and confused me.

I suppose he could guess much of what was in my mind, for he grinned suddenly, with the old, wicked look.

"What are you afraid of, little Katy?" he asked.

"Why—I am not afraid of anything!" I snapped. "And I am not little, Mr. Marchand."

His smile grew and he came over to recline on the grass, near enough to take my hand away from my tasks. "Ah, but you seem so to me, my Katherine, little and vulnerable and gentle, as all God's best creatures are."

He kissed my palm, and I felt an alarming tingle. "Do you know," he continued slowly, "I have watched you all these months, and I cannot find your heart. Why have you hidden it from me, sweet Katy? Does it not belong to me, after all?"

The moment hung motionless as I knelt, looking at our two hands clasped. I knew that Charles was right. I had been hiding from him, afraid to admit my true feelings for this man, for I had been haunted by guilt about the past. Joanna had accused me of trying to take her husband. That was never true, but the love I felt for Charles Marchand had begun then, in spite of all my caution and all my excellent self-advice. It had been wrong, loving another woman's husband. That woman was dead. Yet, somehow this past year, she had become more of a barrier from her grave, than she had been while living.

"Charles—" I began helplessly.

He shook his head. "I understand what has kept us apart, Katherine. Perhaps it was best, for a time. We both had—things to think out. But now—" he cupped a big hand under my chin and lifted my face, stroking the corner of my mouth with his thumb. "Katherine, I want you. I love you, my dearest, and I mean to have some happiness in my life! No ghosts, no mistakes or regrets from the past are going to stand in my way. Do you understand?"

Dumbly, my throat choked with tears, I nodded. He pulled me over so that I was sitting against his body. His arms were about me. I longed to feel his mouth on mine, to give rein to the leaping fire I had kept so carefully banked all these lonely months.

"It has been a mistake to waste this time when we might

313

have been together," he whispered, drawing me down to lie against his chest. "Truly together, as I want us to be. Do you want that too, beloved?"

"Yes," I whispered. "Yes, I want that too."

Epilogue

Eight years have passed since Charles and I said our vows in the village church, time and enough for the healing of old scars. Yet there are the dreams, and occasionally a reminder of those past days.

Only last week, a hot, drowsy August afternoon, I came face-to-face with the past again. I was in a storage room of our home, clearing out a trunk. Our son Sidney will be going to the University in Lexington very soon, and Eileen and I have spent days starching shirts and trying to match mislaid socks. Sidney has grown into a handsome, serious-minded young man. Charles and I are very proud of him.

I emptied the trunk for Sidney's belongings, lifting out old newspapers that had been used to line the bottom. My hands were still in the act of discarding the paper, as flaring headlines caught my eye.

"DAM BROKEN BY HEAVY RAINS
Thousands Die in Flood"

The paper was dated May 31, 1889. Shuddering, I put the paper aside, but the gates of memory had been wrenched open. I saw again the faces of the dead and dying, heard the screams of terror and the roar of the water.

I thought how even the lives of the survivors had been changed for all time. Life had gone stubbornly on, but along new paths.

Charles and I had been fortunate; we had been given a second chance for happiness. We had found a sweetness and contentment in our love and in our family.

Perhaps we have been able to share that happiness with a few others. Dear Eileen is an indispensable part of our family, and her dearest enemy, Mrs. Potter, has been with us since our marriage. How we depend upon her brusque, loyal good sense. Between Mrs. Potter and Eileen, the children are kept unspoiled.

I should never have thought it possible, but even Lily DeWitt has become, if not a favorite relative, at least a fondly tolerated frequent visitor. Several years ago, Horace ran away with a buxom black-haired waitress from Pittsburgh, whereupon Lily sued for a divorce, and got it, along with the lion's share of poor Horace's worldly goods.

Oddly, it was Lily who brought me word of my old antagonist, Sibyl Blackwood. A few months ago Mrs. Blackwood was arrested for the suspected murder of several of her elderly patients. She was accused of promising 'lifetime care' in return for sums of one thousand dollars and more to certain patients who subsequently enjoyed a very brief life indeed.

Sibyl was not convicted. There was not enough evidence. Nevertheless, the authorities closed down the Blackwood Home for all time.

Lily confided in me that she had suspected from the first that Sibyl was a wicked, sly adventuress, and should have been locked up for life. I did not remind Lily that she and Mrs. Blackwood had been allies in attempting to invalidate Bertha DeWitt's legacy to me, and that Lily had been just as firmly-convinced of *my* criminal leanings at the time. It is best to let bygones be bygones.

But some things will not remain in the past. That rainy spring day in 1889 taught us an unforgettable lesson about the fragility of human life, and the frailty of man's works. When the cruel hand of fate moved, it carelessly swept all but memories and dreams.

Perhaps that is as it should be, for of all things given to man by God, are not memories and dreams the most enduring?

BE SWEPT AWAY
ON A TIDE OF PASSION
BY LEISURE'S THRILLING
HISTORICAL ROMANCES!

THRILLING HISTORICAL ROMANCE BY LEISURE'S LEADING LADY OF LOVE, CATHERINE HART

2131-5	FIRE AND ICE	$3.95 US, $4.50 Can.
2226-5	SILKEN SAVAGE	$3.95 US, $4.95 Can.
2287-7	ASHES AND ECSTASY	$3.95 US, $4.95 Can.

UNDER CRIMSON SAILS

Lynna Lawton

Beautiful, spirited Janielle Patterson had heard of the reckless way pirate Ryan Deverel treated his women. He seduced them with the same abandon with which he plundered ships. To the handsome pirate, women were prizes to be won, used, and tossed away.

Ryan intrigued and repelled Janielle—and when they finally met, she was shocked to discover that her own nature was as passionate as the pirate's!

But while he was driven by desire, she was driven by a fierce hatred. Yet she knew neither of them would rest until she had surrendered to him fully.

LEISURE BOOKS   **2002-5/$3.50**

Make the Most of Your
Leisure Time
with
LEISURE BOOKS

Please send me the following titles:

Quantity	Book Number	Price

If out of stock on any of the above titles, please send me the alternate title(s) listed below:

	Postage & Handling	
	Total Enclosed	$

☐ Please send me a free catalog.

NAME_____
(please print)

ADDRESS_____

CITY_____ STATE_____ ZIP_____

Please include $1.00 shipping and handling for the first book ordered and 25¢ for each book thereafter in the same order. All orders are shipped within approximately 4 weeks via postal service book rate. PAYMENT MUST ACCOMPANY ALL ORDERS.*

*Canadian orders must be paid in US dollars payable through a New York banking facility.

Mail coupon to: **Dorchester Publishing Co., Inc.**
6 East 39 Street, Suite 900
New York, NY 10016
Att: ORDER DEPT.